TRUSTING
THE
Enemy

TRUSTING

THE

Enemy

MELANIE MILBURNE
LOUISE FULLER
MICHELLE SMART

MILLS & BOON

TRUSTING THE ENEMY © 2024 by Harlequin Books S.A.

The publisher acknowledges the copyright holders of the individual works as follows:

ONE HOT NEW YORK NIGHT
© 2021 by Melanie Milburne
Philippine Copyright 2021
Australian Copyright 2021
New Zealand Copyright 2021

First Published 2021
Second Australian Paperback Edition 2024
ISBN 978 1 038 90861 2

THE TERMS OF THE SICILIAN'S MARRIAGE
© 2020 by Louise Fuller
Philippine Copyright 2020
Australian Copyright 2020
New Zealand Copyright 2020

First Published 2020
Second Australian Paperback Edition 2024
ISBN 978 1 038 90861 2

MARRIAGE MADE IN BLACKMAIL
© 2018 by Michelle Smart
Philippine Copyright 2018
Australian Copyright 2018
New Zealand Copyright 2018

First Published 2018
Third Australian Paperback Edition 2024
ISBN 978 1 038 90861 2

MIX
Paper | Supporting
responsible forestry
FSC® C001695

Published by
Harlequin Mills & Boon
An imprint of Harlequin Enterprises (Australia) Pty Limited
(ABN 47 001 180 918), a subsidiary of HarperCollins
Publishers Australia Pty Limited
(ABN 36 009 913 517)
Level 19, 201 Elizabeth Street
SYDNEY NSW 2000 AUSTRALIA

Printed and bound in Australia by McPherson's Printing Group

CONTENTS

One Hot New York Night
Melanie Milburne

MILLS & BOON

Melanie Milburne read her first Harlequin novel at the age of seventeen, in between studying for her final exams. After completing a master's degree in education, she decided to write a novel, and thus her career as a romance author was born. Melanie is an ambassador for the Australian Childhood Foundation and a keen dog lover and trainer. She enjoys long walks in the Tasmanian bush. In 2015 Melanie won the HOLT Medallion, a prestigious award honoring outstanding literary talent.

DEDICATION

To Elida Yesenia DeHaan. I hope you enjoy this book specially dedicated to you!

Best wishes, Melanie xx

CHAPTER ONE

ZOEY SAW HIM the moment she stepped into the London auditorium where the advertising conference was being held. It wasn't hard to make out Finn O'Connell in a crowd—he was always the one surrounded by drooling, swooning women. At six foot six, he was head and shoulders over everyone else, with the sort of looks that could stop a bullet train. And a woman's heart. An unguarded woman's heart, that was.

But, just this once, Zoey allowed herself a secret little drool of her own. She might hate him with a passion but that didn't mean she couldn't admire some aspects of him—like his taut and toned body, his strong, powerful, muscle-packed legs, his impossibly broad shoulders, his lean chiselled jaw or his laughing brown eyes. Other aspects, not so much. If there were an Academy for Arrogance, Finn O'Connell would be top of the class.

As if he sensed her looking at him, Finn turned

his head and glanced her way, his prominent black eyebrows rising ever so slightly above his eyes. Zoey was glad she wasn't easily provoked into a blush, as that mocking gaze moved over her in one slowly assessing sweep. His lips curved upwards in a smile that sent a frisson of awareness right through her body. It was the smile of a conqueror, a man who knew what he wanted and exactly how he was going to get it.

He moved away from his posse of adoring fans and strode purposefully in Zoey's direction. She knew she should whip round and dart out the nearest exit before he could get to her, but she couldn't seem to get her feet to move. It was as if he had locked her in place, frozen her to the spot with the commanding force of his dark brown gaze. She always tried to avoid being alone with him, not trusting herself to resist either slapping him or throwing herself at him. She didn't know why he of all people should have such an effect on her. He was too confident, too charming, too polished, too everything.

Finn came to stand within a foot of her, close enough for her to smell the expensive citrus notes of his aftershave and to see the devilish *ah, now I'll have some fun* glint in his eyes. 'Good morning, Ms Brackenfield.'

His bow and mock-formal tone stirred the hornet's nest of her hatred. The blood simmered in her veins until she thought they would explode. Zoey straightened her spine, steeled her gaze and set her mouth into a prim line. 'Looks like you've got your love life sorted for the next month.' She flicked her gaze in the direction of the group of women he'd just left, her tone rich with icy disdain.

His smile broadened and the glint in his eyes intensified to a sharp point of diamond-bright light that made something at the base of her spine fizz. 'You do me a disservice. I could get through that lot in a week.' His voice was a deep, sexy baritone, the sort of voice that made her think of tangled sheets, sweaty bodies, panting breaths, primal needs. Needs Zoey had ignored for months and would keep on ignoring…or try to, which was not so easy with Finn looking so damn sexy and standing within touching distance.

Being in Finn's company made her feel strangely out of kilter. Her usual *sang froid* was replaced with a hearty desire to slap his designer-stubbled face and screech a mouthful of obscenities at him. She raised her chin a fraction, determined to hold his gaze without flinching. 'One wonders if you have a revolving door on your bedroom.'

Finn's gaze drifted to her mouth, his indolent half-smile sending another frisson through her body. 'You're welcome to check it out some time and see for yourself.'

Zoey gripped the tote bag strap hanging off her

shoulder for something to do with her hands, her heart skipping a beat, two beats, three, as if she had suddenly developed a bad case of arrhythmia. 'Does that line usually work for you?' Honestly, if her tone got any frostier, they would have to turn on the heating in the auditorium.

'Always.' His lazy smile sent a soft, feathery sensation down the back of her neck and spine, and her willpower requested sick leave.

Zoey could see why he had a reputation as a playboy—he was charm personified in every line of his gym-toned body. But she *would* resist him even if it killed her. She stretched her lips into a tight, no-teeth-showing smile. 'Well, I'd better let you get back to your avid fans over there.'

She began to turn away, but he stalled her by placing his hand lightly on her wrist and a high-voltage electrical charge shot through her body. He removed his hand within a second or two, but the sensation lingered on in her flesh, travelling from her wrist, up her arm and down her spine like a softly fizzing firework.

'I was expecting to see your dad here. Or maybe I've missed him in the crowd.' Finn turned and scanned the auditorium before meeting her gaze once more. 'He mentioned in a text the other day about catching up for a coffee.'

Zoey couldn't imagine what Finn would have in common with her father other than they both ran advertising agencies. And as to having a coffee with him, well, if only it was caffeine her father was addicted to. It was no secret her dad had a drinking problem—he had disgraced himself publicly a few too many times in spite of her efforts to keep him from harming the business.

Brackenfield Advertising was her birthright, her career, everything she had worked so hard for. She would do almost anything to keep the business on track, which meant sometimes feeling a little compromised when it came to managing her father. And right now, her father was at home nursing yet another hangover. And it wasn't from indulging in too much caffeine.

'My father is…catching up on work at home today.'

'Then maybe you and I could grab a coffee instead.'

'I'm busy.' Zoey lifted her chin and narrowed her gaze to flint. 'I didn't know you and my father were bosom buddies.'

His lips quirked in an enigmatic smile. 'Business rivals can still be friends, can't they?'

'Not in my book.' Zoey pointedly rubbed at her wrist, annoyed her skin was still tingling. One thing was for certain—she would *never* be Finn O'Connell's friend. He was a player, and she was done with players. Done for good. She pulled her sleeve back down over her wrist. She hadn't been touched by a man in months. Why should Finn's touch have such an impact on her?

She couldn't deny he was potently attractive. Tall, lean and toned, with an olive complexion that was currently deeply tanned, he looked every inch the sophisticated, suave self-made business-man. Enormously wealthy, today he was casually dressed—as were most delegates—his crew-neck lightweight cotton sweater showcasing the breadth of his broad shoulders and his navy-blue chinos the length and strength of his legs.

But, while Finn looked casual, nothing about his approach to business was laid back. He was fo-cussed and ruthlessly driven, pulling in contracts so lucrative they made Zoey's eyes water in envy.

Zoey could sense his sensual power coming off him in waves. She was aware of him as she was aware of no other man. She had known him for a couple of years or so, running into him at various advertising functions. He had been her only rival for an account a few months ago and it still infu-riated her that he'd won it instead of her, mostly because she knew for a fact he had a friend on the board of directors of the company—a female friend.

'I hear you're pitching for the Frascatelli ac-count,' Finn said with another mercurial smile. 'Leonardo Frascatelli is only considering three ad companies' pitches for his campaign. A battle between friends, yes?'

Zoey blinked and her stomach dropped. Oh no, did that mean he was vying for it too? With only three candidates in the running, she'd been confident she was in with a chance. But what would happen to her chance if Finn was in the mix?

The Italian hotel chain was the biggest account she had ever gone after, and if she won it she wouldn't have to worry about her dad frittering away the business's assets any more. She would finally prove to her father she had what it took to run the company. She ran the tip of her tongue over her suddenly carpet-dry lips, her heart beating so fast it threatened to pop out of her ribcage. She could *not* lose the Frascatelli account.

She. Could. Not.

And most certainly not to Finn O'Connell.

Zoey was flying to New York that evening to present it the following afternoon. Her presentation was on her laptop in the cloak room along with her overnight bag. Did that mean he was flying over there too? 'I can't think of a single set of circumstances that would ever make me consider being friends with you.'

'Not very creative of you,' he drawled, his gaze sweeping over her in an indolent fashion. 'I can think of plenty.'

Zoey gave him a look that would have sent a

swarm of angry wasps ducking for cover. 'I can only imagine what sort of ridiculous scenario a mind like yours would come up with—that is, of course, if you can get it out of the gutter long enough.'

Finn gave a rich, deep laugh that sent a tingle shimmering down her spine. Drat the man for being so incredibly attractive. Why couldn't he could have one just one physical imperfection? His mellifluous voice was one of the first things she had noticed about him. He could read out loud the most boring, soporific financial report and she would be hanging on his every word. His smiling dark brown eyes made her lips twitch in spite of her effort not to be taken in by his practised charm.

His mouth was nicely sculptured, his lips not too thick or too thin but somewhere perfectly in between. A mouth that promised erotic expertise in its every delicious contour. A mouth she had to keep well away from. No way was she joining the conga line to dive into his bed. No freaking way.

'I wouldn't dare to describe how my mind works.' He gave a slow smile and added, 'I might shock you to the core of your being.'

The core of her being was still recovering from his lazy smile, thank you very much. There was a fluttery sensation between her legs, and she hated herself for being so weak. So what if he was smouldering hot? So what if he made her feel more of a woman than she had ever felt just by looking at her with that sardonic gaze?

She *had* to resist him. She would be nothing more than a notch on his bedpost, a fleeting dalliance he would view as yet another conquest.

'Nothing about you would shock me, Finn. You're so boringly predictable, it's nauseating.' Not strictly true. He kept her on her toes more than any man she'd ever met. He constantly surprised her with his whip-smart repartee. She even—God forgive her—enjoyed their sparring. It gave her a rush, a secret thrill, to engage in a verbal scrap with him because his quick-witted mind more than matched her own.

Finn's eyes kindled, as if her carelessly flung words had thrown down a challenge he couldn't wait to act upon. 'Ah, well then, I'll have to lift my game to see if I can improve your opinion of me.' His lips curved in another smile that curled her toes inside her shoes.

'Finn!' A young blonde woman came tottering over in vertiginous heels with her hand outstretched, waving a business card held in her perfectly manicured fingers. 'I forgot to give you my number. Call me so we can catch up soon?'

Finn took the card and slipped it into his trouser pocket, his smile never faltering. 'Will do.'

The young woman looked as if she had just won the mega-draw lottery, her eyes so bright they could have lit up a football stadium. She gave Finn a fingertip wave and tottered back off to join her gaggle of friends.

Zoey rolled her eyes and, turning to one side, made vomiting noises. She straightened to lock gazes with Finn. 'Really?'

'She's an intern. I'm mentoring her.'

Zoey choked on a cynical laugh. She didn't know what annoyed her more—his straight face or his assumption she would be fooled by it. 'In the boardroom or the bedroom?'

His eyes never left hers, his mouth twitching at the corners with amusement. 'Your jealousy is immensely flattering. Who knew behind that ice maiden thing you've got going on is a woman so smoking-hot for me?'

Zoey curled her hands into fists, her anger flaring like a flame doused by an accelerant. It formed a red mist before her eyes and made each of her limbs stiffen like the branches of a dead tree. He enjoyed goading her—she could see it in his eyes. He liked getting a rise out of her and never wasted an opportunity to do so. He was playing her, and she was a fool to respond to him. But how was she supposed to ignore him? He wasn't the sort of man you could ignore. Oh, how she would love to slap his face. How she would love to kick him in the shins. How she would love to rake her nails—*her unmanicured nails*—down his face.

And, God help her, how she would love to sleep with him to see if he was as exciting a lover as gossip had it. Not that she would ever act on such a desire. Since being cheated on by her long-term boyfriend, Rupert, she was completely and utterly over men. She had given her all to her ex and had been completely blindsided by his betrayal. She didn't want the complications and compromises of a relationship any more.

But whenever she was anywhere near Finn O'Connell every female hormone in her body went into overdrive. She became aware of her body in his presence—of the tingles and flutters and arrows of lust almost impossible to ignore. But ignore them she must. Sleeping with the enemy was not in her game plan.

Zoey flashed him a livid glare, her chest heaving with the effort to contain her rage. 'I wouldn't sleep with you if you paid me a squillion pounds.'

His dark eyes danced and his confident smile irked her beyond endurance. 'Oh, babe, you surely don't think I'm the kind of man who has to pay for sex?' He stepped closer and placed two fingers beneath her chin, locking his gaze on hers. 'Can you feel that?' His voice lowered to a gravelly burr, his eyes holding hers in a mesmerising lock.

'F-feel what?' Zoey was annoyed her voice wobbled but her heart was leaping about like a mad thing in her chest, his fingers on her face sending a wave of scorching heat through her body.

Finn stroked his thumb over the circle of her chin, his warm minty breath wafting across her lips, mingling with her own breath like two invisible lovers getting it on. 'The energy we create together. I felt it the minute you walked into the room.'

No way was she admitting she felt it too. No way. Zoey disguised a swallow, her heart-rate accelerating, her inner core tingling as if he had touched her between the legs instead of on her chin. Why wasn't she stepping back? Why wasn't she slapping his arrogant face? She was under some sort of sensual spell, captivated by the feel of his thumb pad caressing her chin in slow strokes. Intoxicated by the clean, freshly laundered smell of his clothes, the citrus top notes and the sexy bergamot base note of his aftershave. She could feel the forcefield of his sensual energy calling out to her in invisible waves.

Her senses reeled from his closeness, his dangerously tempting closeness. She was acutely aware of his touch, even though it was only the pad of his thumb—it felt like a searing brand, the warmth seeping through her flesh travelling to her feminine core in a quicksilver streak.

Zoey had been celibate for months. She hadn't even thought about sex for weeks and weeks on end. Now, her mind was filling with images of being in bed with Finn in a tangle of limbs and crumpled bed linen, her body slick with sweat and glowing from earth-shattering pleasure. And she was in no doubt it would be earth-shattering pleasure. Being near him like this made her body pulse with longing—a raw, primal longing she wished she could block out, anaesthetise or bludgeon away. It was a persistent ache between her legs, a pounding ache in time with her heartbeat, an ache his touch triggered, inflamed, incited.

But somehow, with a mammoth effort, she got her willpower to scramble back out of sick bay. 'You're imagining it…' Zoey licked her lips and pulled out of his hold, rubbing at her chin and shooting him a frowning look through slitted eyes. 'If you ever put your hands on me again, I won't be answerable for the consequences,' she added through tight lips.

He gave a mock-shudder, his playful smile making his eyes gleam. 'Listen, babe, you'll be the one begging me to put my hands on you. I can guarantee it. *Ciao.*'

He walked away without another word and Zoey was left seething, grinding her teeth to powder, hating him all the more, because she had a horrible feeling he might be right.

CHAPTER TWO

FINN WAS STANDING in line waiting to go through the business class security checkpoint at London Heathrow airport when he saw Zoey Brackenfield two people ahead of him. He had sensed her presence even before he saw her—it was if something alerted him the minute he stepped into her orbit. It had been the same at the conference that morning—he had sensed her in the room like a disturbance in an electromagnetic field. A shiver had passed over his scalp and run down his spine, as if some sort of alchemy was going on between them—otherwise known as rip-roaring lust.

Finn always looked forward to seeing her at various advertising gigs. He enjoyed getting a rise out of her, which was amusingly easy to do. She was prickly and uptight, and flashed her violet gaze and lashed him with her sharp tongue any chance she got. But he knew deep in his DNA that underneath the prickly façade she was as hot for him as he was for her. Their combative repartee had been going on for months and he knew it was only a matter of time before she gave in to the desire that flared and flickered and flashed between them.

Zoey took out her laptop from its bag and put it on a tray to go through the scanner, her striking features etched in a frown. He noticed the laptop was exactly the same brand and model as his— even the light grey bag was identical. *Great minds think alike,* he mused, and stepped up to take a tray from the stack.

She placed her tote bag on another tray and stood waiting—not all that patiently. She shifted her weight from foot to foot, pushed back her left sleeve and glanced at the watch on her slim wrist, then pushed her mid-length silky black hair behind one shoulder. She was dressed in black leather trousers that clung like a glove to her long, slim legs and taut and shapely little bottom. Her silky baby-blue V-necked blouse skimmed her breasts and, when she turned on an angle in his line of vision and bent over to take off her high-heeled shoes, he caught a glimpse of her delightful cleavage and a jab of lust hit him in his groin.

As if she sensed his gaze on her, she straightened and met his gaze, her frown intensifying, her eyes narrowing, her lips pursing.

Finn smiled and pushed his laptop further along the conveyor belt, then he reached to unbuckle his belt to put it on the tray with his watch and wallet and keys. Zoey's eyes followed the movement of his hands as he slowly released his belt, and two spots of colour formed on her cheeks. But then she bit her lip and whipped back round as if she was worried he was going to strip off completely. If only they'd been alone, he'd definitely have done that, and enjoyed watching her strip off too.

There was a slight hold-up, as one of the people in front of Zoey had forgotten to take the loose coins out of their pocket. By the time Zoey walked through to collect her things from the conveyer belt, Finn's things had come through as well. She barely gave him a glance, and snatched up her laptop and tote bag and scurried off, but she was soon stopped by one of the random check personnel. She blew out a breath and followed the uniformed man to be electronically swabbed.

Finn absently put his laptop back in the carrier bag, his gaze tracking to Zoey as if drawn by an industrial-strength magnet. She was so damn cute he could barely stand it. But the people coming through behind him in the queue meant he had to get his mind back on the task at hand. He hitched the laptop bag over his shoulder then put his belt back on and slipped his wallet and phone and keys in his trouser pockets.

His gaze flicked back to Zoey and the frustrated look on her face brought a smile to his lips.

Those random checks were so random, he got called over every time he flew, but today was apparently his lucky day. No pat-down for him, but, hey, he wouldn't mind if it was Zoey doing the patting down.

Zoey was finally given the all-clear and gathered her things and stalked past, her head at a proud height, her gaze pointedly ignoring him.

'Got time for a drink?' Finn asked, catching up with her in a couple of easy strides.

'No, thank you. I don't want to miss my flight.' Even the sound of her heels click-clacking on the floor sounded annoyed.

'What flight are you on?'

She told him the carrier and the time, but it wasn't the same as his, and he was vaguely aware of a little stab of disappointment deep in his gut. Who knew what seven and a half hours in her company might have produced? He got hard just thinking about it.

'Good luck with your pitch,' he said with a smile. 'May the best person win.'

Zoey stopped walking to look up at him, her violet eyes like lethal daggers. 'If it were a level playing field, I would've won the last time we were pitching for the same account. Tell me, did you sleep with someone to swing the board's decision?'

'I don't have to resort to such tactics, babe, I just do a damn good job. Yours was a good pitch, though. And I really liked the dog food commercial you did a while back. Cute…real cute.'

She rapid-blinked in an exaggerated way, one of her hands coming up to her chest as if to calm her heart rate down. 'Oh. My. God. Did I just hear you give me a *compliment*?'

Finn chuckled at her mock-shocked expression. 'What? Doesn't anyone ever tell you how brilliant you are?'

'Not that I can remember.' She gave him a haughty look and added, 'But no doubt you've been hearing that said to you from the moment you were born.'

If only she knew how far from the truth that was. Finn had rarely seen either of his parents since he was six years old. They'd found the task of raising a child too restrictive for their hippy-dippy lifestyle—especially when he'd got to school age. They hadn't been able to handle the responsibility of waking up early enough after a night of drinking and smoking dope to get him ready for school or to pick him up afterwards, so they'd dumped him on distant relatives.

They had been given another couple of chances to get their act together during his childhood, but Finn had finally got tired of it by the time he was thirteen. He'd soon been shipped back to his relatives, who hadn't exactly welcomed him back with open arms. He couldn't recall too many compliments coming his way growing up, but he had got the message loud and clear that he'd been an encumbrance, a burden no one had wanted but kept out of a sense of duty.

'You'd be surprised,' Finn said with a hollow laugh.

Zoey looked at him for a beat or two longer, her forehead still creased in a slight frown. Then she shifted her gaze and glanced at her boarding pass. 'I'd better get to my gate…'

She walked off without another word and Finn felt again that strange little niggle of disappointment. He gave himself a mental shake and strode towards his own departure gate. He needed to get a grip. Anyone would think he was becoming a little obsessed with Zoey Brackenfield. He wasn't the type to get too attached to a woman—to anyone, when it came to that. His life in the fast lane left no time for long-term relationships. A long-term relationship in his mind was a day or two, tops. Any longer than that and he got a little antsy, eager to get out before it got too claustrophobic. Maybe he was like his freedom-loving parents after all. Scary thought.

It was almost three in the morning by the time Zoey got to her New York hotel. She had slept a little on the flight and watched a couple of movies rather than tweak her pitch on her laptop. She knew from experience that last-minute tweaks often did more harm than good. Her nerves would take over, her self-doubts run wild, and before she knew it the presentation would be completely different from her original vision.

Besides, she really loved travelling in Business Class. The way her father's business was currently going meant that travelling in style and comfort might not be something she would be doing too much longer, so she figured she might as well enjoy it while she could. No doubt Finn O'Connell had no worries on that score. She could just imagine him lying back on his airbed, sipping French champagne and chatting up the female cabin crew. *Grr*.

Zoey had a shower to freshen up and dressed in a bathrobe with her hair in a towel, turban-like, on her head, placing the laptop bag on the writing desk in the suite. She unzipped the bag and took out the laptop and laid it on the leather protector on the desk. She opened the screen and turned it on and waited for it to boot up. A strange sensation scuttled across her scalp as the screen became illuminated. She leaned forward, blinked her weary gaze and peered at the unfamiliar screensaver.

The unfamiliar screensaver...

Zoey's heart leapt to her throat, her legs went to water and her hands shook as though she had a movement disorder. This wasn't her laptop! She was in New York without her laptop. The laptop with her pitch on it.

Don't panic. Don't panic. Don't panic. She tried to calm herself down but she had never been a star pupil at mindfulness. Fear climbed her spine and spread its tentacles into her brain like a strangling vine. She was going to lose the contract. She was miles away from her laptop. What was she going to do? *Breathe. Breathe. Breathe.* Zoey took a deep lungful of air and stared at the laptop, praying this was a nightmare she would wake from at any moment.

But wait…all was not lost. Her presentation was in the cloud. But still, her laptop had a lot of personal information on it, and she didn't want to lose it. Besides, her pitch was first thing tomorrow morning and she couldn't be sure there would be another laptop she could use. And it would look unprofessional to turn up so ill-prepared.

Who owned this one?

Her mind spooled back to the security check at Heathrow and something cold slithered down the entire length of her spine. Could this be Finn O'Connell's laptop? Her stomach did a flip turn. Oh, no. Did that mean he had hers? She had a sticker on the back of her laptop with her name and number on it but there was nothing on the back of this computer.

The screensaver was asking for a password. She

drummed her fingers on the desk. Did she need a password to check if it was his computer? Maybe there was something in the laptop bag that might be enough of a clue as to whose computer it was. She reached inside the bag and took out a couple of pens and a collection of business cards. One, from a woman called Kimba, had a red lipstick kiss pressed to the back with a handwritten message below it:

Thanks for last night, Finn. It was unbelievable.

Zoey wanted to tear it into confetti-sized pieces and only just stopped herself in time. Double *grr*. What a player. He probably had lovers all over the world.

But at least it solved the mystery of whose computer Zoey had in her possession...or did it? The bag was the same as hers. No doubt there were other laptop bags exactly the same as this one. How could she know for sure this was Finn's computer inside his bag? It had been crowded at the security checkpoint and so many laptops looked the same. Besides, he hadn't phoned or texted her to tell her he had hers. Maybe someone else had hers and this was a complete stranger's!

Zoey searched further in the laptop bag and pulled out a bright orange sticky note attached to a computer technician's card. The sticky note had the words 'temporary password' written on it and below it a series of numbers and letters and dashes and hashtags. She stared at it for a long moment, a host of rationalisations assembling in her head. She needed to know for sure if this was Finn's laptop. She had a password but whether it was Finn's or not was still not clear. This could easily be someone else's laptop accidentally put in his laptop bag.

She had to know for sure, didn't she? She had to check to see if it was actually Finn's laptop, right? She would call the airport once she knew one way or the other. She figured, if it turned out to be his, all she had to do was call him and ask him to meet her for a quick swap-over. There wouldn't be any delay that way, as he was probably in New York by now too.

Zoey stuck the note to the screen of the laptop and held her fingers over the keys. *You shouldn't be doing this.* She rolled her left shoulder backwards, as if she was physically dislodging her nagging conscience. Her fingers moved closer to the keyboard and her heart began to thud, a fine sweat breaking out across her brow. She could only imagine how nauseating it would be to read his emails. No doubt hundreds of gushing messages from his many lovers telling how wonderful he was. Could she stomach it? No. Definitely not.

Zoey got up from the desk, folding her arms across her body to remove them from temptation.

It would be wrong to read his personal messages—
anyone's, for that matter. Was it even a crime?

But then a thought crept into her brain… Could
she just click on Finn's pitch? Just a teensy-weensy
little peek? No. That would be taking things a little
too far. She was a morally upright citizen. She believed in doing the right thing at all times and in
all circumstances. And yet…this was her chance
to get a heads-up on what his pitch looked like. He
would never know she'd checked…

But *she* would know, and that was something
that didn't sit well with her. The competition had
to be fair and equal and, if she looked at his pitch
and made last minute changes to hers once she
got her laptop back and subsequently won the account, how victorious would she actually feel? It
would be a hollow victory indeed. She wanted to
win the pitch on her own merit. She had fought too
hard and for too long to be taken seriously. If she
were to cheat to get to the top, then she would be
devaluing everything she had worked so hard for.

Zoey glanced back at the laptop, her teeth chewing at her lower lip. 'You can stop looking at me
like that, okay?' She addressed the laptop sternly.
'I'm not doing it. I would hate it if he did it to me.'

Yikes! But what if he was doing it to her at this
very moment?

Zoey let out a stiff curse. Those last few emails
she sent to her ex were not something she wanted

anyone else reading, and certainly not Finn O'Connell. She walked back to the computer and slammed it shut. 'There. Who said I can't resist temptation?'

As long as she could resist Finn O'Connell just as easily.

After dinner was served and then cleared away on the flight, Finn took out his laptop and set it up before him in his business class seat. But as soon as he opened it he knew something wasn't right. For one thing, there were food crumbs all over the keys, which was strange, because he never ate at the computer. Besides, it had only just come back from his tech service people, who had serviced one of his faulty programs, and they always returned it spotless.

He pressed the 'on' button and an unfamiliar screensaver came up. Shoot. He had someone else's laptop.

Someone who had gone through the security check at the same time.

He turned the computer over and found a sticker on the back with Zoey's name and number on it. A smile broke over his face and he closed the laptop with a snap. What were the chances of them switching laptops?

As much as he was tempted to have a little snoop around Zoey Brackenfield's laptop, he was going to resist. Who said he couldn't be a chivalrous gentleman? She had a right to her privacy; besides, he could do without any more animosity from her. He genuinely liked her. She was feisty, determined and talented, and he admired her all-in work ethic. She was in a still largely male dominated field, but she didn't let it intimidate her. A couple of her projects he'd seen had been nothing short of brilliant.

Finn showered and shaved once he got to the penthouse suite of his hotel. He had yet to call Zoey about the laptop mix-up, but considering it was the middle of the night he figured it could wait until a decent hour. Clearly, she hadn't discovered the mix-up because he had no missed calls or text messages from her.

He had got a text message from Zoey's father, however, mentioning something about a business matter he wanted to discuss with him. Finn couldn't decide if it was one of Harry Brackenfield's increasingly regular drunken, middle-of-the-night texts or if there was a genuine reason behind his request for a meeting. Either way, it could wait. He had much more important business on his mind— getting his laptop back and seeing Zoey again.

But as Finn was coming out of the bathroom his phone buzzed from where he'd left it on the bedside table earlier. He walked over to scoop it up and saw Zoey's name come up.

'Good morning,' he said. 'I believe have something of yours in my possession.'

'Did you do it deliberately?' Her tone was so sharp, he was surprised it didn't pierce one of his arteries. 'Did you switch them at the airport?'

Finn walked over to the windows to look at the view of the city that never slept. The flashing billboards and colourful lights of Times Square were like an electronic firework show. 'Now, why would I do that? It's damned inconvenient for one thing and, secondly, dangerous to have my personal data in the hands of someone who doesn't have my best interests at heart.'

'I want it back. Now.' Her tone was so strident and forceful, he could almost picture her standing in her hotel room visibly shaking with anger.

He let out a mock-weary sigh. 'Can't it wait until morning?'

'It *is* morning,' she shot back. 'Where are you staying? I'll come to you right now.'

'Now is not convenient.'

There was a silence in which all he could hear was her agitated breathing.

'Have you got someone with you?' Zoey asked.

'You might not believe this but I'm all by myself.' Thing was, he was all by himself more often than not just lately. He was the first to admit his sex life needed a reboot. The hook-ups were not as exciting as they used to be. None of his lovers captivated him the way he wanted to be captivated. The way Zoey captivated him. His focus on her was stuffing up his ability to sleep with anyone else. But that was easily fixed—he would convince her to indulge in a hot little hook-up. Problem solved.

Zoey made a scoffing noise, as if in two minds whether to believe him about his solitary status. 'Then there's no reason I can't come by and get my computer and give you yours.'

'Why can't you wait until a decent hour? Or are you worried I'm going to hack into your computer, hmm?'

There was another tight little silence, punctuated by her breathing.

'Y-you wouldn't do that…would you?'

Finn let out an exaggerated sigh. 'Your low opinion of me never ceases to amaze me. Look— I'll compromise and bring your laptop to you rather than you come out in the wee hours. Where are you staying?'

She told him the name of the hotel, which was only a block away. 'How long will you be?' she added.

'Don't worry, babe. I know you're impatient to see me, but I won't keep you waiting much longer.'

'It's not you I want to see, it's my computer.' And then the phone clicked off.

* * *

Zoey tugged the damp towel off her head and threw it on the bed, her fury at Finn knowing no bounds. She wouldn't put it past him to have deliberately switched their computers. He never failed to grasp an opportunity to get under her skin. No doubt he'd been trawling through her emails and photos and pitch presentation without a single niggle of his conscience. She, at least, had felt conflicted enough not to do it, even if it had been a close call in terms of self-control. She shut down his computer and put it back in the laptop bag and firmly zipped it up.

But deep down she knew she had made the choice not to snoop because she respected him professionally, even if she had some issues with how he lived his private life.

Or maybe her issues with his private life were because she was envious of how easily he moved from one lover to the next. She had been unable to stomach the thought of sharing her body with anyone since her ex had cheated on her. Well, apart from Finn, which was both annoying and frustrating in equal measure, because he was the last person she wanted to get naked with under any circumstances. However, it was a pity her body wasn't in agreement with her rational mind.

The doorbell sounded before Zoey had time to

change out of the hotel bathrobe into clothes. She clutched the front opening of the bathrobe together and padded over to the door. 'Is that you, Finn?'

'Sure is.'

Zoey opened the door and found him standing there with her laptop bag draped over one shoulder. He didn't look one bit jet-lagged—in fact, he looked ridiculously refreshed and heart-stoppingly gorgeous. He had recently showered and shaved, his brushed back thick, dark hair still damp. The tantalising notes of his aftershave drifted towards her, reminding her of a sun-baked citrus orchard with crushed exotic herbs underfoot. She held out her hand for her computer. 'Thank you for dropping it off. I won't keep you.'

He held firm to the laptop resting against his hip, one prominent dark eyebrow rising in an arc. 'Aren't you forgetting something?'

Zoey looked at him blankly for a moment. He flicked his gaze towards the writing desk behind her, his expression wry. 'I'll give you yours, if you give me mine. Deal?'

Zoey was so flustered at seeing him at this ungodly hour and looking so damn hot, she'd completely forgotten she had his computer. 'Oh…right, sorry…' She swung round and padded over to the desk to pick up the laptop. But then she heard the soft click of the suite door close behind her and a tingle shot down her spine. She turned to face him, her pulse rate picking up at the sardonic look in his eyes. 'I don't remember asking you into my room.'

'I know, and it was most impolite of you to not at least offer me a drink, since I walked all this way in the dark to bring you your laptop. I could have been mugged.' His eyes had a devilish gleam and her pulse rate went up another notch.

Zoey gave him a look that would have withered a plant. A plastic plant. 'Fine. What do you want? Erm, to drink, I mean.'

She was in no doubt about what he really wanted. She could see it in eyes, could feel it in the air—a throbbing pulse of sexual energy that pinged off him in waves, colliding with her own energy, stirring a host of longing and need that threatened to consume her. She felt it every time she was in his presence, the dark, sensual vibration of mutual lust. It horrified her that she was in lust with him. Horrified and shamed her. How could she possibly think of getting it on with him? He was a playboy. A man who had a freaking turnstile on his bedroom door. It was lowering to admit she was so attracted to him. What sort of self-destructive complex did she have to lust after a man she didn't even like?

'Coffee. I'll make it.' Finn sauntered over to the small coffee percolator near the mini-bar area. His take-charge attitude would have annoyed her normally, but she was tired and out of sorts, and the thought of someone else making her a coffee was rather tempting.

'Fine.' She sank to the small sofa in front of the television, wondering if she should have put up more of a fuss and insisted on him leaving. She realised, with a strange little jolt, she had never been totally alone with him before. There had always been other people in the background such as at conferences or at the airport the previous day.

One thing she did know—being alone with Finn O'Connell was dangerous. Not because he posed a physical threat to her safety but because she wasn't sure she knew how to handle such a potently attractive man at close, intimate quarters. At six-foot-six, he made the hotel room seem even smaller than it actually was. And, while she was no midget at five-foot-ten, she was currently barefoot and wearing nothing but a bathrobe.

Being so minimally attired made her feel at a distinct disadvantage. She needed the armour of her clothes to keep her from temptation. And temptation didn't get any more irresistible than Finn O'Connell in a playful mood.

Within a short time, the percolator made its gurgling noises, and the delicious aroma of brewed coffee began to tantalise Zoey's nostrils. Finn poured two cups and brought them over.

'Here you go. Strong and black.'

Zoey frowned and took the cup from him. 'How did you know how I take my coffee?'

His eyes twinkled. 'Lucky guess.'

Her lips twitched in spite of her effort to control her urge to smile back at him. The last thing she wanted to do was encourage him…or did she? The thought trickled into her head like the coffee had done in the machine just moments ago.

The dangerous thought of exploring the tension between them hummed like a current. It was a background hum, filtering through her body, awakening her female flesh to sensual possibilities. Possibilities she had forbidden herself to consider. Finn was a player, a fast-living playboy who had 'heartbreaker' written all over his too-handsome face. She had already had her heart broken by her ex. Why would she go in for another serve? It would be madness…

But it wouldn't be madness if she set the terms, would it? Why shouldn't she allow herself a treat now and again? She had given so much to her ex and got nothing back. Why not indulge herself this time with a man who didn't want anything from her other than hot no-strings sex?

Finn picked up the writing desk chair and placed it close to the sofa where she was sitting. He sat on the chair and balanced his right ankle over his other thigh in a casual pose she privately envied. Zoey had never felt more on edge in her life. Edgy, restless…excited. Yes, excited, because what woman wouldn't be excited in Finn's arrantly male presence?

Zoey sipped her coffee, covertly watching him do the same. Her eyes were drawn to the broad hand holding his cup, her mind conjuring up images of those long, tanned fingers moving down her body…touching her in places that hadn't seen any action for months on end. Places that began to tingle as they woke up from hibernation.

She sat up straighter on the sofa, almost spilling her coffee. 'Oops.' She caught a couple of droplets rolling down the side of her cup before they went on the cream linen sofa.

'Too hot for you?' Finn asked with an enigmatic smile, his eyes glinting.

You're too hot for me. Zoey put her cup on the lamp table next to the sofa, her hand not as steady as she would have liked. 'No, it's fine. I'm just jet-lagged, I guess.'

He leaned back in his chair until it was balanced on the back legs only, his gaze measuring hers. 'Did you sleep on the plane?'

Zoey nodded. 'I'm glad I did now. If I'd realised you had my computer on the plane, I would have been in a flap of panic. It was bad enough finding out when I did, but at least it was only for a short time.'

There was a pulsing silence broken only by the

sound of his chair creakily protesting at the way it was balanced. Finn rocked forward and the front legs of the chair landed on the carpet with a thud. 'So, how did you figure out it was my computer?'

'There was a business card in the laptop bag with a lipstick kiss on it from a woman called Kimba.' She picked up her coffee with a roll of her eyes. 'I'm surprised there was only one card. I was expecting hundreds.'

He gave a laugh and leaned forward to place his coffee cup on a nearby table. 'I do clean it out occasionally. But that wasn't all that was in the bag.'

Zoey brought her gaze back to his. 'You're crazy for leaving your password on a sticky note. What if someone else had got your laptop?'

His mouth curved upwards in a smile, making his eyes crinkle attractively at the corners. 'I had my laptop serviced yesterday and they reset the password. I haven't had time to reset it again.' He reached for his coffee cup, took a small sip and then balanced it baseball-style in his hand. 'So, did you read my emails? Have a little snoop around?'

Zoey could feel heat storming into her cheeks and put her coffee back down on the table. 'Of course I didn't. Did you read mine?'

He placed his hand on his heart. 'Scout's honour, I didn't. I was tempted, sure, but I figured it was a pretty low thing to do.'

She bit down on her lower lip before she could

stop herself. For reasons she couldn't explain, she believed him. He might be a charming player in his free time, but he was scrupulously honest in business. He had built from scratch an advertising empire that was one of the most successful in the business. She might not like him, but she couldn't help admiring him for what he had achieved.

Finn took another sip of his coffee. 'Did you look at my pitch?' His eyes held hers in a penetrating lock that made her scalp prickle.

Zoey sprang up from the sofa as if one of the cushions had bitten her on the bottom. 'I admit I was tempted, seriously tempted, but I didn't do it. Besides, I already know you're going to win.' She was doomed to fail with him as an opponent. It was galling to think he was going to win over her yet again. Would she ever get a chance to prove herself? She drew in another breath and released it on a defeated sigh. 'I think I haven't got a chance against you.'

'Come now, it's not over till it's over.' He got up off the chair and placed his coffee cup on the table with a loud thwack. 'You haven't even presented yours and you're giving up? What sort of attitude is that in this business? You have to believe in yourself, Zoey, no one else will if you don't.' His tone sounded almost frustrated, a frown deeply carved on his forehead.

His unexpected reaction surprised Zoey into a defensive mode. She curled her lip, her eyes flashing. 'Thanks for the pep talk, O'Connell. But I don't need you to tell me how to live my life.'

He raked a hand through his hair, leaving track marks amongst the thick strands. 'Look, I know things are a little messy with your father right now. But...'

Messy? She didn't need Finn to tell her how messy things were—she lived the cringeworthy reality every single day. Watching her father go from hero to zero, picking him up after every binge drinking session, covering for him when he missed a deadline, making excuses to clients when he failed to show up for a meeting... The list went on. Zoey tightened her arms around her middle until she could barely breathe. 'I'd like you to leave. Right now.'

Finn held her stormy gaze with unwavering ease. 'I admire your father. In his day, he was one of the best in the business but—'

'Get. Out.'

'I'd leave if I thought that's what you really wanted.'

Zoey thrust up her chin, her eyes blazing, her body trembling with forbidden longing. A longing she was desperately trying to control. 'Oh, so now you're an expert on what I want? Don't make me laugh.'

Finn stepped up to within a few centimetres of her, not touching her but standing so close she could see the detail in his eyes—the tiny flecks of darker brown like a mosaic, the pitch-black rim of his irises as if someone had traced each circumference with a felt-tip marker. He said nothing, did nothing, his expression almost impossible to read except for a diamond-hard glint in his eyes. Her eyes drifted to the sensual contour of his mouth and something deep in her core fluttered like the wings of moth—a soft, teasing reminder of needs she had ignored for so long. Needs Finn triggered in her every time she was near him, erotic needs that begged to be assuaged.

Zoey became aware of the heat of his body, aware of the energy crackling in the small distance between their bodies. *Touch him. Touch him. Touch him.* The mental chant sounded in her head, the need to do what her instincts demanded a relentless drive she suddenly couldn't control. Her hands went to the rock-hard wall of his chest, her fingers clutching at his T-shirt until it was bunched in both of her hands.

One part of her brain told her not to get any closer, the other part said the exact opposite. The push and pull was like a tug-of-war in her body. She was drawn to him like an iron filing to a powerful magnet, the sheer irresistible force of him overwhelming any blocking tactics on her part—if she could have come up with one, that was. Her rational mind was offline, and her body was now dictating the way forward. It had taken control and was running on primal instinct, not on rationality and reason.

One of her hands let go of his T-shirt and went to the back of his head. She stepped up on tiptoe and got her mouth as close to his as was possible without actually touching it. She didn't know why she was flirting so recklessly with danger. She didn't know why she was putting herself so close to temptation when her ability to resist him was currently so debatable.

But some wicked little imp inside her egged her on to see what would happen. She knew it was dangerous, infinitely dangerous, but oh, so wickedly thrilling to have him teetering with her on a high wire of self-control, not sure who was going to topple off first.

Her heart was beating like a tribal drum, the same erotic rhythm that was pulsing insistently between her legs. 'You think I can't wait for you to kiss me, don't you? But do you know what's going to happen if you so much as place your lips on mine?'

Finn still didn't touch her; his hands were by his sides but his hooded gaze communicated the effort it took not to do so. 'I'm going to kiss you back like you've never been kissed before, that's what.' His voice was deep and husky, his sensual promise sending a shiver cartwheeling down her spine.

Driven by that same little inner demon, Zoey

moved a fraction closer, breathing in the vanilla and coffee scent of Finn's breath, her senses rioting. 'You think you're irresistible. That no woman with a pulse could ever say no to you. But I can resist you.'

Could she? Maybe, but why did she have to? They wanted the same thing—no-strings sex, an exploration of the lust that flared between them. What could be wrong with indulging her neglected senses in a simple hook-up with him?

Finn nudged his nose against hers—the tiniest nudge, but it sent a shockwave through her entire body. 'You're not saying no to me, you're saying no to yourself. You want me so badly, I can feel it every time I see you.'

Zoey fisted her hand in his hair in an almost cruel grip. 'I didn't think it was possible to hate someone as much as I hate you.'

His lips slanted in an indolent smile. 'Ah, but you don't hate me, babe. You hate how I make you feel. And I make you feel smoking-hot.'

'I feel *nothing* when I'm around you.' *Liar, liar, pants literally on fire.* On fire with lust.

He gave a low, deep chuckle and placed his hands on her hips, tugging her forward until she was flush against his rock-hard body. 'Then let's see if I can change that, shall we?' And his mouth came down firmly, explosively, on hers.

CHAPTER THREE

ANY THOUGHT OF pushing him away flew out of Zoey's head the moment his mouth crashed down on hers. Besides it being too late, deep down she knew she had intended this to happen from the get-go.

She wanted him to kiss her.

She wanted to push him over the edge.

She wanted him to be as desperate for intimate contact as was she.

His lips were firm, insistent, drawing from her an enthusiastic response she hadn't thought herself capable of giving to a man she didn't even like.

But what did like have to do with lust? Not much, it seemed.

The sensual heat of his mouth set fire to hers, his tongue entering her mouth with a bold, spine-tingling thrust that made her inner core contract with an ache of intense longing. His tongue duelled with hers in an erotic battle that sent her pulse rate soaring. She kissed him back with the same fierce drive, feeding off his mouth as if it was her only source of sustenance. Never had a kiss tasted so good, felt so good. It made every cell in her body throb with excitement.

One of Finn's hands went to the small of her back, drawing her even closer to his pelvis. The rigid press of his erection sent another wave of longing through her body. She made a sound at the back of her throat, a desperate whimpering sound of encouragement, and pushed further into his hardness, her arms winding around his neck, her fingers delving into the thickness of his hair.

Finn tilted his head to gain better access to her mouth, one of his hands cupping the side of her face. His tongue flicked against hers, calling it back into play, teasing her to a point where she was practically hanging off him, unable to stand on her own, for her legs were trembling so much. Never had she felt such ferocious desire. It pounded through her with each throbbing beat of her blood.

The taste of his mouth, the texture of his skin against her face, the feel of his hands on her hip and her cheek, sent her senses sky-rocketing. She needed to be closer. Ached to be closer. Would die if she didn't get closer.

Zoey unwound her arms from around his neck, tugging his T-shirt out of his jeans and placing her hands on his muscled chest, still with her mouth clamped to his. Her tongue danced with his in a sexy tango that made hot shivers go down her spine like a flow of molten lava.

Finn lifted his mouth off hers, looking at her with his dark, mercurial gaze. 'How am I doing so far? Have I changed your mind, or shall I stop right now?'

'Shut up and keep doing what you're doing,' Zoey said, dragging his head back down so her mouth could reconnect with his.

The kiss went on and on, more and more exciting, more and more intense, leaving her more and more breathless, aching with want and wondering why the hell she had rebuffed him earlier. *This* was what she wanted. This passionate awakening of her senses, catapulting her into a maelstrom of delicious feeling. Feelings that she had forgotten she could feel but which she was feeling now even more intensely than ever before.

Finn lifted his mouth off hers only long enough to haul his T-shirt over his head, tossing it to one side before his lips came back down on hers with fiery purpose. His breathing was heavy, the primal, growling sounds he made in his throat ramping up her own arousal. One of his hands slipped between the front opening of her bath robe to claim her left breast. She gasped at the contact of his hands on her naked flesh, her body erupting into flames.

'Yes…oh, yes…' Zoey hadn't realised she had

spoken out loud until she heard the sound of her desperate plea. 'Don't stop.'

Finn's eyes blazed with lust and he brought his mouth down to her breast, circling her nipple until it rose in a tight bud. He took it in his mouth, sucking on her with surprising gentleness, the sensation sending her senses spinning out of control. She grasped at his head, her spine arching in pleasure, her lower body tingling, tightening in anticipation of his intimate possession.

He lifted his mouth off her breast and held her gaze in an erotically charged lock that made the backs of her knees tingle and flames leap in her feminine core. 'I want you.' His bald statement was the most exciting, thrilling thing she had ever heard.

'Yeah, I kind of guessed that.' Zoey rubbed against him, shamelessly urging him on. 'But I don't want to talk. I want to do this.' She placed her mouth on his chest, circling her tongue around his hard, flat nipple, delighting in the salty taste of his skin. She began to go lower, drawn to the swollen length of him, driven by some wicked force within her. She had to taste him. *All* of him.

Finn made a rough sound at the back of his throat and captured her by the upper arms. 'Wait. I have other plans for you right now.'

He ruthlessly tugged the bath robe fully open, sliding it down her arms and untying the belt so it dropped to the floor at her feet. His hungry gaze devoured every inch of her flesh but, instead of shrinking away from him, Zoey stood under his smouldering gaze, relishing every heart-stopping moment of seeing the raw, naked lust on his face. She was empowered by the way he was looking at her, as if she was some sort of sensual goddess that had materialised before him. She was giddily excited by the rampant desire she triggered in him—the same out-of-control desire he triggered in her.

'I want to see you naked. Fair's fair.' Zoey surprised herself with her boldness. Who was this wild and wanton woman blatantly stating her needs?

Finn held her gaze with his smouldering one. He unsnapped the stud button on his jeans and rolled down the zipper, the *zzzrrruuppt* sound sending a shiver skating down her spine. He stepped out of his jeans, and then out of his black form-fitting undershorts, and her heart rate went off the charts.

Zoey sucked in a breath, devouring every proud inch of him with her gaze. 'Mmm…not bad, I suppose.'

Finn gave a laugh and grasped her by the hips again, tugging her against his potent heat. 'I've wanted to do this for months.' He began to nibble on her earlobe, the teasing nip of his teeth making her shudder with pleasure.

'So, let's do it.' Zoey could hardly believe she was saying it, but it was all she wanted right now. *He* was all she wanted right now. To have his potent, powerful body ease the desperate, clawing ache of her female flesh.

Finn pulled back a little to look into her eyes with a searching expression. 'Are you sure this is what you want?'

Zoey rubbed up against him again, her gaze sultry, delighting in the way he snatched in a breath as if her body thrilled him like no other. 'I want you, Finn. I don't know how to make that any clearer.'

'While we're on the topic of clarity—you know I'm not in this for the long haul, right? I don't do long-term relationships. It's not my gig—never has been, never will be.'

Zoey stroked her hand down his lean jaw. 'Yes, well, that's lucky, because I don't either. Or at least, not any more.' She stroked the length of his nose and then outlined the contour of his mouth and added, 'This is exactly what I need right now. A one-night stand with a man who won't call me tomorrow and want a repeat.' She tapped his lower lip with her fingertip. 'Deal?'

Something shifted at the back of his gaze— a tiny flicker, like a sudden start of surprise, but quickly concealed. 'Deal.' His mouth came down to hers in a hard, scorching kiss, the heat inflamed all the more by the erotic press of their bodies.

Zoey opened to the commanding thrust of his tongue, her arms winding around his neck, which brought her tingling breasts tighter against his chest. The sprinkling of his chest hair tickled her soft flesh and his guttural groan as he deepened the kiss made her toes curl into the carpet at her feet. She had never felt such overwhelming desire for a man, such intense longing, it consumed her from head to foot.

Finn walked her backwards to the bed, his mouth still pressed firmly against hers. He laid her down and stood looking at her for a long, breathless moment, his body in full arousal making her inner core coil and tighten with lust.

Being taller than most of her friends, Zoey had her share of body issues, always feeling gargantuan compared to her petite friends. But with Finn's ravenous gaze moving over her she felt like a supermodel and, for the first time in for ever, proud of her feminine curves and long limbs. 'Had your fill?' she asked in a coquettish tone.

'Not yet.'

He leaned down over her, resting his hands either side of her head, his gaze capturing hers. 'You're beautiful—every delicious inch of you.'

'Yes, well, there are quite a few inches of me.'

He smiled and stroked a lazy finger down between her breasts, his eyes darkening to pitch. 'And I am going to kiss each and every one of them.'

Zoey shivered, her need for him escalating to the point of discomfort. She reached up to grasp his head with both of her hands. 'If you don't have sex with me soon, I'm going to scream.'

His brown eyes glinted. 'Then it looks like I'm going to make you scream either way.'

A frisson passed over her body at the erotic promise of his statement, the same erotic promise she could see in his eyes. She had never been all that vocal during sex with her ex. Their love life had become a little routine over the time they'd been together, but she had put that down to the increasing demands of their careers. If she were to be perfectly honest, it had even been a tad boring at times.

'I'm not a screamer, as it turns out.' Zoey wasn't sure why she was spilling such personal information to him.

Finn came down beside her on the bed and placed his hand on her mound. 'Then I guarantee you soon will be.'

He brought his mouth down to her folds and she arched her spine like a languorous cat, unable to speak for the sensations flowing through her. Electric sensations sent ripples of pleasure to every inch of her body. His tongue stroked against the swollen bud of her clitoris, delicately at first, gauging her response, before he increased his rhythm and pressure.

Zoey gasped as lightning bolts of delight coursed through her flesh, the tension building inexorably to a point of no return. A part of her mind drifted above to look down at her body being pleasured by Finn, and was a little shocked at how vulnerable she had made herself to him. The intimacy of what he was doing to her was way beyond what she had experienced before. Rupert had occasionally gone down on her, but he never stayed long enough for her to feel anything more than a few vague flutters.

But with Finn her body was on fire, and the flames were licking at her flesh with tongues of incendiary heat. Zoey arched her spine even further, her legs trembling as the wave of pleasure hit her with a booming crash. Her breathless whimpers became cries, and then an almost shrill scream, as the waves kept coming, one after the other, pummelling her, pounding through her, until she was thrown out the other side, limp, satiated, in a total state of physical bliss.

'Oh, dear God…' She was lost for words, her breathing still out of order, her senses still spinning.

Finn moved back up her body, his eyes shining like dark, wet paint. 'Ready for more?'

'You can't be serious? I'm a come-once-only girl.'

A wicked glint appeared in his gaze. 'Let's see what I can do about changing that.' He sprang off the bed and went to get a condom from his wallet in the back pocket of his jeans. Zoey relished watching him, his gloriously naked body stirring a new wave of longing in her. He tore the foil packet with his teeth, tossing away the wrapper, and then rolled the condom over his erection, glancing at her with that same dancing, devilish glint in his eyes. And Zoey almost climaxed again on the spot.

Finn came back over to her and she reached up and tugged him back down so he was lying over her, his weight balanced on his arms, one of his powerful thighs hitched over hers. He leaned down to kiss her and she tasted herself on his lips, the raw and earthy intimacy of it blowing her mind. His tongue entered her mouth, teasing hers into a duel that mimicked the throbbing energy of him poised between her thighs. He ran one hand down the flank of her thigh in a slow stroke, and then back again, his mouth moving against hers with deeper and deeper passion.

He lifted his mouth off hers to gaze down at her, his breathing heavy. 'I don't think I've ever wanted someone more than I do you at this moment.' His voice was rough-edged, his eyes holding hers in an intimate lock that heralded the sensual delights to come.

Zoey placed her hand at the back of his head, her fingers toying with his hair. 'I bet you say that to everyone you sleep with.' Her tone was teasing but a part of her realised with a twinge of unease—their one-night stand agreement notwith-standing—she didn't want him to look on her as he looked on his other lovers. She wanted to stand apart, to be someone who wouldn't just disappear into the crowd of past lovers, the nameless women he had pleasured and then walked away from with-out a backward glance. The sort of women who gave him business cards with lipstick kisses and 'thanks for the memories' messages.

But exactly what *did* she want?

Zoey didn't want a committed relationship with Finn, or with anyone else for that matter. That part of her life was over. Dead and buried. She could never trust another man, let him into her life, into her body and then find he had betrayed her. She wasn't that much of a fool to lay herself open again to such ego-shredding hurt.

But she did want to feel alive and, right now, she had never felt more so.

Finn brushed a wayward strand of her hair back off her face. 'I haven't said it to anyone and meant it the way I do right now. You drive me crazy.'

'You drive me crazy too.'

'Good, because I would hate it if things weren't equal between us.' He nudged at her entrance, his eyes darkening as he surged into her with a throaty groan.

Zoey gasped in bliss as he drove to the hilt, her body welcoming him, wrapping around him, gripping him as he started thrusting. She was quickly swept away with his fast-paced rhythm, her senses reeling as the friction increased. Sensations shot through her female flesh, darts, flickers and arrows of pleasure that increased with every deep thrust of his body. She gripped him by his taut buttocks, unable to think, only to feel. And, oh, what exquisite feeling. Tingles, fizzes and starbursts of pleasure rippled through her. The tension grew and grew in the most sensitive nub of her body, but she couldn't quite tip over the edge.

Finn brought his hand down between their bodies and began to stroke her swollen flesh with his fingers, the extra friction, right where she needed it, sending her into outer space. Her orgasm was like a meteor strike exploding in her flesh, sending ripples and waves and rushes of pleasure through her body so fast and so furiously, it was almost frightening. Her body had never felt so out of control. It was spinning and thrashing and whirling with sensations that went on and on, the sweet torture making her throw her head back and bite back a scream.

The muffled scream turned into a sob—a laughing sob of disbelief. How could she have experienced such a tumult of the senses with a man she viewed as the enemy?

Finn gave another deep groan and surged deeply, his movements fast, almost frantic, before he finally let go. Zoey gripped him by the buttocks, a vicarious frisson of pleasure passing over her body as she felt the intensity of his release. He collapsed over her, his breathing still hectic, the slightly rougher skin of his jaw tickling her cheek.

After a few moments, he propped himself up on one elbow to look down at her, his body still joined to hers. He brushed back a stray hair from her face, his expression difficult to make out. His eyes moved between hers, back and forth, back and forth, every now and again dipping to her mouth and back again. He brought his index finger to her mouth and tapped her gently on her lips. 'You rocked me to the core.'

'I'm not finished rocking you.' Zoey captured his finger with her teeth, biting down with just enough pressure to see his pupils flare. She opened her bite just enough so she could glide her tongue over the pad of his finger, holding his smouldering gaze.

'Whoa there, babe. I have some business to see to.' He sucked in a breath and pulled away to deal with the used condom.

Zoey lay on her side with her elbow bent, resting her head on her hand, and followed him with her gaze, drinking in the sight of his lean, tanned build and firm muscles. 'Do you have any more condoms with you?' She could barely believe she had asked such a question. Who was this insatiable woman? It was certainly nothing like her former self.

Finn winked at her and picked up his wallet. 'Enough.'

'How many is enough?'

He walked back over to her and sat beside her, one of his hands running up and down her leg. 'What time's your pitch?'

Zoey glanced past him at the bedside clock and her stomach nose-dived. How could so much time have passed? She had completely forgotten about her pitch at nine a.m. 'Oh, shoot. I have to rush.' She brushed his hand away and scrambled off the bed, grabbing the bath robe off the floor and bundling herself into it. 'I have to shower and do my hair and make-up.' And get her scattered senses under some semblance of control.

Finn rose from the bed with an inscrutable look on his face. 'Then I won't keep you any longer.'

Zoey stood toying with the belt of her bath robe as he dressed, her teeth chewing at her lower lip, her body still tingling from his intimate possession. He picked up his laptop bag and slung it over his shoulder, his expression still masked.

'Erm...thanks for bringing me my laptop,' Zoey began but found herself floundering for what else to say. *Thanks for the memories? Thanks for giving me the best two orgasms of my life? Can I see you again?* No. She definitely was *not* saying that.

No way. She had scratched the Finn O'Connell itch and it was time to move on. 'Hope you have a good flight back home,' she added. Urgh. Of course he would have a good flight home, no doubt with the Frascatelli account firmly in his possession.

Finn gave a brief smile that didn't reach his eyes. 'It was my pleasure.' And then he walked out of the suite and closed the door behind him with a definitive click that made Zoey flinch.

CHAPTER FOUR

FINN'S PITCH PRESENTATION didn't go as he'd envisaged. For one thing, his mind was replaying every moment of making love to Zoey Brackenfield instead of focussing on selling his vision for the ad campaign to the client's representative.

The second thing was a niggling sense of irritation that Zoey hadn't expressed a desire to see him again for a repeat session or two. He had expected her to say it before he left her hotel room. Expected it so much that when it hadn't been forthcoming it had stung him in a way he had not been stung before. It was ironic, as usually it was he who sent a lover on her way with no promise of a follow-up. But it was her call, and he had a feeling it wouldn't be long before their paths crossed once again. And he would make the most of it.

The sex had been nothing short of phenomenal, a totally mind-blowing experience, and he wanted more. Ached to have her in his arms again with a throbbing ache so deep and intense, it was distracting him from his work. So much so, he didn't realise the representative from the Frascatelli Hotel corporation was speaking to him.

'I'm sorry,' Finn said. 'I missed that last bit. What did you say?'

The representative closed their meeting with a stiff smile. 'Once Leonardo Frascatelli has a look at the three candidates' presentations for himself, and my order of preference, he will make a final decision and be in touch on who gets the contract. It will be a few days, I should think.'

'Thank you.' At least he might be in with a chance if Leo Frascatelli had the final say, Finn thought with an inward sigh of relief. It was a big account, and he knew there would be ongoing work once this initial campaign was over. He liked to win when he set his mind on a goal. It was why he loved the advertising business—it was an adrenalin rush, a fast-paced creative process with big dividends. He enjoyed the team work and he had some of the best in the business working for him.

But the biggest adrenalin rush he'd experienced lately was his one-nighter with Zoey. The hunger she had triggered in him hadn't gone away in spite of their hot night of sex. It hadn't defused anything. Instead, his hunger for her was even more ravenous than before. She stirred a fervent sexual energy in him, an energy unlike anything else he had experienced with anyone else.

He didn't know what it was about her, but he wanted more. Zoey had said she hated him, but it didn't change the fact that she desired him. And what a scorching-hot desire it was. He shuddered every time he thought of her silky warmth gripping him so tightly, her breathless gasps and cries of pleasure, the almost desperate clutch of her hands on his body. He had felt the same desperation to be as close as it was physically possible to be.

Finn walked out of the meeting room, sure he could pick up a faint trace of Zoey's perfume lingering in the air from when she had pitched earlier that morning. He closed the door on his exit and blew out a long breath.

Boy, oh, boy, did he have the lust bug bad.

Zoey flew back to London later the same day, determined to stick to the plan of no repeats of her completely out-of-character hook-up with Finn O'Connell. But the deed was done and now it was time to move on and not allow herself to think of him. Anyway, he was probably in bed with someone else by now.

As for her pitch, well, it was Finn's fault she had stumbled and garbled her way through it like a rookie intern on her first project. How was she supposed to perform at a peak professional level with her body still tingling from head to foot from Finn's off-the-scale lovemaking?

But then a thought dropped into her head… Maybe that had been his plan right from the start. Maybe he had wanted to sabotage her pitch by scrambling her brain, short-circuiting her senses, until all she could think about was the stroke and glide of his hands on her skin, his powerful body deep within hers, the star-bursting orgasms that had left her body still tingling even hours later.

Maybe even the laptop switch had been deliberate. Seeing him in the queue at Heathrow had certainly flustered her. She had been so intent on getting through security without betraying how much he unsettled her, she had grabbed a computer off the conveyor belt without properly checking if it was hers.

But, as much as she was annoyed with herself over that little mix-up, how could she regret sleeping with him? It had been more hate sex on her part than anything else, but it had totally blown her mind and sent her senses into haywire from which they had yet to recover. How could she regret having the most incredible sex of her life?

Erm…because it's Finn O'Connell?

Zoey closed her eyes in a 'why was I such an idiot?' manner. But she consoled herself that it was only the once and it would not be repeated. There was no way she was going to hanker after him like his posse of fan girls. She had way too much pride.

In fact, she was not going to think about him at all.

Finn had only been back at his office a few minutes when his receptionist-cum-secretary, June, informed him Harry Brackenfield was waiting to speak to him in the conference room. 'He said it's highly confidential and he didn't want to be seen waiting for you in the waiting room,' she added. 'He wouldn't even make an appointment to come back at a more convenient time.'

'That's okay, I'll see him,' Finn said, wondering if he was in for a lecture about sleeping with Harry's daughter. But surely Zoey wouldn't share such private details of her love life with her father? Besides, Harry Brackenfield didn't seem the devoted and protective dad type.

Harry's attitude to Zoey troubled Finn at times. He had overheard Harry at a cocktail party a couple of months ago denigrating a project Zoey had worked on early in her career. Personally, Finn had thought her early work showed enormous talent. It had been a little rough around the edges but that was normal for a newbie. Her later work was nothing short of brilliant, but he had a feeling she wasn't allowed to shine too brightly at Brackenfield, in case her work eclipsed her father's.

Finn walked into the conference room to find Harry seated on one side of the long table, his hands clasped together.

'Morning, Harry,' he said, taking the seat at the head of the table. 'I missed you at the conference the other day. I thought we were going to have coffee to discuss something.'

Harry's eyes shifted to one side. 'Yes, well, I thought it was too public there to discuss what I want to discuss with you.' His gaze moved back to Finn's. 'I want out.'

Finn frowned in confusion. 'Out?'

Harry separated his hands and laid them on the table. Finn noted both of them had a slight tremble. 'I'm offering you a takeover of Brackenfield Advertising. I know you've done takeovers in the past, and I thought you might be interested, since you've been asking me over the last couple of months about how things were going. I'm done. I'm tired of the long hours and my creativity has dried up. I want to take early retirement.'

A tick of excitement ran through Finn's blood. A friendly takeover was the ideal way to acquire a company, but it concerned him that Zoey hadn't mentioned anything about it during their time in New York. And it begged the question as to why. 'Does Zoey know about this?'

A dull flush rose on the older man's cheekbones. 'No. And I insist the deal is off if she's told before the deal is signed off. It's my company and if I want to sell it, then I'll sell it. This is an exclusive offer to you but, if you don't want it, then I'll offer it to someone else.'

The trouble was, Finn did want it. Brackenfield Advertising would be a nice little coup to add to his empire, but it didn't sit well with him that Zoey was in the dark about the takeover. But business was business and, since Harry was the owner and director, what else was Finn supposed to do? Confidentiality was a cornerstone of good business deals and he wanted that company before one of his competitors got it.

Besides, his one-night stand with Zoey was exactly that—a one-night stand. Even if part of him wished it could be repeated. Would this takeover ruin the chances of seeing Zoey again? A niggle of unease passed through him, but he forced himself to ignore it. He wasn't interested in anything long-term even if Zoey was the most exciting lover he had been with in years…possibly ever.

Finn made a generous offer and readily Harry accepted it. It seemed to confirm the older man's keenness to do other things with his life other than work.

'Right, then, it looks like you've got yourself a deal,' Finn said, rising from his seat to offer Harry his hand. 'I'll get my legal people in contact with yours to get the paperwork written up.'

Harry shook Finn's hand. 'Thank you.'

Finn waited a beat before asking, 'Why the secrecy from Zoey? Surely as your only daughter she has the right to know what your plans are going forward?'

Harry's expression became belligerent. 'If she were my son, then maybe it would be different. But she's not. She'll get married and have kids one day soon and then what will happen to the company?'

'Men get married and have kids too and still successfully manage companies,' Finn felt compelled to point out, even if he didn't place himself in that category. The marriage and kids package had never appealed to him, mostly because he had seen first-hand the damage when it didn't work out. 'Anyway, isn't Zoey more a career woman? That's the impression I've always had when speaking with her.'

It was weird because Zoey reminded him of himself—career-driven, single and wanting to stay that way, yet up for a bit of no-strings fun now and again to relieve the tension. The only trouble was, he didn't like the thought of her having fun with anyone else. If she wanted to have fun, then he wanted to be the one to have it with her. For now, at least. Not for ever.

'I'll tell her as soon as the deal is done and dusted,' Harry said. 'And not before.'

'Your call, but I think you're making a big mistake.'

Harry narrowed his eyes. 'Since when have you been such a champion for my daughter? She hates your guts, or haven't you noticed that small detail?'

Finn suppressed a smile. 'Let's say we've been working at our differences.' And having a hot lot of fun doing it too.

'Hey, how did your pitch in New York go?' Millie, one of Zoey's previous flatmates, asked at their bridesmaid dress fitting a few days later. 'I meant to ask you earlier, but I've been distracted by things…'

'Things' being Millie's recent engagement to hot-shot celebrity lawyer Hunter Addison. Madly in love, Millie had already moved out of their flat to live with him. Ivy Kennedy, Zoey's other previous flatmate, had also moved out a few weeks ago to live with her fiancé, Louis Charpentier. They were getting married next month, and Zoey and Millie were both going to be bridesmaids. And, when Millie and Hunter got married a couple of months after that, Ivy and Zoey would be maid of honour and bridesmaid, along with Hunter's young sister, Emma.

'I haven't heard back yet,' Zoey said, twirling from side to side in front of the full-length mirror in the bridal store's fitting room. 'I don't think this shade of blue suits me.'

'Are you nuts?' Millie laughed. 'You look stunning in it. And it really makes your violet eyes pop.'

What had made Zoey's eyes pop was seeing Finn O'Connell naked in her hotel room. Even though she had insisted their hook-up be a one-off, it still rankled a bit he hadn't called or texted her since. It was perverse of her to hope for a repeat when she had been the one to issue the once-only terms.

'I don't know...' She swished the long skirt of the dress from side to side, her mind wandering back to how it felt to have Finn's hands gliding over her naked body...

'Hey, earth to Zoey,' Millie said. 'You've got such a far-away look in your eyes. Did something happen while you were in New York?' She waggled her eyebrows meaningfully. 'Like with a man, for instance?'

Zoey flattened her mouth and frowned. 'What on earth makes you think that?'

Millie's face fell at her sharp tone. 'Sorry. Is it your father, then?'

Zoey let out a serrated sigh. 'I didn't mean to snap at you, it's just...'

'Tell me.' Millie touched her on the arm, her expression concerned. 'Has your dad been binge drinking again?'

'I haven't seen him since I got back from New

York, so I don't know, but on balance I would say probably he has been.' She chewed at her lip and then added, 'I had a one-night stand.'

Millie's eyes went so wide, they could have moonlighted as Christmas baubles. 'Seriously? Who was it? How did you meet? What was it like? Will you see him again?'

Zoey twisted her mouth and fiddled with the shoestring strap of the bridesmaid dress. 'I'll probably see him again, but not like that.' She met her friend's eyes in the mirror. 'It was Finn O'Connell.'

Millie frowned. 'Your competitor for that other project? But I thought you hated him.'

Zoey gave her a wry look. 'Yes, well, it wasn't so long ago that you hated Hunter Addison and look where that led.'

Millie's expression was sheepish but glowing with happiness too. *'Touché.'* But then her frown came back. 'Are you saying you *feel* something for Finn O'Connell?'

'Of course not!' Zoey laughed. 'What a crazy question to ask.'

'You must have felt something otherwise you wouldn't have slept with him. You haven't had a date since you broke up with Rupert. Finn must have made you feel something to—'

'I felt lust.'

'And now?'

Zoey unzipped the dress. 'And now, nothing. It was a one-night stand and I don't want to repeat it.'

'Was it that bad?'

'Unfortunately, no.' Zoey sighed and stepped out of the dress and hung it back on the padded hanger. 'No wonder that man has a conga line of women waiting to fall into bed with him.'

'That good, huh?'

'Indescribable.' Zoey stepped into her jeans and pulled up the zip. 'But I'm not getting involved with a playboy.'

'They make wonderful fiancés once they fall in love,' Millie said. 'You only have to look at Louis and Hunter to see that. You couldn't ask for a more devoted partner. Did I tell you Hunter is helping my mother with her literacy problems? He's so patient with her, and I love him all the more for being so wonderfully supportive.'

'Hunter is a one-in-a-million guy and I'm happy for you.' Zoey reached for her top and pulled it over her head, then shook out her hair. 'But I'm not interested in a long-term relationship. Been there, done that, thrown away the trousseau.'

Millie gave her a long, measuring look. 'I know Rupert broke your heart cheating on you the way he did. But you can't stop yourself from falling in love with someone again out of fear. I wake up each day feeling so blessed I found love with

Hunter. It would be so wonderful to see you happy again too.'

'Yes, well, maybe I wasn't all that happy with Rupert,' Zoey said, slipping her feet back into her shoes.

It was slowly dawning on her that her relationship with her ex had had some serious flaws which she had chosen not to notice at the time. It was sleeping with Finn O'Connell that made her realise how boring and routine things had become with Rupert. But, rather than address it at the time, she had blithely carried on until it had got to a humiliating showdown, finding him in bed—in *their* bed—with another woman.

'But you were with him for seven years.'

'Yeah, don't remind me,' Zoey said, rolling her eyes. 'I wished I'd left before he made such a fool of me.' She blew out a breath and added, 'I think I got too comfortable in my relationship with him. He told me he loved me daily and I believed it, more fool me. I should know by now you can never trust a word a man says.'

'Not all men are like Rupert.'

'Maybe not, but you only have to look at my father to see he's cut from the same cloth,' Zoey said. 'Says one thing, does another. He told me he was going to rehab the last time we had dinner. But did he do it? No. And lately he's been avoiding me. Ignoring my texts and not answering my calls. I should be relieved at the reduced contact with him, but I know him well enough to know he's up to something he knows I won't approve of. Fingers crossed it's not a new lover young enough to be his daughter. Urgh.'

'Oh, Zoey, I'm sorry you've been let down so much by your dad. But losing your mother when you were so young must have really devastated him.'

Zoey hated being reminded of the loss of her mother when she'd been only four years old. One day her mum had been there, the next she wasn't. Carried away in an ambulance after falling from her horse while Zoey had been at kindergarten, dying three days later from severe head injuries, never having regained consciousness. Zoey hadn't had the chance to say goodbye. She hadn't even been allowed to go to the hospital or to the funeral. Her father had insisted she stay at home with the hastily engaged nanny—one of many, along with various stepmothers who had come and gone during her childhood.

'Yes, well, I lost her too, and do you see me drinking myself into a stupor and making a complete and utter fool of myself? Besides, his drinking has been a fairly recent thing. His last marriage break-up with his wife Linda seemed to be the trigger. She was the first woman he really cared about since mum. Another good reason not to fall in love. It's not worth it.'

Millie sighed. 'I'm sure your mum would be so proud of how you watch out for your dad and of all you've achieved professionally.'

Zoey picked up her tote bag from the chair. 'Yes, well, all I've achieved will be for nothing if I don't get this contract. Come on. I need a coffee.'

All this wedding preparation stuff was seriously messing with her head. Her two best friends had fallen in love with wonderful men—even a hardened cynic like her had to admit Hunter Addison and Louis Charpentier were worth giving up singledom for. But she had been so stung by Rupert's betrayal, and wondered if she would ever allow herself to trust a man again. She had given so much to her relationship with him, been there for him in every way possible, only to find it had all been for nothing. How could she open herself again to such excruciating pain and humiliation?

Finn was in his home office a couple of days later reading through the now mutually signed takeover contract Harry Brackenfield's lawyer had sent via courier. There was a cooling off period of a week, but he knew Harry wouldn't back away from the deal—not with the eye-watering amount of money Finn had paid. But Finn had made plenty of money over his career and the odd gamble now and again wouldn't harm the coffers. Brackenfield Advertising needed a thorough overhaul and a bit of dead wood would have to go. It was a business, after all, and a business was all about profit. That was the bottom line.

Finn's rescue cat, Tolstoy, was sitting on his desk with a scowl on his face. The battle-scarred Russian blue hadn't quite forgiven him for leaving him with the housekeeper when he flew to New York. Tolstoy had pointedly ignored him for the first three days and now, on day five, was only just softening towards him, in that he now tolerated being in the same room as him.

Finn slowly rolled a pen across his desk. 'Go on, you know you want to.' The pen rolled in the direction of the cat's paw, finally coming to a stop against a paperweight, but all Tolstoy did was give him an unblinking stare.

'Still mad at me, huh?' Finn opened the top drawer on his desk and took out a length of string and dangled it in front of the cat's face. 'What about this?'

Tolstoy continued to stare at him, his one green eye nothing short of scathing.

'You know something?' Finn said, dropping the string back in the drawer and closing it. 'You remind me of someone. She looks at me just like that.' He went back to the paperwork on his desk, reading through the fine print with studied concentration… Well, it would have been a lot easier to concentrate if his mind hadn't kept drifting to Zoey.

His phone buzzed beside him on the desk and he picked it up with a quick glance at the screen. It wasn't Zoey but Leo Frascatelli, which could only mean good news. 'Finn O'Connell.'

'Finn, I have a proposition for you,' Leo said. 'I've had a look at the three pitches and I've chosen you and Zoey Brackenfield as equal first. I couldn't choose between you, so I want you to work together on the campaign. Is that doable?'

It was doable but was it wise? Finn hadn't seen her since New York and with each day that had passed the ache to do so had got worse. It was so out of character for him to be hankering after a follow-up date with a lover. Working with Zoey would bring her back into his orbit but it would ramp up the temptation to sleep with her again. And again. And who knew how many more times? He wasn't normally one to mix business with pleasure. But he was prepared to risk it because the Frascatelli project was a lucrative one even if the profits would be split two ways.

'Sure. Have you talked to Zoey yet?'

'Not yet. I thought I'd run it by you first. Do you think she'd be open to working with you? I've heard good things about her work.'

'She's extremely talented,' Finn said. 'How about I run it by her and let you know?'

'That would be great. Nice to talk to you, Finn.'

'You too.'

Finn clicked off his phone and looked at Tolstoy. 'Tell me I'm not an idiot for agreeing to work with Zoey on this account.'

The cat gave him a lugubrious stare.

Zoey decided to check in on her father on her way home from her dress fitting with Millie. Calling on him unannounced was always a little risky, not to mention stressful, but she was pleasantly surprised to find him in good spirits, and thankfully there was no obvious appearance that he'd been recently indulging in the alcoholic ones.

'Zoey, I was just about to call you. I have some good news.' He waved her inside, his face beaming.

She gave him the side-eye on the way in. 'Please don't tell me you're getting married again.'

'No, no, no.' He chuckled and closed the front door. 'It's way more exciting than that. I've sold the business. I got a takeover offer I couldn't refuse. I've just signed off on it.'

Zoey looked at him in shell-shocked silence, her thoughts flying off at tangents. *Sold?* How could the business be sold? She opened and closed her mouth, unable to find her voice for a moment. How could her father have done such a thing without even consulting her? Did she matter so little to him? Did he care nothing for her? She narrowed her eyes, her heart beating so heavily she could feel it pounding in her ears. 'What do you mean you've sold it? Are you sure you haven't been drinking?'

'Zoey.' His tone was that of an adult speaking to a cognitively dull child. 'I've only been drinking because of the stress of trying to run the business on my own. This will mean I can finally relax and—'

'But you wouldn't have had to run it on your own if you'd let me be a director!' She swung away with her hands clasped against her nose and mouth, trying to get her breathing under control.

How could this be happening? She had worked so damn hard. Covering for her father when he didn't meet a deadline. Filling in for him at meetings when he was nursing yet another hangover. She had compromised herself on so many occasions in an effort to keep the company's reputation intact. How could he go behind her back and sell the business without even talking it over with her first?

Zoey lowered her hands to stare at him with wild eyes. 'I can't believe you've done this. How could you…you betray me like this? You know how much the company means to me. Why didn't you discuss it with me? Why deliver it as a fait accompli?'

'Because I knew you would be against it, especially when you hear who's behind the takeover.'

Zoey stared at her father, her scalp prickling with unease. 'And are you going to tell me who this person is?'

'Finn O'Connell.'

'Finn O'Connell?' Zoey gasped. 'You can't be serious. Not him. Anyone but him.'

'I approached him and he jumped at the chance. He's had his eye on the company for a couple of months, asking me how things were going and so on. That's why I gave him first dibs.'

'A couple of months?' Zoey's voice came out as a shriek and her stomach churned fast enough to make butter. If what her father said was true, Finn had slept with her knowing he had his eye on her father's business. He had not said a word to her.

Not a single word.

Not even a hint.

Her father's betrayal suddenly didn't seem half as bad when she had Finn's duplicity to get her head around. Her hatred of him had gone on the back burner after their night of passion, in fact she had even wondered if it could be downgraded to mild dislike rather than pure unmitigated hatred.

But now her rage towards him was a tornado brewing in her body, making her physically shake with the effort to keep it under some semblance of control. Her head was pounding with tension, as if her temples were clamped in the cruel blunt jaws of a vice. She opened and closed her hands, her fingers feeling tingling and slightly numb, as if their blood supply had been cut off in the effort to keep her heart pumping. 'I—I can't believe that man would stoop so low.'

'Zoey, it's a business deal, there's nothing personal about it,' her father said in that same annoying 'adult to dull child' tone. 'Finn is keen to expand his business. He's done other highly successful takeovers. Anyway, I've lost the fire in my belly for the ad game. It's a perfect time for me to take early retirement, and you should be happy for me instead of harping on as if I've mortally wounded you.'

'You have mortally wounded me!' Zoey's voice rose in pitch, her eyes stinging with tears she refused to shed. She would *not* cry in front of her father. He would see it as a weakness and berate her for it, using her emotional response as yet another reason why he had sold the business out from under her. She took a couple of deep breaths and lowered her voice to a more reasonable level. 'What I'd like to know is, what happens to me? To my career?'

'You can work for Finn.'

Over my dead and rotting body. Zoey kept her

expression under tight control but her anger towards Finn was boiling inside her belly like a toxic brew. She had never loathed someone more than she did Finn O'Connell at that moment. And she couldn't wait to tell him so to his too-handsome face. 'That's not going to happen,' she said. 'Not unless he gives me an offer I can't refuse.'

But she would refuse it anyway on principle. She would beg on the streets before she would have Finn lauding it over her as her boss. Oh, God, her boss. Could there be a worse form of torture?

'If Finn O'Connell wants something badly enough, he doesn't mind paying top dollar for it.'

Zoey gave an evil gleam of a vengeful smile. 'Oh, he'll pay for it. I'll make damn sure of it.'

CHAPTER FIVE

ZOEY DECIDED AGAINST calling Finn because she had
a burning desire to see him in person. What she
had to say to him was not suitable for a phone conversation. She wanted to see every nuance on his
face, read every flicker of his expression, to gain
some insight into whether he felt compromised by
what he had done. She suspected not, but she had
to know for certain. The fact he'd slept with her
whilst knowing he was in the process of taking
over her father's business churned her gut.

Why, oh why, had she fallen for his practised
charm? Could there be a more humiliating experience?

But when she got to his office the smartly
dressed middle-aged woman at the reception desk
informed her Finn was working at home that day.

'What's his address, then?' Zoey asked. 'I'll
see him there.'

The woman gave Zoey an up and down, assessing look, her lips pursing in a disapproving manner. 'I'm afraid I can't give you that information. But, if you'd like to make an appointment, Mr O'Connell will see you when he's next available. However, it might not be for a week or two.' She gave a tight smile that didn't reach her eyes and added, 'As you can imagine, he's a very busy man.'

Zoey ground her teeth so hard she thought she'd be on a liquid diet for the next month. She drew in a breath, releasing it in a measured stream, and leaned her hands on the desk, nailing the other woman's gaze. 'Listen, there's no point looking at me like that. I already have his phone number. What I have to say to him needs to be said face to face.'

'Then why don't you just video call him?'

'And have him hang up on me? No way. I want to see him in person. Today. Within the next half hour, if possible. I don't care how busy he is, either in his private or professional life, but I am not leaving this office until you give me his address.'

The receptionist arched her brows, her posture as stiff and as unyielding as a bouncer at a nightclub. 'Your name is?'

Zoey straightened from the desk, furious she was being treated like one of Finn's love-struck bimbos. 'Zoey Brackenfield.'

The woman's expression underwent a rapid change, her haughtiness fading to be replaced by a look of delighted surprise. 'Oh, so *you're* Zoey Brackenfield.' She shot up from her ergonomic chair and held out her hand across the reception counter, a smile threatening to split her face in two. 'How lovely to meet you. I just adored the dog food commercial you did a while back. I started feeding my dog that brand because of you. It was just fabulous.'

'Thank you,' Zoey said, briefly shaking the woman's hand. But, compliments aside, she refused to back down and added in a pointed tone, 'His address?'

The woman shifted her lips from side to side, her eyes beginning to twinkle like fairy lights. 'I'd be happy to give it to you. No doubt you want to discuss the takeover.' She picked up a pen and wrote the address on a sticky note and handed it across the desk. 'It's about time Finn met his match.'

Zoey took the sticky note with a grim, no-teeth-showing smile. 'Oh, he's more than met his match.' And then she whipped round and left.

Finn lived in a leafy street in Chelsea in a gorgeous Georgian-style three-storey mansion. There was a small formal front garden with a neatly trimmed box hedge set behind a shiny, black wrought-iron fence. There were three colourful window boxes at the first-floor level, lush with vermillion pelargoniums and yellow-hearted purple pansies and trailing blue and white lobelia. But Zoey wasn't here to admire the view, even if part of her was as green as that box hedge with envy. If the outside visage was any measure, it was a dream of a house. What a pity such an arrogant jerk owned it.

Zoey pushed open the front gate and marched up the path to the front door and placed her finger on the brass doorbell button and left it there. She heard it echoing through the house and after a few moments the sound of firm footsteps from inside.

Finn answered the door with a welcoming smile. 'Ah, just who I was about to call. Come in.'

Zoey pushed past him, her chest heaving. She waited until he'd closed the door before she turned on him. 'You despicable, double-crossing jerk. How dare you buy—?'

'I take it you've heard about the takeover?' His expression was neutral, no sign of guilt, shame or conflict. Even his tone was irritatingly mild.

She clenched her hands into tight fists, her gaze blazing. 'I'm just dying to hear your explanation about why you didn't tell me you were taking over my father's company the night we…we…' She couldn't say the words without wanting to slap him.

'You've got it all wrong, babe. Your father approached me and offered to sell only a couple of days ago.'

Zoey stood rigidly before him, her blood boiling. How could she believe him? Why should she believe him? 'Did you do it deliberately? The whole laptop switch thing, the one-nighter, the secret takeover...was it all just a game to you? Was *I* just a silly little game to you?'

A muscle in Finn's jaw flickered just the once, as if he was holding back a retort. He let out a slow breath and made a placating gesture with one of his hands. 'Look, nothing was deliberate, other than I agreed to buy your father out when he came to me the other day. I couldn't tell you about the takeover because he didn't want me to. He insisted on absolute secrecy or the deal was off. If you want to be angry with anyone, it should be him.'

'I am angry with him!' Zoey said. 'But I'm even more furious with you. You should have given me the heads up. I had a right to know.'

'That's not the way I do business,' Finn said with annoying calm. 'Your father wanted to keep it under wraps and, while I didn't necessarily agree with it, I respected his decision. Besides, you supposedly hate my guts, so why would I jeopardise the takeover by letting you in on it? You might have leaked it to someone to stop me from—'

'When did he approach you? Before or after we...we...had sex?'

'After.'

Zoey wasn't quite ready to believe him even

though she found, somewhat to her surprise, that she desperately wanted to. 'But he said you'd had an eye on the company for a couple of months.'

'I'm interested in all of my competitors,' Finn said. 'I've run into your father a few times over the last couple of months and we talked shop, but I did not at any time make him an offer. He came to my office a couple of days after we got back from New York.'

'So…so why did you sleep with me?'

'I slept with you because it was what we both wanted.' His eyes contained a dark glitter that sent a shiver skating down her spine. 'And I would hazard a guess and say you want to do it again.'

Zoey coughed out a disdainful laugh. 'You're freaking unbelievable. Your ego is so big it deserves its own zip code. Its own government.' She jabbed her index finger into his rock-hard chest. 'You disgust me.' Jab. 'I hate you more than anyone I know.' Jab. Jab. 'You played me right from the start.' Jab. Jab. Jab. 'But I won't let you—'

'What?' He grabbed her hand before she could aim another jab at his chest. 'Tempt you into bed again? You want me just as much as I want you. That night was something out of the ordinary for both of us. That's why you're here now instead of calling me on the phone to tear strips off me. What you want to tear off me is my clothes. You couldn't keep yourself away, could you, babe?'

Zoey tried to pull out of his hold but his grip tightened and a tingling sensation ran down the backs of her legs like a flock of scurrying insects. Not fear, not panic but lust. And how she hated herself for it. 'Let go of me before I slap your arrogant face.'

Finn tugged her closer, his gaze holding hers in a smouldering lock that sent another shiver scuttling down the backs of her legs. 'I'm not averse to a bit of edgy sex now and again but I draw the line at violence.' He placed his other hand in the small of her back, bringing her flush against him, allowing her to feel the potency of his arousal. And she almost melted into a liquid pool of longing right there and then. 'So, how about we make love not war, hmm?'

Zoey watched as his mouth came down, as if in slow motion, but she didn't do anything to resist. She couldn't. She was transfixed by the throbbing energy between their hard-pressed bodies. His body was calling out to hers in a language older than time. The language of lust—full-blooded, primal lust that craved only one outcome.

His lips met hers and something wild and feral was unleashed inside her. She opened her lips to the bold thrust of his tongue, welcoming him in, swept up in the scorching moment of madness, driven by desire so scorching it was threatening to blister her skin inside and out. Her lips clung to his, her free hand grasping the front of his shirt, her lower body on fire. Giant leaping flames of fire raged throughout her pelvis.

Never had she wanted a man like this one. He incited in her the most out of control urges, turning her into someone she didn't recognise. He turned her into a wanton woman who didn't care about anything but assuaging the raging desire overtaking her body. She fed off his mouth, her tongue playing with his in a catch-me-if-you-can caper, then sent another wave of heat through her female flesh. Her inner core flickered with sensations, hungry, pulsing sensations that built to a pulsating crescendo.

Finn released her other hand, winding both his arms around her, one of his hands going to the curve of her bottom, pushing her harder into his erection. 'No one drives me as wild with lust as you. No one.'

'I'm not sleeping with you again,' Zoey said breathlessly against his mouth. *But I want to so much!* Every cell in her body wanted him. Every pounding beat of her heart echoed with the need for more of his touch. Every inch of her flesh was vibrating with longing. Intoxicating, torturous longing.

'Who said anything about sleeping?' His mouth came back down firmly, desperately, drawing from her an even more fervent response.

Zoey placed her hands in his hair, tugging and releasing the thick black strands, relishing the sounds of his guttural groans as he deepened the kiss even further. One of Finn's hands moved up under her top, cupping her bra-clad breast, his thumb rolling over the already tightly budded nipple. Tingling sensations rippled through her flesh, the covering of lace no match for the incendiary heat and fire of his touch.

But somehow through the enveloping fog of desire a tiny beam of reality shone through. She was falling under his spell again, melting like tallow in his arms, and she had to put a stop to it while she still could. If she still could. Her pride depended on it.

Zoey pulled out of his hold and swiped a hand across her mouth as if to remove the taste of him from her lips. 'No. This can't happen. Not again.'

Finn shrugged as if it didn't matter either way and that made her hate him all the more. How dared he not be as affected by their kiss as her? Her whole body was quivering with need. A pounding need that threatened to overrule her self-control. 'Fine. Your call.'

Zoey stepped a couple of paces away, wrapping her arms around her still throbbing body. 'You must be out of your mind to think I would sleep with you again after what you've done.'

'All I've done is buy a company that was in

danger of falling over,' Finn said. 'You know it's true, Zoey. Your father isn't capable of running the business any more. He's burnt out and ready to retire and he can do it more than comfortably with the price I paid to buy him out.'

'But *I'm* capable of running it,' she shot back. 'He had no right to sell it to you without even discussing it with me.'

'That's something you'll have to settle with him. But you and I have other business to discuss first.' He gestured to a sitting room off the large foyer. 'Come this way.'

Zoey wanted to refuse but something about his expression told her it would be wise to stay and hear him out. Besides, her job was on the line. She had to know what her options were, if there *were* options available to her. But her mind was reeling so badly with shock, anger and bitter disappointment she couldn't think clearly.

What would happen to her career now? She had pictured a long, productive career at Brackenfield Advertising, hopefully one day taking over as director. Proving to her father—and, yes, even proving to herself—she had the ability, drive and talent to do it.

But it had all been ripped out from under her.

All her plans, her hopes, her dreams and aspirations were hanging in the balance.

Zoey followed Finn down the long, wide hall

into a beautifully decorated sitting room off the spacious hall. The polished timber floor was covered by a huge Persian rug that only left about a foot of the floorboards showing around the edges of the room. She stood for a moment, struck by the décor, the luxury carpet threatening to swallow her up to the ankles.

There was a fireplace with a marble mantelpiece above and two luxurious white sofas and a wing chair upholstered in a finely checked fabric for contrast. Various works of art hung on the walls—most of them looked like originals—and the central light above was a crystal chandelier with matching wall lights positioned at various points around the room to provide a more muted lighting effect.

The room overlooked a stunning, completely private back garden with espaliered pear trees along the stone boundary wall. Neatly trimmed, low border hedges ran either side of the flagstone pathway, which led to an outdoor eating area, the light-coloured wrought-iron setting in the French provincial style. No expense had been spared in making the property a showpiece. It was stylish, ultra-luxurious and commodious. The sitting room alone could have swallowed up half of her flat and left room to spare.

It occurred to Zoey that if she didn't keep her job in some form or the other she wouldn't have enough to pay her rent in the long term. Without Ivy and Millie chipping in now they had both moved out, it made for a very tight budget indeed. She would be able to manage for a few months, quite a few months, but what then? How long could she expect to survive? She certainly wasn't going to ask her father for any hand-outs, nor bunk down at his house. She would rather sleep under a sheet of cardboard on the streets.

Finn walked over to a cleverly concealed bar fridge in a cabinet below a wall of bookshelves. 'Would you like a drink?'

Zoey stood at some distance, not trusting herself to be any closer to him. 'A brandy—make it a double. I have a feeling I'm not going to like what you've got to say.'

'Now now, there's no need to be so dramatic,' he chided gently. 'You might be pleasantly surprised in what I have to tell you.' He poured two snifters of brandy into two ball-shaped glasses and then came over to her to hand her one. 'There you go.'

Zoey took the glass but wasn't able to avoid touching his fingers as she did so. The lightning bolt of sensual energy shot up her arm and went straight to a fizzing inferno in her core. Every moment of their scorching night of passion rushed back to her in a flash, as if her skin would never forget the intoxicating intensity of his touch. It was burned, branded into her flesh, and she would never forget it and never become impervious to it. How could the merest brush of his fingers cause such an eruption of longing? She took a large sip of brandy, but it burned her throat, and she began to cough and splutter.

Finn took the glass back from her and patted her on the back. 'Whoa, there. Better take it a little more slowly.'

Zoey shrugged off his hand and glowered at him, her cheeks on fire. 'I want to know what you plan to do with the staff, myself included.'

He idly swirled the contents of his glass, his gaze watching the whirlpool he created in a calm fashion before his gaze fixed back on hers. 'There will, of course, be some trimming—'

'And no doubt I'll be the first to go.'

He held her glare with the same implacable calm, his eyes giving nothing away. 'That will depend.'

Zoey narrowed her eyes to paper-thin slits. 'On what?' Whether she had a fling with him? Was he going to hold her to ransom, offering to keep her on the staff if she gave him access to her body? If so, he had another think coming. And, frankly, so did her body, which was already threatening to betray her and jump at the chance of another night in his arms.

One side of his mouth tilted in a sardonic smile, a knowing glint reflected in his eyes. 'Not on that.'

Zoey suppressed a shiver. 'I don't believe you.'

'I may be a little ruthless at times, but black-mail isn't my style.'

He probably didn't have to resort to blackmail since he only had to crook his little finger and women would flock to him. And Zoey had to be careful she didn't join them, which would have been a whole lot easier if he wasn't so impossibly, irresistibly attractive. She kept her gaze trained on his. 'At the risk of repeating myself, I don't believe you.'

Finn put his brandy glass down, as if he had lost interest in it. He met her gaze with his now inscrutable one. 'I had a call from Leo Frascatelli this afternoon.'

Zoey's heart sank like an anchor. Not just any old anchor—a battleship's anchor. She had lost the contract. Lost it to Finn O'Connell. Oh God, could her circumstances get any more humiliating? He had taken everything from her—her father's business, her career hopes and dreams and the Frascatelli contract. If it wasn't bad enough Finn had bought Brackenfield Advertising out from under her, now she would have to stomach his gloating over winning the account she had hoped would be hers.

She threw him a livid glare, her top lip curling. 'Congratulations. Who did you sleep with to nail that little prize?'

One side of his mouth curved upwards in a half-smile, his dark eyes shining with a mysterious light. 'No one. I was just about to call you about the call from Leo before you showed up on my doorstep in a towering rage.'

'Spare me the brag-fest or I might vomit on your nice cream carpet.'

'It would be no more than Tolstoy has done in the past.'

Zoey frowned. 'Tolstoy?'

As if he had heard his name mentioned, a Russian blue cat with only one eye came strolling into the room, the tinkling of his collar bell overly loud in the silence. The cat completely ignored Finn and came padding over to Zoey, winding around her ankles and bumping its head against her with a mewling sound.

'Zoey, allow me to introduce you to Tolstoy,' Finn said.

Zoey bent down to stroke the cat's head. 'Oh, you darling thing. But you look like you've been in the wars.' Tolstoy purred like a train and bumped his head against her petting hand. 'Aren't you a friendly boy, hey?'

'You have the magic touch, it seems,' Finn said. 'He normally hates strangers. He usually runs away and hides, or worse, attacks them.'

Yes, well, look who was talking about having the magic touch. Zoey was still tingling from head to foot from Finn's heart-stopping kiss. She straightened from petting the cat and met Finn's unreadable gaze. 'How long have you had him?'

'Five months. I found him injured on my way home one night and took him to a vet. They traced the owner via the microchip, but they no longer wanted him. So, I took him in. And paid the eye-watering vet bills.'

'Oh…that was…nice of you.'

Finn's mouth flickered with a wry smile. 'You sound surprised that I can be nice on occasion.'

Zoey elevated her chin. 'I'm sure you can lay on the charm when you want things to go your way. But just for the record—it won't work with me.'

Finn waved to the sofa nearest her, his lips twitching and his eyes twinkling. 'Take a seat. I haven't finished telling you the good news about the Frascatelli account.'

Zoey sat on the sofa and some of the tension in her body dissipated as the deep feather cushioning dipped to take her weight. Tolstoy jumped up beside her, nudging her hand to get her to continue petting him. She absently stroked the cat, but she fought against the temptation to relax. She was in enemy territory and she had to avoid a repeat of what happened between her and Finn the other night.

Anyway, what good news could there be? She had lost the account to Finn. But why had he found out first and she had not even been told her pitch had been unsuccessful? 'Are you friends with Leonardo Frascatelli?' she asked, eyeing him suspiciously.

Finn sat on the opposite sofa, one arm resting on the arm rest. He hitched one leg over the other, resting his ankle on his bent knee in a relaxed pose. His gaze wandered to the cat she was stroking beside her and a flicker of a wry smile passed across his lips. 'We're casual acquaintances but he is too much of a professional to allow any nepotism to influence his decision. He couldn't decide between your pitch and mine, so he's asked both of us to do it. How do you feel about working with me on the account?'

Zoey stared at him in numb shock, a combination of dread and excitement stirring in her blood. 'You mean we *both* won it?' Her voice came out like a squeak and Tolstoy suddenly started and jumped off the sofa. And, twitching his tail, he stalked out of the room with an air of affronted dignity.

'Yep, and he asked me to run it by you first to see if you're willing to share the contract with me,' Finn said. 'It'll mean working together a fair bit but I'm game if you are.' The enigmatic light in his eyes played havoc with her already on-edge nerves. What would 'working with him' entail?

Zoey moistened her paper-dry lips, her heart

kicking against her breastbone at the thought of being in Finn O'Connell's company for extended periods. Could she do it? Could she take on this project—this enormously lucrative project—and come out the other side with her pride intact?

'I—I'm having trouble understanding how this will work. I mean, you now apparently own Brackenfield Advertising. Am I going to be working under the Brackenfield banner or—?'

'The Brackenfield banner will no longer exist.' His tone was brutally blunt. 'I want you to work for me. The Frascatelli account can be your trial period. If all goes well, you can stay on with me. But if you'd like to explore other options, then that's fine too. It's up to you.'

Zoey sprang off the sofa and began to pace the floor in agitation. Brackenfield Advertising would no longer exist? Her job, her future, her career path was now under Finn O'Connell's control. Could there be anything more galling than to be totally under his command and authority? She spun round to face him, her chest pounding with rage. 'I didn't think it was possible to hate someone as much as I hate you. You've taken my future from me. You've stolen my father's company from me and—'

'I paid well above what I should have for your father's business,' Finn said, rising from the sofa with indolent ease. 'It's not been firing at peak performance for months and you damn well know it.'

'I've done my best, but my father wouldn't make me a director, so I was completely hamstrung,' Zoey fired back. 'Plus, I was always covering for him when he missed a deadline or failed to show up at a meeting. But I had it under control. I was bringing in a more or less steady stream of work and—'

'Look, all credit to you for caring about your father, but you're not helping him by covering for him all the time,' Finn said. 'He needs to face his demons and get some help before it's too late. And you're currently in the way of him getting that help.'

On one level, Zoey knew what he said had an element of truth to it. But she hated him too much to give him the satisfaction of telling him so. She thrust her hands on her hips and upped her chin, her eyes throwing sparks of ire at him.

'What would you know about my situation? You with your mouth full of silver spoons and oozing with privilege! You haven't any idea of the struggle it is to keep someone you love from making a complete ass of themselves.'

Something flickered over his face, a quiver of inner conflict at the back of his eyes. 'I know more about that than you probably realise.' His voice contained an odd note she had never heard him use before. A disquieting note, a chord of emotional pain buried so deep inside you could only hear its faint echo ringing in the silence.

Zoey opened her mouth but then closed it again when he turned to pick up his brandy glass from where he had left it. He studied the contents of the glass for a moment, then gave her a sideways glance. 'You speak of my privilege? There are no privileges, no silver spoons, when your parents drink and smoke every penny that comes in the door.'

He gave a grim smile and continued, holding the glass up. 'See this? One drink was never enough for either of my parents. If they had one, they had to have twenty.' He put the glass down with a dull thud. 'And don't get me started on the drugs.'

Zoey swallowed a tight stricture in her throat, ashamed of herself for making assumptions about his background. From what he had said so far, *she* was the one who had grown up with the silver spoons and privilege. 'I'm sorry. I didn't realise things were like that for you…'

Finn turned to put the glass of brandy down again, his expression becoming masked, as if talking about the past was something he found imminently distasteful. 'I'll give you five days to decide what you want to do regarding the Frascatelli project.'

His manner and tone had switched to brisk and businesslike efficiency with such speed, Zoey was a little slow to keep up. She was still musing over his disadvantaged childhood, marvelling at how he had built an advertising empire that was one of the most successful in the world. An empire she was being invited to join…if she could stomach working with him on the Frascatelli project first.

But how could she refuse? It was a project she had dreamed of working on ever since she'd first heard about it. She would have to keep strict boundaries around their working relationship. There could be no repeats of the other night. And her self-control would have to go to boot camp to get back in shape for the months ahead. Finn O'Connell was known to be a demanding boss, but a generous one.

Besides that, she needed a job.

'I'll give my answer now, if you don't mind.'

Finn held her gaze for a long beat, nothing in his expression suggesting he cared either way what her decision was. Zoey drew in a quick breath and released it in a single stream. 'I accept your offer. However, there are some rules I'd like to stipulate first.'

A marble-hard look came into his eyes and the base of her spine tingled. 'Come and see me in my office first thing tomorrow and we'll talk some more. But just to give you the heads up—I'm the one who makes the rules.'

'But I want to talk to you now.'

'Not now.' There was a note of intransigence in his tone and he pushed back his shirt cuff and gave his watch a pointed glance before adding, 'I have to be somewhere soon.'

Zoey gave him an arch look. 'A hot little hook-up waiting for you, is there?'

His unreadable eyes flicked to her mouth for a heart-stopping moment before reconnecting with her gaze. 'Tomorrow, nine a.m. sharp.' He gave a dismissive on-off smile and led the way to the door. 'I'll see you out in case you can't find your way.'

Zoey brushed past him. 'Don't bother. I can find my own way out.' And she marched out of the room, down the hall and out of the front door, giving it a satisfying slam on her exit.

Finn released a long breath and scraped a hand through his hair. He wasn't sure what had led him to reveal to Zoey the shabby little secrets of his parents' life choices. It wasn't something he bandied about to all and sundry. Everyone had a right to a little privacy, and he guarded that aspect of his life with religious zeal. He had spent too many years of his childhood wishing his parents were different. And, as Zoey did with her father, he too had enabled his parents at times in a bid to keep some semblance of normal family life together.

But it had backfired on him time and time again. His parents were addicts and they had only ever fleetingly taken responsibility for their cravings. A week or two here and there, a month, once even three months of being sober, but then they would drift back into their habits and he would be shipped off to relatives again. In the end, he had drawn a line in the sand and told them straight out—get clean or get out of his life. They'd chosen to get out of his life.

Tolstoy peered round the corner of the sitting room, his one-eyed stare wary. Finn bent down and scooped the cat up before it could turn its back on him. 'You're a traitor, do you hear me?' He stroked the soft fur of the cat's head and was rewarded with a rhythmic purr. 'But she is rather irresistible, isn't she?'

The cat nudged his hand and purred some more. Finn gave a crooked smile and continued stroking him. 'I'm glad you've forgiven me but I'm not sure if Zoey's going to.' He set the cat back down on the floor and Tolstoy sat and gave one of those gymnastically complicated leg-in-the-air licks of his nether regions.

Finn had all along considered Zoey's position when it had come to the takeover of her father's company, but he was a man of his word, and since Harry Brackenfield had insisted on secrecy that was what Finn had adhered to. There was a part of him that completely understood her angst and disappointment. Besides, didn't he know all about having your heart set on something only for it to be ripped away? But business was business and he didn't allow emotion to muddy the waters. He wanted to expand his own company and taking the best people from Brackenfield was a sure way to do it.

And Zoey was high on that list.

Finn had cut short his time with Zoey just now, not because he wanted to but because he needed to. There was only so much he was willing to reveal about his background and he was surprised he had revealed as much as he had. He wasn't used to letting people in to the darker aspects of his life. He didn't get close enough to people to share things he wished he could forget. There was no point revisiting the train wreck of his childhood. It never changed anything other than to make him feel even more bitter about his parents' lack of love and care for his well-being.

It was one of the reasons he had ruled out having a family of his own. Not because he didn't think he would do a good job as a father—after all, it wouldn't be too difficult to lift a little higher than the abysmal benchmark his father had set—but because he genuinely didn't want anyone needing him, relying on him, expecting him to be someone he knew he couldn't be. He didn't have the emotional repertoire for such a long-haul commitment. He was too ruthless, too driven, too independent and too self-sufficient.

He enjoyed being a free agent. He had never desired a long-term partner. The thought of developing lasting feelings for someone made him uneasy. Loving someone who didn't or couldn't love you back was too terrifying. He had been there as a child and never wanted to experience that sinking sense of loss again. He found that, within a week or two of being with someone, he began looking for a way out once the thrilling, blood-pumping chase was over. Time to move on to more exciting ventures.

But somehow, with Zoey, Finn sensed a different dynamic going on between them. She excited him in ways no one else had managed to do. Her stubborn prickliness both amused and frustrated him, and her feistiness was the biggest turn-on he had experienced. She was whip-smart and sharp-tongued and sensationally sexy, and he knew working with her was going to be one of the most exciting periods in his life. He didn't normally mix business with pleasure—the pitfalls were well-documented—but this time he was making an exception for an exceptional woman.

And he couldn't wait to start.

CHAPTER SIX

ZOEY ARRIVED AT Finn's office the following morning right on the stroke of nine a.m. She had spent a restless night ruminating over her situation, agonising over whether she was being a fool for agreeing to work with him. It would mean close contact, hours of close contact, and who knew what such proximity would produce? Another firestorm of lust? It must not happen. She must not give in to temptation. She must not be hoodwinked by Finn's charm and allure.

She. Must. Not.

Finn's middle-aged receptionist-cum-secretary smiled as Zoey came through the door. 'Good morning, Ms Brackenfield. Finn will be here shortly—something must have held him up. He's normally bang on time. Can I get you a coffee while you wait?'

Something had held him up, had it? Like a sleepover with one of his avid fans? Zoey painted a polite smile on her face while inside she was seeth-ing. No doubt some other foolish young woman had capitulated to his practised charm. No way was Zoey going to fall for it a second time—even if it had been the most spectacular sex of her entire life. 'No, thank you. Erm…please call me Zoey. Sorry, but I didn't catch your name the last time.'

'June,' the older woman said with a smile. 'Con-gratulations on the Frascatelli account. Finn told me you'll be sharing the contract with him. Are you excited?'

A part of Zoey was far more excited than she had any business being, but not just about the Fra-scatelli contract. The traitorous part of her that couldn't think of her night of passion with Finn without a frisson going through her body. The wild and reckless part of her that still smouldered and simmered with longing. 'I'm sure it will be an in-teresting experience,' she said, keeping her expres-sion under tight control.

June's eyes danced. 'I'm sure you'll get on to-gether famously.' She glanced behind Zoey's shoulder to the front entrance and added, 'Ah, here he is now.'

Zoey turned to see Finn striding through the door looking remarkably refreshed and heart-stop-pingly handsome as usual. He obviously hadn't spent a sleepless night ruminating over what lay ahead. He had probably bedded some young nubile woman and had bed-wrecking sex while Zoey had spent the evening in a state of sexual frustration. One taste of him and she was addicted. How did it happen?

And how on God's sweet earth was she to control it?

He was wearing a charcoal-grey suit with an open-necked white shirt and looked every inch the suave man about town who didn't have a care in the world. Or did he? His revelation about his less than perfect childhood had totally stunned her. Never would she have envisaged him as the product of disadvantage. He had made such a success of his company, he had wealth beyond most people's wildest dreams and he had no shortage of female attention—hers included.

If only she could turn off this wretched attraction to him. If anything, it was getting worse, not better.

'Morning,' Finn said, encompassing both his receptionist and Zoey with a smile. 'Come this way, Zoey.' He glanced back at June and added, 'Hold my calls, June. And can you reschedule tonight's meeting with Peter Greenbaum? Zoey and I are having dinner instead.'

Dinner? Zoey ground her teeth behind her impassive expression. The arrogance of the man. He hadn't even asked her.

'Will do,' June said, reaching for the phone.

Zoey waited until she was alone with Finn in his office before she took him to task. She gave him an arch look. 'Dinner? Funny, but I don't recall you asking me to dinner.'

'I didn't ask.' He flicked her a glance on his way to his desk. 'But I'm telling you now. Take a seat.'

Zoey stayed exactly where she was. 'I'm not going to be ordered about by you. I have other plans for this evening.'

He shrugged off his jacket and hung it in a slim-line cupboard against the wall. Then he came and stood behind his desk with his hands resting on the back of his ergonomic chair, a flinty look in his eyes. 'Cancel them. We have work to do.'

She folded her arms across her middle. 'Work? Are you sure that's what's on the agenda?'

His eyes drifted to her mouth and then back to her eyes, an indolent smile lifting up one side of his mouth. 'Work is on my agenda but who knows what's on yours?'

Zoey wasn't one to blush easily, but she could feel heat pouring into her cheeks. She lifted her chin and glued her gaze to his, determined not to be the first to look away. 'Before we begin working together, I think we need to set some ground rules.'

He rolled back his chair and sat down, leaned back and made a steeple with his fingers in front of his chest, his gaze unwavering on hers. 'I told you last night, I'm the one who makes the rules. You get to follow them.'

Zoey came over to stand in front of his desk and, leaning her hands on it, nailed him with a steely glare. 'Let me get something straight—I will *not* be ordered around by you.'

He slowly rocked his chair from side to side, his fingers still steepled in front of his chest. And, judging from his expression, he was seemingly unmoved by her curt statement. 'If you can't follow simple instructions then you won't have a future working for me once we finish this project.'

Zoey pushed herself away from his desk with an unladylike curse. 'Why do I get the feeling you only bought Brackenfield Advertising to have me under your control?'

He raised one dark eyebrow. 'My, oh my, what a vivid imagination you have.' He released his steepled fingers and leaned forward to rest his forearms on the desk. 'I told you why I bought it. It was about to go under. I was doing your dad a favour. And you too, when it comes to that.'

'I'm surprised you wanted to help him given he's nothing but a rotten drunk like your parents.'

The ensuing silence was so thick and palpable Zoey could feel it pressing on her from all four corners of the room. Nothing showed in Finn's expression that her words had upset him in any way, yet she got the sense that behind the screen of his eyes it was a different story. Shame coursed through her at her uncharitable outburst. She knew nothing of his parents' issues other than the small amount he had told her. And, given her own issues with her father, she understood all too well how heartbreaking it was to see a parent self-destruct, and feeling so useless to do anything to prevent it.

'I—I'm sorry,' Zoey said. 'That was completely uncalled for.'

Finn lifted his forearms off the desk and leaned back in his chair. 'What I told you last night was in confidence. Understood?'

She couldn't hold his gaze and lowered it to stare at the paperweight on his desk. 'Understood.' She bit down into her lower lip, wanting to inflict physical pain on herself for being so unnecessarily cruel.

Finn pushed back his chair and went over to the window overlooking a spectacular view of the Thames and Tower Bridge. He stood with his back to her for a moment or two, his hands thrust into his trouser pockets, the tension in his back and shoulders clearly visible through the fine cotton of his shirt.

He finally released a heavy-sounding breath and turned back to face her, his expression shadowed by the light coming in from the window now behind him. 'I probably don't need to tell you how hard it is to see your parents make a train wreck of their lives.'

'No…you don't.'

He took his hands out of his pockets and sent one through the thickness of his hair, the line of his mouth grim. 'My parents were hippies, flower children who suddenly found themselves the parents of a baby they hadn't planned on having, or at least not at that stage of their lives. They were barely out of their teens and had nothing behind them. So, when it all got too much, they drank or smoked dope to cope.'

He screwed up his mouth into a grimace. 'One of my first memories was trying to wake them both so I could have something to eat and drink. I think I was only three. It took me a long while—ten years, actually—until I realised they were completely unreliable. I gave them a couple of chances to lift their game but of course, they couldn't live without their addictions. So, I finally drew a line in the sand when I was thirteen and gave them a choice. It was no big surprise they chose the drink and drugs.'

Zoey's heart contracted at the neglect he had suffered, and another wave of shame coursed through her for being so mean. How awful for such a small child to witness his care-givers acting so irresponsibly. How frightening it must have been for him to not be sure if he was going to get fed each day. 'I'm so sorry… I can't imagine how tough that must have been for you. To not feel safe with your own parents. To not know if you're even going to be fed and taken care of properly. How on earth did you survive it?'

Finn made a gruff sound in the back of his throat. 'I was farmed out to distant relatives from time to time. I would go back to my parents when they dried out for a bit and then the cycle would start all over again. By the time I got to my teens, I knew I would have to rely on myself and no one else to make something of my life. I studied hard, got a couple of part-time jobs, won a scholarship to a good school and the rest, as they say, is history.'

Zoey found herself standing in front of him without any clear memory of how she'd got there. But something in her compelled her to touch him, to reach out to him to show that she of all people understood some of what he had experienced. She placed her hand on his strong forearm, her fingers resting against hard male muscles, and a flicker of molten heat travelled in lightning-fast speed to her core.

'Finn…' Her voice got caught on something in her throat and she looked up into his dark brown eyes and tried again. 'I'm so ashamed of how I spoke to you. I admire you for overcoming such impossible odds to be where you are today. It's just amazing that you didn't let such an awful start in life ruin your own potential.'

His hand came down over hers and gave it a light squeeze, his eyes holding hers. 'For years, I did what you do for your father. I filled the gaps for them, compensated for them, made excuses for them. I just wanted a normal family and was prepared to go to extraordinary lengths to get it. But it was magical thinking. Some people aren't capable of changing, no matter how many chances you give them, so why wait around hoping one day they will?'

Zoey glanced at his hand covering hers and a faint shiver passed through her body. His touch on her body was a flame to bone-dry tinder. She could feel the nerves of her skin responding to him, the tingles, the quivers, the spreading warmth. She brought her gaze back to his to find him looking at her with dark intensity, his eyes moving between hers then dipping to her mouth.

The air seemed suddenly charged with a new energy, a vibrating energy she could feel echoing in the lower region of her body. A pulse, a drum-beat, a blood-driven throb.

She hitched in a breath and went to pull out of his light hold but he placed his other hand on the top of her shoulder, anchoring her gently in place. Anchoring her to him as surely as if she had been nailed to the floor. 'Finn…' Her voice came out in a barely audible whisper, her heart picking up its pace.

Finn's hand moved from her shoulder to cradle one side of her face, his thumb moving like a slow metronome arm across her cheek. Back and forth. Back and forth. A rhythmic, mesmerising beat. 'I'm guessing this is not part of your list of rules?' His voice was low and deep and husky, his eyes dark and glinting.

Zoe moistened her lips, knowing full well it was a tell-tale signal of wanting to be kissed but doing it anyway. Her eyes drifted to his mouth and a wave of heat flooded her being. 'That depends on what you're going to do.'

He tilted her face up so her eyes were in line with his. 'What do you think I'm going to do?'

'Kiss me.'

'Is that a request or a statement?'

Zoey stepped up on tiptoe and planted her hands on his broad chest, her fingers clutching at his shirt. 'It's a command,' she said, just within a hair's breadth of his lips.

Finn brought his mouth down on hers with a smothered groan, his other arm going around her back like an iron band. Her body erupted in a shower of tingles as she came into contact with his rock-hard frame, every cell throbbing with anticipation. His lips moved with increasing urgency against hers, his tongue driving through the seam of her lips with ruthless determination.

Zoey welcomed him in with her own groan of delight, her tongue playing with his in a sexy tango that sent her blood thundering through the network of her veins. The scrape of his rough skin against the smoothness of hers sent a frisson through her body, the erotic flicker of his tongue sending a lightning bolt of lust straight to her core. Molten heat flooded her system. Desire——hot, thick, dark desire——raced through her female flesh and drove every thought out of her mind but the task of satisfying the burning ache of need.

How had she thought one night of passion was ever going to be enough? It wasn't. It couldn't be. She needed him like she needed air. Needed to feel the explosive energy they created together, to make sure she hadn't imagined it the first time. It didn't mean she was having a fling with him, it didn't mean she was like one of his gushing fans— it meant she was a woman with needs who wanted them satisfied by a man who desired her as much as she desired him.

And what fervent desire it was, firing back and forth between their bodies like high-voltage electricity.

Finn walked her backwards to his desk, bending her back over it, ruthlessly scattering pens and sticky-note pads out of the way. He stepped between her legs, his expression alive with intent, and she shuddered in anticipation. 'If this is on your rules list then you'd better say so now before it's too late.'

'It's not… Oh, God, it's not…' Zoey could barely get her voice to work, so caught up was she in the heart-stopping moment. She wrapped her thighs hard around his body, her inner core pulsating with wet, primal need.

He leaned over her; one of his hands anchored to the desk, the other tugging her blouse out of her skirt to access her breast through her balcony bra. There was just enough of the upper curve of her breast outside the cup of lace for his mouth to explore. But soon it wasn't enough for him and he tugged the bra out of the way so his lips and tongue could wreak further havoc on her senses.

Zoey writhed with building pleasure on his desk, a part of her mind drifting above her body to look down on the spine-tingling tableau below. It was like an X-rated fantasy to have Finn feasting on her body in such an unbridled way. But in a way he *was* a fantasy. He wasn't the type of man she could see a future with, even if she was interested in a future with a man. He was too much of a playboy, too much of a charmer, for her to want to be with him any length of time.

But she wanted this. Wanted him with a burning, aching need that was beyond anything she had felt before. It pounded through her body, hammered in her blood, throbbed between her legs.

'I haven't been able to stop thinking about this since the last time we were together,' he said, kissing his way down her abdomen. 'Tell me to stop if you don't want me to go any further.'

Stop? No way was she letting him stop. Not while her body was quivering with longing, aching with the need to find release. 'Please don't stop…' Her voice was breathless, her spine arching off the desk as his hand drew up her skirt to bunch around her waist. 'Please don't stop or I'll kill you.'

A lazy smile backlit his gaze with a smouldering heat. 'Then, in the interests of occupational health and safety, I'd better do as you command.' He brought his mouth down to her mound, his fingers moving aside her knickers, his warm breath wafting against her sensitised flesh in a teasing breeze. 'So beautiful…' His voice was so low and deep, it sounded as if it came from beneath the floorboards.

His lips moved against her feminine folds, soft little touches that sent her pulse rate soaring. Shivers coursed down her legs and arms, flickers of molten heat deep in her core. He caressed her with his tongue, the slow strokes a form of exquisite torture, ramping up the pressure in her tender tissues until it was impossible to hold back the tumultuous wave. It crashed through her body as if a hurricane were powering it, booming, crashing waves that sent every thought out of her brain short of losing consciousness.

She bit back the urge to cry out, vaguely recalling Finn's receptionist was only a few metres away on the other side of the office door. Zoey was reduced to the pulsing pleasure of her primal body, transported to a place where only bliss could reside. The aftershocks kept coming, gradually subsiding to a gentle rocking through her flesh like the lap of idle waves on the shore.

Finn straightened her clothes into some sort of order, his expression one of glinting triumph. 'That was certainly a great way to start the day.' He held out his hand to help her up off the desk.

Zoey took his hand, her cheeks feeling as if they could cook a round of toast. She slipped down off his desk but grasped the front of his shirt. 'Not so fast, buddy. I haven't finished with you yet.'

Something dark and hot flared in the backs of his eyes. 'Now you've got my attention.'

Zoey pushed him back against the desk, stepping between his legs as he had done with her moments earlier. 'Lie down,' she commanded like a dominatrix, goaded on by the dark, sensual energy throbbing in her body—the same dark, sensual energy she could see reflected in his gaze.

Finn stood with his buttocks pressed against

the desk, his hands going to her upper arms. 'You don't have to do this.'

Zoey planted a firm hand on the middle of his chest. 'I said, lie down.'

He gave an indolent smile, his eyes holding hers in a spine-tingling lock. 'Make me.'

Zoey kept her gaze trained on his and reached for his zipper, sliding it down, down, down, watching the flicker of anticipation in his eyes, feeling the shudder that rippled through him against the press of her hand. 'Here's one of my rules. You don't get to pleasure me unless I can return the favour. Got it?'

Finn gave another whole-body shudder, his eyes dark and as lustrous as wet paint. 'Got it.'

'Good.' Zoey pushed him down so his back and shoulders were on the desk, his strongly muscled thighs either side of hers. She freed him from his underwear and bent her head to take him in her mouth, teasing him at first with soft little flicks of her tongue against his engorged flesh. He groaned and muttered a curse, his body quaking as she subjected him to her wildest fantasy.

She stroked her tongue down his turgid length, then circled the head of his erection, round and round and round, until he muttered another curse. Then she took him fully in her mouth, sucking on him deeply, not letting up until he finally capitulated in a powerful release that rattled every object still sitting on his desk. It thrilled her to the core of her being to have him prostrated before her with the same blood-pounding pleasure he had given her.

Zoey stepped back from him with a sultry smile, feeling that at last she had him where she wanted him. Totally under her power. 'You're right. It was a great way to start the day.'

Finn dragged himself off the desk, but it looked as though his legs weren't quite up to the task of standing upright. He sent a hand through his hair, leaving deep grooves, his expression one of slight bewilderment. He gave a slow blink as if recalibrating himself, a mercurial smile lifting the edges of his mouth.

'I think I'm going to enjoy working with you way more than I anticipated.' He reached out his hand and picked up one of hers, bringing it up to his mouth, his eyes still locked on hers. He pressed a light kiss to each of her bent knuckles, the delicate caress sending a shower of shivers cascading down her spine.

The reality of what had just happened between them suddenly hit Zoey with the force of a slap. She pulled her hand out of his before she was tempted to do another round of off-the-charts office sex with him. How could she have let her wild side out to such a degree? The wild side she hadn't even known she possessed. It was like looking at a totally different person—a *femme fatale* who was driven by earthly drives and pleasures.

How long could this go on? She was supposed to be working on a project with him—an important project—not making out with him every chance she got. She didn't want to join the long list of Finn's temporary lovers. The flings who came and went in his life with such startling frequency. She hadn't had a fling in her life—she had only ever been in a couple of committed relationships before her ex. She wasn't even sure she liked the idea of casual sex. Where was the humanity in using someone's body to satiate her own desires? Where was the dignity of behaving like an animal without a theory of mind, only driven by raw, primal urges?

'Speaking of work…' Zoey straightened her clothes in a back-to-business manner before bringing her gaze back to his. 'I—I want to make something perfectly clear. I'm not having a fling with you. What happened here—' she waved her hand in the vague direction of his desk '—can't happen again. It's…it's totally unprofessional. It has to stop. Now.'

'Fine. Your call. But let me know as soon as you change your mind.'

Something about his smiling eyes told her he was in no doubt of the struggle she was undergoing. The struggle to keep her hands off him, to be the disciplined professional she had trained herself for so long and hard to be. He had undone it with a single kiss, dismantled her armour like a hurricane through a house of cards.

'I won't be changing my mind,' Zoey said, pointedly ignoring his desk, for it seemed to mock her prim-sounding tone. So too did the secret, silent tremors of her body, the intimate muscles still flicking, kicking, tingling with tiny aftershocks. 'I don't want the distraction, for one thing, nor do I want everyone gossiping about me as your latest squeeze. It would be nothing short of humiliating. I'm here to work and that is what I intend to do.'

'We could always keep it a secret,' Finn said, his gaze unwavering on hers as if reading every betraying nuance on her face.

Zoey folded her arms across her body, desperate to restore some much-needed dignity. She had lost so much ground by falling yet again under his potent sensual spell. As tempting as it was to consider a secret liaison with him, what would happen once it was over? For it would all too soon be over—there was nothing more certain than that. Besides, neither of them wanted anything long-term. That part of her life was over. She had drawn a thick black line through it.

Now wasn't the time to erase it. Now was the time to concentrate on her career, to fulfil her ambitions without the distraction of a relationship.

And a relationship of any duration with Finn would be one hell of a distraction. 'Secrets have a habit of becoming exposed,' she said.

'Not if we're careful.'

But that was the problem right there—she lost her ability to be careful when she was around Finn O'Connell. He triggered something reckless and dangerous in her and she *had* to control it. 'Thanks, but no.'

Finn gave an indifferent shrug and moved back to his desk. He straightened the objects he had pushed aside earlier with maddening casual ease, as if he made hot, passionate love to women on his desk every day. But then, he probably did, and Zoey had now joined their number. *Urgh.* Why had she allowed herself to be swept away on a tide of passion with a man she hated?

But you don't hate him.

The thought dropped into her head and stunned her for a moment. What did she feel for him apart from unbridled lust? Her hatred had cooled a little, more than a little, and in its place was a growing respect for all he had achieved given his difficult childhood. She even had to admit she actually liked some aspects of his personality. His drive and ambition were similar to her own. He worked hard, played hard and could be hard-nosed about business decisions, but didn't she secretly admire that single-mindedness?

And she couldn't forget about his battle-scarred cat. Finn had a caring side, a side he obviously didn't show to people too easily, but Zoey had seen it and liked what she saw.

But Finn had been late this morning and it niggled at the back of her mind that he could well have come straight from another woman's bed. Could she bear the thought of him delivering passionate, planet-dislodging sex so soon after being with another woman?

It reminded her too much of the humiliation of what her ex had done to her. Rupert had made love to her the very same morning before she'd come home and found him in bed with another woman later in the day. The discovery of them in her own bed had made her sick to her stomach. She couldn't rid her brain of the image of their naked bodies wrapped in each other's arms.

Finn pulled his chair out and indicated for her to sit on the chair opposite his desk, his expression now back in business mode. 'Let's nut out a few preliminary ideas for the Frascatelli project.'

Zoey sat on the chair and smoothed her skirt over her knees. 'Can I ask you something first?'

'Sure. Fire away.'

She ran the tip of her tongue across her lips, her gaze drifting to his mouth almost of its own volition. 'Erm…' She gave herself a mental shake and asked, 'Why were you late this morning?'

One corner of his mouth lifted in a half-smile. 'You can blame Tolstoy. I let him outside for a bit of sunshine in the garden, but he climbed up one of the trees and refused to come down.'

Relief swept through Zoey in a whooshing wave that made her slightly dizzy. He hadn't been with another woman. Yay. But then she thought about poor Tolstoy who didn't look strong enough to hold his own outdoors. 'Oh, did you get him back in?' She had a sudden vision of the poor cat getting run over or beaten up by another cat.

'Yeah, eventually.' His smile turned rueful. 'Next time, I'm getting a dog, they're way more obedient.'

'Why did you call him Tolstoy?'

'Because our relationship is one that oscillates between war and peace. We're currently in a war phase but there are peace negotiations in process.' He gave a grin and added, 'I'm hoping for a truce by this evening.'

Zoey laughed. 'Then I hope you're successful.' She was the first to admit he had a great sense of humour. 'I really liked him. He's quite adorable, notwithstanding his war wounds.'

'He was quite taken by you.' Finn's gaze held hers in a spine-tingling lock. 'His loving behaviour was completely out of character. I've had to stop entertaining at home because I'm worried he'll scratch someone. He only just tolerates my house-keeper because she feeds him fillet steak.'

'That must seriously cramp your style. I mean, not being able to have…erm…guests over.' She glanced at his mouth and wondered who would be the next woman to kiss those sculptured lips. Who would be the next woman to scream with pleasure in his arms?

His gaze dipped to her mouth and one side of his mouth came up in a half-smile. 'I manage.'

There was a moment or two of silence.

Zoey tore her gaze away from his mouth and shifted her weight in the chair. 'So, what's your vision for the project?' There—who said she couldn't be single-minded?

He leaned forward to pick up a gold pen from his desk and then leaned back in his chair, flicking the button on the top of the pen on and off. His gaze held hers in an unmistakably intimate tether that made her blood tick and roar in her veins. 'What are the four principles of advertising a product?'

Zoey disguised a swallow. 'Erm…attraction, interest, desire, action.' Exactly what Finn had done to her. Attracted her, piqued her interest, made her desire him and spurned her into action. Sensual, racy action she still couldn't quite believe she had taken. And—God forgive her for being so weak—action she wanted to take again.

A knowing smile ghosted his mouth, his dark eyes containing a smouldering glint that made her heart skip a beat and something topple over in her stomach. 'Foolproof, right?'

She licked her lips again before she could control the impulse. 'Yes.'

He tossed the pen he was clicking back down on the desk. 'We need to work on those principles but ramp up the heat. Most well-travelled people are familiar with the Frascatelli hotel chain in Europe, but we need to show the brand as never before. Leo, as you know, wants to build his brand here in the UK. We need to aim not just for the wow factor, but to convince people a Frascatelli hotel is the only place to stay. Agreed?'

Zoey nodded. 'Agreed.'

They discussed a few more ideas back and forth and Zoey was pleasantly surprised at how well he listened and took on board her opinions. He didn't interrupt or discount what she had to say but encouraged her to expand her ideas, to take them a little further out of her comfort zone. It was nothing like the brainstorming sessions she conducted with her father. Her father had dismissed her opinions, ridiculed her and belittled her when her ideas hadn't aligned with his. But with Finn it was an exhilarating process and she was disappointed when he brought the meeting to a close. The time had grown powerful wings and flown by.

Finn pushed back his chair to stand. 'Let's go away and each do our thing and we'll toss our ideas together some more over dinner tonight. Okay?'

'Okay.' Zoey rose from her chair and hunted around for her bag. She picked it up off the floor and hung the strap over her left shoulder, adding, 'Did you have somewhere in mind? I'll meet you there.'

'Let's do it at my place. It'll be more private. And Tolstoy will enjoy seeing you again.'

Do it? More private? The *double entendre* made Zoey arch her brows. 'We'll be working, not…not doing anything else.'

'But of course,' he said with an enigmatic smile. 'Your call, right?'

Zoey lifted her chin, determined to resist him no matter how irresistible he was. And on a scale of irresistible he was way up at the top.

And she had better not forget it.

CHAPTER SEVEN

FOR THE REST of the day, Finn found his thoughts drifting to the explosive little interlude with Zoey in his office. He couldn't look at his desk without picturing her there, nor could he get his mind away from the image of her going down on him. His whole body shuddered in remembrance, the pleasure so intense it had shaken him to the foundation of his being. Their mutual lust was heady and addictive, and yet Zoey seemed to want him with one hand but push him away with the other.

It was her decision. He wasn't the sort of man to force himself on a woman if she was feeling a little conflicted. But he suspected she was holding him off because she was frightened of the passion he stirred in her. When it came to that, he was a little frightened himself of the things she triggered in him.

Mixing business and pleasure was something he had always shied away from in the past but in

Zoey's case he was prepared to make an exception. He wanted her and he knew damn well she wanted him. He was sure it was only a matter of time before she would be back in his arms. For how long, he couldn't say. His flings were short, brutally short, but he suspected a brief liaison with Zoey was not going to douse the flames of lust she evoked in him any time soon.

Their two explosive encounters had made him even more in lust with her. He wanted her with a ferocity that was all-consuming. She filled his thoughts like an obsession. Her wild sensuality sent a shockwave through his senses, making him thrum with the aftershocks for hours.

Somehow Zoey had done what no other woman had done before—she had taken control of their relationship, dictating when and even if, it would progress.

And the most disturbing thing of all was that he *wanted* it to progress. Wanted it badly. Not for ever, because he wasn't a for ever guy, but he wanted her for now. A fling was all he would offer, but so far, she was holding him at bay on that count. Was that why he was so captivated by her? The thrill of the chase had never been more exciting. The sex was beyond description. The drumming need to have her again was relentless, stirring his senses into a frenzy as soon as he saw her.

Yes, a short fling would be just the thing to

get her out of his system. He couldn't allow a woman—even one as beautiful and delightfully entertaining as Zoey Brackenfield—to get under his skin for too long. Commitment of that sort was anathema to him, but then, apparently it was for her too.

Had someone broken her heart? Her father hadn't mentioned anything to him about a boyfriend, but then Harry didn't often talk much about Zoey other than to criticise her. Finn got the feeling Harry was one of those parents who had no idea how to love and value their offspring. And, unfortunately, Finn knew better than most how that felt.

Finn walked out of his office for the day, and June looked up from her desk with a twinkling smile. 'Zoey Brackenfield is rather stunning, isn't she? Those unusual violet eyes, that beautiful mouth, that gorgeous complexion. How on earth do you keep your hands off her?'

He kept his expression bland, but his lower body leapt at the mention of Zoey's physical attributes. Her beautiful mouth had been around him that morning and had just about blown the top of his head off with its wild magic. She had made him punch-drunk with pleasure. Shaken him, rattled him, scrambled him. And he couldn't wait for her to do it again.

'She's not the fling type.'

'And you're not the marrying type.' June gave a little shrug and added with a sigh, 'Pity.'

Finn affected a laugh. 'Well, nor is she, as it turns out.'

June's eyes danced as if they were auditioning for a reality TV dance show. 'Oh, even better.'

'Why's that?'

'Because she's nothing like all the other women who look up to you like you're some sort of rock god. She's seeing the real you, not the idealised you. She's seeing you as an equal, and that makes for a much better relationship in the long term.'

'Ahem.' Finn pointedly cleared his throat. 'Who said anything about a long-term relationship?'

June's smile was undented by his savage frown or curt tone. 'Just putting it out there.'

'I pay you to work for me, not to comment on my private life.'

'And just how satisfying has your private life been over the last few months?'

'Very satisfying.' But not before he had met Zoey. Finn suddenly realised he hadn't felt properly alive before he met her. His day to day, week to week, month to month routine had gradually become so humdrum. He hadn't noticed until Zoey had brought colour, energy and zing to his life. Their occasional meetings at various advertising gigs had been the bright spots in his otherwise routine existence. And just lately she had awakened a dormant part of him, stirring it into living, breathing vitality.

'Zoey Brackenfield is a breath of fresh air,' June said, as if reading his thoughts. 'I think she'll be an asset to the company.' Her smile became enigmatic. 'Who knows how she will shake this place up, hey?'

Who indeed? But, if what had happened between him and Zoey so far was any indication, all he could say was, *Bring it on*.

Zoey dressed with care for her dinner at Finn's house. She spent ages on her hair and make-up, making sure she looked her best. She wasn't game enough to question why she was going to so much trouble—after all, she was supposed to be keeping things strictly business between them.

But every time she thought of him—which was way too often for her liking—her mind filled with images of them in his office making mad, passionate love. Her body remembered every glide of his hands, every stroke and flicker of his tongue against her most tender and sensitive flesh. She shivered as she recalled the taste of him, the feel of him, the velvet and steel power of him and how he was completely undone by her caresses. Which was only fair, seeing how undone she had been by his.

She was starting to realise she had seriously

misjudged Finn in every way possible. She had
accused him of betraying her over the takeover
of her father's company, but a subsequent conversation with her father had confirmed what Finn
had said—her father had approached Finn, not
the other way round. There was so much more to
Finn than she had first thought. He had a depth of
character that intrigued her and pleased her. He
wasn't the shallow, self-serving man she had assumed him to be.

Zoey picked up her evening bag and gave herself one more glance in the full-length mirror. The
black dress wasn't new, but it outlined her curves
without revealing too much cleavage. She had
washed and blow-dried her hair, leaving it loose
and wavy around her shoulders. Her make-up was
understated apart from smoky eyeliner and a vivid
slash of red lipstick.

'You'll do,' she said to her reflection. 'But don't
get any funny ideas about tonight. It's a working
dinner, nothing else.'

Finn answered the door to her dressed in camel-
coloured trousers and a casual white shirt that
highlighted the width of his shoulders. His hair
was still damp from a recent shower and his jaw
freshly shaven. 'Wow. You look good enough to
eat,' he said with a glinting smile.

Zoey suppressed a shiver and stepped across

the threshold, shooting him a narrow glance on the way past. 'Don't even think about it, O'Connell. I'm here to work, not play.'

'Spoilsport.' Finn grinned and then closed the door behind her. 'Come this way—I'm just putting the finishing touches to our meal.'

Zoey followed him to the well-appointed kitchen at the rear of the house, its bank of windows overlooking the garden. She looked at the various items he was preparing on the large island countertop—fillet steaks marinated in red wine and herbs, a melange of green vegetables, potatoes Dauphinoise, as well as a delectable cheese board with seasonal fruit. 'Impressive. I didn't know you were so domesticated. I thought you'd get your housekeeper to do that for you.'

'She only comes in to clean once a week and to look after Tolstoy when I travel.'

Zoey glanced around the room. 'Where is he?'

'Sulking upstairs.' Finn reached for a couple of wine glasses in a cupboard and then placed them on the countertop. 'I wouldn't let him go outside after this morning's *contretemps*.' He held up a bottle of red wine. 'I have white if you'd prefer.'

'Red is fine, thank you.' Zoey perched on one of the stools next to the island bench.

He poured two glasses of the red wine and handed her one, holding his up to hers in a toast. 'So, to working, not playing, together.' There was a hint of amusement lurking in the background of his dark brown gaze.

Zoey clinked her glass against his, something in her stomach pitching. But would *she* be able to stick to the rules? Her lower body quivered with the memory of his lovemaking, little pulses and flickers that reminded her of the exquisite magic of his touch. And how much she wanted to feel it again. 'Cheers,' she said, her gaze slipping away from the smouldering heat of his.

Finn took a sip of his wine and then placed the glass down as he continued preparing their meal. 'I'm interviewing the key staff at Brackenfield over the next month. I'll offer redundancy packages where it's appropriate, but I plan to do a complete restructure to streamline things to increase efficiency. As a result, some jobs will no longer exist.'

Zoey frowned. 'But some people have been with us for decades. You can't just get rid of them.'

'It's nothing personal, it's a business decision. Increasing profit and mitigating losses have to take priority over everything else.'

'Oh, and I suppose you'll suddenly decide my job no longer exists,' Zoey said, shooting him a glare.

'On the contrary, I'm going to keep you.' He wiped his hands on a tea towel and added, 'June would never speak to me again if I let you go.'

'Could you at least discuss with me first some of the decisions you're making over staff? I know everyone and their skill set and their personal circumstances.'

'Your opinion is likely to be too subjective,' Finn said. 'I don't care what a person's circumstances are—what I care about is whether they are capable of doing their job. I'm running a business, Zoey, not a charity.'

Zoey put her glass of wine down on the counter with a loud thwack. 'Running a business doesn't have to be all about profit. You wouldn't have a business if it weren't for the people you employ. How can you expect to get the best from them if you only see them as cogs in a wheel instead of as human beings? People who have families to feed, difficulties to overcome, mortgages and rent to pay—'

'And I suppose the way you and your father have run Brackenfield Advertising with all that touchy-feely stuff has worked well for you?' His gaze was direct, hard and penetrating.

Zoey couldn't hold his gaze and jumped down from the stool to walk over to the windows and look at the garden lit up with various lights. Anger rumbled through her at his cold-hearted approach to business but, as he said, had her father's way been any better?

Her father had pretended to care about his employees but had exploited them on many occasions, just as he'd exploited her, relying on her to do his work for him, to cover for him, to make excuses for him. She had bent herself out of shape to please him, to keep the company going, yet it had all been for nothing. Just as she had done for Rupert—over-adapting to make things work, when all the time behind her back he was cheating on her.

'I didn't have much to do with running the company,' she said, still with her back to Finn. 'My father refused to make me a director, believing it was a man's job, not a woman's, and especially not a young woman's. He wanted a son, not a daughter, and has spent the last twenty-eight years reminding me of his bitter disappointment.'

She swung round to look at him and added, 'So, maybe if I'd been able to do things my way, we wouldn't have had to sell to you at all.'

Finn let out a long sigh and came over to where she was standing. 'Your father's a fool for not giving you more responsibility. But, even if you had been able to do things your way, it doesn't change the fact that businesses have to produce profit otherwise they go under. And then everyone loses— owners, staff, shareholders, even the community at large.'

Zoey flicked him an irritated glance from beneath partially lowered lashes. Everything he said was true to a point, but how could she stand by and watch long-term staff be dismissed as if they didn't matter? They mattered to her. 'I just think there are ways to conduct a restructure without destroying people's lives, that's all.'

Finn reached for one of her hands and held it between both of his. 'Look at me, Zoey.' His voice was low and had a softer quality in it than she had heard before. She lifted her gaze to his and her pulse rate picked up as his thumb began a gentle stroking over the back of her hand. His touch was electrifying, sending tiny shivers down her spine. 'It's not my goal to destroy people's lives,' he went on. 'My goal is to—'

Zoey pulled roughly out of his hold. 'Make money. Yeah, yeah, yeah. I heard you the first time.' She rubbed at her hand in a pointed manner, shooting him another glare. 'I've put everything into my father's business. I've worked so damn hard, and you come sweeping in and want to change it all. There'll be nothing left to show for all the sacrifices I've made. Brackenfield Advertising will be swallowed up by your company. It will be as if it never existed.'

'I'm not sure what your understanding of a takeover is, but it's not like a merger,' Finn said, frowning. 'And, let me remind you, this was a friendly takeover, not a hostile one. Your father couldn't wait to sign on the line once I named a sum.'

'But you didn't even give me a hint of what was

going on.' Zoey banged her fist against her chest for emphasis. 'Why was I kept out of the loop? You had the chance to tell me and yet you didn't.'

He muttered a curse not quite under his breath. 'It seems to me this anger of yours is misdirected. You need to address this with your father, not me. I told him he should involve you, but he wouldn't hear of it.'

Zoey swung away from him, wishing now she hadn't agreed to have dinner with him. 'You don't understand how hard this is for me. I've waited all my life for a chance to prove myself to my father and you've come marching in and taken it all away.'

'Why is it so important for you to prove yourself to him?'

Zoey momentarily closed her eyes in a tight blink, her arms wrapped around the middle of her body. 'Because he's all the family I've got.'

Finn came up behind her and, placing his hands on the tops of her shoulders, gently turned her to face him. His gaze had softened, his expression etched in concern. 'What about your mother?'

Zoey let out a ragged sigh. 'She died when I was four. Horse accident. I was at nursery school when it happened. She never regained consciousness. My father didn't let me see her in hospital or allow me to go to her funeral. He thought it would upset me too much. But it upset me more by not being able to say goodbye to her.'

Finn wrapped his arms around her and brought her close against his body. He rested his chin on the top of her head, one of his hands gently stroking the back of her head in a comforting manner. 'I'm sorry. That must have been pretty tough on you.'

Zoey leant her cheek against his broad chest, the citrus notes of his aftershave tantalising her nostrils, the steely strength of his arms around her soothing and protective.

'I was lucky that I had nice stepmothers and nannies over the years. Dad remarried several times, I guess in the attempt to have the son he always wanted, not that it ever happened. Only one of his new wives got pregnant but she had a miscarriage and didn't try again, but left him soon after.' She sighed and added, 'I've never been enough for my dad. He wanted a son to pass the business on to and instead got me. And now it's too late.'

'He should be more than happy with you,' Finn said, kissing the top of her head. 'And what's this talk of it being too late?' He eased her away from him to look down at her with a reproving frown. 'You don't need your father to be successful. You can do it on your own. You're talented, Zoey, really talented. You bring a lot of innovation to your projects. They're fresh and original, and I'm sure it won't be long before you get the credit you deserve.'

Zoey basked in the glow of his confidence in her. It was so rare for her to hear praise other than from her close friends and hearing it from Finn, whom she respected and admired professionally, was like breathing in clean air after a lifetime of pollution. 'It's nice of you to say so.'

His brows lifted in a mock-surprised manner. 'Nice? Me?'

Zoey gave a rueful smile. 'You're nice enough to allow me to bore you with all my baggage.'

He lifted her chin with the end of his finger, his eyes dark and unwavering on hers. 'I'm beginning to think it's impossible for you to ever bore me.' His gaze dipped to her mouth and the atmosphere tightened as if all the oxygen particles in the room had disappeared.

Zoey moistened her lips, her eyes going to the sculpted perfection of his mouth. Her lips began to tingle in anticipation, and a soft but insistent beat of desire fluttered like wings deep in her core. 'Oh, I don't think I'm all that exciting…' She touched his lean jaw with her fingers, trailing them down to his lips. 'You, on the other hand…' Her voice dropped down to a whisper.

He captured her hand and held it up to his face, pressing a kiss to the middle of her palm, his eyes still holding hers. 'Is this working or playing?' His tone was gently teasing, his smile doing serious damage to her resolve to resist him.

But how could she resist him? He was a drug she hadn't known she had a penchant for until she kissed him the first time. Now her ardent need of him was a driving force that refused to go away. Every time she was around him, the craving intensified.

Zoey pressed herself a little closer, her lower body coming into intimate contact with his growing erection. 'I don't know why this keeps happening between us. I keep telling myself I won't give in to temptation and then I go ahead and do it.'

'I can tell you why.' He smoothed his hand down from below her shoulder blades to the small of her back, pressing her harder into his arousal. 'Because we both want each other.'

Zoey let out a shuddery breath, the heat of his body calling out to hers with a fierce, primal energy. 'I don't want a relationship with anyone right now. Maybe not ever.'

He tipped up her chin, locking his gaze back on hers. 'Why?'

She bit down into her lower lip, those horrid images inside her head of her ex with his new lover torturing her all over again. 'My ex cheated on me. It had been happening for months. I came home and found him in our bed with her.' She closed her eyes in a tight blink and then opened them again to add, 'He'd even made love to me that same morning. Told me he loved me and all.'

Finn held her apart from him, his frowning gaze holding hers. 'That is truly despicable. I'm not surprised you're so against getting involved with anyone again.'

Zoey looked at his chin rather than meet his gaze. 'I thought things were fine between us. I mean, we'd been together for years. But, looking back, there were lots of red flags I didn't notice at the time.' Her gaze crept back to his. 'It's only since you and I hooked up that I've realised how boring my sex life with him was. Maybe that's why he strayed. I wasn't exciting enough for him.'

Finn grasped her by the upper arms in a gentle but firm hold. 'Don't go blaming yourself for his shortcomings, Zoey. You're by far the most exciting lover I've ever had. He was the one who chose to cheat rather than discuss any concerns he might have had. You're better off without him.'

'Yes, well, I know that, but I just don't feel ready to date seriously again.'

'The life of having hook-ups isn't always what it's cracked up to be,' Finn said with a rueful grimace. 'It too can get a little boring.'

Zoey arched her eyebrows. 'Don't tell me the hardened playboy is looking for more permanent pastures on which to graze?'

He gave a crooked smile. 'Not a chance.' His hands slipped back down to hold her by the hips. 'But I'm not averse to having the odd extended fling from time to time.'

Zoey began to toy with one of the buttons on his shirt. 'How long do your, erm, extended flings normally last?' She flicked him a glance and added, 'I'm asking for a friend.'

Finn laughed and brought her closer to his body. 'Well, let's see now... I had one that lasted for a month once, but it was a long time ago.'

'Were you in love with her?' The question was out before Zoey could monitor her tongue. Was he capable of loving someone to that degree? Or was love something he avoided out of the fear of being hurt as his parents had hurt him?

'No. I've never experienced that feeling.'

'Would you recognise it if you did?'

'Would you?' His gaze was suddenly too direct, too penetrating, for her to hold.

Zoey looked back at the button she was playing with on his shirt. 'I'm not sure... I really thought I was in love with Rupert, but I can see now that I just cared about him as a person.'

She glanced up at him again. 'My two ex-flatmates have both recently fallen madly in love with their partners. I don't think I felt anything like what they feel for their new fiancés. And I am doubly sure Rupert never, ever looked at me the way my friends' fiancés look at them. As if the world would be an empty place without them in it.'

Finn slid one of his hands up to the nape of her neck, his fingers warm and gentle against her skin. 'Love can be a beautiful thing when it happens.'

She angled her head at him. 'So, you actually believe it can happen?'

His fingers splayed through her hair, sending a shiver down her spine. 'I too have a couple of friends who've been lucky enough to find love with each other.' His lips made a twisted movement. 'But of course, whether it lasts is another question. So many marriages end in divorce.'

'But your parents didn't divorce?'

He made a soft, snorting noise. 'They never tied the knot in the first place. They broke up a couple of times but drifted back together as drinking and drug buddies. Or so I'm told—I haven't seen them since I was thirteen.'

Zoey frowned and reached up to touch his face with her hand. 'I can only imagine how devastated you must have been by them behaving so irresponsibly. Do you know why they became like that? What were their backgrounds like? People who grow up in difficult circumstances often replicate them in their own lives as adults.'

Finn removed his hand from her hair and placed it on the top of her shoulder. His expression became stony, impenetrable. 'I get a little tired of people who excuse their appalling behaviour on their backgrounds. We all have choices in how we behave.'

'I know, but it can be really hard for some people to push past the stuff that happened to them, especially in early childhood,' Zoey said. 'Children's brains can be affected by witnessing violence or experiencing abuse. It can have a lifelong impact.'

Finn stepped away from her as if the conversation was causing him discomfort. He scraped a hand through his hair, his mouth tightly set. 'Look, I know you mean well, but if you're thinking I'll ever have a nice, cosy little reunion with my parents, then you're completely mistaken. I want nothing to do with either of them or the relatives that brought me up.'

Something in Zoey's stomach dropped. 'Why are you so hard on your relatives? Were they…abusive?' She hated even saying the word, wondering if Finn had suffered at the hands of his carers in the most despicable way.

He gave a short, embittered laugh. 'Depends what you mean by abusive. No one ever laid a hand on me, and I was always fed and clothed, but I was left in no doubt of how much of an inconvenience I was to them. I got passed around three or four families over the years. No one wanted to keep me any length of time. They had their own kids, their own tight little family unit, and I didn't belong.'

'Oh, Finn,' Zoey said. 'What about your grandparents? Did either set have—?'

'My father was disowned by his parents for his lifestyle choices. My mother's parents had me for the occasional weekend in the early years but found the task of taking care of a young child too taxing, especially a child born out of wedlock. They were highly religious and were not averse to telling me I was the spawn of the devil. Both of them died within a couple of years of each other and I was farmed out to various great-aunts and great-uncles.' He gave a grim smile and added, 'The only contact I have with any of them is when they ask for money.'

Zoey frowned. 'Do you give it to them?'

He came back to place his hands on her shoulders, his eyes meshing with hers. 'I don't want to talk about my family any more. This is what I'd rather do.' And he brought his mouth down to hers.

CHAPTER EIGHT

FINN WONDERED IF he would ever tire of kissing Zoey's soft and responsive lips. He loved the taste of her, the smell of her skin, the touch of her hands, the way her body pressed against his, as if she wanted to melt into him completely.

But it wasn't just the physical closeness with her that stirred him so deeply. It was the strange sense of camaraderie he felt with her. Both of them were only children who hadn't had things easy and both of them were relentlessly driven to achieve, to prove something to themselves, to leave an indelible mark on the world. He had never felt such affinity with anyone before and it made him wonder if he was getting too close to her. He was allowing her too much access to his locked-down emotional landscape. The barren wasteland of his childhood was normally something even he didn't revisit. But he had allowed Zoey in and it had changed something in their relationship.

Relationship? Was that what this was between them? He didn't do relationships as such. Not the ones that stretched into the future without an end point. He only conducted temporary relationships that didn't go deep enough to engage his emotions. The sort of emotions that made him vulnerable in the way he had been as a child—wanting love, needing it, craving it and yet repeatedly being denied it.

He had taught himself to ignore the human need to be loved. To ignore the need to be connected in such a deep and lasting way to another person. The sort of love that made your bones ache to be with the other person. The sort of love that filled your chest and made it hard to take a breath without feeling its tug. The sort of love that could be snatched away when you needed it the most, leaving you empty, abandoned, vulnerable. And that most awful word of all—lonely.

Finn was not the 'falling in love with your soul mate' type. He had never pictured himself growing old with someone, having a family and doing all the things that long-term couples do. His career was his focus, continuing to build his empire that provided more money than he could spend and gave him more accolades than he could ever have dreamed of receiving.

And yet, with Zoey's mouth beneath his, and her arms around his body, her soft whimpers of pleasure made him wonder if going back to his casual approach to sex was going to be as exciting as it once had been. He was finding it increasingly hard to imagine making love with someone else. Found it hard to imagine how he would desire anyone else with anywhere near the same fervour he had for her. It was as relentless as his drive to succeed, maybe even more so. And that was deeply disturbing.

Zoey lifted her mouth off his to gaze into his eyes. Her cheeks were flushed, her lips swollen from the pressure of his, and he could not think of a moment when she had looked more beautiful. 'I hope the dinner you've been preparing isn't burning to a crisp.'

Finn had completely forgotten about the meal—the only hunger he felt was for her. A rabid hunger then clawed at his very being. He framed her face with his hands and kissed the tip of her nose. 'You have the amazing ability to distract me.'

Her lips curved in a smile. 'Likewise.' But then a tiny frown flickered across her forehead and she added with a slight drop of her gaze, 'I'm not sure what's happening between us…'

Finn knew what *he* wanted to happen—more of what was already happening. The electric energy of being intimate with her, the blood-pumping passion of holding her, the thrill of his senses each time he looked at her. He wanted her like he had wanted no one before. But would the occasional hook-up with her truly satisfy him? For the first time in his life, he wanted to indulge in a longer relationship. Not long-term, but longer than he normally would.

But would Zoey agree to it?

'What do you want to happen between us?' Finn could barely believe he was asking such a loaded question. A dangerous question. He was giving her control over the very thing he *always* controlled— when a relationship started and when it ended.

She ran the tip of her tongue across her lips, her gaze creeping back up to meet his. 'Nothing permanent.'

Nothing permanent. Hearing his own words coming out of her mouth should have delighted him, and would have delighted him if anyone other than her had said it. He was the one who normally set the rules of a relationship, and yet this time Zoey wanted that privilege. And, because he wanted her so badly, he would give it to her without question. 'Okay. So, a fling for as long as we both want it. Does that sound workable?'

Her teeth sank into the fleshy part of her lower lip for a moment. Then her eyes meshed with his with a spark of intractability. 'As long as we both agree to be exclusive. That for me is not negotiable.'

Finn couldn't agree more. He hadn't been too

keen on an open relationship—call him old-fashioned, but he wasn't into sharing, especially when it was Zoey, the woman of his sensual dreams and fantasies. The thought of her with anyone else churned his gut, which was surprising to him, because he had never considered himself the jealous type. He had no time for possessive men who thought they owned a woman, but something about Zoey made him want her all to himself.

'It's a deal-breaker for me too. I might be fairly casual with how I conduct my sex life, but I have never played around on a current partner.'

A smile flickered at the edges of her mouth and her arms wound back around his waist. 'I've never had a fling before. I've always been in long-term relationships. Don't you find it ironic that you're the opposite?'

Finn gave a wry grin. 'Believe me, the irony hasn't escaped me.' He brought her closer, hip to hip, pelvis to pelvis, need to need. 'I have an idea. Can you clear your diary for next week?'

'I might be able to, why?'

'I want to be alone with you, somewhere without distractions,' Finn said. 'How does Monte Carlo sound?'

Her eyes lowered from his, her teeth beginning to chew at her lower lip. 'It sounds lovely but…'

He tipped up her chin, so her gaze met his. 'But?'

A flicker of something passed through her gaze. 'It's tempting.'

'That's the whole point.'

She gave a half-smile. 'It sounds wonderful. I haven't been there before, but I've always wanted to go.' But then her smile faded and a frown took up residence on her forehead. 'But what about Tolstoy?'

'I'll get my housekeeper to look after him.' He gave a grimace and added, 'It'll put the peace negotiations back a bit, but hopefully he'll forgive me.'

Zoey made a sad face. 'Poor boy. Cats don't like change and regularly punish their owners when there's a change of routine.'

'Yes, so I'm finding out. You're the only person I've been able to have here since I got him. It will seriously curtail my social life if he doesn't improve his attitude.'

Zoey studied him for a moment. 'If he's turning out to be so much trouble, why haven't you given him to someone else?'

'After all the money I spent on him? No way. He can damn well adjust. I've had to.'

Her lips began to twitch with another smile. 'You love him.'

Finn hadn't really thought about it before, but it suddenly occurred to him that he had developed an attachment to that wretched cat. The thing wasn't even cute and cuddly. It looked more like something out of a horror movie. But he had grown to look forward to seeing Tolstoy at the start and end of each day, even if he wasn't the most congenial housemate. 'Yeah, well, maybe I've developed a mild affection for him.'

Zoey's smile became playful. 'So, the ruthless businessman has a heart after all. Who knew?'

Finn gave her a look. 'Not so big a heart that I would consent to taking him with me to Monte Carlo. I do have my limits. Besides, I want you to myself. My villa is private and secluded, and I often go there when I need to work on a deadline. And, given that Leo Frascatelli has plans for a hotel revamp in Nice, which is only a few minutes' drive away, we can do some on-site research.'

A tiny frown tugged at her forehead. 'But won't having me there be a distraction?'

Finn pressed a kiss to her mouth. 'A shocking one, but I think I can handle it.'

A sparkling light came into her eyes and her arms moved from around his waist to link around his neck. 'You think you can handle me?' Her tone was teasing, her touch electric, and he wished he could clear his diary for a month instead of a week and spend it alone with her. 'You have no idea what you're letting yourself in for, O'Connell.' She pressed her lips against his for a brief moment, making him desperate for more. 'Don't say you weren't warned.'

'Warning heeded,' Finn said and brought his mouth back down on hers.

The following day, Zoey met up with Ivy and Millie for a quick catch-up over a drink after work. She always looked forward to catching up with her friends but, since they had both become so happily engaged, she felt a little on the outer. The irony was, she had once been the marrying type. It was why she had been with Rupert for so long—seven years. Every year that had passed without him presenting her with an engagement ring she had made excuses for him. He was under the pump at work…he wasn't ready for marriage yet…he wanted to pay off some debts first. She had spent years of her life waiting, only to have her loyalty and commitment thrown back in her face.

And now, she was the one who didn't want to settle down.

'Millie told me about your little hook-up in New York with Finn O'Connell,' Ivy said with a smile. 'You do realise I fell in love with Louis after a one-night stand?'

Zoey gave her a droll look. 'I'm not going to fall in love with Finn O'Connell, okay?' She was in lust with him and it was wonderful. She had never felt like this before, so alive and in touch with her body. When he had first suggested the trip, she had been assailed with doubts. Would she be setting herself up for hurt by spending such concentrated time with him? But she reassured herself it was just a fling. She was the one in control and she would stay in control. Five days with him in Monte Carlo would be divine. It was just what she needed right now, a chance to put some of her past disappointments aside and enjoy herself by living in the moment.

Millie leaned forward to pick up one of the nibbles from the plate in front of them. 'How will you stop yourself? I said the same thing about Hunter. When love strikes, it strikes, and you can't do anything to stop it.'

Zoey topped up her wine from the bottle on the table. 'I don't think I've ever been in love, or at least not like you two are. What I felt for Rupert was… I don't know… I told him I loved him plenty of times, and he did me, but…'

'But?' Millie and Ivy spoke together.

Ivy blew out a little breath and twirled the wine around in her glass. 'I think I might have been in love with the idea of being in love. Of being important to someone, you know? Really important to them, not just someone they lived with who did the bulk of the cooking and cleaning and was available for sex whenever they wanted it.' She gave the girls a wincing look and asked, 'Too much information?'

'You've never really talked about your relationship with Rupert so honestly before,' Ivy said.

'Maybe acknowledging the problems you had with him will help you to not to repeat the mistakes in a future relationship.'

'That's exactly what I'm doing,' Zoey said. 'I'm doing what I want for a change. That's why a fling with Finn O'Connell is perfect for me right now. We want the same things—a no-strings, no-rings, no-promises-of-for-ever fling.'

'So, will you bring him to my wedding as your plus-one?' Ivy asked, looking hopeful.

Zoey gave a short laugh. 'I'm not sure a romantic wedding would be Finn O'Connell's thing at all. Besides, I don't want to broadcast it too publicly that I'm having a fling with him.'

Ivy and Millie exchanged speaking looks. Zoey frowned at them both. 'What?'

'Are you sure a fling is all you want from Finn?' Ivy asked, with a look of concern. 'Have you really changed that much to go from having a long-term relationship history to wanting nothing but flings with people who take your fancy?'

'Of course I've changed,' Zoey said. 'No offence to you two, but I can't see myself settling down with someone any more.' The inevitable hurt, the vulnerability, the crushing disappointment when the person you had committed your life to let you down. Why would she sign up for that? It was better this way, she had way more control.

'I think it's sad that you feel that way,' Ivy said.

'I can't wait to spend the rest of my life with Louis. To think I might have missed out on feeling like this about someone and have him feel the same way about me is too awful to contemplate.'

'But what if Finn wants more?' Millie chimed in.

'Not a chance,' Zoey reassured her and reached for a marinated olive from the plate. 'He's a playboy with no desire to settle down.' She popped the olive in her mouth and chewed and swallowed. 'Look, be happy for me, okay? I'm spending the next five days with him in Monte Carlo. It's kind of a working holiday but there'll be plenty of time for...other stuff.'

Millie and Ivy exchanged *can you believe this?* looks and Zoey rolled her eyes. 'What is it with you two? No one is going to fall in love, okay?'

'We just don't want you to get hurt, Zoey,' Millie said. 'You've been through a lot with Rupert and your dad. The last thing you need is to get your heart broken again.'

'Don't worry, it won't get broken.' Zoey wondered now if it was her pride that had been hurt rather than her heart when it came to her ex.

And, as long as she kept her pride intact during her time with Finn, she would be perfectly safe.

Finn and Zoey flew the next day from London to Nice and then drove the twenty-minute drive to his villa in Monte Carlo in a luxury hire car. Zoey stepped out of the car and gazed at the Belle Époque style three-storey villa, with glossy, black wrought-iron balconies on the two upper levels. She had thought his London home was stunning, but this was on a whole new level.

'Oh, wow, it's lovely...' she said, shading her eyes with her hand from the brilliant sunshine to take in the view over the water in the distance.

Finn placed his hand on the small of her back to guide her forward towards the villa. 'I'm glad you like it.'

'How could anyone not?' She stepped inside the villa and turned a full circle in the marble foyer. A large crystal chandelier hung from the tall ceiling. The floor was beautifully polished parquetry, partially covered with a luxurious Persian rug that picked up the black and white and gold theme of the décor. A large gilt-edged mirror on one wall made the foyer seem even more commodious than it was, and that was saying something, because it was huge. There were works of art on the walls that very much looked like originals and there were fresh flowers in a whimsical arrangement on a black-trimmed marble table in front of the grand, sweeping staircase.

Zoey turned back to face him. 'Oh, Finn, this is truly the most amazing place. How long have you had it?'

'A year or two. It was a little run-down when I bought it, but it's come up well.'

'It certainly has.'

'Why don't you have a look around while I bring in the bags?' Finn said. 'The garden and pool are that way.' He pointed to the right of the grand staircase, where she could see a glimpse of lush green foliage through a window.

Zoey walked through the villa until she came to a set of French doors leading out to the garden and pool area. Finn hadn't been wrong in describing the villa as secluded and private—the pool and garden were completely so. A tall hedge framed two sides of the property, and the twenty-metre pool in the centre overlooked the sparkling azure-blue of the Mediterranean Sea in the distance. The garden beds in front of the tall hedges either side of the pool were a less structured affair with scented gardenias and colourful azaleas. There was an al fresco dining and lounge seating area on one side, and a cleverly concealed changing room and shower and toilet nearby.

Zoey bent down to test the water temperature of the pool just as Finn came out to join her. 'Fancy a swim?' he asked.

She straightened and smiled at him. 'Don't tempt me.'

He came over to her and took her by the hands, his warm, strong fingers curling around hers. 'Look who's talking. Do you know the effort it took for me to keep my hands off you during that flight?'

A frisson coursed through her body at the glinting look in his dark gaze. 'It took an effort on my part too.'

He brought her closer to the hardened ridge of his growing erection, his hands settling on her hips. A shockwave of awareness swept through her body, desire leaping in her core with pulsing, flickering heat. 'Take your clothes off.' His commanding tone sent her pulse rate soaring.

'What, here? What if someone's watching?'

He smiled a devilish smile. 'I'll be the only one watching.'

Zoey shivered in anticipation, for she knew without a single doubt he would more than deliver on the sensual promise glinting in his gaze. 'I've never gone skinny dipping before. In fact, there's quite a few things I haven't done before I met you. You seem to bring out a wild side in me I didn't know I possessed.'

'I happen to like your wild side.' He brought his mouth down to the shell of her ear, gently taking her earlobe between his teeth and giving it a soft bite. A shiver raced down her spine with lightning-fast speed and a wave of longing swept through her. He lifted his head to lock his gaze back on hers and added, 'It turns me on.'

Zoey moved her lower body against the proud

ridge of his arousal, her blood thrumming with excitement. 'You turn me on too.' She began to unbutton his shirt, button by button, leaving light little kisses against each section of the muscled chest that she uncovered. 'You taste like salt and sun and something else I've never tasted before.'

He became impatient and tugged his shirt out of his jeans and pulled it over his head, tossing it to one side. 'And do you like it?'

'Love it.' She pressed another kiss to his right pectoral muscle. 'I think I might be addicted to it.' She circled his flat male nipple with the point of her tongue, round and round and round. He made a growling sound deep in his throat and she lifted her head to give him a sultry smile. 'Steady... I'm only just getting started.'

'Yeah, well, so am I.' Finn slid the zipper at the back of her sundress down to just above her bottom. The dress slipped off her shoulders and fell to her feet, leaving her in just balcony bra and lacy knickers. He ran his hands over the curve of her bottom, bringing her back against his hardened flesh, his eyes darkening with unbridled lust.

'I'm not taking the rest off until you take off your jeans and underwear.'

His mouth tilted in a smile and he stepped back to strip them. 'Happy now?'

Zoey drank her fill of his gloriously tanned and toned and aroused body, her insides coiling tightly with lust. 'Getting there…' She stroked her fingers down his turgid length in a lightly teasing manner, and he sucked in a harsh-sounding breath and closed his eyes in a slow blink. She cupped him in her hand and massaged up and down, emboldened by the flickers of pleasure passing across his features.

He made another growling sound and pulled her hand away. He reached around her to unfasten her bra, tossing it in the same direction as the rest of his clothes. He hooked his finger in the side of her knickers, drawing them down until they were around her ankles. She stepped out of them and he ran his hungry gaze over her lingeringly while her body throbbed and ached for his possession. No one had ever made her feel so proud of her body. No one had ever triggered such sensual heat and desire in her flesh. No one had ever made her want them with an ache so powerful. It consumed her totally, it drove out every thought but how to get her needs satisfied. It turned her into a wild and wanton being, driven by primal urges.

Finn cupped her breasts in his hands, moving his thumbs over her already peaking nipples. Her flesh tingled at his touch, tingling sensations coursing through her body in an electric current. She made a soft sound of approval, her breathing increasing as the tingles travelled all the way to her core. He bent his head to caress her breast with his lips and tongue, the exquisite torture making her breathless with excitement. His touch was neither too soft or too hard but perfectly in tune with her body's needs.

It was as if he was reading her flesh, intuitively understanding the subtle differences and needs in each of her erogenous zones. He brought his mouth to her other breast in the same masterful manner and a host of sensations rippled through her. Delicious sensations that made her legs tremble and her heart race.

Finn lifted his mouth from her breast and gazed down at her with smouldering eyes. And, without a word, he scooped her up in his arms and carried her to the sun loungers, laying her down on the largest one, which was the size of a double bed. He came down beside her, one of his hands caressing her abdomen, moving slowly, so torturously slowly, towards the throbbing heat of her mound.

'I love watching how your pupils flare when I touch you like this,' he said in a husky tone. 'You have such expressive eyes. They are such an unusual colour, like winter violets. They're either shooting daggers at me or looking at me like you are now.' He brought his mouth down to the edge of hers and teased her with a barely touching kiss. 'Like you can't wait for me to be inside you.'

'Newsflash,' Zoey said, stroking her hand down the length of his spine, her own body on fire. 'I can't wait. Please, please, please make love to me before I go crazy.'

He tapped a gentle finger on the end of her nose. 'Safety first.' He pushed himself up off the lounger and went to get a condom from his wallet in the back pocket of his jeans. Zoey watched him apply it, her need for him at fever pitch.

He came back and joined her on the lounger, his weight propped on one elbow, his other hand stroking her from the indentation of her waist to the flank of her thigh and back again. 'Now, where was I?'

Zoey pulled his head down so his mouth was just above hers. 'You were here.'

Finn's mouth covered hers at the same time he entered her with a deep, thick thrust that made her shiver from head to foot. The movement of his body in hers was slow at first, then built to a crescendo. Her senses rioted, her feminine flesh gripping him tightly, the exquisite tension in her swollen tissues building and building. She rocked with him, her legs tangled with his, her hands stroking the hard contours of his back and shoulders. And then, as she got closer and closer to the point of no return, she grasped him by the buttocks and arched her spine to receive each driving thrust of his body.

Finn slipped his hand between their bodies, caressing her intimately to push her over the edge of the cliff to paradise. She fell apart with a sobbing, panting cry that rent the air, her body quaking as the pulsating sensations went through her. Her orgasm was powerful, overwhelming, earth-shattering and mind-altering, and it went on and on, faded a little and then resumed with even more force. Finn rode out the second wave of her pleasure with his own release, his deep, urgent thrusts triggering yet another explosive orgasm that left her breathless, panting and wondering how on earth her body was capable of such intense pleasure.

Zoey flung her head back against the sun lounger, her chest still rising and falling, the warmth of the sun on her face and the heat of Finn's body lying over her a blessed weight, anchoring her to the earth. It didn't seem possible to experience such profound pleasure without a price to pay and she suddenly realised what it might be. Her earlier hatred of Finn had faded to a less potent dislike, then somehow it had morphed into a deep respect of him. A growing admiration for the things he had overcome to become the man he was today.

And there was another step she was desperately trying to avoid taking—the step towards love. Not just the friendship or casual love, but the sort of love that sent down deep roots into your very being until you couldn't move or breathe without feeling it. The sort of love that made it impossible to imagine life without that person by your side. The sort of love her friends were experiencing with their partners.

A once in a lifetime love.

The sort of love Zoey had never experienced before… How had she settled for all those years with her ex when she hadn't felt anything like what she was beginning to feel for Finn? The feelings inside her were like the first stumbling steps of a toddler learning to walk. Tentative, uncertain, unstable. But how could she be sure it was actually the real deal—love? What if she was confusing great sex with long-lasting love? It was an easy mistake, and many women made it, becoming swept up in the heady rush of a new relationship when the sex was exciting and fresh and deeply satisfying.

Finn propped himself up on one elbow and used his other hand to cup one side of her face. 'You've gone very quiet.' His gaze held hers in an intimate lock she found hard to hold. 'I hope it's a good quiet, not a bad quiet.'

She lowered her gaze to his mouth and gave a flickering smile. 'It's not often in my life that I become speechless.'

He tipped up her chin to mesh his gaze with hers. 'Same.' His thumb brushed over her lower lip in a slow caress that made her whole mouth tingle. 'You're breathtaking, do you know that?' His voice had a husky edge and his eyes darkened to pitch. 'No one has ever got under my skin quite as much as you.'

'Good to know I'm not the only one who feels like that,' Zoey said, gently caressing his strong jaw. 'But, given this is just a fling, I think we need to be careful we don't start confusing good sex with something else.'

'I'm not confused, but are you?' His tone was playful but there was a faint disturbance at the back of his gaze. A shifting shadow, fleeting, furtive.

Zoey stretched her lips into a confident smile. 'Not so far.'

His eyes moved back and forth between hers as if he was looking for something. 'Better keep it that way, babe. I don't want to hurt you.' There was a roughened edge in his voice. 'That's the last thing I want to do.'

'Ah, but I might be the one who ends up hurting you,' Zoey countered in a teasing tone. 'Have you considered that?'

There was another tiny flicker at the back of his gaze but then his expression became inscrutable. 'I guess I'll have to take my chances.' And he sealed her mouth with his.

CHAPTER NINE

LATER THAT EVENING, Finn brought a bottle of champagne and a cheese and fruit board out to the terrace overlooking the sparkling lights of Monte Carlo and the moonlit sea in the distance. Zoey was leaning against the stone balustrade, her long, dark hair lustrous around her shoulders, her face turned towards the golden orb of the moon. She was wearing a long white shoestring-strap sundress that showcased every delicious curve of her body. He wondered if he would ever get tired of looking at her. His pulse leapt every time he came near her, the memory of their lovemaking stirring his blood anew.

The rattle of the glasses on the tray he was carrying alerted her to his presence and she turned round and smiled, and something in his chest stung like the sudden flick of a rubber band. Maybe it was the moonlight, maybe it was the passionate lovemaking earlier…or maybe it was a warning he needed to rein it in a little.

Her comment earlier about the possibility of her hurting him would have been laughable if anyone else had said it. He never allowed anyone close enough to give them the power to hurt him.

But Zoey was getting close, a little too close for comfort.

She knew him intimately, far more intimately than any other lover. And that intimate physical knowledge had somehow given her the uncanny ability to tempt him into lowering his guard. He had brought her away to spend concentrated time with her because he wanted continuity rather than having one night here and one night there.

Having her to himself, day upon day, night upon night, had deepened his desire for her and also made him appreciate how talented she was and how she hadn't been given a proper chance to shine. He had a plan for her irrespective of the timeframe of their fling—he wanted her on his creative team going forward. He didn't want her to disappear out of his life once their fling was over. Whether she would agree to it was another question, but he would make her an attractive offer, one she would be a fool to refuse.

A part of him was a little disquieted about the lengths to which he was prepared to go in order to keep her. He normally kept his emotions out of business. He hadn't built his empire by being swayed by his feelings but by concentrating on the facts. But the fact was, Zoey was a one in a million person and he didn't want to lose her to someone else. She would be an asset to his business and, since his business was his main priority, he would do anything to keep her. Almost anything.

'Ooh, lovely, a moonlit champagne supper,' Zoey said. 'You really know how to spoil a girl. But then, you've had plenty of practice.'

'Some women are harder to impress than others,' Finn said. 'But worth the effort in the end.'

'And which category am I in?'

'You're in a category of your own.'

Zoey was the first woman he had brought here, and right now he couldn't imagine bringing anyone else. It would seem…odd, tacky…almost clichéd. He knew it was how she saw him. As some well-practised charmer who slept his way through droves of lovers. And there was some uncomfortable truth in her view of him. That was the way he lived his life and he would no doubt go back to that lifestyle once their fling was over.

Finn frowned as he placed the tray on the table and took the champagne out of the ice bucket. The kicker was, what if he didn't want it to be over any time soon? What if Zoey wanted to end it before he did? What if the possibility of her hurting him became a painful, inescapable reality? What if that little elastic band flick in his chest became a thousand flicks? Ten thousand? More?

'Is something wrong?' Zoey asked, catching the tail end of his frown.

Finn gave a crooked smile. 'What could be wrong? I've got the most beautiful woman with me on a perfect night in Monte Carlo.'

Her gaze slipped away from his and her hand left his arm to scoop her hair back behind one shoulder. 'I guess I'm just one of many you've brought here.' She walked back over to the balustrade and stood with her back to him, her slim shoulders going down on a sigh.

Finn put the champagne bottle back in the ice bucket and came over to her. He placed his hands on the tops of her shoulders and turned her to face him. 'You're the first person I've brought here.'

Doubt flickered in her violet gaze. 'I find that hard to believe, given your reputation.'

'It's true, Zoey. I've only just had the renovations done and there hasn't been time to entertain a guest before now.'

'But you'll bring others here once our fling is over.'

Finn removed his hands from her shoulders and frowned. 'Is that a crime?'

'No.' She gave a stiff little smile and added, 'I'll have other lovers too.'

The sting in his chest was not the flick of a rubber band this time but a whip. Finn walked back to open the champagne, a frown pulling at his forehead. He wasn't a card-carrying member of the double standards club, but right now he was having trouble handling the thought of her making love with anyone else. He pulled the cork of the champagne with a loud pop and poured some in each of the glasses, but he had never felt less like drinking it. He brought the glasses over to where she was standing and offered her one.

She took it with another smile and then clinked her glass against his. 'Let's hope my future lovers are as exciting as you.'

Finn put his glass down on the edge of the balustrade without taking a sip. 'For God's sake, Zoey,' he said with a savage frown.

She arched her eyebrows in an imperious manner. 'What? You're being a little touchy, are you not? I'm simply stating a fact. We'll both go back to our normal lives once we end our relationship. In fact, you've done me a favour in breaking my self-imposed man drought. I haven't been with anyone since I broke up with my ex and wondered if I would ever take a lover again. But you've helped me get back in the dating game.'

He scraped a hand through his hair and muttered a curse not quite under his breath. 'Glad to be of service.'

'Why should the mention of my future lovers be an issue for you? You'll probably have dozens after me, hundreds even.'

One thing Finn knew for sure—none of them would be half as exciting as her. 'I'm not sure you'll find the casual dating scene as fulfilling as you think.'

'Does that mean you don't find it so?'

Finn hadn't found it so for months but wasn't going to admit it to anyone. He was barely ready to admit it to himself. Admitting it to himself would mean he would need to change how he lived his life, and he wasn't sure he wanted to explore the possibility of doing that in any great detail. He was used to being alone, apart from brief flings. He was used to being self-sufficient. He was used to having the control to start or end a relationship on his terms. Sharing that control with another person was in the too-hard, too-threatening basket.

Finn took one of her hands and brought it up to his chest. 'I don't want to think about you with anyone else, not while we're having such a good time.' He gave her hand a gentle squeeze. 'You're having a good time, yes?'

Her lips curved in a smile. 'I can't remember when I've enjoyed myself more.'

Finn placed his arms around her and gathered her close, resting his head on the top of her head. 'Nor me.'

The next few days were some of the most memorable of Zoey's life. They spent considerable time in

Nice, looking at the hotel Leo Frascatelli was currently redeveloping. The hotel was situated close to the sweeping arc of the beach and had various restaurants and bars that made the most of the spectacular view. It was in the process of extensive renovations, which were now close to being completed, to coincide with the launch of the advertising campaign.

On another day they toured the ancient fortress town of St Paul de Vence, high up in the hills behind Nice, strolling hand in hand up and down the narrow cobblestoned alleys, wandering in and out of the galleries and artisan shops. They went to the renowned perfume village of Grasse, where Finn bought her some gorgeous fragrances to take home. They had a leisurely lunch in the resort town of Cannes, famous for its international film festival, and then visited the ancient market place in Antibes, and gazed at the jaw-droppingly expensive yachts moored in the port.

Being in Finn's company every hour of the day, whether they were sightseeing, working or dining or making love, made Zoey realise how dangerously close she was to falling in love with him. He treated her like a princess and yet still managed to make her feel his equal in every way. He was tender and caring, looking at her with such focussed concentration at times, she began to wonder if he was developing a stronger attachment to her than he was prepared to admit.

And, unless she was seriously deluding herself, she had seen that same look on her friends' fiancés' faces. A look so tender and caring it made her blood sing with joy. Every time she tried to imagine a future without him, a wave of dread swept through her. He was an attentive and considerate and exciting lover and, as much as she had teased him over one day moving on to other lovers, she was beginning to realise it would be near impossible for her to do so without disappointment. Acute, heart-wrenching disappointment. For who could possibly compare to him and his exquisite lovemaking?

But it wasn't just his lovemaking she would miss. She enjoyed listening to his insights into the advertising business. She felt inspired by his work ethic and stamina. And, while he was a hard task master when they were working together on their creative approach to the Frascatelli account, she found herself rising to the challenge, enjoying the repartee and exchange of ideas. He encouraged her to be bold in her vision, bolder than she had ever been, and it freed her to explore and stretch her creativity in a way she had never done before.

But a tiny seed of doubt kept rattling around her brain over her future working for him. Becoming one of his employees was not the same as owning and operating her own business. How could she operate in a business that was no longer hers?

But, then it had never been hers—her father had seen to that.

The takeover would take some weeks to finally settle, in terms of which staff would be let go and which would move across to Finn's company. Could she work with him in the long term once their fling was over? How would it feel to see him every day but not in their current context? He would go back to his playboy lifestyle and she would have to learn to be indifferent to him. Indifferent to the many women who came and went in his life. She would have to pretend it didn't bother her, pretend he didn't matter to her other than as an employer.

But he did matter.

He mattered more than she wanted to admit. But it was beyond foolish to hope she might matter to him too.

On their last night in Monte Carlo, Finn took Zoey to a restaurant near the Monte Carlo casino and the stunning Hotel de Paris. They were seated at their table with drinks in front of them, waiting for their meals to arrive. He had been quieter than normal for most of the day and she hadn't been game enough to ask why. Over the last few hours, she'd often found him looking into the distance with a slight frown on his face.

Was he thinking of ending their fling now they'd had this concentrated time together? His flings were notoriously short—some only lasted a day or two. What right did she have to hope he would want her for longer? That he might have come to care for her the same way she had come to care for him?

Care? What a mild word to use when what she felt for him was much stronger, much deeper, much more lasting.

Much more terrifying.

Love was a word she had never thought to use when it came to Finn O'Connell. But now it was the only word she could use to describe how she felt about him. It wasn't a simple, friendship love, although she did consider him more of a friend now than an enemy. It was an all-consuming love that had sprouted and blossomed over the last few days, maybe even before that. The first time they made love had triggered a change in her attitude towards him, and not just because of the explosively passionate sex. The union of their bodies had triggered a union of their minds, their interests, their talents and even their disappointments about some aspects of their childhoods. Zoey had sensed an emotional camaraderie with him she had not felt with anyone else.

Was it silly of her to hope he felt the same way? That he would want to continue their fling…maybe even call it a relationship rather than a fling and one day allow it to become permanent?

How had she fooled herself that she never wanted to settle down? She wasn't cut out for the single-and-loving-it club. She longed for deep and lasting love, a love that could help overcome the trials and tribulations of life. A love that was a true partnership, a commitment of two equals working together to build a happy and productive life. A family life where children were welcomed, loved, supported and encouraged to grow and be all they could and wanted to be. Zoey had denied those longings until she'd met Finn, but now those deep yearnings were not to be so easily ignored.

Finn reached for her hand across the table, his fingers warm around hers. The candle on the table reflected light back into his dark brown eyes and cast parts of his face in shadow, as though he were a Gothic hero. How could she have thought she wouldn't fall in love with him? How could she have thought she would be immune to his charismatic presence, his admirable qualities, his earth-shattering lovemaking? He was everything she wanted in a life partner but had never thought to find. It wasn't enough to have him as a temporary lover. How could she ever have thought a fling with him would quell the need he evoked in her?

Zoey looked down at their joined hands, his touch so familiar and yet still as electrifying. She glanced up to meet his gaze and found him looking at her with unusual intensity.

'There's something I want to run by you.' His voice was low-pitched and husky.

Zoey disguised a swallow, her heart giving a tiny leap in her chest. Could her nascent hopes be realised after all? Did he want to extend their fling, to make it a little more permanent? 'Yes?'

There was a moment or two of silence. His gaze slowly roved over her face, as if he were memorising her features one by one. His thumb began to stroke the fleshy part of her thumb and a shiver coursed down her spine. His gaze finally steadied on hers. Dark…enigmatically dark. 'How do you feel about becoming my partner?'

His partner? Zoey blinked, as if a too bright a light had shone in her eyes. Her heart jumped. Her stomach flip-flopped. Her pulse tripped and began to sprint. 'Y-your partner?' Her voice stumbled over the word, her thoughts flying every which way like a flock of startled birds.

Surely he didn't mean…? Was he proposing to her? No, surely not? He would be more direct if he was proposing marriage, wouldn't he? Should she ask? No, definitely not. Her heart began to thump so loudly she could hear its echo in her ears, feel its punch against her ribcage. 'I—I don't quite understand…'

'My business partner.' His mouth slanted in a smile. 'I don't just want you to come and work for me, I want you to work with me—alongside me. These last few days have shown how we work brilliantly together and how we balance each other so well. I know we'll make a great creative team.'

A great creative team… He was offering her a stake in his business, not in his personal life. Her heart sank. He was talking business, but she was hoping for happy-ever-after. How could she have thought it would be anything else? Zoey pulled her hand out of his before he felt it trembling against his. Her whole body was beginning to tremble, not with excitement but an inexplicable pang of disappointment. She gave herself a hard mental slap. How could she have thought he was going to propose *marriage* to her? He wasn't the marrying type. She had fooled herself into thinking those tender looks he'd been giving her meant something more. How could she have been such an idiot?

He was offering her a dream—a different dream.

A dream career, working with him in one of the most successful agencies in the world.

A business partnership.

Not the dream partnership she most wanted— a lifelong partnership of love and commitment.

'Wow… I'll have to think about it for a day or two…' Zoey gave a fractured laugh and added, 'For a moment there, I thought you were proposing something else.'

There was a thick beat of silence.

'I hope you weren't unduly disappointed?' His gaze was marksman-steady, but the rest of his expression was inscrutable.

Zoey picked up her wine glass to do something with her hands. She kept her features under strict control. No way would she show him how disappointed she was. She had way too much pride for that. He had always been upfront about his level of commitment. She was the one who had gone off-script and begun wishing for the moon and the stars and the rarest of comets too. She was the one who had deluded herself into thinking they had a future together. Finn had never promised a future, only a fling. 'Why would I be disappointed?'

'Why indeed?'

She took a generous sip of wine and kept the glass in her hands, watching one of her fingers smoothing away the condensation marks on the side. 'You seem to have come to this decision rather quickly.' She glanced at him again. 'I mean, there must be other people you've considered letting into the business before now?'

'No one quite like you.'

Zoey looked at the contents of her glass again.

'I'm hugely flattered. More than a little gobsmacked, actually.' She gave another cracked laugh. 'I've been working alongside my father for ten years and he never once offered me a directorship. I've only been sleeping with you for just over a week and you're offering me a dream proposition.'

'This has nothing to do with us sleeping together.' His tone was adamant, his expression flickering with sudden tension.

Zoey raised her eyebrows and forced herself to hold his gaze. 'Doesn't it?'

Finn sat back in his chair and picked up his wine glass. 'This is strictly a business decision. You're extremely talented and haven't yet had that talent properly tapped. You will bring to the company new energy and innovation. I have a good creative team but with you on board it will be brilliant.' He took a sip of wine and put his glass back down, his eyes holding hers and added, 'Besides, I don't want to lose you to someone else.'

He didn't want to lose her. If only he meant those words the way she wanted him to. Zoey ran the tip of her tongue over her dry lips. 'It's certainly a wonderful opportunity. But will my name be on the company letterhead or just yours?'

'Come on, Zoey, you know about branding better than most,' he said with a frown. 'I've spent years building my company's name and reputation. I'm not going to change it now. The deal I'm offering you is generous enough without that.' He named a sum that sent her eyebrows up again. 'How does that sound?'

'It sounds almost impossible to resist.' Just like he was, which was why she needed more time before she signed on the dotted line. 'But I'd still like a day or two to think it over.'

'Fine. But don't take too long. I want to get things on the move as quickly as possible.'

'I understand, but a lot has happened in a short time,' Zoey said. 'The takeover, us getting involved, now this. It's a lot for me to process.'

Finn reached for her hand again. 'Your father was a fool not to allow you more control in his company. If he had given you more creative freedom, then he wouldn't have felt the need to sell to me.'

'It would have been nice if I'd been involved in the process.'

'I'm involving you now.'

Zoey couldn't hold his gaze and stared at her wine instead. 'What if he doesn't stop drinking even though he's no longer running the company?'

Finn placed his hand over hers. 'Look at me.'

She lifted her gaze with a sigh. 'I can't help worrying about him.'

He stroked the back of her hand with his thumb. 'He's not your responsibility. If he doesn't choose to get the help he clearly needs, then it won't be your fault. You have to step back and let him face the consequences of his choices. There's no other way.'

Zoey knew he was right, but the knowing and the doing were as far apart as two sides of a giant chasm. 'He's the only link I have left to my mother. The only person I can ask about her to keep my fading memories of her alive.'

'Tell me about her. What was she like?' His tone was gentle, his gaze equally so.

Zoey gave a wistful smile. 'She was funny and a bit wild at times.'

'Now, why doesn't that surprise me?' His tone was dry.

She smothered a soft laugh and continued, 'She loved to cook, and she made Christmas and birthdays so special.' Her smile faded, her shoulders dropping down on a sigh. 'I missed her so much. I still miss her. She left a hole in my life that nothing and no one can ever fill. I don't think I've ever felt as loved by anyone else.'

'Not even by your father?'

Zoey rolled her eyes. 'No.'

'What about before your mum died? Did you feel loved by him then?'

Zoey thought about it before answering, casting her mind back to the early years before tragedy had so cruelly struck. 'It's funny you should ask that… I've never really thought about this before, but he was a lot warmer to me back then. He wasn't as physically demonstrative as my mum was, but I don't remember feeling like he didn't love me. I'm a bit like him in that I'm not comfortable with showing physical affection.'

'You could have fooled me.'

Zoey could feel her cheeks warming. 'Yes, well, I did tell you, you have a very strange effect on me.'

'Likewise.' His eyes glinted.

She looked down at their joined hands and returned the caress by stroking the strong, corded tendons on the back of his hand. A shiver passed over her at the thought of the pleasure his hands gave her, the pleasure that thrummed in her flesh even now like a plucked cello string.

Why had she thought she could keep her emotions out of a fling with him? Her emotions had been engaged right from the start. 'Losing my mother changed everything between my father and me. It was like the bottom fell out of our world that day. I know it certainly fell out of mine.' She glanced up at him and gave a twisted smile. 'I still see my stepmothers. I haven't told my father, though. He doesn't part with his exes on good terms. But they were each good to me in their own way and I missed having them around––especially the last one, Linda. She's a lot like my mother, actually.'

'Maybe your father was worried about losing

you too,' Finn said. 'It can happen after a sudden loss. People become terrified it might happen to someone else they love, so they tone down how they feel to protect themselves.'

Zoey wondered if Finn had done the same after his parents had chosen their drinking and drugs lifestyle over him. 'You could be right, I suppose, but I'm not riding my hopes on it. I'm twenty-eight years old. I don't need to hear my father say he loves me every day.'

'But it would be nice if he showed it in some way.' Finn's hand squeezed hers, his gaze holding hers in an intimate tether that made something warm flow down her spine.

'Yes…'

Finn released her hand and signalled to the waiter for the bill. 'We'd better have an early night. We have a lot of work to do when we get home to London.'

Later that night, Finn reached for Zoey in the dark, drawing her close to his side. He breathed in the scent of her hair, his blood stirring as she nestled into him with a sigh. Their lovemaking earlier had been as passionate as always, but something had changed—or maybe he had changed. It hadn't felt as basic as smoking-hot sex between two consenting adults but a mutual worship of each other's bodies. He began to wonder if he would find anyone else who so perfectly suited him in bed. Their lovemaking got better and better, the pleasure, the intensity, the depth of feeling—all of it made him realise how shallow and how solely body-based his other encounters had been.

Zoey was not just a convenient body to have sex with—not merely yet another consenting adult to have a good time with then say goodbye to and never think of again. He wondered if there would be a time when he wouldn't think of her. She filled his thoughts to the exclusion of everything else.

Finn had never been much of a fan of sleepovers in the past. The morning-after routine got a little tiresome, the attraction of the night before fading to the point where he often couldn't wait to get away. But with Zoey it was completely different. He enjoyed waking up beside her each day, enjoyed the feel of her body against him, enjoyed seeing her sleepy smile and feeling her arms go round him.

But he was surprised she hadn't jumped at his offer of a business relationship last night over dinner. Surprised and disappointed she hadn't been as enthusiastic as he'd hoped. It was a big step for him to take and one he had never taken before. He had run his company singlehandedly from the get-go and had resisted bringing anyone else on board. But he knew Zoey's gifts and talents would be an asset to him and he couldn't allow her to take them elsewhere. He was impatient for her answer so he could get things in motion. There were legal things to see to, paperwork to draw up, contracts to sign—all of it would take time. He had pushed their flight back a couple of hours, determined to get her answer before they went home to London.

Zoey snuggled against him and opened one sleepy eye. 'Is it time to get up yet?'

'Not yet. I delayed our flights a couple of hours.'

She rolled onto her tummy, her slim legs entwined with his. She traced a slow circle around his mouth, making his lips tingle. 'Oh? Why? So we can loll about in bed all morning?'

Finn captured her hand and held it against his chest. 'I want your answer. Today. Before we fly back to London.' He didn't want to waste any more time. He had to know one way or the other.

Her hand fell away from his face and her expression clouded. 'I told you I need to think about it. There's a lot to consider.' She moved away from him and, throwing back the doona, got off the bed, wrapping herself in her satin bathrobe and tying the waist ties.

'Like what?' Finn frowned, rising from the bed as well. He picked up his trousers and stepped into them. 'I'm offering you an amazing opportunity. What's taking you so long to decide?'

Zoey turned away. 'I don't want to talk about it now. Stop pressuring me.'

Finn came up behind her and took her by the

shoulders and turned her to face him. 'But I want to talk about it now.'

Her chin came up and a stubborn light shone in her eyes. 'Okay, we'll talk, but you might not want to hear what I have to say.'

'Try me.' He removed his hands from her shoulders, locking his gaze on hers.

She drew in a deep breath and let it out in a steady stream. 'What you're offering me is an extremely generous offer. Hugely generous. But it's not enough. I want more. Much more.'

Finn choked back an incredulous laugh. 'Not enough? Then I'll double it.'

Her gaze continued to hold his with unnerving intensity. 'I'm not talking about the money, Finn.'

He looked at her blankly for a moment. If it wasn't about money, then what was it about? 'Since when is a business deal not about money?'

'I don't just want to be your partner in business.'

A prickly sensation crawled across his scalp. 'Then what do you want?'

Twin pools of colour formed in her cheeks, but her eyes lost none of their unwavering focus. 'I want to be someone important to you.'

'You *are* important to me,' Finn said. 'I've offered you a deal that would be the envy of most people in our field.'

'But why did you offer it to me?'

'I told you before—I don't want to lose you.' He

scraped a hand through his hair and added, 'You'll be a valuable asset to me.'

A hard look came into her eyes. 'And what happens once our fling is over? Will I still be an asset to you then?'

'Of course. Our involvement ending doesn't change that. Why should it? This is purely a business decision.'

She gave a hollow laugh, her expression cynical. 'You still don't get it, do you? You talk about your business decisions, but you won't talk about your feelings.'

'Okay, I'll talk about my feelings,' Finn said. 'I feel insulted you aren't jumping at the chance to come on board with me. You complain about spending years pushed to the sidelines by your father, with your talent withering on the vine, and here I am offering you a deal to die for and you're deliberating.'

Zoey walked a little further away, her arms going across her body. 'I don't think I can work with you once our fling is over. It will be too… awkward.'

'Why? We're both mature adults, Zoey. We're not teenagers who can't regulate their emotions.'

She flicked him a glance over her shoulder. 'I think it's best if we end it now before it gets any more complicated.'

Finn stared at her for a speechless moment. End

it? Now? The prickly sensation on his scalp moved down the length of his spine and down the backs of his legs. He wanted to move towards her but couldn't get his legs to work. He wanted to insist she change her mind, to beg her to reconsider…but then he realised he would be demeaning himself in pleading with her to stay with him.

His days of begging and pleading with anyone were well and truly over.

'Okay, we'll end it if that's what you want,' Finn said, trying not to think about what that would look like, how it would feel to see her and not be involved with her. 'But the directorship offer is still on the table.'

Zoey turned to face him, her expression difficult to read. 'I can't accept it, Finn. I can't work with you.'

He frowned so hard his forehead hurt. 'You work brilliantly with me. Hasn't the last few days shown you that? We make a great team, Zoey, you know we do. Why would you walk away from that?'

'I'll call Leo Frascatelli and tell him I'm handing the account over to you,' Zoey said. 'I'll find another job somewhere and—'

'Do you want me to beg? Is that what you want?' Finn said through tight lips. Never had he felt so out of balance. So out of kilter. So desperate, and yet so desperate not to show it. Emotions he didn't know he possessed reared up inside him,

clamouring for an outlet. Hurt, grief, despair…
loneliness at the thought of losing her. Of not seeing her every day, of not making love to her.

'No, Finn, what I want is for you to feel about
me the way I feel about you.'

Finn approached her and, unpeeling her arms
from around her body, took her hands in his. He
searched her face for a moment, his thoughts in a
tangled knot. 'Are you saying you…?' He didn't
want to say the word because he couldn't say it
back. He had never told anyone he loved them,
not since he was a child. And look how his love
had been rewarded back then—with abandonment.
Brutal abandonment. Loving someone to that degree gave them the power to hurt you, to leave
you, to destroy you.

'I used to think I hated you,' Zoey said. 'But,
after getting to know you more, I realised I was
actually quite similar to you in some ways. That's
why I was so confident I could have a fling with
you without involving my feelings—but I was
wrong, so very wrong.'

'Zoey…' He took an unsteady breath. 'Look,
you know I care about you. I enjoy being with you.
But I'm not willing to commit to anything more.
We agreed on the terms—a fling for as long as
we both wanted it.'

'But I don't want it now.' She pulled out of his

hold and stepped back. 'There's no point continuing a relationship that isn't working for me.'

'How is it not working?' Finn asked. 'We've just spent five wonderful days together and you say it's not working?'

'I'm not talking about the sex. It's been perfect in every way, but one day that will come to an end, because that's how your casual flings work. You don't commit in the long-term, you don't want it to be for ever. But casual and uncommitted isn't enough for me any more. I can't be with you knowing you'll end it when someone else catches your attention.'

No one had captured Finn's attention like Zoey. No one. And he wondered if they ever would. But she was asking too much. Long-term commitment wasn't in his skill set. He no longer had the commitment gene. He had erased it from his system. He didn't want to feel so deeply about someone that he would promise to spend the rest of his days with them, always wondering if they would walk away without a backward glance. He strode away a couple of steps, his hand rubbing at the corded tension in the back of his neck.

'What did you think I was proposing last night over dinner?' He gave a bark of cynical laughter. 'Marriage?'

Zoey let out a long sigh. 'You know, I did for a moment think you were considering something a little longer term between us. You've been so wonderful to me over the last few days, so attentive and, yes, loving, even if you don't want to call it by that name. I wondered if you were falling in love with me, rather than just being in lust with me.'

'Marriage was never and will never be on the table.'

'Which is why we have to end this now. I want for ever, Finn. Is it unreasonable to want someone to love me for a lifetime? I want a man to commit solely to me. To love me and treasure me, not just as a sexual partner but as a life partner. I want a partner in life, not just a partner in bed or in business.'

'The latter two are the only ones I can offer. Take it or leave it.'

Zoey hugged her arms around her body. 'You told me a while back when we were talking about my dad it was pointless to expect someone to change if they weren't capable of it. So, I'm going to take your advice—I'm not going to waste any more of my life hoping you'll change because I'll get even more hurt in the end.'

How like her to throw his own words back at him, Finn thought. Words he had lived by for years and which he'd found perfectly reasonable. But now they contained an irony that cut to the quick. Stinging him in a way he never expected to be stung. He was losing her on both counts—

she wanted to end their fling and she was reject-ing his business proposal.

It was a novel experience for him, being on the other end of a break-up. The one who was left, not the one who was doing the leaving. That hadn't hap-pened since he'd been a kid. But he refused to show her how much it affected him, how much it disap-pointed and riled him to have the tables turned. 'If you want to end our involvement, then end it. But you're making a big mistake in walking away from the chance to be in business with me. I won't be of-fering it again if you suddenly change your mind.'

The determined light came back into her eyes. 'I won't change my mind.' She turned and began to gather her things together.

'What are you doing?'

'I'm packing. I'll make my own way back to London.'

'Don't be ridiculous, Zoey,' Finn said. 'There's no need for such histrionics. I've booked our flight for eleven a.m. You don't need to rush off now.'

She folded an article of clothing and held it against her stomach. 'I think it's best we make a clean break of things, starting now.'

He wanted to stop her. To convince her to rethink her decision, to have just a few more hours with her before they went their separate ways. But the words were stuck in the back of his throat, blocked behind a wall of pride. 'Have it your way, then.'

Finn shrugged himself into a shirt and shoved his feet into his shoes and made his way to the door.

'Aren't you going to say goodbye?' Zoey asked.

Finn gave her a cutting look. 'I just did.' And he walked out and closed the door behind him with a resounding click.

Zoey bit down on her lower lip until she thought it would bleed. How could she have thought it would be any different between them? Finn was never going to change, just like her ex had refused to change. And she would be a fool to live in hope Finn would one day develop feelings for her. How many years would she have to wait? One? Two? Seven? Ten?

It was better this way, better for her to make a new start, to put her lost hopes and dreams behind her and forge her own way forward.

Finn was angry at her for not accepting his offer but that came out of his arrogance in believing she couldn't resist any terms he presented her. She could resist. She had to resist, otherwise she would be reverting to old habits. Her old self had toed the line, adapted, lived in hope but been too afraid to embrace her own agency. Too afraid to voice her needs and instead had kept them locked inside.

But Zoey was no longer that person. She had morphed into a person who took charge of her own destiny, who openly stated her needs and was prepared to live with the consequences if they failed to be met. She would no longer stay with a man in the hope of happy-ever-after. And certainly not a man like Finn who didn't even believe in the concept of a once-in-a-lifetime love.

Zoey packed and was out the door and in a taxi within half an hour. It was no surprise Finn didn't return to the villa and try and beg her to change her mind, but she was heartbroken all the same. All her life she had yearned to be loved, to be treasured and valued, and now she had been denied it yet again. By the one man with whom she thought she could be truly happy.

'You were right,' Zoey said to Ivy and Millie a few days later when they caught up for coffee. 'I fell in love with Finn.'

Ivy and Millie leaned forward in their chairs. 'And?' They spoke in unison, hopeful expressions on their faces.

Zoey shook her head and sighed. 'And nothing. I broke things off.'

'Oh, hon, I'm so sorry,' Ivy said. 'What happened?'

'He doesn't feel the same way and I was too stupid to realise it. I thought he was about to propose to me over dinner on our last night in Monte Carlo but he was only offering me a business deal.'

Millie's eyes rounded. 'A business deal? Oh,

Zoey, I really feel for you. Under different circumstances that would have been so good. I don't suppose you accepted?'

Zoey screwed up her face. 'I can't possibly work with him now. Can you imagine how hard it would be to see him every day? To hear other staff talking about his latest squeeze in the tea room?' She picked up her latte from the table in front of them. 'I'm looking for a job elsewhere.'

'But what about the account you were working on with him?' Millie asked. 'The Frasca whatsit?'

'Frascatelli,' Zoey said. 'I forfeited it to Finn.'

'I know how upsetting it is to be in your position—we both do, don't we, Millie? But was that wise?' Ivy asked. 'You wanted that project so badly.'

'Maybe not wise, but necessary,' Zoey said with another sigh. 'I never thought I'd fall for anyone the way I've fallen for Finn. He's the only man I could ever imagine spending the rest of my life with but he's dead set against commitment.'

'But he committed to you during your fling, didn't he?' Millie asked. 'I mean, it was exclusive between you, wasn't it?'

'Yes, I insisted on that,' Zoey said. 'And, what's more, I trusted him implicitly.'

'Well, it shows he can commit,' Ivy put in. 'But maybe he needs more time to realise what he feels for you. You've had a bit of a whirlwind affair.

Maybe he hasn't yet come to terms with how he feels. Commitment-shy men can be a bit slow to realise how they feel.'

But how long would she have to wait? Years, as she'd waited for her father to change? She was done with waiting, wishing and hoping for change. 'Finn treated me with the utmost respect and consideration. I know this sounds strange, but I *felt* like he was growing to love me, you know? That's why I thought he was going to pop the question. God, I feel like such an idiot now.' She groaned. 'How can a man make love to you so beautifully and not care about you in some way?'

'I wish I could say it will all work out in the end like it did for Millie and I,' Ivy said. 'But that's probably not all that helpful to you now, while you're hurting so much.'

'Has he contacted you since you came back from Monte Carlo?' Millie asked.

'A text message to inform me of the meetings he's having with the Brackenfield staff,' Zoey said. 'No doubt he's going to fire half of them and not feel even a twinge of conscience about it.'

'The deal Finn offered you,' Millie said. 'Surely he wouldn't have offered it to you unless he didn't think you'd be an asset to the company? It's a huge compliment to you. I just wonder if you're being a bit hasty in rejecting it out of hand.'

'But he only wants me to be an invisible director,' Zoey said. 'My name won't be on the letter-head—he told me so. I've worked for ten years for the Brackenfield name and now it's going to completely disappear, swallowed up by him.'

'You can't talk him into a compromise?' Millie ventured.

Zoey drained her coffee before answering. 'Finn O'Connell doesn't know the meaning of the word.' And her days of compromising were well and truly over.

Zoey called in on her father on her way back from coffee with the girls to find him halfway through a bottle of wine. And it wasn't his first. There was an empty bottle on the bench.

He held up a glass, swaying slightly on his feet. 'Have a drink to celebrate my retirement.'

'Dad, I'm not here to celebrate anything,' Zoey said. 'I'm here to tell you I won't see you again unless the next time it's in a rehab clinic. Your choice—the drink or me.'

He frowned, as if he couldn't process what she was saying. He scratched his head and frowned. 'But you always visit me.'

'I know, and it's going to stop,' Zoey said. 'For years I've visited you, I've had countless lunches or dinners with you, I cover for you, I make excuses for you—and what have I got in return? You continue to drink and embarrass me. Not only that, you sold out on me to Finn O'Connell. I waited for years for you to promote me, to allow me to reach my potential, but you never did. Why am I so unimportant to you?'

He put the glass down, a frown still wrinkling his brow. 'You're not unimportant…'

'But the drink is more important,' Zoey said. 'You wanted a son. You've made no secret of that and instead you got me. And I tried to be the best daughter I could be but it's not enough. I'm not enough for you.' Just as she hadn't been enough for her ex. And as she wasn't enough for Finn, and how that hurt way more than anything.

'You are enough for me…' Her father looked at her with bloodshot eyes, his voice trembling. 'When I lost your mother…' His hand shook as he rubbed at his unshaven face. 'I kept thinking I might lose you too. I—I found it hard to be close to you after that. I seem to lose everyone I care about. I know I always carry on about wanting a son but that was the way I was brought up. A son to carry on the family name was my dream, but when your mother died, well, that dream was shattered. And when Linda left me a few months ago I began to drink to numb my feelings. I lost interest in everything. Work was just a burden. I couldn't wait to offload the company.'

So, Finn had been right about her father, Zoey thought. He had told her that her dad was most likely protecting himself from further hurt after losing her mother. Was that what Finn was doing too? Protecting himself after the rejection of his parents' love? Strange that he would have such insight into her father but not have it into himself. Or maybe he did have it but just didn't love her. She had been a convenient fling partner but not someone he loved enough to spend the rest of his life with her in marriage.

'Will you promise to get help?' Zoey asked her father, determined not to back down.

He gave a stuttering sigh. 'I've made promises before and never kept them…' He winced as if in deep pain and added, 'But if it means losing you…'

Tears began to roll down his face and Zoey went to him and hugged him, fighting tears herself.

It would be a long journey but at least her father had taken the first painful step.

CHAPTER TEN

FINN IMMERSED HIMSELF in work over the next four weeks to distract himself from Zoey's decision to end their fling. But the endless meetings with the Brackenfield staff were a constant reminder of her. He found it hard to decide on who to keep and who to let go. His emotions kept getting in the way.

Yes, his emotions, those pesky things he never allowed anywhere near a business decision. He offered generous redundancy packages to some, far more generous than they probably deserved. But he kept thinking of Zoey, how she saw the staff as people beyond their desks, people with families and loved ones and worries and stresses to deal with in their personal lives.

But he had his own stress to deal with in his personal life—the stress of missing Zoey.

He missed everything about her—her smile, her laughter, her feistiness when she didn't agree with him on something, her touch, her kisses, the explosive way she responded to his lovemaking. There was a constant ache in his chest, a dragging ache that distracted him during the day and kept him awake at night. He had never reacted to a break-up so badly. But then, he had always been the instigator of his previous break-ups with casual lovers. He never allowed anyone the power to hurt him, to abandon him—he always got in first. Was that why his break-up with Zoey was so hard to handle? He hadn't seen her as a casual lover— she was in a completely different category, but he wasn't exactly sure what it was.

Finn hadn't even thought of taking another lover. His stomach turned at the thought. So much for his playboy lifestyle. He was turning into a monk. A miserably lonely monk. He spent most evenings with only his one-eyed cat for company.

Finn felt a strange sense of camaraderie with his battered and brooding cat. Tolstoy had been hurt in the past and went out of his way to avoid further hurt. That was why, when Finn had gone away to New York and then Monte Carlo, Tolstoy had punished him on his return. Fear was behind that behaviour, fear of being permanently rejected. But, since Finn had been home every evening over the last month, Tolstoy had built up enough trust to lose some of his guardedness. It occurred to him then that Tolstoy loved him and was terrified he might not come back.

Why hadn't he realised that before now?

Maybe it wasn't Finn's dented pride that was causing this infernal pain in his chest. Maybe he was a little more like his cat than he realised. Didn't they say pets and owners became alike? Finn didn't like to think of himself as the sort of man who couldn't move on after a woman had ended a fling. He knew how to let go—he'd been doing it without a problem for years.

But this didn't feel like a cut and dried case of injured male pride.

It felt like something else…something he had never felt before…something that was threatening the entire basis on which he lived his footloose and fancy-free life. Something beyond a fleeing attraction…something deeper—a sense that if he never saw Zoey again he would be missing something essential to his existence. Without her, he would not be the person he was meant to be. He would be stunted in some way, reduced, lacking. She inspired him, enthralled him, delighted and fulfilled him.

Zoey hadn't said the words 'I love you' out loud but she had told him she had developed feelings for him. Feelings that had grown from negative to positive. Feelings he had rebuffed out of fear. Why hadn't he seen that until now? He was as one-eyed as his cat not to have seen it. He'd been afraid to love her in case he lost her and yet he had lost her anyway. He had spent his whole life avoiding love, avoiding emotional attachment in case he was rejected. But he had rejected the most amazing love from the most amazing woman. The only woman he could envisage having permanently in his life. The only woman with whom he wanted a future.

Zoey *was* his future.

Zoey decided there was no more painful thing than watching one of your best friends get married, knowing you would never experience the same exhilarating joy. It was a month since she'd left Finn in Monte Carlo and, apart from the odd email or text message regarding business issues, she had not seen him in person.

Zoey listened as Ivy and Louis exchanged vows under an archway festooned with white and soft pink roses. The love they felt for each other was written all over their glowing faces, both of their voices poignantly catching over the words, 'Till death do us part'. Zoey wasn't a habitual weeper but seeing such depth of emotion in the young couple made tears sting at the back of her eyes. She had so dearly hoped that one day she would stand exactly as Ivy was doing, exchanging vows with the man she loved with her whole heart. But instead, her heart was broken, shattered by the realisation Finn would never love her.

Zoey heard Millie begin to sniffle beside her, no

doubt eagerly awaiting her own wedding day the following month. But if there was anything positive to be had out of the pain of the last few weeks it was this—her father was in full-time residential rehab and his estranged wife Linda had been visiting him every day. It was wonderful to see her dad finally taking responsibility for his drinking and, while it would take a while for Zoey to feel close to him, she knew things were heading in the right direction.

Ivy and Louis's reception was a joyous affair and Zoey got swept up in the celebrations, determined not to allow her own misery to spoil her friends' special day.

'Time to throw the bridal bouquet!' the Master of Ceremonies announced. 'Single ladies, please gather in the centre of the room.'

Millie nudged Zoey. 'Go on. That means you.'

Zoey rolled her eyes. 'No way.'

Millie grabbed her by the arm and all but dragged her to where the other young women were eagerly assembled. 'Come on. Ivy wants you to be in the circle. And make sure you catch it.'

Why? There was only one man Zoey wanted to marry and he was the last man on earth who would ever ask her. But Millie had a particularly determined look in her eye, so Zoey stepped into the circle with a sigh of resignation. The band struck up a rousing melody to get everyone cheering and

Zoey had never felt more like a fish out of water. The other women were right into the spirit of the event, cheering and whooping and jumping up and down, arms in the air, hoping for Ivy's bouquet to come their way.

Zoey, on the other hand, was trying to hide behind a larger woman, hoping to avoid the floral missile. The drum roll sounded, the women in the centre of the room became almost hysterically excited and Zoey closed her eyes, figuring she wouldn't catch the bouquet if she couldn't see it. But then something soft and fragrant hit her in the face and she reflexively caught it in her hands. She stared at the bouquet she was holding while the crowd cheered and clapped around her.

But she had never felt so miserable in her life.

Zoey finally managed to escape all the noise and cheering by slipping out of the venue to the garden, where there was a summer house covered in a rambling pink clematis. She sat on the padded seat inside the summer house and looked at the bouquet still in her hands.

'I'm really glad you caught that,' Finn O'Connell said, stepping out of the shadows.

Zoey blinked as if she was seeing things. The way her heart was carrying on, he might as well have been a ghost. 'Finn? What are you doing here? I didn't know you were invited.'

'I gate-crashed,' he said with an inscrutable

smile. 'May I join you?' He indicated the bench seat she was sitting on.

Zoey shoved a little further along the seat, the bouquet still in her hands—or at least what was left of it. She had been shredding it without realising, the petals falling like confetti around her. Her pulse was thumping at the sight of him, her senses reeling at his closeness. 'Why are you here?' She gave him a sideways glance. 'It's not very polite to gate-crash someone's wedding. If it's a business matter, then surely it could have waited?'

He removed the now sad-looking bouquet from her hands and set it to one side. 'It is a business matter—our business.' His dark gaze held hers in a tender lock. 'Zoey, my darling, I have come to realise what a damn fool I've been. I've been fighting my feelings for you for months, even before we got involved. But I was too frightened to admit it even to myself, let alone to you.'

He took her hands in both of his. 'I love you madly, deeply, crazily. My life is empty without you. Just ask Tolstoy. He's witnessed every miserable minute of me moping about my house for the last month. Please forgive me for not telling you sooner. For not realising it sooner.'

Zoey swallowed, her heart beating so hard and fast, she felt light-headed. 'I can't believe I'm hearing this…' Her voice came out as a shocked whisper. Shocked but delighted.

He gave a self-deprecating smile. 'I can't believe I'm saying it. I never thought I would fall in love with anyone. I didn't think I had the ability to until I met you. But you are the most wonderful person and I can't imagine being without you. Please say you'll marry me.'

'You want to get married?' Zoey gasped.

Finn got off the bench and knelt down in front of her, holding her hands in his. His eyes looked suspiciously moist, and her heart swelled until she could barely take a breath. 'My darling Zoey, will you marry me and make me the happiest of men?'

She threw her arms around him with a happy sob. 'Oh, Finn, I will, I will, I will. I love you, love you, love you.'

Finn rose from the floor of the summer house, bringing her to stand upright with him. His arms came round her, his expression as joyful as her own. 'I love you so much. I will never get tired of saying it. I want you to come back and work with me. I want your name as well as mine on the letterhead. We'll hyphenate them—Brackenfield-O'Connell Advertising. It's got quite a ring to it, hasn't it?'

'You mean you don't want me to change my name to yours after we get married?'

His arms tightened around her. 'I don't want to change anything about you, my darling girl.'

'Oh, Finn, I never thought I could be so happy,'

Zoey said, gazing up into his eyes. 'Being at Ivy and Louis's wedding has been like torture. Seeing them so happy made me realise how miserable I was without you. And when I accidentally caught the bouquet just then, I wanted to curl up and hide. Millie just about frogmarched me out there to join in. I thought it was a little mean of her at the time, because she knows how unhappy I've been.'

Finn's eyes began to twinkle. 'I heard she's a fabulous jewellery designer. Do you think she'll design our rings for us? She seems the most helpful and obliging sort of person.'

Zoey's eyes widened. 'Oh, my God, she knew you were going to propose! No wonder that bouquet came straight at me. She made sure it did. But she's normally hopeless at keeping a secret.'

He grinned. 'I might have mentioned to her I was dropping by to see you.' He brought his mouth down to hers in a lingering kiss. He finally lifted his mouth off hers to smile down at her. 'How soon can we get married? I don't want to wait for months on end.'

'Nor do I,' Zoey said. 'But I thought you never wanted to get married. And what about kids?'

'I never envisaged making a family with anyone before I met you,' he said. 'But the idea is increasingly appealing. I bet you'll be the most beautiful mother in the world.'

'And you the most amazing father,' Zoey said.

'Speaking of fathers…did you know my dad has been in rehab for the past month? He's doing really well so far.'

'I'm really glad for you and for him,' Finn said. 'And I've even thought of contacting my parents to ask them about their backgrounds. You got me thinking that there may be more to their behaviour than I thought.'

He brought her even closer, his gaze tender. 'You have taught me so much about love and caring about people. I found it near impossible to trim down the staff from Brackenfield in the takeover.'

Zoey hugged him again. 'I'm glad you found your heart. I knew it was there inside you somewhere.'

He tipped up her face to look deeply into her eyes. 'It was there waiting for you, my darling.'

* * * * *

The Terms Of The Sicilian's Marriage
Louise Fuller

MILLS & BOON

Books by Louise Fuller

Harlequin Modern

Vows Made in Secret
A Deal Sealed by Passion
Claiming His Wedding Night
Blackmailed Down the Aisle
Surrender to the Ruthless Billionaire
Revenge at the Altar
Craving His Forbidden Innocent

Secret Heirs of Billionaires

Kidnapped for the Tycoon's Baby
Demanding His Secret Son
Proof of Their One-Night Passion

Passion in Paradise

Consequences of a Hot Havana Night

Visit the Author Profile page
at millsandboon.com.au for more titles.

Louise Fuller was a tomboy who hated pink and always wanted to be the prince—not the princess! Now she enjoys creating heroines who aren't pretty pushovers but are strong, believable women. Before writing for Harlequin she studied literature and philosophy at university, and then worked as a reporter on her local newspaper. She lives in Tunbridge Wells with her impossibly handsome husband, Patrick, and their six children.

DEDICATION

For my wonderful husband, Patrick.
Still impossibly handsome, and still pressing
all the right buttons...

PROLOGUE

THE BAR WAS starting to empty.

Across the room, the blonde sitting at the counter with her friend looked over and gave Vicenzu Trapani a slow, lingering smile. A smile that promised a night, or quite possibly more, of unparalleled, uncomplicated pleasure.

Under normal circumstances he would have smiled back and waited for her to join him. But nothing was normal any more, and he wasn't sure he was ever going to smile again.

Picking up his glass, he stared down into the dark gold liquid. He didn't normally drink bourbon, particularly when he was back in Sicily, but it had been Ciro who had caught the bartender's attention. Ciro who had snapped out the order before Vicenzu's own numbed brain had even fully registered where they were. Ciro who had commandeered the table in the corner and pushed him into a seat.

They had left the meeting and come straight to the bar. Vito Neglia was their lawyer, and an old family friend, but today he had also been their last hope.

A hope that had been swiftly and brutally extinguished when Vito had confirmed what they already knew.

There was no loophole. Cesare Buscetta had acted within the law.

He was the new and legitimate owner of both the Trapani Olive Oil Company and the beautiful, beloved family estate where Vicenzu and Ciro had spent an idyllic childhood.

Vicenzu's fingers tightened around his glass. The family estate he still called home.

Home.

The word stuck in his throat and, picturing his mother's expression as he'd handed the keys over to the agent, he felt his stomach lurch.

It had broken his heart, having to do that to her, and the memory of her bewildered, tear-stained face would be impossible to forget. The reason for it impossible to forgive.

'We must fix this.'

Ciro's voice broke into his thoughts and, looking up, he met his brother's gaze—and instantly wished he hadn't.

Ciro's face was taut with determination, his green eyes narrow with a certainty he envied…eyes that so resembled their father's that he had to look away.

His stomach tightened. Ciro was his younger brother, but he was his father's son. Whip-smart, focused, disciplined, he could have taken over the business and run it with his eyes shut—hell, he could have turned it into a household name overnight. And, had their father been cut from different cloth, that was exactly what would have happened.

But Alessandro Trapani had not been a cut-throat man. To him, family had mattered more than global domination.

Or had it?

Vicenzu felt his stomach lurch again and, pushing away the many possible but all equally unpalatable answers to that question, he lifted his glass to his lips and drained it swiftly.

Meeting his brother's gaze, he nodded.

'We have to get it back. All of it.'

Ciro's voice was quiet, but implacable, and Vicenzu nodded again. His brother was right, of course. Cesare Buscetta was not just a thief, he was a bully and a thug. But it was too soon...feelings were still too raw.

He'd tried to explain that to his brother—had reminded him that revenge was a dish best served cold. Only Ciro couldn't wait—*wouldn't* wait. His need for vengeance was white-hot, burning him from the inside out. He wanted revenge *now* and he needed his brother to play his part.

'Vicenzu?'

For a moment he closed his eyes. If only he could turn back time. Give his father back the money he'd borrowed. Be the son his father had needed—wanted.

But regrets were not going to right the wrongs that had been done to his family and, opening his eyes, he leaned back in his chair and cleared his throat. 'Yes, I know what I have to do and I'll do it. I'll take the business back.'

His chest tightened. It sounded so simple—and maybe it would be. After all, all he had to do was get a woman to fall in love with him.

Only this wasn't *any* woman. It was Immacolata Buscetta—the daughter of the man who had hounded his father to death and robbed his beautiful, always-laughing mother of her husband and her home.

There was not much to go on. Cesare was a protective father, and by all accounts his eldest daughter was a chip off the old block—as ice-cold as she was beautiful. Who better than her to pay for the sins of her father?

He felt a sudden rush of fury. He would make her melt. Seduce her, then strip her naked—literally and metaphorically—and make her his wife. He would take back what belonged to his family and then, finally, when she was his—inside and out—she would discover why he had really married her.

A fresh round of drinks arrived and he picked up his glass.

Ciro's eyes met his. 'To vengeance.'

'To vengeance,' Vicenzu repeated.

And for the first time since his father's death he felt alive.

CHAPTER ONE

'OH, MY, DOESN'T she look beautiful?'

Without changing the direction of her gaze, Immacolata Buscetta nodded, her insides tightening with a mixture of love and sadness.

'Yes, she does,' she said softly, addressing her response to the Sicilian matron who was standing beside her, clutching her handbag against her body with quivering fingers.

Actually, privately she thought 'beautiful' was too mundane a word to describe her younger sister. Her stunning, full-skirted traditional white wedding dress was beautiful, yes, but Claudia herself looked beatific.

Not a word Imma had ever used before, and she would probably never use it again, but it was the only one that remotely came close to capturing the blissful expression on her sister's face.

Imma's heart gave a small twitch and she glanced over to where Claudia's new husband was greeting some of the one hundred carefully selected guests who had been invited to celebrate the marriage of Claudia Buscetta to Ciro Trapani on this near-perfect early summer's day in Sicily. There would be another hundred guests arriving for the evening reception later.

Of course Claudia was in a state of bliss. She had just married the man who had stormed their father's citadel and declared his love for her like some knight in a courtly romance.

But it wasn't Ciro's impassioned pursuit of her sister that was causing Imma's insides to tighten and her heart to beat erratically. It was the man standing next to the newlyweds.

Ciro's brother, Vicenzu, was the owner of the legendary La Dolce Vita hotel in Portofino. Like pilgrims visiting a shrine, members of royalty, novelists looking for inspiration, divas and bad boys from the world of music and film—all eventually made their way to his hotel.

Her throat tightened. And Vicenzu was the baddest of them all.

His reputation as a playboy and pleasure seeker stretched far beyond the Italian Riviera and it was easy to see why.

Reluctantly, her gaze darted towards him again, drawn like a moth to the flame of his absurdly beautiful features.

He was standing slightly to one side, taking advantage of an overhanging canopy of flower-strewn greenery, which made him both screened from view and yet still the most conspicuous person there.

With dark hair, a teasing mouth and a profile that would grace any currency, he stood out among the stocky Sicilian and Italian businessmen and their wives—and not just because he was a head taller than most of them.

Glancing up through her eyelashes, she felt a cool shiver tiptoe down her spine. In their formal suits and dresses, quite a few of the guests were perspiring beneath the heat of the sun, but he looked effortlessly cool, the impeccably fitted white shirt hugging his lean, supple body and perfectly setting off his dancing dark eyes.

At that moment he turned, and those same dancing eyes met hers, and before she had a chance to blink, much less move, he was sauntering towards her, a lazy smile pulling at the corners of his mouth.

'Immacolata…' He made a disapproving face. 'You don't play fair, do you, Ms Buscetta.'

'Play fair?' She stared up at him, her pulse beating with fear and fascination, trying to look calm and unaffected. How could he talk about being fair, looking like that? 'I don't understand.'

Up close, his beauty was so startling it felt like a slap to her face. His eyes, that beautiful, curving mouth, the clean-cut lines of his features… All made her mind go completely blank and made her feel bare, *exposed*, in a way that no other man ever had.

'Playing hide-and-seek without telling me…' He shook his head. 'That was sneaky.'

'I wasn't hiding,' she lied, desperately wanting to turn and walk away and yet held captive by the soft, baiting note in his voice. 'I was looking after my guests.'

'Not all of them,' he countered. 'I was feeling very neglected. Quite light-headed, actually. In fact, I think we might need to go somewhere quiet so you can put me in the recovery position.'

She felt her cheeks go red and, hating this instant and—worse—visible response to the easy pull of his words, she lifted her chin and glanced pointedly past his shoulder. 'There are cold drinks on the terrace, and plenty of seating.'

He grinned. 'Don't you want to know why I'm feeling so light-headed?'

'No, thank you. I'm perfectly fine as I am.'

'I couldn't agree more,' he said slowly.

As he spoke his eyes meandered over her body in a way that made her feel breathless and on edge. Fighting to keep control she glanced down at the lapel of his jacket. 'Vicenzu, I—'

His eyes glittered. 'It's okay. I get it. You thought I was just a pretty face, but now we've got to know each other a bit better you're starting to like me. It happens all the time. But don't worry—I'm not going to tell anyone.'

Her face flamed. 'Actually, I was just going to tell you that you've lost your boutonnière,' she said stiffly. 'Now, if you'll excuse me, I need to check on—on something. In the kitchen.'

Before he could say anything she turned and began walking blindly away from his mocking gaze, her panicky response to him echoing in her ears.

Panicky and prim and gauche.

Gritting her teeth, she smiled mechanically as people greeted her. What was the matter with her? She was an educated woman, had been top of her class at business school, and she was the daughter of one of the most powerful men in Sicily, soon to be CEO of her father's latest acquisition. So why had she fled like a rabbit from a fox?

But it hurt to look at him—and hurt even more to look away, even though that was what she'd been doing her very best to accomplish ever since he'd arrived at the church.

Only as they were maid of honour and best man,

there had been no avoiding his laughing dark eyes during the service.

It had been equally impossible not to be swept along by the beauty and romanticism of the ceremony, and as a shaft of sunlight had gilded his extremely photogenic features she had briefly allowed herself to fantasise that it was her wedding, and Vicenzu was her husband...

Her pulse twitched. It was nearly five years since she'd been remotely attracted to anyone, and her response to him was as shocking as it was confusing.

Three times she'd lost her place in the order of service, distracted by his gaze—a gaze that had seemed never to leave her face, making her tremble inside.

But no woman—particularly one who had zero actual hands-on experience of men—would consider Vicenzu Trapani husband material. Unlike the rumours about her father's links to organised crime, the stories about him were not just idle gossip. On first impressions alone it was clear he'd earned his flirtatious reputation.

Not that it mattered, she told herself quickly as she skirted around the chattering guests. She had absolutely no intention of falling in love with anyone ever again—and especially not with a man whose behaviour was as provocative as his smile.

All she had to do was ignore her body, and him, for the next couple of hours and concentrate on what really mattered today: Claudia and her new husband.

Plucking a chilled mimosa from a passing waitress, she fixed her gaze on Ciro.

He certainly looked the part. Like his brother, he was tall, dark and handsome, but the resemblance was superficial.

Where Vicenzu was all languid grace and rolled up

shirtsleeves, Ciro wore his suit like custom-built armour, and the imperious tilt of his jaw hinted at an inner confidence and determination that had clearly driven the stratospheric rise of his retail empire.

It was that business success which had persuaded her ultraprotective Sicilian father, Cesare, to agree to the swiftness of this marriage. That and the fact that Ciro came from exactly the kind of respectable background her father craved for his daughters.

The Trapanis were a good, solid Sicilian family, trusted and respected, with a good, solid Sicilian family business to their name. A business that Alessandro Trapani, Ciro's father, had just sold to her father, along with his beautiful home.

Imma felt her shoulders tense. She didn't know all the details of the sale. Despite having groomed her to follow in his footsteps, Cesare was both controlling and secretive about many areas of the business he had built from the ground up.

In his words, old man Trapani had 'got into a mess financially' and wanted a quick sale. Probably it was those same money worries that had led to Alessandro's collapse and tragic, untimely death two months ago.

Her eyes were drawn to the petite woman talking to Claudia. Ribs tightening, she felt an ache of sympathy for her.

With her cloud of dark hair and almond-shaped eyes, Audenzia Trapani must have been exquisite when she was younger, and she was still a beautiful woman. But there was a fragility to her now, and a stillness—as though she was holding herself tightly inside.

Her gaze was still hovering on the older woman when she suddenly became aware that she was being watched.

Looking up, she felt as if her skin had turned inside out. Vicenzu had joined his brother and was staring at her again, his eyes locked on her with an intensity that almost made her flinch.

'Immacolata!'

She turned, relief battling with regret. Her father was bearing down on her, and she felt a familiar rush of love and frustration.

Like a lot of Sicilian men of his generation, Cesare was compact—a solid-bodied barrel of a man. The muscles of his youth were turning heavy now, and yet it would never do to underestimate him on the grounds of age. Cesare was a force of nature. Still handsome, vigorous and uncompromising, a powerful and some thought intimidating presence at any occasion.

'Papà.' She smiled, hoping to deflect the criticism she knew was coming. As he kissed her on each cheek she inhaled the potent mix of cigar smoke and citrusy aftershave that remained in every room he visited long after he'd left.

'Why are you not with your sister?' He frowned. 'Today of all days I want to show both my beautiful daughters off to the world.' His dark eyes softened. 'I know it's hard for you, *piccioncina mia*, watching your sister leave home, and I know you think it's all been too quick, that she's a little young to be married...'

Imma felt her smile tighten, and her father's voice seemed to fade into the hum of background chatter. It wasn't just Claudia's youth that made her feel anxious about the speed of her marriage. It was something more personal: a promise made...

Only neither her father nor her sister wanted to hear her tentative reservations about how fast everything had moved. Cesare had pursued and married their own mother at the age of seventeen, and as for Claudia— she was a dreamer.

And now her dreams of love and a handsome husband and a beautiful home had all come true.

But what about my dreams? Imma flexed her fingers against her cool glass, trying to ignore the pulse of envy beating inside her chest. *When will they come true?*

Hard to say when she actually had no dreams. No idea what she wanted. No idea who she even was.

For her, there had never been any time for thinking about such things. She had always been too busy. Trying to be some kind of mother to Claudia, studying hard at school and then university, and always mindful of the wishes of her father. For without a son to fulfil *his* dreams Cesare had made her the focus of his ambitions.

All his ambitions—including having his say on her choice of future husband, and that was never going to be some local boy made good, like Ciro Trapani, or his rakish older brother.

Not that Vicenzu would ever be interested in her, she thought, her gaze fluttering fleetingly over the perfect angles of his profile. Being in charge of her father's household and a mother figure to Claudia had made her seem far older than her years. And, although she actually shared her sister's shyness, her brief, disappointing interactions with men—she couldn't really call them dates—had left her so wary that she knew her shyness came across as remoteness or disdain.

Hardly qualities that would tempt a man like Vicenzu who, if the internet and the tabloid press were to be believed, was like catnip to women.

But why would she even want to let anyone get close

to her? She was tired of being hurt and humbled. Tired of men running a marathon from her when they realised her surname was Buscetta. Tired of never being good enough, pretty enough, desirable enough for them to face up to her father and fight for the right to be with her.

But her sister's beautiful, romantic wedding was not the time to be letting such thoughts fill her head and, taking a quick, calming breath, she looked up at her father.

'Just at the beginning, Papà.' She took his hand and squeezed it.

Cesare smiled. 'You've been like a mother to her, but marriage is right for Claudia. She doesn't have the temperament for studying or business.'

Imma nodded, her momentary stab of envy instantly swamped by remorse. More than anyone Claudia deserved to be happy, for although their father indulged his youngest daughter, he also found her easy to ignore. Now, though, for the first time in her life, she was in the spotlight.

'I know,' she said quietly.

Cesare grunted. 'She's a homebody and he's a good man for her. Strong, dependable, honest.'

Her father's chest swelled and she could tell he was almost bursting with satisfaction that his daughter had made such a good match socially.

'Come.' He held out his arm. 'Let's go and join your sister—it's nearly time to eat.'

'Where have you been?' It was Claudia, hurrying towards her, clutching the hem of her dress. 'I was just about to send Ciro to find you.'

There was a slight unevenness to her voice, and Imma felt her heart squeeze. She might be a married woman now, but Claudia was still and would always be the little sister she'd comforted whenever she was sad or hurt. Papà was right. Today of all days Imma needed to be there for her—because tomorrow she would be gone.

Pushing back against the ache in her chest, Imma took her sister's hand.

'I just wanted to check in on Corrado,' she said quickly.

Corrado was the Buscettas' Michelin-starred chef, and he had been extremely put out by Cesare's insistence that other Michelin-starred chefs must be flown in at incredible cost from all over the world to help him cater for the wedding breakfast.

But Cesare had been unrepentant. It was his daughter's wedding, and no expense would be spared. He wanted the whole of Sicily—no, make that the whole of Italy—rendered speechless with envy and awe and so, as usual, it had been left to Imma to pour olive oil on troubled waters.

'No, there's nothing wrong,' she added as Ciro and Vicenzu joined them. 'It's just difficult for him, having to share his kitchens, and I didn't want him sulking in any of the photographs.'

'If he does that he'll be looking for a new job,' Cesare growled. 'And he can forget about references. In fact, he can forget about working, full stop. If he doesn't have a smile pinned on his face every second of today I'll make sure he never works again.'

A short, stunned silence followed this explosion. Claudia bit her lip and Ciro looked confused. Vicenzu, on the other hand, seemed more amused than unnerved.

'Of course he won't be looking for another job, Papà,' Imma said firmly. 'Corrado has been with us for ten years. He's one of the family—and we all know how much you value family.'

'And we share those same values, Signor Buscetta.'

Imma glanced sharply over at Vicenzu. For a few half seconds she had been distracted by her father's outburst, but now she felt her stomach swoop down like a kite with a broken tail.

He sounded and looked sincere, and yet she couldn't help thinking he was not. Quickly, in case her father began thinking along the same lines, she said, 'Isn't that how we all ended up here today?'

As she pasted a smile on her face, her father grunted. 'Forgive me. I just want everything to be perfect for my little girl.'

'And it is.' Ciro took a step forward, his deep voice resonating in the space between them. 'If I may, sir, I'd like to thank you for making all this so special for both of us.' He turned to Claudia, who was gazing up at him, her soft brown eyes wide with adoration. 'I promise to make my marriage to Claudia equally memorable.'

Beaming, his good humour restored, Cesare slapped him on the shoulder and then, flicking his ostentatious gold watch free from his cuff, he glanced down at it.

'I'll hold you to that. And now I think we should go and eat. *Ammuninni!*'

Her father held out his arm to Imma, but as she moved to take it Vicenzu sidestepped her, his dark hair flopping over his forehead, his mouth curving into a question mark.

'May I?'

Imma felt her father tense. She knew his opinion of Ciro's older brother. Vicenzu's hedonistic lifestyle and his reputation as a *donnaiolo*—a playboy—had been her father's one and only real objection to Claudia's marriage.

Before she could reply, Cesare said stiffly, 'I think I would prefer to escort my daughter myself.'

There was a short silence, and then her heartbeat accelerated as Vicenzu's teasing dark eyes rested on her face.

'But what would Immacolata prefer?'

Imma froze, his words pinning her to the ground as if he had cast a spell rather than asked a question. Around them the air seemed to turn to stone, and she could sense Claudia's mouth forming an *O* of shock.

No one, certainly not her father, had ever asked about Imma's preferences before, and she had no idea how to respond. But she did know that her father was expecting her to refuse Vicenzu, and maybe it was that assumption, coupled with a sudden longing to indulge in a little impulsive behaviour of her own, that made her turn to Cesare and say calmly, 'I think you should escort Audenzia, Papà. That would be the right and proper thing to do.'

More importantly, it was exactly the right thing for her to say. When he was a young man, her father had just wanted to be rich and powerful, but now what he wanted most was to be accepted in society on an equal footing by people like the Trapanis.

'Of course—you're right,' he said, and Imma felt her heart begin to beat faster as Vicenzu held out his arm.

'Shall we?' he said softly.

Her heart bumping into her ribs, she wondered how he managed to imply so much in two little words. And then, doing her best to ignore the hard swell of his bicep, she followed Claudia and Ciro towards the circus-tent-sized marquee, where the wedding breakfast was being held.

Inside it was impossibly romantic, and Imma felt her stomach flip over as Vicenzu led her to their flower-strewn table. She was already regretting defying her father. Vicenzu Trapani probably flirted in his sleep and she needed to remember that—not let the emotion of the day or his dark eyes suggest anything different.

'So, Vicenzu,' she said quickly, before he had a chance to speak, 'I've heard so much about your hotel. Tell me...how many people work at La Dolce Vita?'

Dropping down next to her, he frowned. 'Well, Immacolata, that's a tricky one. Let me see... I guess, on a good day, probably about forty percent of them.'

The smile tugging at his mouth was impossible to resist, and of their own accord her lips started to curl upward, like the sun rising in the morning sky.

'I know—you think they should all be working. And you're right. I need to crack the whip a bit.'

As his smile slowly unfurled, she felt her stomach flicker like a flame in a breeze. 'I meant—' she began.

He was grinning now. 'I'm just teasing. The answer is I don't know or care. All I know is I get to enjoy your company for the foreseeable future. And, as you're the most beautiful woman in this tiny, unassuming tent...' he glanced mockingly around the vast marquee '...that makes me the luckiest man on earth.'

A cool shiver ran over her skin. Her heart was suddenly beating so fast she felt it might burst free of her ribs.

'Really?' She met his gaze calmly, even as his words resounded inside her head.

'Really. Truly. Absolutely. Unequivocally. Did I say that right?'

She saw his eyes light up as she smiled. 'Yes, only that doesn't make it true.'

'But why would I lie?'

His tone was still playful, but he was staring at her intently.

'Look, I'm not good for much—just ask anyone who knows me…'

He leaned forward so that he was filling her view, and she felt her skin grow hot and tight as he stared down at her steadily.

'But I am a connoisseur of beauty, and you are a very beautiful woman.'

For a second or three the world seemed to stop—or at least the hubbub in the tent faded to a dull hum beneath the uneven thump of her heartbeat. He probably said that to every woman he met, and yet she couldn't stop herself from hoping that he was telling the truth.

He took her hand and she felt her stomach flutter. But he didn't kiss it. Instead he turned her arm over and examined the skin on her wrist.

'What are you doing?' she asked.

'Looking for chinks in your armour,' he murmured.

There was a brief shifting silence, and then he glanced up as waiters began filing into the marquee.

'Great—it's time to eat.'

His eyes met hers, soft and yet intense in a way that made her breathing knot.

'Let's hope the food is as delectable as my hostess,' he said. 'I don't think I've ever been hungrier…'

The food had been incredible. Seven courses accompanied by a note-perfect string quartet. Then there had been speeches, and now Claudia was leaning into Cesare as they slowly circled in the traditional father-and-daughter dance.

But Imma had barely registered any of it. Not the food, nor the music or the toasts. Of course she had gone through the pantomime of raising her glass to her mouth and smiling and nodding, but inside she had been too busy trying to work out the enigma that was Vicenzu Trapani.

She'd expected to like him—*obviously*. A man didn't get the kind of reputation he had for no reason. And this must be how he was with every woman. She was no different in her response to his easy charm and lush beauty.

And yet although she had wanted to find him shallow and spoilt, flirtatious and flippant—and he was all of those things—she felt she might have misjudged him.

Particularly in those moments like now, when he seemed to forget that she was there and his eyes would seek out his mother at the far end of the table.

Her breathing lost its rhythm. Of course she missed her own mother, but his loss was so recent...still raw.

Glancing over at him, she said hesitantly, 'It must be difficult.'

'Difficult?' He raised one perfect eyebrow.

'Today. I mean, without your father. I know Papà wishes he'd come to him sooner.'

Vicenzu's handsome face didn't change, but she could sense an immediate tightening beneath the surface of his skin.

'It's no harder than any other day.'

The lazy amusement had left his voice and her cheeks grew warm. Wanting to kick herself, she glanced across the dance floor to where Ciro had taken over from Cesare. Watching him gaze down into Claudia's upturned face, she felt an ache of the loss to come.

'I'm sorry, Vicenzu—'

'It's Vicè—and, no, *I'm* sorry.' He frowned, his face creasing without impairing its beauty. 'You're right. It is hard without him, and I should have expected it to be, but I'm an idiot.'

Maybe it was the bleakness in his eyes, or perhaps his earlier defiance of her father, but she felt suddenly protective of him.

'You're not an idiot for missing your father. I miss my mother every day.'

They were so close she could feel his warm breath on her face, see the stubble already forming on his jaw. For a full sixty seconds they stared at each other, wide-eyed, mesmerised by the bond they seemed to have formed out of nowhere, and then, standing up, he held out his hand.

'Maybe not,' he said slowly. 'But I will be an idiot if I leave this wedding without having at least one dance with you.' He hesitated. 'That is if you'll dance with me?'

Her mouth felt dry and her blood was humming in her ears. She could feel a hundred pairs of eyes on her. But her eyes were fixed on his and, nodding slowly, she stood up and took his hand.

CHAPTER TWO

BREATHING OUT, VICÈ pulled Imma against him, keeping his beautiful face blank of expression. It was all part of the plan, he told himself. The first step in his great seduction of Immacolata Buscetta.

But inside his head a war was raging between the man he was and the man he was trying to be and needed to be.

No change there, then, he thought irritably.

Except this time there would be no second chances.

It should be easy—and had it been any other woman it would have been. Women liked him. He liked them. But Imma wasn't like other women. She was the daughter of his enemy—and as such he'd expected to hate her on sight.

Everything he'd seen and heard about her in advance had made that seem likely. He'd expected her to be cool and reserved, less overtly aggressive than Cesare, but still her father's daughter. And she was definitely a princess. Watching her with her staff, it had been clear to him that her quiet words and the decisive up-tilt to her jaw held the same authority as a royal command.

Her dark, demure dress seemed to confirm the message that she wanted to be taken seriously—only it couldn't hide her long, coltish legs.

He felt his chest rise and fall.

And as for that long dark hair... It might be neatly knotted at the nape of her neck but he could all too easily imagine running his fingers through its rich, silky length, and her bee-stung parted lips definitely seemed to contradict the wariness in her green eyes.

In short, she was beautiful. Just not the cold, diamond-hard beauty he'd anticipated.

And that was the problem.

He'd wanted to go in for the kill—do it quickly and cleanly like a shark—only it was turning out to be so much harder than he'd anticipated. Particularly with Imma's smooth, supple body pressed against his.

His chest tightened and, catching sight of his mother's face again, he closed his eyes, wishing it was as easy to shut out the confusion he felt on the inside.

Could he do this? Could he actually pull this off?

They were the questions he'd been asking himself for weeks now—ever since he and Ciro had sat in that bar drinking bourbon.

Ciro was his brother and his best friend. There was less than a year between their birthdays, so he couldn't remember a time when Ciro had been smaller, weaker, slower than him.

Maybe he never had been.

It had certainly felt that way for most of his life.

Opening his eyes, he watched his brother dance past, his hand wrapped around Claudia's waist, his face gazing down into hers.

He looked every inch the devoted husband—and he would look that way right up until the moment when he told his new wife the truth and her world came tumbling down.

And, even though he would have preferred to take things more slowly, when the time came he would do the same to Imma. He wanted vengeance every bit as much as Ciro.

His heart stilled.

His father had not been a critical or judgemental man, but he remembered once as a child they had been in Palermo, and a stocky man with a sneering smile had got out of a car and Alessandro's eyes had narrowed.

Sensing his son's curiosity, his father had told him he was a man 'without honour'. He had never forgotten the man's name or his father's words. Coming from his mild, gentle father, they had shocked him.

Now they choked him.

Cesare Buscetta had hounded and humbled Alessandro to death. He needed to pay for his crimes, and it was Vicenzu's job—*his duty*—to make that happen.

'Excuse me, Imma…'

It was Ciro, a small apologetic smile playing around his mouth. His eyes met momentarily with his brother's.

'It's time for Claudia to go and change, and apparently you said you would help her—'

Imma was frowning, and she seemed dazed—almost as though she'd been woken from a dream. 'I'm so sorry… of course I did. Would you mind?'

'Vicè?' His brother frowned too. 'Imma's talking to you.'

'Yeah, I heard, bro.' Feeling Ciro's gaze on his face, he softened his voice and stared down at Imma until he saw a flush colour her cheeks. 'I mind tremendously, but I'll forgive you as long as you come right back.'

As she lifted her face and looked up at him his chest tightened painfully. He'd sworn an oath with Ciro and he was going to keep it—but it would be so much easier if she had eyes of a different colour.

Watching her walk away, he gritted his teeth.

It wasn't fair. Why did her eyes have to be *green*? And not just green but the exact lush green of the No-cellara olives that grew so abundantly on his family's estate. Olives he had helped pick as a child. Olives his father had nurtured and loved almost as much as he had nurtured and loved his family.

It was one of his earliest memories—that first time he'd been allowed to join his father and the other estate workers for the harvest.

He had been so proud when he'd shown his father his haul, and Alessandro had not so much as hinted that the fruit he'd picked was too small and not ripe enough.

It had been that way for his entire life—his father covering up his mistakes, never holding him account-able, always giving him another chance. He couldn't even pinpoint when it had first started.

Had it been at school? When he'd got into trouble for trading tips on how to kiss girls in exchange for getting his homework done? Or when he'd got drunk and driven a tractor around the olive groves? He'd written off the tractor, and some of the estate's oldest trees—but, just like on all the other occasions when he'd messed up, Alessandro had simply sighed and shaken his head.

Something bitter rose in his throat—the burning anger that had been swirling inside his chest since his mother's distraught phone call.

If only his father had told him the truth about Buscetta he would have been able to help. It could have been his chance to make amends. It wasn't as if he was still a child. He didn't need protecting from the truth.

And then, just like that, he felt his anger drain away swiftly, like water spiralling down a plughole.

To his father he had still needed protecting.

That was why Alessandro had kept both his financial and his health worries to himself. Vicenzu glanced over at his brother. And that was why Ciro was so insistent that they seek revenge on Buscetta.

Unlike him, his brother had always been independently successful on a scale that far surpassed their father, and the idea that Alessandro hadn't thought Ciro man enough to take on his father's problems had incensed his younger brother.

The truth was actually the opposite, he thought numbly. His father had known that he'd be able to rely on Ciro, but he hadn't wanted to confide in one son and not the other, so he'd sacrificed himself so that *he*, Vicenzu, wouldn't feel inadequate.

It was yet another reason for him to feel guilty.

'How's it going?'

Glancing up at his brother, he shrugged. 'It's going fine, I think.' He leaned forward and picked up a *confetti* from a nearby table. It was a traditional gift for the wedding guests. His mother still had hers from her own wedding. Five pastel-coloured sugared almonds—a reminder that married life was both sweet and bitter—and five wishes for the new husband and wife.

Health, wealth, happiness, children and a long life.

His shoulders tensed. Now, thanks to Buscetta, his parents' wishes had withered like olives exposed to a hard frost.

He sensed Ciro's impatience even before he heard it in his voice. 'You *think*? What does that mean?'

He felt a flicker of irritation—and envy. Ever since he could remember people had wanted to make his life easy. Not just his parents, but his friends and pretty much every woman he met. Ciro too. Until now. Now his brother was so on edge, so picky and demanding all the time.

But Claudia had always been the easier sister to seduce. She was younger, naive in the extreme, and had clearly been groomed for marriage. All Ciro had had to do was get past her monstrous father. Okay, that had sounded tough on paper, but in reality Cesare had laid out the red carpet for him.

Obviously.

His brother ticked all the boxes, whereas Vicenzu just owned a hotel. It might be the most celebrated hotel in the Western hemisphere—part sanctuary, part crash pad for its hard-partying, glamorous A-list clientele— but still...

And, of course, there was his reputation—

'Vicè!' His brother's voice tugged him back into the present. 'I thought seduction was supposed to be your area of expertise?'

'It is.' He turned towards his brother, his hands itching to both hit him and hug him. As usual, he went down the path of least resistance. '*Scialla*—just chill, Ciro, okay?' Grabbing his brother by the shoulders, he pulled him into an embrace. '*Festina lente*, bro.'

'There's no time for chilling, *bro*,' his brother said irritably. 'And quoting Latin at me doesn't change the facts. We agreed—you agreed—'

'Yeah, and I'm doing it.'

'Do it faster.' They were facing each other and their eyes met. 'I don't want to be stuck in this marriage for any longer than I have to be.'

'I know.'

Ciro held his gaze. 'Look, ever since I was a teenager I've watched women climb over each other to get to you. Immacolata Buscetta will be exactly the same. So just do this for Mamma, and for Papà, and then everything will go back to how it was before.'

Except it wouldn't.

They would have avenged their father, but nothing could bring him back to life. They would have the business and their home, but their mother still wouldn't have her husband.

He glanced over to where Audenzia was sitting, sipping coffee. His parents had been so devoted to each other they had never spent a night apart during their forty years of marriage. He'd always feared falling short of their ideal, and now he was having to seduce a woman he hated into marrying him.

'I can't help feeling that Papà wouldn't like this,' he said quietly.

Ciro stared at him. 'Maybe not—but he's not here to ask, is he? And if you're having second thoughts, maybe you should ask yourself why that's the case.'

The pain was sharp and humbling. And just what Vicenzu needed to clear the confusion from his mind.

He had made and broken enough promises in his life.

This time he would do whatever it took to keep one.

It was dark when Ciro and Claudia finally left.

'He will take care of her, won't he?'

Vicè was standing next to Imma at the edge of the

marquee. Having waved off the happy couple, most of the guests had already gone back inside, but she had wanted to wait until the car had disappeared.

He felt a rush of anticipation—like that moment on a rollercoaster ride just before the track dropped down. Now that it was close, he just wanted to make it happen.

'Yes, of course,' he lied.

She nodded. 'You don't have to wait with me,' she said, glancing back at the distant car, her green eyes tracking its progress. 'I know it's silly, but it's the first time she's gone away without me.'

'I want to wait.' He hesitated. 'And there's nowhere I'd rather be than here.' Taking her hand, he gently pulled her closer. 'With you.'

Her eyes lifted to his face, and there was a faint frown on her brow as she tugged her pashmina closer to her body. He felt his blood start to hum. He'd bet his last sugared almond that she was trying to hide how aroused she was by his words.

'I don't think we know each other well enough for you to say that,' she said quietly.

'So let's get to know each other better.' He took a deep breath. 'Let's go somewhere more private.'

She looked up at him, her green eyes wide with confusion and a curiosity that made his groin turn to stone.

He nodded. 'I know it's sudden, and I'm guessing you think I do this kind of thing all the time. But I don't. Usually I'm just looking for fun—but not today. Not with you.'

She bit her lip, and for a moment he thought he'd gone too far, too fast.

'Look, forget it,' he said quickly. 'I must be crazy, suggesting something like that—'

She nodded slowly. 'Yes, you are.'

He felt her fingers tighten around his.

'But maybe it's about time I did something crazy too.'

His heart gave a leap, and he felt shock mingling with confusion. He couldn't believe she was agreeing with him.

'I should say goodbye to Papà first—'

'No.' He squeezed her hand. 'Don't go back in— please.' There was no way he was going to let her talk to Buscetta before she left. 'My driver's out front. We can call your father on our way to the airport.'

She stared at him for a moment, and then she smiled. 'Or we could go completely crazy and take my father's helicopter...'

Leaning back into the cream leather upholstery, Vicè breathed out slowly. The Buscetta helicopter was rising up into the dark sky, its rotor blades whipping up the discarded *coriandoli* so that for a moment he felt as if he were in a snow globe—a sensation exacerbated by the feeling of his world being turned upside down and shaken vigorously.

He could hardly believe it.

That Imma had agreed to his impulsive suggestion that they get to know one another seemed fantastical enough, but for her to more or less commandeer her father's helicopter in order to make their escape seemed too preposterous to be true.

And yet that was exactly what was happening.

At that moment Imma turned and smiled at him, her eyes bright with eagerness and pleasure at her part in the adventure, and he felt his heart jump, his body responding to her sudden and thrilling abandonment of the normal expected preliminaries.

Well, perhaps not all of them.

Remembering that this was supposed to be a seduction, he lifted her hand to his mouth, feeling her pulse dart under the skin like a minnow in a pond.

'Will this thing make it to the mainland?' he asked softly.

'The mainland?' she repeated.

He held her gaze, his eyebrow curving upward at the question in her voice.

He and Ciro had accepted that Buscetta would never countenance Vicenzu courting Imma. Plus, the second brother falling in love with his other daughter was so implausible it would almost certainly hint at some kind of plot, so they'd decided that it would be better to present him with a fait accompli.

His shoulders stiffened. Of course before he'd even thought about how he was going to make that happen Ciro, being Ciro, had already proposed to Claudia and started the process of arranging the paperwork for their marriage.

But seducing a woman was not something Vicè consciously did—normally it just happened. He had no idea how to cold-bloodedly reproduce that organic process, so he'd left it to the last minute—like he did everything else in his life.

Not that he'd told his uber-efficient brother that.

Arriving at the wedding, he'd decided to seduce Imma and then use his reputation as leverage for their marriage. It would be a delicate balancing act. She'd know he wouldn't be Cesare's choice for her husband. But nor would her father want her to be viewed as just another notch on Vicenzu's bedpost. And obviously his plan wouldn't work if they kept their liaison private, which was why he needed it to play out in public.

And where better to find maximum publicity than at his celebrity-studded hotel with its inbuilt entourage of photographers?

'I thought I was taking you back to mine,' he said.

'To the Dolce Vita?' She looked confused. 'I thought you wanted to go somewhere private.'

Good point, he thought, his shoulders tensing.

It was a rookie error—except he wasn't a rookie. As Ciro had so pointedly remarked earlier, this was supposed to be his area of expertise.

Glancing out of the window, he felt his pulse slow as he realised he'd made another error in assuming he was calling the shots. Imma might not be planning to go back to his hotel, but they were clearly not just flying in circles so...

'I do,' he said. He let his gaze linger on her face. 'And I should have realised that totally rules out my hotel. But ever since you walked into that church behind your sister I haven't been able to think straight.'

Watching her chew at her lip, he felt his heart kick against his ribs.

'I'm guessing you have somewhere in mind,' he said softly.

He felt her fingers move against his and, glancing down, was almost shocked to see her hand entwined with his. Holding hands was not his thing, but his parents had always done it and his ribs tightened as he pictured his mother sitting alone at the wedding. That was another crime to chalk up to Cesare Buscetta's relentless greed.

But as he felt the ever-present trickle of anger start to rise and swell he pushed the memory away. His anger would wait. Right now he needed to focus on the task in hand.

Closing his grip around her fingers, he gently pulled her closer. 'So where are you taking me?'

No doubt Imma had some favourite boutique hotel in mind—somewhere quiet, intimate—and actually that might work for him. They could lie low until he had her eating out of his hand, and then he could discreetly tip off the paparazzi.

He felt her gaze on his face.

'Papà has a villa on Pantelleria…'

Pantelleria. Unlike most people in the world, he'd heard of the island—but, like most of the population, he'd never set foot on it. Why would he? It was basically a black volcanic speck in the Mediterranean between Sicily and Tunisia.

'Right…' He nodded, holding his easy smile in place. 'Your father isn't going to have a problem with that?'

She hesitated, her face tensing a little as though she was weighing up what to say next.

'He bought it as a kind of hideaway, somewhere to get away from work—only he's not very good about handing over the reins, so he never really goes there. But Claudia and I love it. It's just so beautiful—and very private.'

Her eyes seemed to grow even more opaque.

'But if you've changed your mind I can get Marco to—'

She was close enough that he could feel her small, firm breasts through the thin fabric of his shirt, and the tiny shivers of anticipation scampering over her skin. Seducing Imma at a hideaway on a remote island owned by Buscetta himself was about as far away from ideal as it could get, but he didn't want to jeopardise this mood of intimacy between them.

The time for talking was over.

He looked down at the pulse beating erratically at the base of her beautiful throat, feeling his body harden to stone for the second time in as many minutes. Reaching up, he caught her chin with his hand, tilting her face to his. 'Nothing's changed.'

He could make it work—he *would* make it work.

Needing to defuse any indecision she might still be feeling, he did the first thing that came into his head. Lowering his mouth to hers, he kissed her.

Whatever he'd been expecting when his lips touched hers, it wasn't what actually happened. For a brief second or two she stilled against him, her mouth softening beneath his, lips parting on an intake of breath, and then her hand slid over his neck, fingers pressing lightly against his skin as though she was reading Braille.

Barely breathing, he moved his lips over hers, teasing her with the whispering heat of his mouth, the firm tip of his tongue, stirring her senses, tasting her, all the while telling himself that he hated this woman, that she was guilty by association.

But then she moaned softly, shifting against him. Her fingers curled through his hair to grasp his skull, her tongue pushing between his lips, and hunger, hot and powerful, punched him in the gut.

Her scent enveloped him and, breathing in sharply, he made a rough, incoherent sound against her mouth, trying and failing to still the blood pounding through his veins, almost idiotically stupefied by the strength of his desire and hers.

He was hard—very hard—and, framing her face

with his hands, he kissed her fiercely, pulling her closer so that she pressed against him, wanting more of her, needing more of her—

'Miss Buscetta?'

Imma jerked back and they stared at one another dazedly as the pilot's voice filled the cabin.

'We'll be coming in to land in about five minutes. There might be a few crosswinds, but nothing to worry about.'

With a hand that trembled slightly, Imma pressed the intercom. 'Thank you, Marco.'

Vicenzu breathed out unsteadily, blindsided by her response, and utterly floored by his own.

He had wanted so much more than just her mouth. And, judging by the dull ache in his groin, he still did.

His heart beating out of time, he struggled to pull his brain back online. 'Imma—'

Her green eyes fluttered to his face, wide and startled. The curves of her cheeks were flushed with desire, or embarrassment, or maybe both.

He swore inwardly. 'I'm sorry. I didn't expect—I didn't mean for that to happen—'

Actually, what he hadn't expected was for it to feel like that—for her to be so gloriously responsive, so fierce, so sweet, so everything he'd ever wanted in a woman.

But how was that possible?

He was only supposed to be seducing this woman to avenge his family.

'I understand.'

She inched backwards, slipping her hand free of his. He watched her fold it back into her lap, his heart beating as violently as if he'd just sprinted for a finishing line. Only for once—incredibly—he didn't appear to be on the winner's podium.

'Imma—'

'Please.' She held up her hand and her beautiful mouth no longer looked soft and kissable but pinched, as though she was trying to hold something in. 'I don't need to hear it.'

'Hear what?'

Her face was pale and set, and there was a tension to her body he recognised. It was as though she was bracing herself for bad news.

'I've heard it all before,' she said, staring past him. 'Let me guess. You're worried things are moving too fast. Or maybe you respect me too much? That's always popular.'

He frowned. Her words made no sense. 'I don't understand—'

She ignored him. 'You know, back at the wedding I thought you were different. But I guess when it comes to the crunch you're just like everyone else.'

The bitterness in her voice was unmistakable now.

'I'm sorry for taking up so much of your time, Signor Trapani. But don't worry. You can go back to your precious hotel and the rest of your "sweet life" now. Just tell Marco where you need to go and he'll take you.'

There was a slight judder as the helicopter touched down, and before he had a chance to respond, even to absorb her words, she'd pulled off her seat belt and was out of the door and gone.

He stared after her, shock and outrage swirling up inside him, and then he was wrenching himself free and following her into the warm night air. She was moving fast, and he found himself having to run to catch up with her.

He'd never run after a woman metaphorically, let

alone in reality, and the fact that he was having to do so made his irritation intensify with every step.

'Imma!'

She carried on walking and, frustrated by the sight of the smooth, untroubled knot at the nape of her neck, he caught her arm, jerking her round to face him.

'Where's all this coming from? All I said was—'

Her eyes narrowed and she shook his hand off. 'I heard you the first time.'

Watching the bow of her mouth tremble, Vicè felt his breath hitch in his throat. Before her anger had been crimped, confined by a forced politeness, now she was clearly furious.

'Look, I get it. It was a wedding. You were bored, or curious—maybe both. But I do have feelings and I am done with being picked up and dropped like some toy.'

She glared at him, her hands curling into fists. 'But I suppose I should be thankful that at least one Trapani brother has the courage of his convictions.'

His jaw clenched. Being compared unfavourably to Ciro was such a frequent occurrence he rarely even reacted any more, but Imma's criticism, delivered in that clipped, dismissive manner, somehow got under his skin, so that suddenly he was having to rein in his temper, usually so slow to rise.

'Meaning?' he said.

Her lip curled with contempt. 'I mean, unlike you, Ciro's not scared of my father.'

Listening to her words echo in the silence, Imma felt slightly sick.

She hadn't meant to say that out loud, only there was no real point in continuing with this farce.

Vicenzu Trapani was a beautiful liar, and she was an unforgivable idiot.

What was worse, for just a few short hours she had actually started to hope…started to think that Vicè was different—that, incredibly, like Claudia, she had met a man who was prepared to stand proudly beside her.

And not just any man—a man who was in a class of his own. Cool, glamorous, and with a smile that made her body ache and a mouth that turned her inside out.

Remembering her uninhibited response to his kiss, she felt her skin grow warm. She had kissed men before—three, to be precise—but Vicè's kiss had been like nothing she'd ever experienced, and if Marco's disembodied voice hadn't interrupted she would have gone on kissing him forever.

Her cheeks burned as she replayed that sound she'd made when he'd pulled her against his hard body. It had felt so good, so right—but clearly not good or right enough for him to want to continue.

She hung on to her temper as he took a step towards her, his eyes narrowing like chips of volcanic rock.

'*Scared*? Of your *father*? Let me tell you something, Imma. I feel many things for your father, but fear isn't one of them. I'm no more scared of him than Ciro is.'

Gone was the handsome easy-going playboy. The skin across his cheekbones was tight, like a ship's sail in a strong wind. But it was the rawness in his voice that convinced her that he was telling the truth.

And just like that her own anger turned to air.

'I thought you'd changed your mind.' She swallowed. 'Like all the others.'

There was a beat of silence and she heard him breathe out unsteadily.

'I panicked,' he said.

His dark eyes found hers, and the naked heat in them sent a jolt through her body.

'But not because I wanted to back out. I thought I'd come on too strong.' He hesitated, and then, reaching out, took her hand and pulled her closer. 'I meant what I said earlier. I want to get to know you better.'

As he gazed down at her she felt her pulse begin to beat a little faster.

'And if you still want that too then I won't let anything or anyone—including your father—get in the way of that happening. Do you understand?'

Her heart was pressing against her ribs. It was what she'd wanted to hear for so long—and, more importantly, it was clear he meant it.

Nodding slowly, she let him pull her into his arms.

CHAPTER THREE

'So, who are these "others"?'

Glancing up at Vicè, Imma frowned. Neither of them was hungry, but they were drinking wine on the vast terrace next to the pool. Or rather he was drinking. She was too jittery to do anything but clutch the stem of her glass. Besides, just looking at him made her tongue stick to the roof of her mouth.

Watching him languidly stretch out his long legs, she felt knots form in her stomach. He was so perfect, with his dark poet's eyes and panther-like grace...

Trying to stay calm, she gazed past him. It was a bad idea. Somebody—probably Marianna, the housekeeper—had lit some candles, and the twitching flames made the curves of his face even more dangerously appealing.

Accompanying the darkness was the lightest of breezes—a whisper of dry air from Africa—and on it came the scent of the roses and jasmine that Marianna cherished in the garden that surrounded the villa on all sides.

The undiluted romance of it all sent a tremor through her blood.

She cleared her throat. 'Others?'

He picked up his wine glass, lounging back in his

seat, his dark eyes roaming her face. 'Earlier, you said something about me changing my mind "like the others".'

'Oh, that…' She felt a prickle spread over her skin and down her spine. 'It's nothing, really.'

How could someone like him truly understand? But he held her gaze.

She sighed. 'Just that my dates were always ever so keen on me—until they worked out who my father was. And then—'

'Oh, I see,' he said softly.

She nodded. 'Papà has a reputation. Friends in low places. I'm sure you've read the stories about him?'

He shook his head, his eyes gleaming. 'Too busy reading about myself.'

The teasing note in his voice made her skin sting. Pulse quickening, she glanced away. What was he thinking when he looked at her like that? And why did her body like it so much?

Reaching across the table, he took her hand. 'Look, what they can't find out they make up. It's not important.'

His voice was gentle but his dark eyes were burning into her, the intensity of their focus accelerating her already racing pulse. He was everything she wanted, but everything she feared. Compelling. Confident. Curious about her.

She had never talked like this to anyone. Her father's moods were too changeable and Claudia was so young and innocent.

She felt his fingers tighten around hers.

'Those men had no right to judge you, *cara*.' His beautiful mouth twisted. 'Believe me, I know. People think because they read about you that they know you, but they don't.' His eyes met hers. 'They really don't.'

Remembering the stories she'd read about him, she felt a twinge of guilt. How could she complain about being judged when she was guilty of doing the same to him?

'And those people don't know you,' she said, her words tumbling over themselves. 'The real you. You're funny, and smart, and kind, and sweet…'

Her voice petered out. Beside her, Vicè leaned back a little, his expression midway between surprise and amusement—unsurprising, given that she'd sounded like some teenage fangirl.

Cringing inwardly, she frowned. 'Look, maybe this wasn't such a good idea. I'll get Marco to drop you back to your hotel—'

Reaching over, he tugged her towards him. Then he smiled…a slow, flickering smile like a candle being lit that made a pulse of excitement beat beneath her skin.

'*Cara*, forget about my hotel…you're the sweetness in my life.'

Oh, she liked him so much—and she'd almost ruined everything with her stupid accusations. But this was all so new and different. She was different with him. More impulsive and open. Bolder.

Her body tensed. Only not so bold that she was looking forward to facing her father.

Picturing Cesare's outburst, she shivered. He would be angry enough about her leaving the wedding early, but his fury would be visible from space when he found out she had left with Vicè and come here. Particularly as he'd hinted that he was finally ready to talk about her role at Trapani.

'How mad is he going to be?'

Her chin jerked up. 'How did you know what I was thinking?'

'Just a guess.' He sighed. 'Come on, let's go inside. I think you need something stronger than wine.'

Inside, he poured two glasses of grappa and, dropping down beside her on the sofa, handed her one. 'Look, I feel like this is my fault. Why don't I call him? Explain—'

'No, absolutely not.' She shook her head. She could think of nothing that would antagonise Cesare more.

Leaning forward, Vicè stroked the curve of her cheekbone with a tenderness that made her skin melt.

'I'm not scared of him, Imma.' His face stilled as though something had just occurred to him. 'Are *you*?'

She shook her head. 'Of course not. Papà just doesn't like surprises. He has plans for me. Expectations. Your father's business—he wants me to run it.'

He lifted his glass. 'And you don't want to.'

It was a statement, not a question. And just for a moment his eyes seemed to narrow. But when he lowered his glass she realised he was just curious.

'Yes, I do. It's a wonderful business. And it's the least I can do for Papà. I want to be there for him.'

Her pulse skipped. Her father was going to be apoplectic, but it was the aftermath of his rage she was dreading.

He would become even more controlling—particularly regarding her matrimonial choices. Claudia could have her Ciro, but Cesare wanted Imma to marry well—and by 'well' he meant to a man nearer his own age, whose wealth was equal to the GDP of some small country.

Love hadn't been mentioned.

She shivered inside. She couldn't disappoint her father. He needed her to fulfil his dreams.

All she wanted was just one night for herself.

An experience that was hers and hers alone.

An experience she would remember forever—an encounter that would imprint on her body and mind to help her through years of dutiful marriage to a man she didn't love.

Tonight she wanted fire and ecstasy. She wanted to understand her own needs and desires…be in charge of making that small but important change from sheltered, uninformed virgin to a woman who had experienced the storm of passion.

Picking up her glass, she saw her hand was shaking a little. Her body was humming…fear mingling with desire. Fear of missing out. Fear of giving in to what she wanted.

And she wanted Vicè.

Her hunger, her need for him, was like a tornado inside her, upturning everything in its path so that her skin could barely hold it in.

And by bringing Vicè here she had already sealed her fate. Her father was going to come down on her hard and fast. So shouldn't she make sure it was for something that mattered?

And what mattered more than choosing your first lover?

This might be her last opportunity to make that choice and she was choosing Vicè. Because he was handsome, charming, and most importantly she trusted him.

'But I want to be here with you too,' she said slowly. 'And I don't care how angry that makes him.'

. Their gazes locked.

'He has no reason to be angry.'

His dark eyes held her fast and heat shivered down her spine.

'Nothing's happened.'

Something stirred deep inside her, and she took a steadying breath.

'Nothing's happened *yet*,' she said softly.

Her hunger for him was like the lick of a flame. Only he could put out the fire.

The glass in her hand was shaking. Reaching over, he took it from her.

'Are you saying you want something to happen?' he asked.

His eyes were steady on her face, his expression intent, as though he was trying to read her mind.

She didn't know where to start, or how to ask for what she wanted. But she knew that she wanted to share it, feel it, with him—with this man. With Vicè.

She nodded. 'Yes, that is what I'm saying.'

Her belly clenched. She sounded so formal, so uptight, but she couldn't help it. Her body was just so wound up, so hot and tight with hope and need and anticipation. And fear of rejection.

Her stomach was a ball of nerves. 'It's just that I'm scared—'

'Of being hurt?' He gave her a crooked smile. 'It's a risk, and I guess it's a particularly big risk with someone like me...someone with my history.' His dark, mocking face was suddenly serious. 'But if it makes you feel better I think I'm the one in danger here. You make me feel things I've never felt, want things I've never wanted before—'

Heat surged over her skin, lifting the hairs on her

arms, making her breasts tingle and tighten. So many choices had been made for her already. So much decided and dictated. This night with Vicè would be hers, and hers alone.

'I want them too,' she whispered. 'I want you.'

But he was gorgeous and sexy, and he had his pick of beautiful, experienced women. Would he really want someone so inexpert and gauche?

For a moment she thought about telling him the truth. Only what if it changed things between them?

Vicè might be a playboy, but he was also a Sicilian. What if beneath the languid posturing he retained an old-school Sicilian attitude to taking a woman's virginity? What if he backed off?

She made up her mind.

Being here with him was straight out of a fantasy, and raising the topic of her virginity would introduce a cool reality she wasn't ready to face yet.

'Shall we go somewhere even more private?' she said softly. 'More intimate…'

Vicenzu stared at her in silence, a pulse beating in his throat, her voice replaying inside his head.

Intimate.

He felt his belly flip over.

Intimate.

The word brushed against his skin. It made him think of subdued lighting, soft laughter and naked bodies.

His own body turned to granite as she bit her lip.

'Imma, are you sure?' Holding her gaze, he softened his voice. 'I know my reputation, and I don't want you to think that's why I'm here.'

She shook her head. 'I don't think that.'

She was staring up at him, her face expressionless, but he could hear the nervous edge in her voice and knew she was trying to sound calmer than she felt.

It was understandable. Given how protective Buscetta was about his daughters, it was unlikely she did this kind of thing very often—and certainly not under her over-controlling father's nose. Clearly being here, in her father's lair, was spooking her.

Her cheeks were flushed and her dark hair was coming undone from the knot at her neck. He studied her face, lost momentarily in the delicacy of her features and the flame in her eyes. He felt his pulse accelerate. He could do this, but he needed to take charge, keep it light—not let her beauty get in the way of what was really happening here.

'I'm happy to wait, *cara*. Well, maybe happy is pushing it.' He grimaced. 'Obviously I'd be in a lot of pain—'

She laughed then, and for a moment he almost forgot why he was there. It was such a lovely sound. All he could think about was how to make her laugh again.

But then he blanked his mind as she stood up, pulling him to his feet.

'I might just freshen up.'

She seemed more nervous now they were in her bedroom, and he kissed her softly on the mouth.

'Good idea. I'll wait here. Take all the time you need.'

Actually, he was the one fighting for time. He needed to put some distance between himself and Imma otherwise...

As the door closed he began unbuttoning his shirt,

and then, frowning, he pulled out his wallet. He was checking he had condoms when he noticed he had a notification on his phone. It was a voicemail from Ciro.

'Vicenzu, it's me... Look, I can't do this for much longer. I've fulfilled my part. She's going to sign the house over to me today. You need to get your side done, and quickly. Whatever it takes to get the business back, do it. Because I don't know how much longer I can keep the pretence up.'

He thought about the edge to Imma's voice.

Then he pictured his mother sitting alone at the wedding.

Taking back his father's business and their family home would go a long way towards making her smile again. And it would wipe the smile off Buscetta's face at the same time.

He knew what his mother would say. That two wrongs didn't make a right.

His jaw tightened. No, they didn't. On this occasion two wrongs would make two rights.

Hearing the door to the bathroom open, he texted Ciro quickly, then tossed his phone onto a chair. Composing his face, he looked up—and his breath stalled in his throat.

Imma was standing in the doorway, her long dark hair hanging loose over her shoulders.

Her naked shoulders.

Actually, she was entirely naked except for a tiny pair of cream lace panties—a fact that his groin had apparently registered several moments before his eyes.

His body hardening to stone, he stood hypnotised by her small rounded breasts and rose-coloured nipples. Her skin was the colour of the purest cold-pressed virgin olive oil, and just looking at it made his ribcage tighten around his chest.

He was used to nudity, and blasé about beauty, but there was a vulnerability to her pose that had everything and nothing to do with sex.

His pact with Ciro was forgotten. And his anger and grief and guilt—everything that had propelled him to this softly lit room—was swept away by a need he had never experienced before.

He stared at her, dry-mouthed, feeling the blood throb through his body.

She took a step forward, reaching out to touch him.

'Wait,' he said gently. 'Let me look at you first.'

She looked up at him, and he took his time absorbing her beauty.

Expression shuttered, he stepped closer and stroked the curve of her cheek. 'Don't be shy. You're beautiful.'

'So are you.'

Heat flared inside him as she touched his chest, her warm fingers sending shock waves over his skin. Leaning forward, he brushed his mouth lightly over hers, sliding his hand through her hair.

It wasn't a kiss—more a prelude to a kiss. She drew a quick breath and her eyes met his. Then, taking his hand, she led him to the bed.

He stripped quickly and slid in beside her. As he ran his hand lightly down her arm, she shivered against him.

'Are you sure about this?'

Heart pounding, Imma stared up at his beautiful face. She had never been surer about anything. Her whole body felt as though it was clamouring for him.

But as he shifted closer she felt a rush of panic. Up close and naked, there seemed to be even more of him than before. His limbs seemed more solid, and—she glanced down at his erection—he was very hard, and bigger than she'd imagined.

Her pulse accelerated. This wasn't going to work. Vicè had a wealth of sexual experience. No doubt he was expert at all kinds of lovemaking and used to sophisticated, skilful lovers. But beyond the mechanics of sex she knew absolutely nothing.

'Yes, I'm sure. Are you?'

'Am *I* sure?' He seemed to consider her question, frowning. Then, 'Yeah, of course.'

His hand moved to cover her hip, his fingers gliding over the crest of bone in a way that made her skin tingle.

'I mean, as long as you respect me in the morning...' he added.

His eyes gleamed and she started to laugh.

Dipping his head, he brushed his mouth against her. 'Tell me what you want.' His voice was warm with desire. 'What you like.'

She didn't know what she liked. She didn't know where to start. Where it would end.

'I like this...' Her finger trembled against the curve of his jaw. 'And this...' She touched his chest, the smooth contours of his muscles. 'And this.' She flattened her hand against the trail of fine dark hair that ran down the centre of his stomach.

He sucked in a breath, his pupils flaring.

'I like that too,' he said unsteadily and, lowering his mouth, he kissed her.

He kissed her lightly, then more deeply, slowing

the kiss down, slowing her pulse and her breath, kissing her so that she forgot her doubts, forgot his past—forgot everything except the touch of his mouth and the heat of his skin and the unchecked hunger in his dark eyes.

He cupped her breasts, gently thumbing each nipple, and then, taking his weight on his knees and elbows, he grazed the hardened tips with his mouth, his warm breath sending shock waves of desire up and down her body so that her stomach clenched around the ball of heat pulsing inside her.

She arched against him, pressing herself closer, wanting more of him. His fingers were sliding over her skin now, in slow, measured caresses that made a moan of pure need rise up in her throat.

Would it be like this on her wedding night? Would her husband make her feel like this? That nameless man who was yet to be chosen for her. She took a breath, fighting panic, and instantly felt him still against her.

'*Cara...*' He shifted his weight. 'Is this okay? Do you want me to stop?'

'No.' She splayed her hands on his chest, feeling his quickening heartbeat through her fingertips. 'I don't want you to stop. Please, don't stop.'

She couldn't admit the truth. It would be crazy to admit that she wanted this to last forever—for him to be that nameless man, to be her husband.

Reaching up, she brought his face down to hers and kissed him slowly, deepening the kiss as he pushed against her.

His hand moved across the outside of her leg, then between her thighs. Shivering, she shifted closer, lifting her hips, pressing against the hard contours of his knuckles, seeking him, wanting him to ease the ache inside her.

'Your skin is like silk,' Vicè murmured.

He pulled her closer, moulding her body against his, his mouth finding hers—and then he felt her hand enclose the heavy weight of his erection.

He cut off a groan, catching her hand in his, blood thundering in his ears.

'Not yet...not me.' Pushing her gently back on the bed, he leaned over her, kissing her deeply. 'This is all about you.'

Hooking his thumbs into her panties, he slid them down her legs. Now she was completely naked.

'Look at me,' he said softly.

Her eyes locked with his and he felt his heartbeat accelerate.

His breathing staccato, he began again at her face, tracing the outline of her lips with his tongue, kissing the curving bones of her cheeks, and then he lowered his mouth to her throat, tracking the pulse beating frenetically beneath the smooth skin, moving with deliberate, sensuous slowness down to the swell of her breasts.

Her hands slid through his hair and she pushed his head against her nipple, moaning softly as she arched her body up to meet his lips.

His heart missed a beat. He was desperately trying to centre himself. Trying to stay detached. But she was just so beautiful, so eager and responsive. He couldn't stop himself from responding to her. His need for her was like a fever in his blood.

Her nipples were taut and he sucked first one and then the other, nipping the swollen ruched tips, his erection so hard now it was almost horizontal.

Ignoring the ache in his groin, he found her mouth again, kissing her slowly, sliding his hand down over her waist and through the triangle of curls, gently probing the slick heat between her thighs.

Imma felt her head start to spin. She had never felt anything like this before. His fingers were moving inside her, his thumb brushing the nub of her clitoris, sending oscillating tremors over her skin.

Shivering, she moved against his caress, chasing the pulse beating in his hand, wanting, needing something *more* to fill the urgent hollowed-out ache inside her.

'You're killing me,' he said hoarsely.

She reached again for his groin. This time he didn't stop her, and as her fingers wrapped around his hard, swollen length, he groaned against her mouth.

'Ti voglio,' she whispered. 'I want to feel you inside me. *Ti prego.'*

Gritting his teeth, he shifted his weight and reached over to the bedside table. She heard a tearing sound. Dazed, she watched him slide a condom on.

He gazed down into her face and the dark passion in his eyes made hunger rear up inside her.

Lowering his mouth, he kissed her breasts again, licking her nipples and drawing them into his mouth, and then she felt the blunt head of his erection pushing between her thighs.

It was too big. She tensed. It would never fit inside her.

Her hands pressed against his chest, and he stopped moving, shifting his weight minutely.

'It's okay,' he murmured. 'Take your time. You just need to get used to me.'

His voice calmed her, but it was the hunger etched on his face that made her start to move against him.

Taking a breath, she parted her legs further. She arched upward, straining for something she didn't understand, something just out of reach, something that would satisfy the insistent clamouring of her body.

He moved above her and instinctively she opened her legs wider, her breath jerking in her throat as he rubbed the tip of his erection against the bud of her clitoris. Curling her arms around his shoulders, wanting to feel all of him inside her, she lifted her hips and he pushed into her.

There was a moment of sharpness and she tensed—must have tensed, because he stilled above her. Not wanting him to suspect her virginity—or, worse, stop—she pulled him closer and began to move against him, trying to regulate her breathing as her body stretched to accommodate him.

He was fully inside her now, and his mouth found hers as he matched himself to the rhythm of her breathing. As he started to increase his pace she felt the pulse inside her accelerate in time to his movements.

She was panting now, lunging up towards him. Muscles she hadn't known she had were straining, pulling apart, fraying, and she gripped his shoulders as her whole body suddenly splintered in a rush of pleasure so intense she could have wept.

And then he was thrusting into her, clamping her body to his, his groans mingling with her ragged breathing as he tensed, shuddering helplessly against her.

His hands tightened in her hair and he kissed her

face, murmuring her name against the damp skin of her neck. *'Sei bellissima,'* he said softly.

She smiled, suddenly shy beneath his dark gaze. 'Was it okay for you?'

'Was it okay for me?' He laughed. 'I've never been asked that before. It was more than "okay", *cara*. It was incredible.'

'I didn't know it could be like that,' she said slowly.

How could she have imagined such dizzying pleasure was right there, at her fingertips? Her cheeks felt warm. Or rather at *his* fingertips. She had wanted it to be amazing but she had completely underestimated how it would feel, the bliss of being touched, the heat of his mouth…

His eyes roamed her face. 'What's it been like before?'

Her heart gave a jump. She could lie, but it was done now. They had made love. There was no need for secrets between them.

'It wasn't like anything.' She took a breath. 'There was no "before". You're my first—my first lover.'

Her first lover.

Vicè stared at her in silence, made mute by shock and disbelief.

She'd been a virgin.

He couldn't have been any more stunned if she'd thrown a bucket of cold water in his face.

His head was spinning. With an effort, he replayed the time they had just spent in each other's arms.

When he'd entered her—he gritted his teeth, *her actual first time*—her body had been tight, and there had been moments when she'd tensed, moments when he had felt her hesitate.

But he'd put it down to nerves over having sex with somebody new. He hadn't thought she had no experience whatsoever.

Suddenly his skin could barely contain the chaos inside his body.

He was frustrated with himself for not realising, and he felt guilty for not taking it more slowly, more gently—he would have done if he'd known. He was angry too, incomprehensibly. Angry with Ciro, for putting him in this position, but mostly with Imma.

He swallowed against the rush of questions rising in his throat.

Why hadn't she told him?

Why hadn't she said anything?

It made no sense.

But there was nothing he could do about it now. No magic spell to turn back time.

'I am?' He frowned. 'Sorry, I thought… I mean, I know you went to university, so…'

She shrugged casually, her hands trembling as she spoke. 'I didn't live in halls. My father bought me an apartment and insisted on my bodyguards going everywhere with me.'

'So those "others" you mentioned…you didn't…?'

Imma shook her head. 'I never wanted any of them in that way. Not like I wanted you.' She hesitated. 'Is it a problem?'

She was staring up at him, and the expression on her face made him swear silently. He needed to make this all right, and fast, or risk blowing everything.

Shaking his head, he touched her cheek. 'Quite the

contrary.' His face twisted. 'I can't believe I'm saying this, but I like it that I'm your first.'

Imma stared at him, her pulse beating out of time.

'Actually, I'm a little embarrassed by how happy it makes me feel,' he added.

Her stomach clenched and blood rushed into her pelvis. Her body was rippling back to life as he pulled her closer.

Breathing out unsteadily, he buried his face in her neck. 'Imma, do you think it's possible for two people to fall in love in a single day?'

Her heart lurched against her ribs. His dark eyes were soft and steady on her face, but she could hear the shake in his voice.

She took a deep breath. 'I do,' she said softly.

'And could you maybe see yourself saying *I do*?' He stared down at her. 'If I asked you to marry me.'

'You don't have to marry me,' she said shakily. 'It was my decision not to say anything. I should have told you I was a virgin—'

'That's not why I want to marry you.'

His arms tightened around her, and she knew he was telling the truth.

'I know it sounds crazy, but I have to marry you—there's no other option for me.'

The poetry of his words made her heart swell.

She was too choked to speak, but as he lowered his mouth to hers she leaned into him, her hands threading through his hair, and kissed him fiercely.

They made love again, and afterwards she fell asleep in his arms.

She was still wrapped in his arms sometime later,

when she woke in the early hours, and for a moment she lay on her side, watching Vicè sleep.

There were no words to describe how she was feeling. She was happy—had never been happier—but 'happy' felt too ordinary, too small a word to describe what had just happened.

It was everything she'd wanted for her first time. He had wanted her for herself, just as she had wanted him, and his desire had made her feel sensual. Confident. Powerful. Even when her body had dissolved into hot, endless need.

She still felt as if she was glowing inside.

And it wasn't just the sex.

It was Vicè.

She had fallen helplessly in love with him. And, incredibly, he felt the same way about her. He must do to have proposed.

Her heart trembled.

She might not have his experience, but she had learned enough about the world to know that a man like Vicè didn't propose marriage after every sexual encounter.

Given his track record with women, he must have been hoping simply to seduce her. It had probably never crossed his mind that he would fall in love any more than it had hers.

Glancing over at him, she felt her throat tighten.

He was so beautiful, so gorgeously masculine, all muscle and smooth golden skin, and he'd been so generous. Remembering how his body had felt, on hers and in hers, her muscles tensed.

Suddenly she was hot and damp and aching.

It had been so good.

Felt so right.

His weight and the press of his mouth…the rush of his heartbeat.

Could she wake him?

She bit her lip. Would that be greedy? Too forward?

He shifted in his sleep, turning his face into the crook of his arm, and she breathed out unevenly.

She was so, *so* happy. The only thing that would make it even more perfect was if she could share her happiness with Claudia. But it was too early—and anyway it was her sister's wedding night.

She frowned. Across the room, she could hear her phone ringing. Slipping out of bed, she picked it up, her heart fluttering with joy. It was Claudia. But of course it was—they had always had the ability to communicate almost telepathically.

She tiptoed out of the bedroom, closing the door softly behind her. 'Hey, you! I was just—'

'Oh, Immie, something terrible has happened.' Claudia's voice was high and trembling.

Imma's breath scrabbled inside her chest. 'Don't cry, *mia cara*. What is it? Tell me.'

'It's all a lie, Immie. He doesn't love me.'

Her heart pounded fiercely. 'Of course he does—'

'He doesn't. He didn't know I was there and I heard him talking on the phone—'

'That can't be right…' The phone felt slippery in Imma's hand and she clutched it more tightly. 'Ciro loves you.'

'No, he doesn't, Immie. He doesn't. He just married me to get revenge on Papà. And Vicenzu is planning to do the same to you.'

The room swayed. For a moment she couldn't breathe. Her lungs felt as though they were full of sand.

It couldn't be true. Claudia must have made a mistake. Vicè wouldn't do that—

But as her sister began to cry she knew that he had.

CHAPTER FOUR

Rolling over onto his side, Vicè shifted against the pillow, his hand reaching across the bed for—

His eyes snapped open.

For Imma.

But the bed was empty.

He raised himself up on his elbow, his pulse accelerating as he heard the sound of running water from the bathroom. He glanced at the clock by the bed, realising how late in the day it was. She must be showering.

Only it wasn't the thought of a naked Imma with water streaming over the soft curves of her body that was making his pulse beat faster. It was the sharp, shocking realisation that he had been reaching out for her—for the daughter of his enemy.

Except she hadn't felt like his enemy—not when she'd been moving on top of him with her hair tumbling over her shoulders and a dazed look in those incredible olive green eyes.

When she'd walked out of the bathroom last night, naked except for that tiny wisp of underwear, he'd forgotten all those weeks of anger and doubt. In that moment he had simply been a man swept away by lust.

He gritted his teeth. But now his feelings were less

simple—they were downright confused, in fact, and for one very obvious reason.

He hadn't signed up for taking her virginity.

In fact, he'd never slept with a virgin before, and if he'd been going to start it wouldn't have been with *this* woman.

Taking Imma's virginity felt like a bond—a connection between them that didn't fit well with the task in hand. And yet...

He might have made a joke of it earlier, but almost against his will—flying in the face of everything he knew to be logical—he liked being her first lover.

His skin felt suddenly hot and taut. Even to admit that privately to himself blew his mind. When had he turned into such a caveman?

But there was no point in pretending. Satisfaction that he had been her first still resonated inside him.

And affected him on the outside too, apparently.

Gritting his teeth, he lifted the sheet away from his erection. He didn't understand what was happening to him. Imma was very beautiful, and she felt even better than she looked. But he was remembering how she'd fallen asleep, with her body curled around his. He let go of a breath he hadn't realised he was holding.

No matter how attractive the woman, or how intense his desire, he had never felt even the slightest impulse to hold any of his lovers in his arms while he slept.

It must have been finding out she was a virgin. There was no other explanation.

Rolling onto his back, he frowned up at the ceiling. He was irritated at having to feel anything but his usual sense of repletion. He certainly hadn't planned on dealing with all this complicated stuff.

But was it really that complicated? So she'd been a virgin? So what?

She was an adult, and she had wanted sex as much as he had. Getting fixated on being her first lover was making him lose sight of what mattered—the fact that for once he'd done what he'd set out to do.

It had been a playbook seduction. He'd used his hands, his mouth, his body expertly to turn her on, touching her and tormenting her until she had melted into him, her moans of ecstasy filling the silent room.

Agreed, her virginity had added a layer of confusion—but surely it would make the likelihood of her marrying him and therefore getting back the business a shoo-in.

He was going to push for the soonest date possible for their wedding. After that, all that would remain would be for him to persuade her to sign the paperwork.

Then it would be done.

Revenge would be theirs.

But he was jumping ahead of himself. His moment of triumph would need to be savoured properly with Ciro, over a cigar, and probably some of that bourbon his brother loved so much. Right now there were other things to savour.

His pulse twitched and he felt hunger course through his veins like a caffeine rush.

So why not simply enjoy the ride?

He glanced over at the bathroom door. Maybe he would join her in that shower, after all…

But just as he was about to throw back the sheet, the door to the bathroom opened. Remembering her entrance last night, he felt his gaze narrow—but this time Imma wasn't naked. In fact—disappointingly—she was fully clothed.

His eyes drifted lazily over the simple white cotton dress she was wearing and he felt a pulse of heat bumping over his skin. He wasn't averse to watching her take it off.

Sprawling back against the pillows, he lifted his eyes to hers and smiled. 'Hi.'

'Hi,' she said quietly.

She didn't move, just stood in the doorway.

'Did you sleep well?'

She nodded. 'Yes, thank you.'

'Are you okay? I mean—'

She nodded again. 'Everything's fine.'

He felt relief slide over his skin. He'd been a little worried that, having had time to think, she might want to do some kind of post-mortem. Clearly, though, she had other things on her mind.

She took a deep breath. 'Vicè, last night you asked me to marry you. I wondered if you meant it? Or if you just got carried away in the heat of the moment?'

'Of course I meant it.' Throwing back the sheet, he got up and walked swiftly around the bed to where she stood in the doorway. 'I want to marry you. I want to do it as soon as possible. Only…'

He hesitated, a rush of triumph sweeping over his skin as her eyes searched his face. *He had done it*. She was hooked. His father's business was as good as his.

'Only what?'

'Only I don't remember you actually saying yes.'

'Oh!' she gasped in a rush. 'Then, yes… I will marry you. But first there's something I want to do.'

There was only a sliver of space between them. Her gaze dropped to his naked body and he felt his groin harden again in time with his accelerating heartbeat. *Really? She was going to...?*

She slapped him across the face.

He swore. 'What the hell—'

'You are a *monster*.'

The softness in her voice was gone, and it was gone from her eyes too. She looked and sounded coldly furious.

'You and that despicable brother of yours.'

She slapped his other cheek, equally hard.

'How could he do that to her? How could you both be so cruel?'

Stunned, his face stinging, he caught her hand as she lifted it to strike him again. A flush of panic and confusion swirled in his chest.

'I don't know what—'

She struggled against his grip. '*Basta!* Enough!' She tugged her hand free. 'I've had enough of your lies. I know none of this is real, Vicenzu. I know because I've read the texts you sent your brother. And I've heard his voicemail.'

She pulled his phone from her pocket and he stared at it in silence. A cold, dull ache was spreading over his skin, turning his blood to ice.

'You didn't bother locking it—but then I suppose you didn't think you needed to. I mean, why would you be worried about *me*? A woman who was stupid enough to gift-wrap her virginity for you.'

'That's not fair!' he snarled. 'If you'd told me, I would have—'

'You would have what?' She folded her arms across her chest, her green eyes wide with contempt. 'Given up? Gone home? *Yeah, right*,' she jeered. 'And forgot-

ten all about taking back your precious olive oil company. I think not. You might be careless about most
things—like the truth…' She paused, her expression
not just hardening, but ossifying. 'But clearly you care
about that.'

He flinched inwardly, the truth of her words slicing
through him to the bone.

But this conversation was always going to happen,
he told himself quickly. It wasn't as if he and Imma had
ever been going to celebrate their ruby wedding in forty
years, like his parents had.

The memory of the last time he'd visited his parents'
home made his spine tense painfully. At the time he'd
vaguely registered that his father looked a little tired
and seemed a little quieter than usual, but it had been
easy—shamefully easy—to just tell himself that his
dad was getting old.

Except now Alessandro would never get old. That
was on him, even more than on his brother, but the person really responsible for this mess was this woman's
father: Cesare Buscetta.

She held up his phone. 'Perhaps you've forgotten
what you wrote? Perhaps you'd like me to read your
text to you? Just to remind you.'

'I know what I wrote, Imma,' he said coldly. He
met her gaze and then, reaching down, picked up his
clothes from last night, pulling them on with deliberate unconcern.

Her eyes were sharp, like shards of broken glass.
'You know what makes all this so much worse? I already *knew* about your reputation with women. I *knew*
you couldn't be trusted. But then we talked, and you
made me believe that people had been wrong about you.

That you weren't some spoilt playboy with nothing in his head except living *la dolce vita*.'

She shook her head, and even though he was angry he couldn't stop his brain from focusing on the way her still damp hair was turning her white dress transparent.

'And I was right.' She stared at him, contempt mingling with loathing in her green eyes. 'You're not just a spoilt playboy—you're also a vicious, unprincipled liar.'

'Says the woman who didn't bother telling me she was a virgin,' he snarled, feeling the dam inside him breaking.

A part of him knew that he was only angry with her because he was in the wrong. He had seduced her. Methodically, cold-bloodedly pursuing her at the wedding, gaining her trust, then using all his charm to woo her into bed.

And all the while he'd told himself that she deserved it. He'd thought he had her all figured out. Thought she was a silent witness to her father's behaviour.

Only then she'd told him she was a virgin, and for some reason that had changed everything. It had made him feel responsible, guilty, and that wasn't fair.

'You should have told me,' he said.

'About my virginity?' Her eyes narrowed. 'Why? What difference would it have made?'

He was in a blind fury now. 'It would have made a difference to me!'

She was either incredibly naive or disingenuous if she thought that any man wouldn't want to know whether a woman had ever had sex before.

'Oh, and this is all about you. You and your stupid vendetta.' Her lip curled. 'You were lying to me, Vicè. And you would still be lying to me now if I hadn't confronted you. Tossing a few rose petals on the bed and lighting some candles wouldn't have changed anything.'

Porca miseria! Vicè stared at her, hearing her words pinballing around inside his brain. He wasn't talking about rose petals and candles. He was talking about the rules of interaction between couples.

'So what if I lied?' he asked. 'You lie all the time. To me. To other people. To yourself—'

'Excuse me?' Her voice was a whisper of loathing.

'All that garbage about your father wishing he could have "helped" mine sooner.' *Helped!* The word curdled in his mouth. 'Turning a blind eye to his arm-twisting doesn't absolve you. It was your monstrous father hounding him, breaking him down month after month, that sent my father to an early grave—as you very well know.'

'That's not true.' She spat the words at him. 'Papà told me what happened. How your father had over-stretched himself. How he came and asked to be bought out. Maybe he didn't want you and Ciro to know the truth.' She gave him a withering glance. 'I mean, why would he? He clearly knew neither of his sons had what was needed to save his life's work.'

Vicè flinched inwardly. One son certainly hadn't.

A stiletto of pain stabbed him beneath the ribs. Pain followed by rage. With her, for seeing what he was so desperate to hide, and with himself for not having been the son his father had needed.

Instead he had been an additional burden in Alessandro's time of need. For in trying to protect him, his son, his father had been left with nobody to turn to.

'Your father is a thief and a thug,' he said slowly. 'He stole the business my great-grandfather founded and the house where my parents lived their whole married life. Thanks to him, my mother lost her husband and her home all in one day.'

Her face turned pale, but then she rallied, lifting her chin so that her gaze was level with his. 'And is your mother in on this too?'

The tightness in his chest was unbearable. *What? No.* My mother is a saint. She's the sweetest person on earth.'

'I thought so.'

Her eyes hadn't left his face, and now there was something unsettling in her steady, stinging gaze.

'That's why we're going to get married,' she said.

He stared at her in confusion. *Get married? She still wanted to marry him?* Surely she was joking?

As though she could read his mind, she gave a humourless laugh. 'What's the matter, Vicè? Have you had a change of heart?' Her eyes narrowed. 'Oh, sorry, I forgot—you don't have a heart.'

Imma swallowed past the lump in her throat. It hurt to breathe. It hurt to speak. It hurt to look into his eyes and see nothing but hatred and hostility where only hours earlier she had thought she'd seen love.

She was such a fool. Had she really believed that this beautiful angry man could see past her defensiveness and gauche manner to what was inside? To value and desire what he saw there?

Their night together had been perfect, unrepeatable, miraculous—so that even when he had pulled her closer, or she had reached out for him, it had felt illusory…like an all too vivid dream.

And now she was living in a nightmare of her own

making, and no amount of daylight was ever going to wake her up.

If only she could go back in time—back to before Claudia had called her, back to that moment when she had been held in the muscular warmth of his arms. When her heart, her pride, had still been intact.

But it was too late for regrets. All that mattered now was making him pay. And she was going to keep telling herself that until it felt true.

His face darkened. 'And you, like the rest of your rotten, corrupted family, have no soul.'

Her eyes blazed into his. 'You are nothing to me now—just as I was nothing to you.'

She'd felt something—something real—but for him it had all been a trick, a con, a hoax.

The pain made her want to throw up.

He took a step forward. 'Great reason to get married.'

'It's about on a par with yours.' Pushing past the pain, she filled her voice with contempt. 'You slept with me under false pretences, Vicè. You faked your way into my bed. At least now we both know what's real and what isn't.'

He shook his head. 'What happened last night in your bed *was* real. You wanted me as much as I wanted you.'

Oh, he was good. He was so convincing—so plausible. Even now, when they both knew the truth, he made it sound as if he really believed what he was saying.

She shook her head. 'Actually, you *wanted* my father's business.'

Breathing out raggedly, she watched his face darken. 'No, I wanted *my* father's business.'

'Then you should have approached me with an offer.'

'I'm not going to pay for what was stolen from me.'

The hardness in his voice pressed against the bruise on her heart. The pain of trying to pretend spread out inside her like a rain cloud. Tears pricked behind her eyes and she blinked them away furiously, determined not to show any weakness in front of him.

'No, *I* paid. With my virginity.'

She felt a rush of shame and misery, remembering how her body had softened and melted from the heat of him.

His flinch was small, fleeting, but she saw it.

'Is that the going price for an olive oil company these days?' she taunted.

A flush of colour crept over his cheeks, but his eyes were cold. When he spoke his voice was colder still. 'For the last time, I didn't know you were a virgin.'

'Don't try and pretend you have a conscience, Vicenzu.' Her simmering pain gave way to an even hotter anger. 'You wanted to marry me and you will. Only it will be on my terms. Not yours. And if you refuse then I will find your mother and tell her exactly how you and your brother have behaved,' she said, her voice shaking slightly. 'I will tell her what kind of men the boys she raised have become.'

Her threat was empty. She wouldn't do it. She didn't want to marry him, and nor would she do anything to hurt Audenzia.

But she wanted to hurt him like he'd hurt her, and this was the only way she could think to do it.

His face hardened and the look in his eyes made her want to weep.

'I thought your father was a monster, but you...you are something else.'

And she had thought Vicenzu was the kind of man

who crossed any number of boundaries, but not ruthlessly or with wanton cruelty.

Jabbing his phone into his chest, she met his gaze head-on. 'Yes, I am. I'm your nemesis, Vicenzu.'

Her face was aching with the effort of blanking out the beauty of his high cheekbones and full mouth... the mouth that had so recently kissed her into a state of feverish rapture.

His eyes narrowed. 'You really are Daddy's little girl, aren't you? Except that he uses threats and then violence to get what he wants.'

Smiling bitterly, she shook her head. 'What happened to *"what they can't find out, they make up"*?'

He stared at her incredulously. 'I wasn't talking about your father.'

'Well, you couldn't have been talking about yourself. Nobody in their right mind could make this up.' Her voice rose. 'How could you do this to me? How could you be so cruel?'

'You think *I'm* cruel?' He took a rough breath, his face hardening. 'Me? No, I'm just an amateur, *cara*.' He typed something into his phone, scrolled down the screen. 'This is the real deal. Here—' Letting his contempt show, he pressed the phone into her hand. 'You like reading my messages? Read these and then tell me who the bad guy is.'

She stared at him. Her lungs felt as if they were on fire. 'I don't need to. *You* are the bad guy, Vicenzu.'

And, sidestepping past him, she walked quickly away—going nowhere, just wanting, needing, to get as far away as possible from his cold-eyed distaste and the wreckage of her romantic dreams.

She half expected him to come after her, as he had

last night. But of course last night he'd been playing her. Last night he'd only come after her because he'd been playing his part, doing whatever it took to get the family business back.

Whatever it took.

Like having sex with her.

The thought that having sex with her had been one step en route to the bigger prize, a means to trap and manipulate her, made her feel sick.

She had wanted her first time to be perfect. To be her choice and not just an expected consequence of her marriage vows. Had wanted it to be with Vicè, because in her naivety—idiot that she'd been—she had liked and trusted him.

And when he'd walked towards her at the wedding, his dancing eyes and teasing laughter trailing promises of happiness, she'd fallen in love with him.

As she reached the terrace tears began to fill her eyes and she brushed them away angrily.

She had been stubborn and vain. Ignoring and defying her father's words of warning and letting herself be flattered by Vicè's lies. Her pain was deserved. But Claudia's...

Her eyes filled with tears again, and this time she let them roll down her cheeks. She had let her sister down. Worse, she had broken her word.

She had been eight years old when she made that promise—too young to understand that her mother was dying, but old enough to understand the promise she was making. A promise to take care of her younger sister, to protect her and keep her safe in the kind of cruel, unjust world that would leave two young children motherless.

She had always kept her word. Protecting Claudia at school, and at home too. Shielding her from the full force of Cesare's outbursts and trying to boost her confidence by encouraging her love of cooking and gardening.

Only now she had broken that promise.

Remembering her sister's stunned, tearful call, she felt another stab of guilt. Claudia was her priority. She would do whatever her sister wanted—help in any way she needed. Then she would face her father.

But first...

Her fingers tightened around the phone in her hand—Vicè's phone.

She found what she was looking for easily—an email from the family lawyer, Vito Neglia, to Ciro and Vicenzu, plus further emails between Alessandro and Neglia.

She scrolled down the screen, her eyes following the lines of text.

It made difficult reading.

Alessandro Trapani had been unlucky—machinery had broken and mistakes had been made. He had taken out a loan with the bank and then his troubles had begun to escalate. There had been accidents at work, then more problems with machinery, and he had started to struggle to meet the repayments.

Her heart jolted as her father's name leapt out from the screen. But she had been right, she thought with a rush of relief. Cesare had offered cash for the business with the proviso that the sale would include the family estate. She took a steadying breath. It was just as her father had told her. Papà had only been trying to help.

She glanced back down at the screen and some of her relief began to ooze away.

Alessandro had refused her father's offer. But then he hadn't been able to pay one of his suppliers—and, with the bank putting increasing pressure on him over the repayments, he'd gone back to Cesare.

This time her father had offered twenty percent less.

With no other options left, Alessandro had had no choice but to accept.

But that was just *business*, she told herself, trying to push back against the leaden feeling in her stomach. Probably if the circumstances had been reversed Alessandro would have done exactly the same.

Clearly Neglia didn't agree with her.

He had done some digging around and, although he had found no direct link to her father, there was clearly no doubt in the lawyer's mind that Trapani employees had been bribed to sabotage the machinery.

And her father had been behind it.

Imma's throat worked as she struggled to swallow her shock. She felt sick on the inside. Her skin was cold and clammy and her head was spinning.

She didn't want it to be true.

But the facts were stark and unforgiving.

Cesare had used bribery and intimidation to ruin a man's business and steal it away from him. The fact that he had also demanded Alessandro's home made her heart break into pieces.

Hot tears stung the back of her eyes. No wonder Ciro and Vicè hated him. But, whatever her father had done, it didn't give them the right to punish her and Claudia, and she hated both of them for that.

Only despite everything she had read, she couldn't

bring herself to hate her father. It wasn't an excuse, but she knew he would have done it for her and for Claudia.

Cesare was not stupid. He'd heard the rumours about his 'friends' and his shady dealings. And she knew that he wanted something different for his daughters. That was why they had been educated at the convent. That was why they'd been raised like princesses in a tower.

And that was why he had used every trick in the book to acquire a 'clean' business and a beautiful family estate—as gifts for his beloved girls.

The world suddenly felt very fragile.

She forced air into her lungs, tried to focus.

She couldn't hate her father, but she couldn't face moving back home either. She needed space, and time to think about all of this—about her part in it and her future.

Her future.

She sank down in one of the chairs, wrapping her arms around her stomach. She felt incredibly, brutally tired. Tired of not knowing who she was or what she wanted.

Her heart pounded. She had thought she wanted Vicè—that he had wanted her. She had been wrong about that too. And yet on one level she didn't regret what had happened. Having sex with him had unlocked a part of herself she hadn't known existed.

She had discovered a woman who was wild and alive and demanding, and she liked that woman. She wanted to find out more about her, and that was another reason she needed time and space.

Time and space—those words again.

She wouldn't have either living at home with Papà. But sooner or later she was going to have to tell him that she had slept with Vicè, and then he would insist on her marrying someone of his choosing.

Her pulse slowed and she sat up straight, biting her lip, listening to the distant sound of the waves.

Maybe, though, there was another option…

Clenching his jaw, Vicè stared around the empty bedroom.

He was still in shock. The script he'd planned for today had unravelled so fast, so dramatically, and in a way he could hardly believe possible.

Just when everything had been falling into place so beautifully.

Everything.

She'd even agreed to marry him.

So how come he was standing here with his face still stinging and her ultimatum ringing in his ears?

Behind him the tangled bed sheets were like a rebuke or a taunt and, feeling as if the walls were starting to shrink around him, he crossed the room, yanking open the door and stepping through it in time with his pounding heartbeat.

It was his fault.

Actually, no, it was hers.

If she had told him the truth about being a virgin in the first place he might not have been so distracted, so caught off balance.

He might even have locked his phone.

His chest tightened. How could he have been so unforgivably stupid and careless? When Ciro found out he was going to go ballistic. He might never speak to him again.

The one consolation in this whole mess was that

Ciro had already managed to get the house back. He knew his brother: Ciro was a fast worker. Claudia had agreed to sign over the house before she'd learned the truth, and those documents would be signed and witnessed by now.

But what did he have to show for himself?

Niente, that was what!

He had nothing.

He gave a humourless smile. He was trapped on an island with a woman who basically wanted to cut off his *palle* and fry them up for brunch.

Glancing back into the bedroom, he ran a hand over his face, wishing he could as easily smooth over the last few hours of his life.

The shock of being unmasked had shaken him more than he cared to admit—as had Imma's threat to speak to his mother. Although now he'd had a chance to cool off he knew she'd been bluffing.

But what had really got under his skin was the sudden devastating loss of the woman who had melted into him just hours earlier.

Gone was the passion, the inhibition of the night, when she had arched against him, her body moving like a flame in the darkness. Now in her eyes he might as well be something that had crawled out from under a particularly dank and slimy rock.

And, even though he knew logically that it shouldn't matter what Imma thought about him, he didn't like how it made him feel. Didn't like being made to feel like he was the bad guy.

There was only one bad guy and that was her father.

From somewhere nearby a phone buzzed twice. Glancing down, he saw that it was his.

It was sitting on a small table and he felt his stomach tense. Imma must have left it for him. Feeling a sharp stab of guilt and misery, he picked it up, swearing under his breath.

His stomach dipped. It was Ciro.

His brother's message was short and to the point.

I can't talk now, but it's all gone belly-up here so you need to pull your finger out.

For a moment he let his finger hover over his brother's number, and then, swearing loudly this time, he pocketed the phone.

He couldn't deal with his brother right now. He had to get his head straight first.

He was clenching his jaw so tightly that it ached.

Nine weeks ago he would have walked away.

But nine weeks ago he still had a father.

Tilting his head back, he closed his eyes. He still couldn't believe that he would never see Alessandro again. His father had been his mentor, his defender—more than that, he had been his hero. He had been the best of men...fair, kind, generous and loving.

Opening his eyes, he breathed out unevenly. He'd given up any hope of ever being his father's equal a long time ago, but he could do this one thing and do it right.

He had let down Papà in life; he would not do so now.

Imma was not going to have everything her own way.

He'd sat around listening to his father and Ciro talk business enough to know that she had overplayed her hand with him, and let her emotions get the better of her. In her anger, she had threatened the very thing he had wanted all along.

He *would* be her husband—but he was not going to walk away empty-handed. He was going to take back the Trapani Olive Oil Company and there would be nothing his future 'wife' could do about it.

He found her out by the pool, staring down at the smooth turquoise surface of the water. In her white dress, and with her long dark hair flowing over her shoulders, she looked as young and untested as her name suggested, and her slender body reminded him of the delicate honey-scented sweet peas that were his mother's favourite flowers.

It was hard to believe she was the same woman who had threatened to tell Audenzia the truth about everything he and Ciro had been doing. He gritted his teeth. Hard, but not impossible.

She turned towards him, folding her arms high across her ribs. But even without the defensive gesture he would have known that she had looked at the emails on his phone.

Her eyes were slightly swollen and she looked pale, more delicate. He felt a pang of guilt, but pushed it away. The truth hurt—so what? His mother had been widowed and forced to leave her home. That was real suffering.

'I read the emails,' she said quietly. 'I don't know what to say except that I'm sorry for how my father acted, and for what I said earlier about talking to your mother.' She took a breath. 'I was angry, and upset, but I want you to know that I would never do anything to hurt her. I know she had nothing to do with this.' Her eyes met his, steady, accusatory. 'I would never punish an innocent bystander.'

Her words stung. No doubt she'd intended they

should. But he was surprised by her apology. He hadn't expected that—not from anyone bearing the Buscetta surname. Only if she thought that was somehow going to be enough...

He took a step towards her. 'And the marriage proposal?' he said softly.

Her green eyes narrowed. 'Yours or mine?' she shot back.

'Does it matter?'

'I suppose not.'

He heard the catch in her voice, and before he could stop himself he said, 'So tell me, Imma, if you're not looking for revenge then why exactly do you want to marry me?'

Her arms clenched and, watching the fabric of her dress tighten over her nipples, he felt his pulse snake, remembering how just hours earlier they had hardened against his tongue.

She shrugged. 'My father is a traditional Sicilian male. Very traditional. Now that you and I have had sex he'll expect us to marry, and if we don't he'll find another husband for me.' Lifting her chin, she twisted her mouth into a small, tight smile. 'Essentially you're the lesser of two evils, Vicè.'

Chewing her words over inside his head, he felt his gut tense. *Wow!* That was a backhander. It certainly wasn't something he'd ever been called before.

She took a quick breath. 'If we marry, then obviously I'll be your wife legally. But in reality you'll just be there. In the background.'

In the background.

He wasn't sure if it was her disparaging description

of his upcoming role or her haughty manner, but he felt a pulse of anger beat across his skin.

'Sounds relaxing. Will I need to get dressed?'

That got to her. She wanted him still. He could see it in the flush of her cheeks and the restless pulse in her throat. Watching her pupils flare, he felt his own anger shift into desire.

Ignoring his question, she said coolly, 'Before we go any further, you should know that I have a condition.'

A condition?

'Is that so?' Taking a step towards her, he held her gaze.

She nodded. 'The marriage will last a year. That's long enough for it to look real. If we manage our diaries, then we shouldn't have to intrude into one another's lives beyond what's necessary.'

He stared at her in silence. All his life women had fawned over him, flattered and chased him. But now Imma was basically treating him like a footstool.

'I have a condition too,' he said silkily.

Seeing her swallow, he felt a flicker of satisfaction.

'I will stay married to you for a year. But I want it in writing now that you will sign the Trapani Olive Oil Company over to me at the end of that year.'

She searched his face. Probably she thought he was joking. When she realised he was being serious, she started shaking her head. 'You can't expect me to—' she began.

He cut her off. 'Oh, but I do. I find managing my diary very dull, so I'll need *some* incentive.'

He enjoyed the flash of outrage in her eyes almost as much as the way she bit down on her lip—presumably to stop herself from saying something she'd regret.

'Is that going to be a problem? Maybe you'd rather go back to bed and thrash all this out there instead.'

Silence followed his deliberately provocative remark, and he waited to see how she would respond, his body tensing painfully in anticipation of her accepting his challenge.

Two spots of colour flared on her cheeks and he saw her hands curl into fists. She wanted to thump him. Or kiss him. Or maybe both.

And, actually, either would be preferable to this tight-lipped disdain.

But after a moment she said stiffly, 'No, I would not.'

'Shame,' he drawled. 'Still, there's always the wedding night to look forward to.'

'Yes, there is.' She lifted her chin. 'But we'll be enjoying it in separate rooms. Just to be clear, this marriage is purely for show, Vicè. You won't be sharing my bed. Or having sex with me.'

Vicè felt his smile harden.

He'd already had to be celibate in the run-up to his brother's wedding. Not out of choice, but Ciro had insisted, and in the end he'd grudgingly accepted that any hint of scandal would ruin his chances of seducing Imma before he had even got to meet her.

Those nine weeks had left his body aching with sexual frustration. And now she was suggesting that that sentence should be extended to a year.

'Obviously you won't be having sex with anyone else either,' she added coldly. 'I won't have my family's name dragged through the mud by your libido.'

Their eyes met. 'I wouldn't worry about that, *cara*. Your father wallows in something far nastier than mud.'

His words drained the colour from her cheeks, but he

told himself that a woman who was prepared to enter willingly into this kind of marriage deserved no compassion on his part.

'That's rich, coming from you,' she said shakily. 'The man who seduced a virgin for revenge.'

He felt his gut twist. But he wasn't going to feel guilty about that. She should have told him—given him a choice about whether to do things differently.

She lifted one slender wrist and gazed down at her expensive gold watch. 'If you're done insulting me, then a simple yes or no will suffice.'

No. Absolutely not. Never. Not if my life depended on it.

He thought about his life before...*la dolce vita*.

A life of leisure and pleasure. A sweet life.

And then he thought about his mother, and his father, and the promise he had made to his brother.

'Yes,' he said.

CHAPTER FIVE

So she really was going to go through with this.

Glancing out of the window of the taxi, Imma felt her fingers tighten around the small posy of lilies of the valley in her lap. Beside her, his dark eyes shielded behind even darker glasses, his fingers pointedly entwined with hers, Vicè sat in silence.

To anyone else he would seem the perfect groom. Young, handsome, intent on marrying the woman he loved.

She swallowed past the ache in her throat. But of course he was good at pretending.

They had left the island and returned to the mainland, 'borrowed' Cesare's private jet and flown to Gibraltar. They had arrived in late last night, and booked into a discreet hotel on the edge of town, near the Botanic Gardens.

Separate rooms, obviously.

Not that it was really necessary. He might be almost painfully attentive in public, but as soon as they were alone he barely lifted his eyes to meet hers, choosing instead to stare at his phone.

And it hurt. Hurt in a way that seemed utterly illogical.

Or just stupid.

Yes, 'stupid' was the only way to describe this hollowed-out feeling of loss for something that had been so fleeting and false.

It didn't help that all the preparations had been so rushed and furtive, but she couldn't risk Cesare finding out and intervening.

Thinking about her father made her chest ache. She loved him still, but right now she didn't trust him—and she didn't trust herself to be around him. She was too angry and confused about everything she had found out, and her desolation and the sense of betrayal were still too raw.

She had no idea what to say or do next. But she did know that she didn't want anything to do with what he'd done to Alessandro. Which was why she'd agreed to hand over the business to Vicè in a year's time.

If she hadn't needed a bargaining chip to get some space and time away from her father she would have handed it over today. She hated owning the thing he wanted—hated knowing that it was the only reason he was here, sitting beside her in the car, on their way to a register office.

Her chest tightened. If they had been other people, or if the circumstances had been different, then maybe all this haste and secrecy would be exciting, impulsive and romantic. But instead it just felt sneaky.

Even though she had texted her father to say that she was at the villa, she kept expecting him to call, demanding to know when she was coming home. Obviously she hadn't told him she was in Gibraltar, and that made her nervous too.

But, judging by the long, rambling and gleeful voice-

mail Cesare had just left her, she had been worrying
for no reason.

He hadn't been fretting over her absence at all; instead he had been shooting boar on the Di Gualtieri
estate.

A shiver scuttled down her spine. Stefano di Gualtieri
was a fabulously wealthy local landowner and the great-
grandson of Sicilian nobility. He was her father's age, and
in her opinion he was a bore of a different kind—and a
snob. But, despite her hinting as much, she knew Cesare
saw him as a possible suitor for her hand in marriage.

Imma exhaled softly, trying to still the jittery feeling in her chest. If her father knew what she was about
to do…

But his prospective anger was not the only reason
she wanted to keep off his radar for as long as possible.
Since reading those emails, her world—everything she
had taken for granted about the man who had raised
her—had begun to look as fragile as the tiny, delicate
bell-shaped flowers in her hand.

She'd thought she knew her father so well. His
moods, his brusqueness, his maddening and stifling
overprotectiveness. Now, though, she felt as if she didn't
know him at all.

Obviously she'd heard the rumours about him, but
her father had always brushed them off: yes, some of
his friends were a little rough. You had to be tough
where he'd grown up—that was just how it was. And
he wasn't going to turn his back on his mates. What
kind of friend would do that?

*'That's why people say these things about me.
They're jealous,* piccioncina mia. *They hate me for*

dragging myself up out of the gutter so they scrape over my past...invent stories.'

It reminded her of what Vicè had said about people making up what they didn't know, and the thought that he had this, of all things, in common with her father made her want to leap out of the car while it was still moving.

Finding out that Cesare had behaved so ruthlessly made her feel sick. But finding out that he'd lied to her had been the reason why she'd finally decided to marry Vicè.

Okay, maybe at first she'd wanted revenge. Part of her still did. And she hadn't been lying when she'd told Vicè that he was the lesser of two evils. Her father would find her a husband, and she shuddered to think who he might choose.

But all her life she had struggled to know herself, and this revelation about her father made her feel she knew herself even less. Marriage to Vicè would at least give her the freedom to think about what she wanted to happen next.

And so this morning they had met with a notary, to complete the necessary paperwork. And now they were on their way to the register office.

Shifting in her seat, she glanced down at her dark blue polka-dot dress. It was the same one she'd worn to Claudia's wedding. And she hated it.

Not because it was a little boring, and cut for an older, more mature woman. But because it was so tied up with the now crushed romantic dreams of her little sister, and those few hours when Imma had mistakenly, humiliatingly, believed that Vicè was interested in her.

She could have bought another dress, but that would

have defeated the object. She needed this reminder of where vanity and self-delusion led. And anyway she wouldn't have known what to buy. What was the correct dress code for a marriage of convenience?

Her stomach clenched—doubt gripping her again. She could stop this now. Tell the driver to pull over... tell Vicenzu to get out.

Only then what?

Go back to the life she'd had?

Pretend that none of this had happened or mattered?

Blanking her mind, she sat up straighter. She didn't know if she could go back to her old life. And where could she go, what could she do, if she didn't return to it?

She didn't know that either. And that was why she would go through with this ceremony.

That way, at least she would have time to find the answers to all the questions swirling inside her head.

Feeling Imma shift beside him, Vicè felt his body tense. She was a good actress. Not for one moment would anyone guess that she was marrying him out of spite.

The solid rectangular shape of his phone pressing against his ribs reminded him of the brief but reassuring message his brother had sent.

Have secured the house. Keep your promise.

He should be pleased—and he was. And yet it would be such a relief if, just for once, his brother messed up. But of course—Ciro being Ciro—he had turned everything around. So now it was just him hurtling towards a broken bridge on a runaway train.

In the street, a group of young men jostled against the car, shoving each other and laughing at some shared joke. They looked so happy. And free.

He bit down on a sudden rush of envy. A week ago that would have been him. Now he was marrying a woman he hated. And she hated him.

But it would be worth it. For in a year the Trapani Olive Oil Company would belong to his family again.

'We're here.'

She turned to face him and smiled, and even though he knew it was for show his breath stuck in his throat. She shouldn't be marrying him like this. Where was her father now? Her bodyguards? Didn't anyone care that she was doing this?

He thought back to the way her face had changed when he had taken her that first time. The directness of her green gaze had clouded over, transforming her from sexy to vulnerable. And in that moment, he'd forgotten about her father, forgotten about his. There had been nothing but the whisper of pleasure skimming over his skin and the white heat building between them.

'We could do this with a bit more style, you know. Take some time,' he said.

'We don't *have* time.' Her voice was clipped. 'My father is binary in the way he approaches life. It's his way or no way. We need to present him with an irreversible fact—like a marriage certificate.' She met his gaze, her green eyes narrowing. 'I know this is a little basic, but unlike you I didn't have a couple of months to work everything out in detail. Shall we go in?'

The ceremony was short and functional.

The registrar, a pleasant woman in her fifties, spoke

her lines clearly, turning to each of them as she waited for their responses.

They had agreed to use English for the ceremony. But although they were both fluent, to her, the unfamiliar words made everything feel even more remote and pragmatic.

'Immacolata and Vicenzu, with your words today, I can now pronounce you husband and wife.' The woman smiled. 'And now you may seal the promises you have made with a kiss.'

Imma's expression didn't change, but Vicè felt her go still beside him. Glancing down, he saw that her green eyes were huge and over-bright, and her slim body was trembling like a wild flower in the wind.

It's just a kiss, he told himself.

And he lowered his head, assuming it would be nothing more than a passing brush of contact. But as their mouths touched he felt her lips part and instantly his body tensed, his insides tightening as a jolt of desire punched him in the gut.

Instinctively he slid his hand over her hip, tilting her face up to meet his and deepening the kiss.

Oh, but he hadn't meant to do that.

It was insane, stupid—beyond reckless—only he couldn't seem to stop himself.

He wanted her…wanted her with an urgency and intensity that was beyond his control.

He heard her breath hitch in her throat and was suddenly terrified that he would lose her—that he wouldn't be able to satisfy his hunger for her sweet, soft lips—but she didn't pull away.

Instead she leaned into him, her body moulding against his, and then he was pressing her closer, one hand sliding down her body, the other threading through her silky, dark hair.

His heart was pounding and his blood was surging through his limbs as an ache of need reared up inside him, pulsing and swelling, blotting out everything but the softness of her body.

From somewhere far away he heard a faint cough and, still fighting his drowning senses, he broke the kiss.

Imma was staring up at him, her green eyes unfocused, her lips trembling, and it was only the presence of the registrar and the two witnesses that stopped him from pulling her back into his arms and stripping that appalling dress off her body.

The registrar cleared her throat. 'Now, if you'd like to join me, we have the register here, all ready and waiting. Once that's signed, we're done.' She smiled. 'I'm sure you have plans for the rest of your special day.'

Vicè nodded. He did. But unfortunately for him, his marriage strictly forbade those plans being fulfilled.

Watching Imma sign the register, his shoulders tensed. It didn't matter that they had just come close to ripping off each other's clothes in public. Judging by the look on his new wife's face, that wasn't about to change any time soon.

Leaning back in her seat, Imma tilted her head sideways, gazing through the window at the cloudless blue sky. Her posture was determinedly casual, but her ears were on stalks and every five seconds or so her skin tightened and her stomach flipped up and over like a pancake in a skillet.

She felt on edge and distracted. And, even though

wild horses wouldn't have dragged it out of her, she knew she was waiting for Vicè to walk back into the cabin.

After the ceremony they had taken a taxi back to the private airfield, Vicè's hand still clamped around hers. But as soon as they had got on board the plane he had excused himself on the pretext of wanting to change into something less formal.

In reality, they had needed to give one another privacy to tell their respective families.

There was the sound of footsteps and instantly her nerves sent ripples of unease over her skin. But it was only the steward, Fedele, bringing a pot of coffee.

'Congratulations again, Signorina Buscetta—I mean Signora Trapani.' The steward smiled down at her. 'Would you like anything to go with your coffee? We have pastries and fruit.'

She shook her head. 'No, thank you, Fedele. But would you please thank the crew again for their kind words.'

It had been easy to tell the cabin crew that she was married, to receive their polite and no doubt genuine congratulations. Sharing the news with her father had been far less pleasant.

As predicted, Cesare had roared. For a good ten minutes he had threatened, reproached her, ranted and railed against her, his frustration and displeasure flowing unstoppably like lava from a volcano.

On any other day she would have tried to soothe him, to be the eye of calm at the centre of his storm.

But not today.

Maybe it had been the strain of the last few hours catching up with her, or perhaps she'd just been worried about letting the truth slip out, but she simply hadn't had it in her, so she had just let him rage until finally he'd registered her silence and said gruffly, 'So this Trapani boy—he loves you, does he?'

'Yes, Papà, he does.'

She'd heard her father grunt. 'And you love him?'

'I do—I really do.'

He'd sighed. 'Well, what's done is done. And if he makes you happy…'

It had been easier to lie than she had thought. Maybe it always was—maybe that was how her father managed to lie to her about Alessandro's business.

It hurt to think about all the other lies he might have told her. Only not as much as it had hurt having to stand next to Vicè at that dismal parody of a wedding and hear him repeat his vows knowing that he meant not one word of them.

She had heard him speaking, heard herself respond. She had watched the registrar smile and watched the witnesses sign the register. But she had felt totally numb, as though her veins had been filled with ice.

Until Vicè had kissed her.

Her heart bumped against her ribs as she remembered.

It had been as if he'd struck a match inside her. His mouth had tasted of freedom, and the warmth of his body against hers had seemed to offer danger and sanctuary all in one.

And just like that she had leaned into him, her body softening like wax touched by a flame. And all she knew was his closeness. And he had been all she wanted.

She shivered as a jolt of heat shot through her and

shifted in her seat, pressing her knees together, trying to ignore the flood of want.

Her cheeks felt hot. Yes, want. She wanted him.

Only how could she?

How could she still want Vicè after everything he had done? The lies he had told... The manipulation... The pretence...

But it didn't matter that it made no sense. It was the truth. And although she might be lying to her father, and to the cabin crew and to the rest of the world, she wasn't going to lie to herself.

The truth was that, even hating him as she did, with every fibre of her being, she still wanted him.

Kissing him should have been complicated.

Except it hadn't felt complicated.

It had been easy. Natural. Right. *Facile come bere un bicchiere d'acqua*, as her father liked to say when he was boasting about some deal he'd made.

But it was clearly just some kind of muscle memory kicking into action. It wouldn't happen again, of that she was certain. She might have been swept along in the moment, captivated by the swift, intoxicating intimacy of that kiss in an otherwise colourless ceremony, but—like the misplaced desire she had felt for Vicè yesterday—it had been just a blip.

'So how did it go? Am I going to be swimming with the fishes? Or did you manage to sweet talk him into accepting me as his son-in-law?'

A shadow fell across her face and, glancing up, she felt her pulse trip. Vicè was next to her, his dark eyes gazing down into her face, a mocking smile pulling at his mouth.

He was wearing a pair of jeans and a slim-fitting

navy T-shirt—the kind of low-key clothes that would make anyone else look ordinary. But Vicè didn't need logos or embellishments to draw the eye. His flawless looks and languid grace did that all on their own.

Dry-mouthed, she watched wordlessly, her heart lurching from side to side like a boat in a storm, as he dropped into the seat opposite her.

'It was fine. How about you?'

Ignoring her question, he picked up the coffee pot. 'How do you like it?' he murmured. 'Actually, no, don't tell me... I already know.'

Her stomach muscles trembled. She knew he was just talking about the coffee, but that didn't stop a slow, tingling warmth from sliding over her skin.

'I'm going to go with no milk and just a sprinkle of sugar.'

He held her gaze, his eyes reaching inside her so that for a moment she didn't even register what he'd said. Or that he was right.

Since agreeing to the terms of their marriage he'd been distant, cool, aloof... Sulking, presumably, at having the tables turned on him. Now, though, he seemed to have recovered his temper, and his dark gaze was lazily roaming her face. She knew it wasn't real but, try as she might, she couldn't stop herself—or her body anyway—from responding to him.

Annoyingly, she knew that he could sense her response and was enjoying it. The hairs on her arms rose. She had dictated the terms of their marriage. She was the one in control. So why did it feel as if he was playing with her?

Suddenly she wondered if she had done the right thing.

'Marianna told you,' she said quickly. She knew her face was flushed, and as he shook his head she frowned.

'She did not,' he said. His eyes hadn't left her mouth. 'But you're my wife, so I assume you want your coffee like your husband. Dark, firm-bodied, and with a hint of sweetness.'

He poured the coffee and held out a cup.

For a fraction of a second she hesitated, and then she took it. 'Thank you,' she said stiffly.

His eyes gleamed and, reaching across the table, he picked up his own cup. He seemed utterly at ease, and she wondered if he was still acting or if his mood really had changed.

It was impossible to tell. Up until a few days ago he'd been a stranger. Yet in the space of those few days so much had happened between them. Big, important, life-changing things.

'Sorry I took so long.' He lounged back in his chair, his dark lashes shielding the expression in his eyes. 'I needed to clear my mind. You know—' he made a sweeping gesture with his hand '—so much emotion after that wonderful ceremony. It was simple and yet so beautifully romantic.'

Hearing the mocking note in his voice, she gave him an icy glare. 'It's all you deserve.'

His gaze locked on hers. 'All I deserve?' He repeated her words softly. 'That's a missed opportunity.'

The glitter in his eyes made her nerves scream. 'What do you mean?'

Tilting his head back, he smiled slowly. 'Just that if I'd known you were trying to punish me I would have suggested something more exciting. Mutually satisfying.'

Her muscles tightened and she felt heat creep over

her cheeks. Stiffening her shoulders, she forced herself to look him in the eye. 'I wasn't trying to punish you. It was the only option under the circumstances. And I don't see why you even care about the ceremony anyway. You seduce virgins under false pretences. You don't do romance.'

Something flared in his eyes. 'I don't care, *cara*. But I can't believe a convent girl like you had that kind of ceremony pinned on her wedding board.'

Without warning he leaned forward and brushed her hair lightly with his fingertips. For a heartbeat she forgot to breathe. And then, as heat rushed through her body, she jerked backwards. 'What are you doing?'

'You have *coriandoli* in your hair,' he said softly, holding out his hand.

She gazed down at the rose petals, felt her pulse slowing. Vicè was wrong. She'd never planned her wedding day. In fact, she'd blocked it from her mind. Why would she want to plan a day that would so blatantly remind her that her life choices were not her own?

No, it had been Claudia—her sweet, overlooked little sister—who had dreamed of marriage and a husband and a home of her own.

Remembering her sister's tears, she curled her fingers into her palms. 'It's sweet of you to be concerned, Vicenzu,' she said. 'But I can have my dream wedding with my next husband.'

Vicenzu stared at her, her words resounding inside his head. *Seriously?* They had been married for less than two hours and she was already thinking about her next wedding? Her next husband?

His chest tightened. The thought of Imma being with

another man made him irrationally but intensely angry. And as his gaze roamed over her tight, taunting smile and the defiance in her green eyes, he felt his body respond to the challenge. To her beauty.

But his response wasn't just about the swing of her hair or the delicacy of her features—the dark, perfect curve of her eyebrows, the full, soft mouth, those arresting green eyes. There was something else…something hazy, elusive…a shielded quality.

Looking at her was like looking through a kaleidoscope: one twist and the whole picture shifted into something new, so that he couldn't imagine ever getting bored with her.

He felt his body harden. It had been a very long time since he'd got an erection from just *looking* at a woman.

Containing his temper, and the ache in his groin, he smiled back at her. 'But I'll always be your first, in so many ways, and that means something—don't you think?'

Watching colour suffuse her face, he knew he had got to her.

Leaning back in his seat, he glanced out of the window. 'So which godforsaken rock are we heading to now?' he asked tauntingly. 'Hopefully one with fewer monkeys and more beaches. I mean, this is our honeymoon, after all.'

'This is *not* our honeymoon.'

She leaned forward, her blush spreading over her collarbone, her narrowed green eyes revealing the depth of her irritation.

'This is business. We need to convince everyone, particularly our parents, that we are in love and that this marriage is real.'

Her mouth twisted.

'Otherwise you won't get your father's olive oil company back. And we both know that's all you're interested in.'

His pulse twitched. *Not true.* Right now he was extremely interested in whether the skin beneath the neckline of her dress was also flushed.

He forced his eyes to meet hers. Had she been inside his head on the flight over to Gibraltar, and in the car on the way to the register office, she would have found herself to be right. He had been furious at having lost the upper hand—having thrown it away, more like— and it had only been the thought of the family business that had kept him going.

Marriage to Imma was just a means to an end. In a year's time he would have his reward and he would have fulfilled his promise to Ciro. Vengeance would be his.

But a year was a long time. And right now, with Imma sitting so close, the business seemed less important than the way the pulse in her throat seemed to be leaping out at him through her skin.

'Fine…whatever.' He shrugged, lounging back and letting his arm droop over the back of his seat with a languid carelessness he didn't feel. 'But I meant what I said about monkeys and beaches.'

She gave him a look of exasperation.

'*Fine…whatever.* If it's such a big deal to you, then you can choose where we go.'

'Okay, then—let's go to Portofino. Let's go to my hotel.'

He'd spoken unthinkingly. The words had just appeared fully formed on his lips before he'd even realised what he was saying. Only now that he had said it, he knew that was what he wanted to do.

She was looking at him with a mixture of shock and confusion, as if he'd suddenly announced he wanted her to sleep in a bath of spaghetti. He felt nettled by her reaction.

For some inexplicable reason—maybe a desire to be on his home turf, or perhaps to prove there was a whole lot more to him than just a pretty face—he wanted her to see La Dolce Vita.

'Is that a problem?' he asked quietly.

But before she could reply, the steward appeared beside them.

'Signora Trapani—Chef would like to know if you're ready for lunch to be served?'

Imma nodded. 'Yes—*grazie*, Fedele.'

The steward began clearing the table.

'*Scusa*—I'm in the way. Here, let me move.'

Moving smoothly, Vicè swapped his seat for the one next to Imma. Taking advantage of Fedele's presence, he slid an arm around her waist, one hand snaking out to clasp hers firmly.

'That's better—isn't it, *cara*?'

She must have had a lot of practice in hiding her feelings, he thought, watching her lips curve into a smile of such sweetness that he almost forgot she was faking.

'You can let me go now,' she said quietly, her smile fading as Fedele disappeared.

'Why? He'll be back in a minute with lunch.'

He pulled her closer, tipping her onto his lap and drawing her against his chest. The sudden intimacy between them reminded him vividly of what had happened in her bedroom.

'Don't be scared, *cara*...' His heart was suddenly hammering inside his chest. 'This is just business...'

'I'm not scared,' she said hotly.

But she was scared. He could feel it in the way she was holding herself. Not scared of him, but of her response to him. Of this tingling insistent thread of need between them.

'Good,' he said softly. 'Because, as you so rightly pointed out, we need to convince everyone this is real— and that's not going to happen if we're sitting on opposite sides of the room. We need to practise making it look real.'

He stared down into her eyes.

'We need to act as if we can't keep our hands off one another. As if we want each other so badly it's like a craving. As if, even though it doesn't make sense, and it's never happened to us before and it's driving us crazy, we can't stop ourselves...'

That pretty much described how he'd been feeling ever since they'd met. How he was feeling right now, in fact. His blood was pounding in his ears and his body was painfully hard. He felt as though he was combusting inside.

Instinctively he lowered his face, sliding his hand into her hair.

'Vicè, stop—'

Stop? He hadn't even started!

Longing and fierce urgency rose up inside him, and as her fingers twitched against his chest it took every atom of willpower he had to stop himself from pressing his mouth to hers.

With an effort, he leaned back, smoothing all shades

of desire from his voice. 'So, are we going to Porto-fino, or not?'

There was a beat of silence, and then she nodded.

He kept his face still. 'I think ten days should be about right for a honeymoon. Or are you thinking longer...?'

'No.'

She shook her head, and he felt his stomach flip over at the sudden hoarseness in her voice.

'Ten days sounds perfect.'

Yes, it did, he thought, his body tensing as she slid off his lap.

Ten days.

And if he had his way every minute of all those days would be spent in bed...

CHAPTER SIX

IT WAS LATE afternoon by the time they arrived in Genoa. At the airport Vicè picked up his car—a surprisingly modest black convertible—and they drove south.

It wasn't just the modesty of his car that was surprising, Imma thought as they left the city's outskirts. Vicè was actually a good driver.

He was certainly nothing like her father. Cesare drove as he lived. Rushing forward aggressively and raging when he was forced to slow down or, worse still, stop.

Vicè drove with the same smooth, fluid grace as he did everything else.

She glanced over at him. They had barely spoken since setting off, but maybe that was a good thing. Every time they talked she seemed to start the conversation feeling in control but end it feeling he had the upper hand.

It didn't help that, despite everything she knew about him, her body persisted in overriding her brain whenever she was near to him.

Remembering exactly how near he had been earlier, on the plane, she felt a coil of heat spiral up inside her. She could tell herself it had been the plush intimacy of the plane or the glass of champagne that had affected her judgement. But it would be a lie to say she hadn't wanted him in that moment.

Only it was going to stop now. It had to.

This marriage might be a lie, but she couldn't lie to herself for a whole year.

She might have agreed theoretically with what Vicè had said on the plane, about making their marriage look real, but she knew she was going to find faking it far more difficult and painful than he would.

For him, those hours in her bed had been a necessary step in his plan to win back his father's business. A trick, a trap, a seduction.

For her, ignorant in her bliss, it had been something more.

He'd taught her about sex. About the sleek warmth of skin, the melting pleasure of touch and the decadent ache of climax.

It didn't matter that he'd been lying to her; her feelings for him had been real. And, even though she knew the truth now, the memory of how she had felt that night remained, overriding facts and common sense.

Admitting and accepting that would stop her repeating the reckless intimacy between them on the plane. But she needed to set some ground rules. Make it clear to him that she *would* play her part—but only in public, and only when absolutely necessary.

Feeling the car slow down, she glanced up ahead. The road was growing narrower and more winding. The palms of her hands were suddenly clammy.

Were they here?

As though he'd read her mind, Vicè turned towards

her and, taking one hand off the wheel, gestured casually towards the view through the windscreen.

'This is it. This is Portofino.'

She wasn't ready, she thought, her heart lurching. But it was too late. They were already cruising past pastel-coloured villas with dark green shutters, some strung with fluttering lines of laundry, others decorated with *trompe l'oeil* architectural flourishes that made her look twice.

The town centre was movie-set-perfect—a mix of insouciant vintage glamour and stealth wealth chic. Beneath the striped awnings of the cafes hugging the *piazzetta*, women in flowing, white dresses and men wearing linen and loafers lounged in the sunlight, talking and drinking Aperol spritz.

It was all so photogenic, so relaxed and carefree. A part of the world where *dolce far niente* was a way of life.

She swallowed, her throat suddenly dry. No wonder Vicè chose to live here. And now she would be living here too. Living here as Signora Trapani.

A shiver wound down her spine. Up until that moment she had been so focused on getting married she hadn't considered what being married would mean for her day-to-day life.

But here in Portofino, with Vicè, she would be free. For the first time ever there were no bodyguards tracking her every move, no Cesare dictating her agenda.

No rules to follow.

No rules at all.

Her stomach flipped over.

It was nerve-racking—like stepping from the safety of a ship onto new, uncharted land—and yet she wasn't scared so much as excited.

She let go of a breath. So much of her life had been spent feeling unsure about who she was, being scared to push back against the weight of duty and expectation. But without noticing she *had* pushed back, she realised with confusion. She had already changed, something shifting tectonically inside her.

How else could she be here with Vicè?

Her stomach knotted.

Much as she might want to flatter herself into believing that she had done so alone, incredibly—unbelievably— he was part of it. He had backed her into a corner and she had come out fighting. She had found another side of herself with him.

Feeling his gaze on the side of her face, she turned. 'It's beautiful,' she said simply.

His expression didn't alter, but she could sense he was pleased with her reaction.

'I'll save the guided tour for another time.'

His lip curved, and she felt his smile curl its way through her pelvis.

'I'm sure you'll be wanting to get out of those clothes.'

Refusing to take the bait, she lifted her chin. 'So what happens at the hotel?'

Shifting in his seat, he changed gear, his smile twitching at the corners of his mouth. 'Well, there are people who come and stay and use the rooms—I call them guests—'

She clenched her jaw. 'I meant what's the plan for us?'

'Relax, *cara*.' He was grinning now. 'We'll just play it by ear.'

'That's not a plan,' she snapped.

Back on the plane, she had told herself that it was a

good idea to come here. La Dolce Vita was a magnet for Hollywood actors, rock stars and rappers, so there was bound to be a bunch of paparazzi hanging around the hotel. Obviously they would be hot news for a couple of days, but it would all die down pretty quickly and then their lives could go back to normal.

'Normal' with the occasional necessary public display of affection.

Now, though, she was starting to see flaws in the plan—the major one being that Vicè didn't appear to have a plan.

'It'll be fine,' he said.

They were heading up a hill now, along a road edged with cypress trees and pines. Away from the town it was quieter, the air heavy with the scent of honeysuckle and lemon trees, and there was a surprising lushness to the greenery around them.

She felt the car slow again, her heartbeat accelerating as he turned between two scuffed pillars.

'Don't worry—I can do all the talking.'

He made it sound so easy. But then, of course, he was good at painting castles in the air.

Remembering how effortlessly he had persuaded her to believe in him, she gritted her teeth. 'As long as you keep to the script and don't contradict me—'

'Spoken like a true wife,' he said softly, stopping the car. Pulling off his sunglasses, he glanced over his shoulder. 'We're here.'

Her heart gave a startled leap and, blinking into the sunlight, Imma looked up and felt her mouth drop open. She'd seen photos, but nothing did justice to the building in front of her.

Surrounded by palm trees, flecked with sunlight, the

peaches-and-cream-coloured hotel oozed Italian Riviera style. But this was more than just a playground for VIPs, she thought, watching a flurry of petals flutter down from the wisteria-draped facade. It was magical, and the knowledge that Vicè was the man behind the magic made her heart hammer in her ears.

She jumped slightly as Vicè opened her door.

'It used to be a monastery, would you believe?'

He gave her one of his pulse-fluttering smiles and she bit her lip. In this mood he was impossible to resist— just like the hand he was holding out to her.

'No, I wouldn't.'

His fingers threaded through hers and she stepped out of the car, her muscles tightening as he slid an arm around her waist.

'It's true. The monks kept getting overrun by pirates, so they abandoned it. Moved further inland.'

'What happened to the pirates?'

'Oh, they're still here.' He smiled, his dark eyes glittering in the early-evening sunlight. 'One of them, anyway.'

The heat of his body matched the heat in his eyes. For a moment he stared down at her, and the pull between them she'd been trying so hard to ignore flared to life inside her.

'*Ehi, capo!* You're back!'

Swinging round, Vicè raised his hand, his smile widening as a young man with streaked blond hair, sleepy brown eyes and an equally wide smile strode towards them.

'Matteo. *Ciao!*'

'I was expecting you two days ago.'

'What can I say? I got distracted.'

As the two men embraced Imma watched in confusion.

Capo? Was Vicè his *boss?*

She tried and failed to picture any of her father's employees talking to Cesare in such a casual, effusive manner. But all she could think about were those emails she had read and his treatment of Alessandro.

She felt her stomach clench. She still wasn't ready to go there, and she was almost grateful when Vicè turned towards her, reaching out for her hand.

'Come here, *cara.*'

He pulled her closer, his dark gaze on her face.

'This beautiful woman is the reason I got distracted. Imma, this is Matteo, the hotel manager here and a good friend. Matteo—this is Imma, my wife.'

Her pulse jumped. Vicè was looking at her—really looking at her—so that it felt as if he was reaching inside of her, claiming her for his own.

'My wife,' he repeated softly.

It was an act, she told herself. It was all for show. Only she couldn't stop her stomach from turning over in an uncontrollable response to the intimacy of his words and the flame in his eyes.

For a split second time seemed to end. Just stop.

She forgot where she was and why she was even there. Around her the air seemed to thicken into an invisible wall, and inside the wall was Vicè, his skin dappled with sunlight, his dark gaze pulling her closer...

'You got married!'

She blinked as Matteo grabbed Vicè in a one-armed hug.

'*Che bello!* That's fantastic news. I'm so pleased for you both.'

'Thank you, bro. It was all a bit *di impulso.*' Glancing over at Imma, he grinned. 'What can I say? She swept me off my feet.'

Imma forced her mouth into a smile. Vicè made it all sound so plausible—no wonder Matteo was beaming at them in delight. But his congratulations were warm and genuine, and it felt wrong accepting them under such false pretences.

She felt a flash of anger. How was she going to do this for a whole year? Smile and lie to every single person she met? It was a daunting prospect, and the wider implications of what she'd agreed to do made her heart cramp.

She felt Vicè's hand tighten around hers.

'Matteo, can you get the bags brought round?'

'Sure, boss.'

'Come on.'

He turned and, still holding her hand, led her away from the hotel to a narrow path that disappeared into the lush undergrowth.

'I'll show you to the villa.'

She let him lead her between the citrus trees and beneath the boughs of myrtle and laurel, but as soon as they were out of sight she jerked her hand away.

'That's enough,' she snapped.

Vicè stopped. His pulse was racing.

In that moment when he and Imma had been talking to Matteo he'd forgotten that their marriage wasn't real. More confusingly, watching her face soften, he'd wanted it to be real.

Pulse slowing, he thought back to when he'd agreed to marry her. At the time he'd been too stunned by her conditions, too determined to get back his father's business, to think about what it would mean to live this particular lie. He'd been lying for so long, to so many people, why would one more matter?

Except now it did.

He wanted to stop, to erase the past and start again.

And not just his marriage to Imma. He wanted to go back—way, way back, to before his father's death—and live his whole life differently.

He turned to face her, his expression benign, one eyebrow raised questioningly. 'Enough what?'

'I don't want you touching me,' she snapped.

'Really?' he said, one eyebrow raised sceptically. 'You didn't seem to have any objections on the plane. You know, when you were sitting on my lap…'

Watching the pink flush rise over her face up to her hairline, Vicè held his breath. Was it embarrassment or desire? Maybe it was embarrassment at her desire?

Briefly he wondered what she would do if he pulled her closer and kissed her. Kissed her until she melted into him and she was his again. Beneath the overhanging greenery, he saw her eyes had darkened but, glancing over at her taut, flushed face, he pushed back against the heat rising like a wave inside his body.

Sadly this wasn't the right time or place.

'In fact, things seemed to be getting quite…*cosy.*' He drew the word out, elongating it deliberately until the colour in her cheeks grew darker.

She ignored his remark and, tipping her head back in the manner of a queen addressing a commoner, she gave him a glacial stare. 'Are you going to show me where we're going or do I have to find my own way?'

He sighed. 'Isn't it a little early in our married life

to start with the nagging, *cara*? Could we at least get
to our one-week anniversary first?'

Whistling softly, he sidestepped, moving past her
furious face.

Coming to Portofino had been a whim. But, watching her reaction as they'd pulled up in front of the hotel,
he had felt his stomach grow warm. She had obviously
been expecting some seedy 'no-tell motel', but he could
tell she was surprised. And impressed.

He breathed in on a rush of pleasure. Was it impressive? He tried to see it through her eyes.

To himself, and to everyone else too—especially his
family—he'd always downplayed how much he cared
about the Dolce, making out that it was more of a hobby
than a business so nobody would suspect that it mattered to him. But Imma's open-mouthed wonder made
him want to stop pretending and tell her how he really felt.

At the villa, he unlocked the door, feeling the usual
rush of conflicting emotions.

He loved the spacious rooms. The polished hardwood
floors, high ceilings and antique Murano chandeliers
all captured the glamour of a bygone era, and the tall
windows caught the gentle sea breeze and offered mesmerising views of the serene cerulean bay.

It was the perfect backdrop for his *dolce far niente*
lifestyle. But it was not home. Home would only ever
be his family's estate in Sicily.

Turning, he found Imma standing at the entrance,
one foot over the threshold. He felt his breath catch.
With her dark hair tumbling over her shoulders, and
anger mingling with apprehension in her green eyes,

she looked some like a woodland nymph who had stumbled across a hunter.

It took him a moment to realise that he was the hunter. Another to realise that he didn't like how that made him feel.

He felt something pinch inside his chest. Revenge was supposed to be sweet, but he hated the guarded expression on her face—*and* knowing that he was the cause of it.

'Okay, this is it. I'll give you a tour of the house first, and then we can just chill for a bit. Maybe have an *aperitivo* and then—'

Distracted by the various and all equally tempting versions of 'and then' playing out inside his head, he broke off from what he was saying and headed towards the kitchen.

He kept the tour brief and factual, opening doors and listing rooms.

'That's it for this level.' He gestured towards the staircase. 'Shall we?'

For a moment she stared warily back at him, as though he was Bluebeard, inviting her to see where he kept his other wives, and then, averting her gaze, she stepped past him. His chest tightened first and his groin next, as he caught the scent of her perfume, and he took a moment to steady himself before following her upstairs.

'There are no guest rooms,' he said. 'Not that we need any.' He gave her a slow, teasing smile. 'Guests on a honeymoon would be a little de trop, don't you think, *cara*?'

'Not on this one,' she said sweetly.

Touché, he thought, holding her gaze. He liked it that

he could get under her skin—metaphorically speaking. Of course, what he'd like more would be to actually strip her naked and lick every centimetre of her smooth, satiny body.

They had reached the top of the stairs.

The large, beautiful bedroom stretched the whole length of this floor, and it was filled with light and the scent from the honeysuckle that grew prolifically in the gardens below. Strangely, though, he could still smell Imma's perfume.

He watched as she stopped and turned slowly on the spot, stilling as she caught sight of their bags sitting side by side at the end of the bed.

'What did you say about the other bedrooms?'

'There are none.'

Catching sight of the vibrant aquamarine sea, he walked towards the French windows and opened them, blinking into the sunlight as he stepped onto the balcony.

'You know, sometimes you can see dolphins swimming in the bay. When the Romans came here there were so many of them they named it Portus Delphini—that's why it's called Portofino.'

Imma came and stood beside him. She was frowning.

'Say that again?'

'Portus Delphini—it means Port of the Dolphins—'

'I meant about the bedrooms.'

He dropped onto one of the chairs that were scattered casually around the balcony, extending his legs and stretching his arms above his head. He was fully aware that she was watching him, waiting for his reply, and the tension in her body made his own body grow taut.

'Oh, that…' he said casually. 'I said this is the only one. This is *our* bedroom.'

'No.' She shook her head, her green eyes narrowing. 'This is *your* bedroom. I will take a room at the hotel.'

Now he frowned. 'At the hotel? How is that going to work?'

She was looking at him as if she wanted to take off her shoes and throw them at his head.

'Very simply. You sleep *here*. I sleep *there*.'

He shook his head. 'You're not making sense, *cara*. We're supposed to be crazily in love. People who are crazily in love don't sleep in separate beds—never mind separate rooms in a different building.'

Eyes narrowing, she put her hands on her hips. 'But we're not in love, Vicè.'

Her voice was tense, and he heard the depth of her hurt and anger.

'Oh, I'm sorry—did you start to believe your own lies? I suppose that's what happens when you never tell the truth.'

His jaw tightened. 'You don't get to lecture me about the truth. Not after that show you put on in *your* bedroom the other night.'

For a moment he thought she was going to slap him again and knew on some level he would deserve it. Knew also that he didn't like this version of himself. Worse, he knew his father would be appalled. Alessandro had been a *gentiluomo*. He had treated everyone with the same quiet courtesy, but had reserved a special respectful tenderness for his wife.

'At least it was only one night,' she said acidly. 'Your whole *life* is a show, Vicè.'

Her blunt words felt like the waves that battered the coastline during winter storms.

He stared at her in silence.

Probably ninety-nine percent of what was written about him was untrue, or at best vaguely based on the truth, but he never bothered demanding a retraction. There was no point. His 'bad' reputation was good for business. And, as Ciro's brother, he had grown so used to unfavourable comparisons that he hardly registered them or even knew how to resent them.

But this woman seemed to know exactly which buttons to press. She made him feel things—good and bad—that no one ever had before. Somehow she'd sneaked under the barriers he'd built against the world, so that he was finding it harder and harder to maintain his usual couldn't-care-less attitude.

With an effort, he tethered his temper. 'I'm well aware we're not in love. But what matters is that we appear to be.'

'In public,' she countered. 'Look, we made an agreement—'

'Yes, we did,' he agreed. 'It's called marriage.'

Her chin jutted forward. 'A marriage that I made clear would not include our sleeping together.'

He shrugged. 'Okay, so go back to your father,' he said.

It was an idle threat. She had already made it clear that was not an option. But as her eyes darted towards the staircase he felt his heart jolt, his mind tracking back to the way she'd looked at him when Matteo had been there.

Her smile had felt like the sun breaking over this balcony in the afternoon. Warm and irresistible and real.

He didn't want her to leave.

In fact, he was determined that she should stay.

Obviously he wanted her to stay, or he wouldn't get his father's business back, but for some reason that seemed to matter less than getting her to share that soft, sweet smile with him in private.

'Let him find you another husband,' he said softly. 'Shouldn't be a problem. There must be a queue of men wanting to marry a woman who walked out on her wedding night. And, if not, I'm sure your *papà* will persuade someone to step up.'

Watching the colour leave her face, he knew she was cornered.

'You did this on purpose—didn't you?' she prompted, her incredible green eyes flashing with anger and resentment. 'You knew there was only one bedroom. That's why you wanted to come here.'

'Me? I'm just a passenger, *cara*,' he said disingenuously. 'This is your itinerary. I go where you tell me.'

Her green eyes flared. 'Well, in that case, you can go to hell!'

'Maybe later.' He glanced at his watch. 'Right now, we need to get ready.'

'For what?'

'We have dinner plans. At the hotel.'

Was he being serious?

Imma gaped at him. They were in the middle of an argument—*no*, scratch that, they were in the middle of a power struggle—and he wanted them to just wrap it up and have dinner together.

As if!

Fury rose up inside her and, lifting her chin, she folded her arms. 'I'm not feeling hungry.'

His eyes met hers, and the sudden dark intensity of his gaze made her breath stall in her throat.

'Oh, I wouldn't worry... I'm sure I can find something on the menu to prick your appetite,' he said softly.

The air between them seemed to thicken, his words making her heart miss a beat in such a maddening and all too predictable way that she wanted to scream. He'd tricked her into coming here. He was vile. Manipulative. Duplicitous.

So why was her stupid body betraying her like this?

Her pulse jolted as he began unbuttoning his shirt.

'What are you doing?'

'Getting changed.' Catching sight of her face, he sighed. 'We have to eat. Well, I do, anyway. And we're going to have to face people sooner or later. So let's get it over with. We'll show our faces, smile, look loved up and then it's done.'

'Fine. Since you put it so nicely,' she said stiffly. 'But just because I'm going to dinner with you it doesn't change anything.'

He looked at her for a long moment. Probably it was a new experience for him. No doubt most women would move continents to have dinner with Vicenzu Trapani.

'Of course not,' he murmured. 'The bathroom's through there. I'll see you downstairs.' His dark eyes met hers, then dropped to her mouth, then lower still. 'Call me if you need me to zip you up. Or, better still, unzip you. I'll be happy to help.'

In the bathroom, she washed quickly and changed out of her dress.

How had this happened? At home, when she wanted

space, she'd run a bath and lie back, closing her eyes and losing herself in the steam and the silence. And now she was here, hiding in another bathroom from another man.

Only wasn't that the reason she had agreed to marry Vicè? To change all that? To be someone different?

It wasn't the only reason.

Her pulse twitched. Did he know the effect he had on her?

Of course.

Vicè was an expert on women—he knew exactly what to look for. He probably thought he had her all worked out, and that when he clicked his fingers she would come running. But he didn't know her at all.

She glanced down at her dress, her pulse beating unevenly. It was new. Her sister had chosen it for her on a shopping trip in Milan. It had been a rare day of freedom for them. Her mouth twisted. Freedom that had included a posse of bodyguards, of course.

She'd been planning to wear it at the evening function after Claudia's wedding. Only in the end she hadn't had the guts to put it on in front of her father.

Glancing down, she felt her skin tighten. The dress was green, a shade brighter than her eyes, and to say that it was 'fitted' was an understatement. Had it looked this clinging in the shop? Probably. But after two glasses of Prosecco she hadn't noticed or cared.

It wasn't her usual style, any more than the black patent skyscraper heels were. But her sister was always wanting her to dress up, and she'd been so excited, so eager for Imma to buy it.

She lifted her chin and met the gaze of her reflection.

She would wear it tonight—for Claudia—and prove to Vicenzu that he knew nothing about her at all.

But as she walked downstairs her bravado began to falter with every step.

Catching sight of him standing with his back to her, his eyes fixed on the sunset lighting up the bay, she felt a rush of panic. Perhaps she should change.

But before she had a chance to retreat he turned and her heart lurched. Suddenly she wasn't thinking about what she was wearing any more. She was too busy marvelling at his blatant masculine beauty.

He was wearing black trousers, a dark grey polo shirt and loafers, and she liked how he looked. *A lot*.

Her throat tightened. She liked how he was looking at her even more.

'Is it too much?' she asked quickly as his dark gaze skimmed her body.

'Not at all.' He hesitated, then took a step forward. 'It suits you.'

His voice was cool, and she wasn't sure what he meant by that remark, but she didn't want to get inside his head to find out. Right now she just wanted to go somewhere, anywhere there were other people—people who would prevent her from doing something stupid.

Even more stupid than marrying him.

Maybe he felt the same way. Or perhaps he was just desperate for company, she thought as he escorted her swiftly and purposefully towards the hotel.

They entered through a side door. 'We'll deal with the paps later,' Vicè said, his hand locking with hers.

It was lucky for him that he was holding her hand so tightly, otherwise she would have scuttled back to the villa. Even without the paparazzi, the experience of walking into this hotel was intimidating. The beautiful decor was the embodiment of relaxed chic, a perfect mix of retro glamour and contemporary cool, but it was still overshadowed by the fame of the guests.

In the space of a minute she counted at least five A-list film stars, two motor racing drivers, a tennis champion and a disgraced former Italian prime minister—and all of them seemed to know Vicè and wanted to offer their congratulations. Even those who didn't were nearly falling over to catch a glimpse of him.

'They're bored with me,' he murmured.

'What?' She glanced up at him in confusion.

'It's you they've come to see.'

Wrong, she thought as they sat down at their table in the restaurant. He was so devastating you could gaze at him for several lifetimes and not get bored.

He was a gracious, natural host, and a master of *sprezzatura*—that ability to make things happen seemingly without effort or any apparent thought. And he liked people…accepted them for who they were.

Watching him stop to speak to a middle-aged couple who were celebrating their wedding anniversary, she felt her pulse slow. Vicè was turning out to be an enigma. And, even though she knew that feeling this way wasn't clever, he was a mystery she found herself wanting to solve.

The view from the panoramic terrace was legendary, and she could see why. In the fading light of the setting sun the curve of the town's pastel-coloured houses looked like something from a dream.

But if the view was enchanting, the food was sublime. She chose *paté di seppia* followed by *zembi au pesto* and savoured every mouthful.

'So you've found your appetite?'

Looking up, Imma blushed.

'It's fine,' he assured her. Leaning forward, he took her hand. 'It's been a long day. You need to eat.'

Watching him kiss her hand, she wondered if it would feel different if he meant it. 'The food is delicious,' she said.

'I'm glad you like it.'

She met his gaze. 'I didn't think it would be so...'

'So what?'

His expression hadn't changed, but she could sense the tension around his eyes.

'So magical here. You've made something remarkable, and you've done it on your own. Your family must be very proud.'

He nodded. 'Of course.'

'So why did you choose Portofino?'

He shrugged. 'I didn't. It chose me.'

It was a perfectly reasonable reply, but she couldn't shift the feeling that there was more to it than what he was saying. But if there was, he wasn't sharing it. He talked easily and amusingly about anything and everything except himself. Then he either made a joke or changed the subject.

When the meal was over Vicè caught her hand.

'Let's get this done.' He eyed her sideways. 'You know we're going to have to kiss? Nothing beyond the call of duty—just enough to make it look real. Are you okay with that?'

She nodded. 'For the cameras, yes.'

She had been expecting a couple of photographers,

but as they walked down the steps of the hotel a crowd of paparazzi rushed forward.

'Vicè, is it true you two only met twenty-four hours ago?'

'Give me a break. I'm good—but not that good.' He grinned. 'It was at least forty-eight.'

There were yells of laughter.

'Aren't you going to kiss your wife, Vicè?'

Her heart leapt as he turned and looked down at her.

'I think I should,' he said softly, his eyes dropping to her mouth.

His hand moved to her back. She felt her stomach disappear as he tipped her head back and stared into her eyes, and then he leaned forward and kissed her.

It was the lightest of kisses, fleeting and gentle. But, staring up into his dark eyes, she felt her brain freeze and her body begin to melt. Pulse jumping, she leaned into him and pressed her mouth against his.

For a fraction of a second she felt his surprise, and then his hand caught in her hair and he was pulling her closer. Her head spun. She could taste his hunger...feel her own hunger flowering with a swiftness that shocked her. Blood was roaring in her ears.

Her fingers slid over his chest, curling into the fabric of his shirt, and she couldn't stop herself from slanting her body against his.

His lips were still moving slowly, deliberately over hers, drawing out the heat that was tightening her stomach so that she was shivering, shaking inside, her body melting with a raw hunger that was as torturous as it was exquisite. And then she was kissing him back, fusing her mouth with his.

The roar of the photographers' voices filled her head.

For a few moments the world turned white. Then she felt his swift indrawn breath, and as he lifted his head she dimly became aware of her surroundings again.

'Okay, that's it for now.' Vicè smiled, and seconds later he was leading her back down the path to his villa.

Her heart was hammering against her ribs and her cheeks felt scalded. It had been supposed to be for show, but as he'd drawn her into the half-circle of his arms she had never wanted anything to be more real.

Had Vicè sensed her unbidden response beneath the performance? The thought made her throat tighten and as they walked into the villa she spun round to face him. 'I can't believe you just did that.'

He arched an eyebrow. 'What did you expect? A peck on the cheek?'

Her voice was shaking. 'That kiss was *way* "beyond the call of duty"!'

And she had kissed him back. Her teeth clenched. She was furious with herself. But to reveal that would reveal her vulnerability, and so, as he dropped down onto the sofa, she directed her anger towards him.

'You love this, don't you? Playing your stupid games—'

His eyes narrowed, and then he was on his feet and moving towards her so fast that she only just had time to throw up a defensive hand.

'*Me* playing games?' He shook his head, an incredulous look on his handsome face. 'I'm not the one playing games here, Imma.'

'What is that supposed to mean?' she hissed.

'It means all this fighting and flirting. You *do* know that eventually we're going to end up back where we started? Naked. In bed.'

Her eyes clashed with his. 'In your dreams.'

'In yours too,' he taunted.

His words made her breathing jerk. She shook her head in denial. 'You are impossibly arrogant.'

'So I've been told. But that doesn't change the facts—which are that you want me as much as I want you. So why don't we skip the fighting and go straight to the sex?'

Cheeks flaming, she stared up at him angrily, the truth of his words only intensifying her need to deny them.

'You didn't want me before—you wanted your father's business. And you only want me now because you can't risk having an affair and blowing our deal. As to what I want—do you really think I'd sleep with you again after everything that's happened?'

'Why not?'

His eyes were fixed on her face, hot and dark, and as she caught the intense heat in them her body began to tremble.

'We're adults. We're both getting what we want from this arrangement. Except each other. But I'm willing to forget the past if you are.'

Forget the past.

For a second she couldn't trust herself to speak. 'Excuse me.' She stepped past him.

He frowned. 'Where are you going?'

'To get some bedding. I'm going to sleep on the sofa.'

For a moment he clearly thought she was joking, and then he swore softly. 'Fine. I'll sleep down here.'

She stumbled slightly, caught off guard by his sudden acquiescence.

'Fine. And, just so you know, from now until we leave, there won't be any more public appearances for the two of us. Show's over, Vicè.'

CHAPTER SEVEN

Rolling onto his back, Vicè savagely punched the pillow behind his head and gazed up at the ceiling.

Newsflash: this sofa might look great, and lounging on it with a Negroni was fine, but it was definitely not designed for sleep.

Not that he was going to sleep any time soon, he thought. Even if his neck hadn't been in agony, his body was wound so tightly he doubted he would ever sleep again. In fact, it had been on high alert ever since Imma had sashayed downstairs earlier and he'd forgotten to breathe.

Gone had been the absurdly staid mother-of-the-bride navy dress and in its place had been a silk number the colour of absinthe that had clung to her body without a ripple, exposing her slim curves and shimmering biscotti-coloured skin.

And then there had been those shoes…

A muscle pulsed in his jaw. It was a toss-up as to whether that dress or her parting shot had rendered him more speechless.

Remembering Imma's words, he felt his muscles tighten.

Show's over.

Wrong, he thought. It wasn't over. This was just an intermission.

Scowling, he shifted onto his side. Just an intermission that was longer than necessary and extremely uncomfortable.

He scowled. How had he ended up here? Spending a night on the sofa while his new wife slept alone in *his* bed?

He couldn't work out what had happened. So he might not be a business tycoon like Ciro, or even his father, but if there was one thing he understood above all others it was women.

He gritted his teeth. Make that all women except Imma.

Take tonight: she had been spitting fire over their sleeping arrangements, storming off into the bathroom when he'd told her about their dinner reservation. But then she'd seemed to calm down and relax over dinner, eating and enjoying her meal even though she'd claimed earlier she had no appetite.

Her mood had shifted a little when they'd walked out of the hotel. She had been jittery—understandably. Like oysters, the paparazzi were an acquired taste. And, unlike him, Imma had very little experience of facing a phalanx of photographers. But he'd warned her that they would have to perform for the cameras and she'd seemed to be up for it.

His pulse began to beat thickly in his blood.

Had he meant to kiss her like that? As if a clock had been counting down to the end of the world and only by kissing her could he stop time and stay alive?

No, he hadn't—and he hadn't expected her to respond like that either.

He'd thought she would play coy, do her 'duty'…

But then she'd leaned into him, her lips parting. And, lost in the sweetness of her mouth and the pliant heat of her body, he had kissed her back.

His groin tightened at the memory.

It had not been a duty kiss. But, *mannaggia alla miseria*, he was only human, and when a beautiful woman was in his arms, kissing him, what was he supposed to do?

He felt his shoulders tense. She thought he'd planned it—that it had been yet another example of him lying to her about his intentions. The truth was that his arousal had been so fast, so intense, he'd lost the ability to think, much less contemplate all possible interpretations of his actions.

In the time it had taken for her to part her lips he'd forgotten about the paparazzi, forgotten their marriage wasn't real. His breath, his body, his whole being, had been focused on the feel of her mouth on his and he had been powerless to stop.

Only there was no way to prove that to her. Not that she would believe him anyway. And could he really blame her?

His chest tightened. Never before had he treated anyone quite so unfairly as he'd treated Imma.

He'd lied to her repeatedly and manipulated her, using every smile and glittering gaze in his repertoire to lure her away from her family and seduce her. Of course she wouldn't believe him.

Sighing, he stared across the darkened living room.

And that was why he would be sleeping on this sofa for the foreseeable future. Or rather *not* sleeping.

He sat up. There was no point in just lying there.

Glancing out of the window, he caught sight of a flicker of light reflected from the surface of the pool and felt a rush of relief, as if someone had thrown him a life jacket. A swim was just what he needed to clear his head and cool his body.

Outside, the warm air clung to his skin. For a moment he stood on the edge of the pool and then, tipping forward, he executed a flawless dive into the water.

For the next forty minutes or so he swam lengths, until his chest and legs ached in unison. Turning over, he floated on his back, his lungs burning.

A huge pale moon hung over the sea, and above him the inky blue-black sky was crowded with stars. The air was heavy with the scent of cypress and honeysuckle and vibrated with the hum of cicadas. It was all impossibly romantic—the perfect setting, in fact, for a wedding night.

All that was missing was his beautiful bride.

He was back where he started.

Grimacing, he turned towards the pool's edge, his limbs stretching through the water. As he pulled himself out and draped a towel around his neck, a tiny speckled lizard darted between the shadows.

But that wasn't what made him catch his breath.

Beyond the shadows, her green dress luminous in the moonlight, her long dark hair hanging loosely over her shoulders, was his wife.

Imma felt her body tense.

Upstairs in the bedroom she had felt trapped. The windows on to the balcony had been open to the sea breeze, but still she had felt hot and panicky.

Back on Pantelleria, marrying Vicè had seemed like

a good idea. She had thought she needed time and space to deal with the consequences of her actions—and his. She'd also naively believed that she could play him at his own game.

But the truth, as she'd so humiliatingly discovered this evening, was that she was out of her depth and floundering.

He was too slick, too good at twisting words and situations to his advantage. And for someone who was so poor at telling the truth he was remarkably good at pointing out dishonesty and hypocrisy in other people— namely herself.

She had known that sleep was beyond her, so she hadn't bothered to undress. Instead she had slipped off her shoes and tried to rest.

Even that, though, had been impossible.

How could she rest in his room? On his bed? And it *was* his bed. She'd been able to smell him. His aftershave and something else…a scent that had made her stomach grow warm and her head swim. Clean, masculine…like salt or newly chopped wood. She had felt it slipping over her face like a veil.

Veil. Her throat had closed around the word like a vice.

With Vicè's denials and accusations still echoing in her head, she had forgotten that this was supposed to be her wedding night.

Some wedding night.

She had never felt more alone, so she had crept downstairs, past the sofa, and gone out into the heavy night air.

She had thought Vicè would be asleep. But he was

not only very much awake, he was standing in front of her. In boxer shorts. Extremely wet boxer shorts.

Her stomach flipped over and for a heartbeat she couldn't move. She no longer seemed to know how to make her legs work. But she did know that no good would come of her staying there.

'Imma. Please, wait—'

Against her will, against every instinct she had, she made her body still. With an effort, she turned to face him. 'Why? So you can make me feel stupid? You don't need to bother, Vicè. Really. I'm already doing a great job of that all on my own.'

He took a step towards her. 'I don't want to make you feel stupid. I just want to talk.'

She looked away, swallowing against the ache in her throat, feeling trapped again. 'Well, that's a lovely idea, but we don't talk. We argue. And I'm tired of arguing.'

'We do talk,' he said quietly. 'That first night at your father's villa we talked a lot.'

She stared at him in confusion. But he was right. They had talked that night about lots of things. Actually, *she* had talked—and that in itself was remarkable.

Usually, she was the listener. When it was just the two of them, Claudia would always be the one chattering on about some recipe she was going to try, and at work, with her father's shadow looming large over everything, her opinions were politely ignored. As for Cesare himself—like most rich, powerful men, he was far too convinced of his own rightness to invite other viewpoints.

A lump of misery swelled inside her. She was getting distracted. *At her father's villa, Vicè had a reason to listen to her.*

'That wasn't real,' she said flatly. 'None of this is real.'

'I am—and you are.' His eyes held hers. 'And so is this thing between us.'

She shook her head. 'There *is* no thing between us, Vicè.'

But of their own accord her eyes fixed on his chest. For a few half seconds she stared at the drops of water trickling down over his smooth golden skin, and then she looked away, her breathing ragged, her denial echoing hollowly around the empty terrace.

She had taken him back to her father's villa thinking that one night with him would give her the answers she needed. Instead it had simply raised more questions. Like what kind of woman could still want a man like him? And how—*where*—was she ever going to find another man who would override the memory of his touch, his kiss?

'Even if there is, we're not going to do anything about it.'

His eyes were steady and unblinking. 'We already have. So why are you still denying how we both feel?'

'Because it doesn't make any sense,' she mumbled.

'Does it have to?'

She looked up at him, made mute by the directness of his words and the complicity they implied.

He was silent for a moment, and then he sighed. 'Look, Imma, I don't want to argue any more than you do, so could we call a truce? Please?'

Her heart contracted. 'Forget the past, you mean?'

He stared at her. 'Not forget it—just put it on hold.'

She frowned. 'We're not talking about a nuisance call. This is my sister's life—her heart.' *My heart.* Her eyes were filling with tears. 'She doesn't deserve what your brother has done to her.'

'Oh? But my father *did* deserve to be hounded in the last few months of his life?'

His voice was suddenly hard, his eyes even harder. *So much for a truce*, she thought.

'And my mother? She deserved to lose her home? Her husband?'

His tone made her shiver.

'Of course not.' She hesitated. 'Is that why you want the business back? For her?'

For a moment he seemed confused, as though he didn't understand her words.

'I want my father back—so does my mother. There's only one reason I want the business, and one reason I want you as my wife—and that's so your father gets a taste of his own medicine.'

She flinched, the scorn in his voice biting into her flesh. This was exactly why she should have turned and walked away when she'd had the chance.

There was a tense, expectant silence, and then Vicè ran a hand over his face.

'I didn't mean that.' He was breathing unevenly. 'What I said about wanting you… I was angry—I *am* angry—but I don't want to hurt you.'

Glancing up, she tensed. His eyes were filled with a kind of bewildered frustration. He was hurting, and his pain cut through her own misery.

Without thinking, she reached out and touched his arm. 'I wish my father hadn't acted like he did, and if I could go back and change one thing in all of this it would be that.'

There was a silence. He stared at her, but he didn't shake off her hand.

After a moment, he said slowly, 'Not what happened between us? You wouldn't go back and change that?'

He sounded confused, disbelieving, and his dark eyes were searching her face as though he was trying to read her thoughts.

Her mind turned over her words. She was suddenly confused herself. But it hadn't occurred to her to regret that night they'd shared. She wouldn't exchange those beautiful, sensual hours in Vicè's arms for anything. And it hadn't been just the heat and the hunger, or even the fact that for those few short hours she had believed he wanted her for herself.

That night with him had been the first time she had consciously defied her father's wishes—not to his face, maybe, but it had felt like it. The first time she had made decisions about her own life.

'No, I wouldn't change that,' she said quietly.

'I wouldn't change it either.'

His eyes held hers and, catching the heat in his dark gaze, she felt a rush of panic. Last time she had willingly walked into the fire. But she couldn't do so again, knowing what she did now.

'I can't do this,' she said. And this time she acted, turning and running swiftly back into the house.

He caught up with her in the living room, his body blocking her escape. 'Where are you going?'

'Anywhere you're not.' She spoke breathlessly.

'For a year?' He looked and sounded incredulous. 'You're going to keep running away from me for a whole year?'

'I'm not like you, Vicenzu. I can't just switch it on and off for the cameras.'

'What cameras?' Holding out his arms, he gestured to the empty room. 'There are no cameras here. There is you, and me—just like there was at the villa on the island.'

Remembering her shock and misery the morning after, she shook her head. 'But you weren't really you. Or maybe you were, and I just thought you were someone else.'

She had been someone else that night too. Someone reckless and uninhibited. And gullible.

His gaze rested intently on her face. 'I don't understand...'

Tears pricked her eyes. 'You don't need to.'

He frowned. 'We're married. I'm your husband.'

Her chest rose and fell as she struggled to breathe. 'I can't believe you can say that with a straight face.' She gazed at him, her heart racing. 'But I suppose it's not surprising you think this is normal. Your whole life is a charade. Why should your marriage be any different?'

Vicè stared at her, a muscle working in his jaw.

'My life was just fine until I married you,' he said slowly.

If she didn't like charades then why was she making him act like some lovesick puppy in public and then relegating him to the sofa when they were alone?

'How is this my fault?' She seemed almost to choke in disbelief.

He stared at her in frustration, her words replaying inside his head. He *didn't* think this was normal. For

him, 'normal' had always been his parents' relationship. Normal, but unattainable.

He was suddenly conscious of his heart hammering
against his ribs.

They had been so happy together, so comfortable,
and yet still sweetly infatuated like the teenagers in love
they had once been. Whereas he—

His body tensed. The idea that he would ever be capable of replicating his parents' marriage had always
seemed too ludicrous to contemplate. So he had done
what he always did—he'd pushed the possibility away,
deliberately choosing a way of life that was the antithesis of theirs.

And his parents had done what they always did too,
indulging him even though he knew that they'd longed
for him to fall in love and settle down.

Remembering his mother's reaction when he'd called
to tell her he was married, he felt his heartbeat slow. It
had been a bittersweet moment. She had been so happy
for him, but also sad that Alessandro hadn't been alive
to see his eldest son finally find love.

What would she say if she knew the truth?

Looking over at Imma, he pushed the thought away,
guilt making his voice harsher than he'd intended. 'This
"charade", as you put it, wasn't my idea.'

She lifted her chin. 'True. But if you'd had your way
I'd have signed over the olive oil company the morning
after we slept together and you and your vile brother
would probably still be toasting your victory in some
bar in Palermo.'

Her description was just about close enough to his
last meeting with Ciro for colour to stain his cheekbones.

Shaking his head, he took a step back, his jaw tightening. 'I don't need this, and I certainly can't live like this for a year.'

'This isn't just about you.'

There was a tautness in her voice, and her mouth was trembling slightly. He realised that she was close to tears.

She sucked in a breath. 'For once I don't want to have to think about what someone else wants or needs. I thought with you—'

As she glanced away he felt his spine stiffen. The events of the last few days must be starting to catch up with her. Or maybe she had been in shock all along.

'You're right. This isn't just about me.' He flattened the anger in his voice, picking his words very carefully, suddenly afraid that the wrong ones would make her run again. 'So tell me what *you* want—what *you* need.'

There was a moment of silence.

'I don't know.' She shook her head. 'I really don't know. I've never known. Maybe if I had none of this would be happening.'

Her shoulders tightened, making her look smaller, wounded, like a bird with a broken wing. Seeing her like that—so diminished, so vulnerable—made him ache inside.

'I doubt that,' he said gently.

He sat down on the sofa, and after a moment, as he'd hoped she would, she sat down beside him.

'There are a lot of reasons why this has happened, *cara*, but you're not one of them.'

She stiffened. 'I know you hate him. My father, I mean. But he's not all bad. He used to be different before...

when my mother was alive. He's just been on his own for too long.'

His pulse stalled. He did hate her father—and yet right now the reason for that hate seemed irrelevant. What mattered more was Imma's pain.

'How old were you when she died?'

'Eight.'

Her stark single-word answer made his heart kick against his ribs. Watching the flicker of sadness in her green eyes, he felt the ache in his chest spread out like a dark rain cloud.

His father's death had felt like something tearing inside him—and he was an adult, a grown man. Imma had had to deal with the loss of her mother as a child.

'He hated not being able to help her,' she said quietly. 'I think that's why he's like he is now. He can't bear the idea of something happening to me and Claudia—something he can't control.'

Vicè felt his stomach clench. In that case he and Ciro had already had their revenge. And just like that his hunger for retribution was gone—diluted and washed away by the tears in her eyes.

'He's your father,' he said. 'Of course he doesn't want to see you hurt.'

It was meant to be a generic response, only for some reason he found himself thinking about his own father. Right up until his death Alessandro had spent his life protecting him, constantly levelling the playing field so that he wouldn't have to compare himself unfavourably to Ciro. In fact, it had been that need to protect his eldest son that had ultimately caused his death.

Something jarred in his chest, as if a depth charge had exploded. He'd made this about Cesare, but it was actually about him. It had always been about him and his failings as a son, as a man.

He forced himself to look over and meet her gaze. 'He loves you.'

She nodded slowly. 'But he still misses my mother. That's why he works so much. Only now he's become obsessed with building up the business, and...' She hesitated, her face tensing. 'It matters to him—his name, his legacy. He's never said anything but I know he wishes he'd had a son. Instead, he's got me. Only I can't ever be good enough. He wants me to be tough and ruthless, but he also wants me to be a dutiful daughter. And then there's Claudia...'

The sudden softness in her eyes cut through him like a blade. 'You're close?' he asked.

She nodded. 'She was so little when Mamma died. We had nannies, but they didn't stay long. Papà was so angry, so exacting. Anyway, she always preferred me. And I didn't mind. I *wanted* to look after her.'

Her voice sounded scraped and bruised. It made something hard lodge in his throat. 'You *have* looked after her.'

'How?' She bit her lip. 'I let her marry Ciro and now he's broken her heart.' A tear slid down her cheek. 'I was supposed to take care of her—'

He caught her hands in his. Her whole body was rigid, braced for disaster. 'You did—you are. But she's not a child any more, *cara*—'

'You don't understand. I promised Mamma, and now I've broken that promise.'

She was crying in earnest now and he pulled her onto his lap, wanting and needing to hold her close, to hold her for as long as it took to make her feel whole again.

His skin burned with shame as he realised the mistake he'd made. Imma wasn't her father's daughter at all. She was just a little girl who had lost her mother and had to grow up fast. A little girl who had been so busy trying to be a daughter and a mother and a proxy son all at once that she had never had time to be herself. He couldn't bear picturing her little face, her anxious green eyes.

Gently, he stroked her hair. *'Va tutto bene, cara,'* he murmured. 'It's going to be okay. I've got you.'

He understood now how her family had pushed their needs ahead of hers. And he had been no better. In fact, he had been worse. Deliberately and ruthlessly using her as a means to punish her father.

His arms tightened and he kept on smoothing her hair until finally she let out a shuddering breath.

'None of this is your fault, Imma,' he said quietly. 'You're a good sister, and a loyal daughter, but you're way more than the sum of your parts. You're an amazing woman. You're beautiful and sexy and strong and smart. You can be anything you want.' Pulling the towel from around his neck, he gently patted the tears from her cheeks. 'And I'll be there, remember? In the background...'

Her lips curved up, as he had hoped they would.

For a moment they stared at each other in silence.

'You didn't sign up for this,' she said quietly.

'Oh, I signed up for everything, *cara.* Kiss-and-tell interview, miniseries, film franchise...'

He was trying to make her relax, maybe enough to trust him. But he was surprised to find that he was also telling the truth.

Her smile flickered. 'I want to be there for Papà and

Claudia, but I want to be myself too. I thought if I could break free just for one night, lose my virginity to someone I'd chosen, then it would all become clear. Who I am. What I want. And maybe somebody would want me for being me.' She screwed up her face. 'It sounds stupid, saying it out loud.'

He shook his head. 'It's not stupid at all.'

He'd left Sicily to do much the same. Not to lose his virginity, but to put as much distance as possible between himself and his parents' carefully managed disappointment—and, of course, Ciro's effortless success.

'I thought it would be so easy.' Her eyes found his. 'And then I met you.'

'You deserve better,' he said slowly. 'You deserve better than me.' He hesitated. 'How is she? Claudia? Is she okay?'

Her smile faded a little and for a moment he didn't think she was going to reply, but finally she nodded.

'She will be. I'll take of her.'

'I know.' His eyes met hers and he was suddenly conscious of her warm hands on his chest. 'And what about you?'

There was a beat of silence.

'Me?' She seemed stunned by the question. 'I don't— It's not—'

'I want to look after you, Imma.' He stopped. 'Look, I messed up. Ciro too. We were wrong. We made this about you and Claudia and that was wrong,' he repeated. 'Our fight is with your father—not you.' His heart began to beat faster. 'I want to make it up to you. What I'm trying to say is… Could we start this year over?'

Her face didn't change, and nor did she reply.

'If you need more time—' he began.

'I don't,' she said quietly.

He felt a rush of misery and regret, but then his pulse leapt as her hand splayed across his chest.

'But if we start again it has to be different. No more lies, Vicè. No more games. Agreed?'

At that moment, with her body so warm and soft and close to his, he would have agreed to just about anything.

'Agreed,' he said hoarsely.

There was a short silence.

Finally, she cleared her throat. 'You should probably get out of those damp clothes…'

Nodding, he made as though to slide her off his lap, but she didn't move. Instead, her eyes met his.

'Or I could help you…' A little shakily, she ran her fingers down his body to the waistband of his shorts. 'Unless you've changed your mind?'

He stared at her dazedly. *What mind?* Like the rest of him, his mind had melted at the feel of her fingertips on his skin.

A flicker of hope went through him like an electric current and he swallowed, his eyes dropping to her mouth, then lower to the swell of her breasts.

'Is that— Do you— I mean, are you saying what I think you're trying to say?'

His usual effortless eloquence had deserted him. He couldn't remember ever feeling so awkward. But he was shaken by the intensity of his desire, paralysed with fear that he had misunderstood her gesture and words.

'Yes,' she said simply.

It was as if a starter gun had gone off in his head.

Framing her face with his hands, he pulled her closer,

his mouth finding hers, and he felt a shiver running over him as her fingers stroked across his skin.

'I've been thinking about this for days...' he groaned against her mouth.

Shock waves of desire were slamming through his body.

'I've been thinking about it too.'

Her breathing was decidedly unsteady now, and she was pushing him back, back onto the sofa.

'Wait, wait... No—not here. Not on this damn sofa,' he muttered.

It was his last conscious thought as, reaching down, he scooped her up into his arms and carried her upstairs.

As he dropped her gently onto the bed Imma sat up, pulling him closer, her mouth seeking the outline of his arousal through the still damp fabric of his boxer shorts. He grunted, his body jerking forward as her fingers slid over his hip bones and she began to move her lips over the swell of his erection.

His hand caught in her hair. 'Imma...' He swore softly.

Imma felt her stomach clench. Her power to arouse him was shockingly exciting, and he was fiercely aroused. Fingers trembling slightly, she tugged at the waistband of his boxer shorts, heat flaring in her pelvis as she slid them over his hips.

She watched his jaw tighten, the muscles of his arms bunching as she ran her tongue around the blunt, rigid tip, taking it in her mouth. The feel of it jerking and pulsating in her mouth made her head swim.

He groaned, his fingers twisting in her hair, and then he jolted backwards, lifting her face and lowering his mouth to hers, kissing her with a hunger that made liquid heat flood her pelvis.

As her hands reached for him, he batted them away. 'My turn,' he said hoarsely.

His eyes were dark and molten with heat. Pulling her to her feet, he dipped his head, kissed her again, taking his time, running his tongue slowly over her lips then between them, tasting her, slowing her pulse.

She felt his hands on her back and then he was unzipping her dress, sliding it over her body, his hands moving smoothly around to cup her breasts, his thumbs grazing the already swollen tips until she was shaking inside.

And then he was nudging her back onto the bed, his mouth on hers, dropping his head to take first one and then the other nipple into his mouth, rolling his tongue over the tight, ruched skin as her hands clutched his neck and shoulders.

She reached for him again and this time he caught her hands, pinning them to her sides. Deliberately he slid down her body. A shiver of excitement ran through her.

'Let me taste you,' he whispered, and her head fell back, her whole body quivering as he parted her with his tongue.

Her body arched, pressing against his mouth. She had never felt anything like this. She was moaning, shifting restlessly against him, desperately seeking more, her body no longer her own. There was nothing except him…nothing but his warm, firm mouth and the measured, insistent press of his tongue.

Helplessly, she pushed against him, chasing that fluttering, delicate ripple of pleasure, and then her pulse quickened and she felt her body tighten inside, tensing as the ripple became a wave and she cried out, shuddering beneath him.

Releasing her hands, he moved up the bed, licking his way up her body to her mouth. 'I want you, Imma.'

She wrapped her arms around his neck. 'I want you too. Inside me.'

He rolled onto his back, taking her with him so that she was straddling the rigid length of him, hard and hot against the ache between her thighs. Reaching over, he fumbled in a drawer, lifting her gently as he rolled on a condom.

Squirming against him, she moved her hands across his body, over his stomach and down lower, taking him in her hand. He pulled her against him, his fingers tightening around her waist as he lifted her up and pushed into her slowly, easing himself in, inch by inch.

His face was tight with concentration and with the effort of holding back. 'Look at me,' he whispered.

Their eyes met and, gripping her hips, he began to move. She moved with him, and their bodies sought and found a steady, intoxicating rhythm that sent arrows of heat over her skin.

Reaching out, he cupped her breast, squeezing her nipple, and then his hand moved to the swollen bud of her clitoris, caressing her in time to his body's thrusts, his dark eyes never leaving hers.

She rocked against him, feeling the heat rising up inside her again, gripping him with her muscles, holding him as the friction grew. Her skin felt hot and tight. She was hot and tight inside. And suddenly she flexed forward, as though she was trying to climb over him.

He pulled her back, his eyes locking with hers, and

then he pushed up one more time and she felt her body arch as he tensed, his hands clamping around her waist, her gasp of pleasure mingling with his groan.

CHAPTER EIGHT

IT WAS LATE when Vicè woke, the distant sound of a motorboat in the bay dragging him reluctantly from his
cocoon of warmth. For a moment he clung on to the
last shreds of sleep, and then slowly he opened his eyes
and turned his head towards the open French windows.

He had forgotten to draw the curtains, and outside
the sky was a marbled swirl of the palest blue and gold,
as beautiful as any Renaissance ceiling. But no sky,
however beautiful, could compete with the woman lying
beside him.

Imma was asleep, her face resting against his shoulder. Her left hand curled loosely on his chest, the other
was resting on the pillow, leaving one rosy-tipped breast
bared to his gaze.

His heart began to beat faster. With her tousled hair
and long dark lashes brushing her cheeks she looked
like a painting. There was a softness to her in sleep, a
hint of the vulnerability beneath the poise that made
him want to pull her close and hold her against him.

He tensed. It was the first time in his life he had felt
that way about any woman, and yet even though it was
new and unfamiliar he didn't feel panic or confusion.
Instead it felt completely natural, like smiling.

But was that so surprising, really?

He might have acted unfairly—ruthlessly, even—but he wasn't a monster, and seeing her cry had horrified him. Naturally he had wanted to comfort her.

His pulse quickened. What had happened next had been completely natural too.

Natural and sublime.

He swallowed, his groin hardening at the memory of how Imma had moved against him. Illuminated in the moonlight, her body had looked like liquid silver—felt like it too.

It had been different from that first time—slower, less frantic, more like riding a wave…an endless, curling wave of pleasure.

But then last time there had been other things in play. Obviously he'd needed to seduce her, but the intensity of his attraction had caught him off guard, made him question his motives so that it had all got tangled up in his head.

Imma had had her own agenda then too. Sleeping with him, losing her virginity, had been her first small act of independence.

Last night, though, it had been far less complicated for both of them.

It had been lust. Pure and simple and irresistible.

There had been no agenda.

He had wanted her and she had wanted him.

Of course they had been fighting it for days—fighting each other for days. But it had been too strong for both of them.

His chest tightened. They had come together as equals and Imma had made him feel things no other woman

had—driven him to a pitch of excitement that had sub-
sumed everything that had happened between them.

Including getting even with her father.

She stirred in his arms and he stared down at her,
replaying that thought, turning it back and forth inside
his head. Yesterday, when she had been so upset, he'd
felt something shift inside him, but he hadn't articulated
it quite so bluntly before. Putting it into words seemed
to make his thoughts move up a gear, give shape to his
feelings.

He felt a rush of relief. Getting even with Cesare
didn't matter any more. His father's business was as
good as his already, and that meant he was free to enjoy
this year with Imma.

Watching her eyelids flutter open, he felt his body
grow even harder.

And he didn't want to waste a second of it.

'Hey,' he said softly.

She stretched her arms, the movement causing the
sheet to fall away from her naked body, sending a jolt
of heat across his already overheated skin. For a moment she stared up at him, her green eyes widening with
confusion, and then she met his gaze.

'Hey...'

Imma stared up at Vicè, her heart pounding. She had
absolutely no idea what to do. Last time she'd been in
the same situation Claudia had called, so she had never
got to this moment of acknowledgement. It had got lost,
swept aside by her sister's revelation. But now there
was nowhere to hide from the truth of what they had
done—what she had done.

Remembering her hoarse, inarticulate cries of pleasure, the way she had pulled his body and then his mouth closer as he'd addressed that relentless ache between her thighs, her cheeks felt suddenly as if they were on fire.

His touch had been electric, every caress sending her closer to the edge, straining for that elusive *something* that would douse the swirling heat at the centre of her body, until finally it had been in her grasp and she had shuddered to stillness in his arms.

She had never felt like that before—not even that first time. It had been beyond anything she'd ever experienced.

As the moonlight had spilled through the windows she had demanded and given pleasure in equal measure, surrendering to the passion he had unleashed. Now, though, in daylight, she felt a little embarrassed.

Understandably.

She had cried all over him, told him things about herself and her life that she had never shared with anyone, and then she'd had sex with him.

Her heart skipped. She'd expected the sex to be incredible—Vicè was a generous, gifted lover. But apparently he was also a good listener. Talking to him had been easy—even about things she had held so close and kept secret from others.

'If it's any help, I don't know how to do the morning-after bit either,' he said quietly.

Swallowing, she looked up into his dark eyes. Her whole life she had been a complicated, contained girl, equal parts fear and ambition, always wanting to push back, but too scared to refuse, to demand, to ask.

But she wasn't scared any more.

'What do you usually do?' she asked.

'That's just it.' Leaning over, he stroked her cheek. 'I don't do anything. Spending the night with someone isn't my thing.' His mouth twisted. '*Wasn't* my thing.'

She stared at him uncertainly, trying to ignore the way her stomach was turning over and over in response to the implication of his words.

'But it is now?' she whispered.

A curl of hair had fallen over her breast and, reaching out, he wrapped it around his fingers, drawing her closer so that her mouth was under his.

'Yes, it most definitely is.'

Was that true? Or was he simply saying what she wanted to hear?

There was a moment of silence.

'You don't believe me?' His eyes searched her face.

'I want to…' She hesitated. There was a coldness in her chest, the chill of doubt. 'It's just that before this— you and me—it wasn't real. You had an agenda—'

Vicè hadn't wanted her for herself then. He'd *needed* to seduce her. Only she'd had no idea. So how could she trust her instincts, her senses, now?

'And you think I had one last night?' He grinned. 'What can I say? I had to get off that sofa somehow.' He glanced down, his smile fading. 'I'm joking, *cara*. That wasn't why—' His face stilled. 'Is this about what I said before? About only wanting you to get at your father?'

He stopped, his jaw tightening.

'Look, maybe right at the beginning, at the wedding, it *was* about getting back at him and getting the business back. But when you came out of the bathroom—' He grimaced. 'I promise you I wanted you so badly I wasn't thinking about your father or my father's olive oil company. Actually, I wasn't thinking, full stop.'

Imma bit her lip. She wanted to believe him, but it was hard. Her father and Claudia both needed her. For support, for protection. She had never felt desirable before—just necessary.

His hand covered hers, and the warmth of his fingers thawed the chill in her chest.

He shook his head. '*Lo so, cara*. I know I haven't given you any reason to trust me, but I meant what I said last night. I can't get you out of my head—you're all I've been thinking about.' His mouth twisted. 'Watching you walk downstairs in that dress, those heels… I actually thought I was going to lose control. I was desperate to get to the hotel, so I didn't make a fool of myself.' He gave her the ghost of a smile. 'Although being a fool is what I do best.'

It was the kind of teasing remark that was typical of him, and yet she couldn't help feeling there was something beneath the banter.

She stared into his eyes. 'You're not a fool.'

'I'm a fool for you,' he said lightly.

She smiled at that and, lifting his hand, he stroked her hair away from her face. 'You know, I think I'm getting pretty good at this morning-after bit,' he murmured.

'Is that right?' Her lips curved upward, caught in the honeyed trap of his gleaming dark eyes and teasing smile.

'Yeah…'

Their eyes met, and then his mouth dropped, and then he kissed her. She felt something stir inside—a flickering heat that made her body ripple to life and tighten in response.

Tipping his head back, he stared down at her, and

then he ran a finger slowly along the line of her collarbone. 'Although I might just need a little bit more practice...'

His voice was warm with desire, and she felt an answering warmth start to spread over her skin as he took her face between his hands and bent his head to kiss her again.

She wanted him, and she was willing to act on that want. She was making a choice and she was choosing Vicè.

It was a feather-light kiss. But then his mouth fused with hers and she whimpered softly as he moved his tensile muscular body over her.

Gripping his hips, she stretched out beneath him. He entered her slowly, giving her time to adjust, inching forward in time with her soft sighs of pleasure. But she needed him *now*—all of him—and she arched upward, pressing herself against the smooth, polished heat of his skin, wrapping her legs around his hips.

She was already aroused, and soon she was growing dizzy, intoxicated by the hard, steady rhythm of his body. A moan of pleasure climbed in her throat, and then a fierce heat blossomed inside her as her muscles tightened around him and she let go in time to his thrust of release.

Later—much later—they sat outside beneath the canopy of wisteria, enjoying a late brunch on the terrace.

'What are you thinking?' Vicè asked.

Turning, Imma smiled. He was staring at her across the table, his dark eyes fixed on her face.

Her pulse skipped. The shock of his beauty never seemed to fade. Any other man would have been eclipsed by the decadent glamour of the Dolce, but in his cream linen trousers, short-sleeved shirt and loafers, he looked like a poster playboy for the Italian Riviera.

With effort, she pulled her gaze away to the view past his shoulder, where huge white yachts floated serenely on an aquamarine sea. 'I was thinking how lucky you are.'

He raised an eyebrow. 'That's crazy—so was I.'

Smiling, she glanced past him at the panorama below. 'You have such a beautiful view here.'

'No, that's not what's beautiful here,' he said softly.

She shook her head. 'Do you ever stop?'

'You made me, remember?' He rolled his eyes. 'You said we had to eat food. Or get dressed or something…'

Their eyes met. She and Vicè had taken a shower together. Her cheeks felt suddenly warm. At first they had just washed one another, but then the soap had got dropped, and then he had shown her other, more inventive and thrilling ways to pass the time beneath the warm, tumbling spray.

'Somebody was knocking at the door. You were naked.'

'It was Matteo,' he protested. 'And he's seen me naked hundreds of times…' He paused. 'You know, at the orgies.'

Her mouth dropped open. 'The orgies—'

'At the hotel. Surely you've read about them?'

He was grinning.

'Oh, very funny, Vicè.'

He got up, moving smoothly around the table to grab her, laughing softly when she tried to bat him away.

'*Cara*, come on. I'm sorry. I couldn't help it. You just look so sexy when you're outraged.'

'I wasn't outraged. I was—'

'Jealous?'

His dark eyes were watching her intently and she felt her pulse jump.

She lifted her chin. 'Curious.'

'Well, you're going to have to stay curious, I'm afraid,' he said softly, and his calm tone was at odds with the slight tightening of his jaw. 'You're mine, and I'm not about to share you with anyone.'

Leaning forward, he kissed her fiercely, parting her lips to deepen the kiss until her head was spinning.

'Vicè...' Closing her eyes, she whispered his name, her voice trembling, her stomach flipping over in frantic response to his words as much as to his mouth, her body screaming in protest as slowly he released her.

Opening her eyes, she found him still watching her, his face impassive again.

'So,' he said. 'How would you like to spend the rest of the day?'

He shifted against her, and as his arm grazed her shoulder blade her heart jerked. Earlier, she'd been worried this wasn't real. Now, though, she could see that a far more likely scenario was her letting it get real in her imagination. Getting ahead of herself, making connections that simply weren't there and never would be.

For her, every soft word and dark glance might feel meaningful, but the truth was Vicè liked to flirt. It was his default setting. He liked sex too, and it was great that sex had unlocked this wild, uninhibited woman hiding inside of her. But the year was supposed to be about discovering who she was, and sex was only a part of that.

Essentially, the facts hadn't changed. Theirs was a marriage of convenience and in a year it would be over.

She needed to remember that. And until it was over she was going to have to set some rules.

First rule: take a step back. Stop allowing the passion she found in his arms to mislead her and make her forget why she had agreed to this marriage in the first place.

Second rule: get out there and do and try everything at least once. How else was she going to work out who she was?

Smoothing her sundress over her knees, she said offhandedly, 'I know I said I didn't want the two of us to go out in public again, but I'd really like to take a proper look around.'

If he noticed the forced casualness in her voice he didn't acknowledge it. Instead he leaned back in his seat and gave her an approving smile. 'Of course, *cara*. It would be my pleasure.'

Imma found the hours that followed both enjoyable and enlightening.

The hotel was larger than she had realised, but still small enough to feel like a private sanctuary, with a decor that cleverly blurred the lines between vintage and contemporary, homely and hip. Chequerboard floors sat alongside huge gilt mirrors and faded hand-painted frescoes of the Dolce's guests and staff.

'My friend Roberto painted them in exchange for my letting him have a room over the winter,' Vicè explained as they wandered out into the lushly beautiful tiered gardens.

There were grander, more opulent, more glamorous hotels, she was sure. But there was something special about the Dolce.

She glanced over at where Vicè stood, joking with

Edoardo, the hotel's legendary seventy-year-old pianist, who played everything from show tunes to swing for the guests sipping *aperitivi* on the terrace.

Unlike most hotels, everything felt authentic, rather than staged to create a certain vibe. But then not many hotels so closely embodied the personality of their owner. The Dolce *was* Vicè, and so, like him, it was effortlessly glamorous, flirty and cool.

'Do you want to dance?'

Vicè had stopped in front of her.

'Edo can play anything. Although I'd steer clear of rap or thrash metal.'

Biting into her smile, she shook her head, feeling suddenly conspicuous as around them everyone seemed to sit up straighter and glance covertly in their direction.

'Maybe later.'

Grinning, he took her hand. 'I'll hold you to that. Come on, I want to show you my favourite view. *Ciao*, Edo.' He turned and waved at the older masn.

'*Ciao*, boss. Maybe catch up with you and Signora Trapani later? At the party!'

Imma frowned. 'There's a party?'

'Not here—on the yacht.' When Imma raised her eyebrows, he shrugged. 'I have a yacht—the *Dolphin*. I keep her down in the bay for guests who like to cut loose. There's a party on board tonight, but obviously I wasn't going to go.'

She felt a ripple of relief—and then, remembering her refusal to dance, she stiffened her shoulders. What had happened to rule number two?

'Why not?' she said quickly. 'I'd like to go.'

'You would? Okay…well, if that's what you want

to do, great.' He shook his head. 'You are full of surprises, *cara*.'

She gave him a quick, tight smile. Full of fear, more
like. How did you even 'cut loose'?

'You're very quiet,' he said a moment later, as he led
her along a shady path. 'If you've changed your mind
about the party—'

'I haven't.' She stared up at him. 'I was just thinking
that you're full of surprises too.'

He eyed her sideways. 'Then you're in a minority of
one. Most people think they can read me like a book.'
His eyes met hers. 'At a guess, I'd say a well-thumbed
easy read—a beach blockbuster, maybe.'

He was smiling, but she had that same feeling she'd
had before—that there was something more than what
he was saying. And suddenly there was nothing she
wanted to know more than what he'd left unsaid.

'That's what you *let* them think.'

He'd let her think that too, at first. Now, though, she
could see that there was more to him—a whole lot more.

Take the Dolce. She might have limited hands-on
business experience, but she understood enough to
know that running one required more than charm and
a sexy smile.

His guests loved him. His staff too. She could sense
real affection and admiration, and they worked hard for
him. He seemed to bring out the best in people. Or at
least reveal their untapped potential.

'You have a gift, Vicè,' she said slowly. 'You've made
this like a wonderful private club that's open to everyone. And you did it on your own.'

He shrugged. 'It's a living. It's not exactly in Ciro's
league. He's Mr Midas.'

They had reached the villa now and, frowning, she followed him upstairs. 'Maybe. But some things are more important than money—and I know you believe that or we wouldn't both be here.'

It felt strange, putting it that way, but it was true. Vicè cared about his father's legacy enough to put aside his distaste and marry the daughter of his enemy. He had wanted revenge on her father, but he had also thrown her a lifeline by agreeing to marry her for a year.

And if revenge was all he was after he certainly wouldn't have agreed to sleep on any sofa.

'You care about your staff, your guests, your family. And it shows. You should be proud of that—of everything you've achieved. I'm sure your family is.'

'Careful, *cara*. I'm already "impossibly arrogant".'

She recognised her own words, but she didn't smile. 'Actually, I don't think you are,' she said quietly.

His eyes locked with hers.

'You're very smart, Imma.' Lifting a hand, he stroked her dark hair away from her face. 'Way too smart for me.'

Her heart began to beat faster and she felt heat break out on her skin. Vicè was wrong. If she was smart she would follow her own rules and stop her body reacting to his lightest touch.

'Not always.' Glancing round the bedroom, she frowned. 'I thought you were going to show me your favourite view?'

'I'm looking at it,' he said softly. He hesitated, his eyes never leaving her face. Then, 'Although I might need to make one small adjustment...'

He took a step towards her and, hooking the thin straps of her dress with his thumbs, he slipped them down over her shoulders. A muscle flickered in his jaw as it slid down her body, pooling around her feet.

Her mouth dried. Caught in the beam of his dark, shimmering gaze, she felt herself melt.

'Perfect,' he said hoarsely.

He leaned over to kiss the bare skin of her throat, and then she was pulling him backwards, onto the bed, all rules forgotten and broken.

'I hope you don't mind, but I bought you something for tonight.'

Leaning forward, Vicè planted a kiss on Imma's lips. As she stared up at him dazedly he sat down on the bed, handing her a large cardboard box wrapped in ribbon.

'I'm going to go and get changed, and then I've got a couple of things to go over with Matteo. Come down when you're ready.'

Ten minutes later he was downstairs, pouring himself and Matteo a glass of wine, his eyes dutifully scanning the guest list.

But his mind was elsewhere.

After they had made love Imma had fallen asleep, but he had been too restless to doze off. Lying next to her soft, naked body had been impossible too, so he'd got dressed and wandered down to the town for the early-evening *passeggiata*.

He'd been wandering through the square, past the cafes and bars, stopping occasionally to greet people, when he'd seen it.

It was the first dress, the first anything, he'd ever bought for a woman.

His mother didn't count.

He hadn't blinked—just walked in through the door

of the boutique and walked out again five minutes later, with the box under his arm and a stupid grin on his face.

It was only now that he was wondering why he'd felt the need to get her a gift. Why he was suddenly so keyed up, so desperate to see her happy.

But wasn't it obvious?

She'd been upset, in tears, and he'd felt guilty. *Great.* He could add it to the teetering pile of guilt he already carried around.

His breath scraped his throat as he remembered their conversation.

Imma thought he was an amazing businessman. A self-made man. The pride of his family. *What a joke.* She'd been closer to the mark when she'd accused him of living a charade.

His whole life was a charade. And the worst part was that his father—the one person who had known his weaknesses, his flaws—had lost his life playing along with it.

He wanted to tell her the truth, but he couldn't bear the idea of losing the respect and trust he'd gained. So now he was trapped in yet another charade.

Only how long would it be before he messed up and she saw him for what he really was? It was only a matter of when, and how, and in the meantime there was nothing he could do but wait for things to fall apart.

'Any problems, boss?'

Glancing at Matteo, he shook his head. He'd barely looked at the names on the guest list, but frankly he didn't care who was going to the party as long as Imma was there.

His stomach knotted.

He wanted to show her that he wasn't just a playboy who used his hotel as a private clubhouse. Okay, it was true that if Ciro had been running the business he would have already turned it into a global chain of luxury hotels. But his business was about more than world domination.

It was about people. Treating people like VIPs. And tonight he wanted to make Imma feel special.

He wanted her to enjoy herself. To relax, to laugh, to smile. More specifically, he wanted her to turn that sweet, shy smile his way.

'It all looks great, Matteo.'

The two men stood up and Vicè clapped his manager on the shoulder.

Matteo grinned. 'Okay, *capo*. I'll catch up with y—' He stopped midsentence, his mouth hanging open.

Turning, Vicè did the same. Imma was hovering in the doorway, biting her lip. Her hair was in some kind of chignon, and with her smoky eye make-up and glossy lips she looked as if she'd wandered off the set of a Fellini film.

And then there was her dress.

Beside him, Matteo whistled softly. 'I'll leave you to it, boss.'

He skirted past Imma, smiling, and Vicè heard the soft click of the door.

She turned, the smile she had given Matteo still on her face. 'Could you finish zipping me up, please?'

'Of course.' Finding his voice, he crossed the room. 'There—done.'

He couldn't stop himself from dropping a kiss to the column of her throat, his body hardening as he felt her shiver of response.

'Thank you for the dress,' she murmured.

'You look beautiful.'

Glancing down, he swallowed. The heavy satin looked like freshly poured cream, and his groin clenched as his brain feverishly rushed to bring that image to life in glorious 3D Technicolor.

'It fits perfectly.'

She smiled. 'You look pretty perfect too.' Her eyes skimmed appreciatively over his dark suit.

Recovering his poise, he made a mocking bow. 'This old thing?' As she started to laugh he held out his arm. 'Shall we go?'

Gazing across the water, Vicè breathed in the fresh, salt-tinged air.

The blunt outline of the motorboat was skimming easily over the indigo waves, the hum of its engine lost in the vastness of the bay. Behind him the glittering bracelet of lights along the Portofino seafront was starting to fade.

He glanced over to where Imma sat beside him. Her green eyes were wide with nerves or excitement or both, her cheeks flushed already from the rushing breeze.

They were on their way to the yacht, and he was still slightly surprised at her eagerness to go. But then nothing should surprise him about this woman who had agreed to be his wife. She had been surprising him ever since she'd walked into that church and refused to meet his eye.

Leaning back against his seat, he studied her profile.

Immacolata Buscetta. Prized eldest daughter of a notorious bully and a thief and a chip off the old block. But Imma was most definitely not what she seemed. The clues had been there. He'd just been too blinkered with anger to do anything more than focus on the obvious.

He had believed what he'd wanted to believe, and the fact that she was not the woman he had thought her to be was unsettling enough. More unsettling still was the fact that had she just walked away he would never have known his mistake.

Never got to know her.

The thought of that happening made his stomach clench.

Or maybe it was the sudden swell of the sea as the motorboat slowed alongside the yacht.

'Party's started,' he remarked as they stepped on board.

He felt a rush of exhilaration beat through his body in time to the music drifting down through the warm evening air. Here, he was king. This was his world. And he loved it. He loved the laughter, the pulsing bass notes and the waiters with their trays of champagne. He loved the buzz of energy and the beautiful women with their sequins and high heels.

His eyes roamed slowly down over Imma's body. Actually, make that one specific woman...

His heartbeat stalled. But who said anything about love?

Turning towards her, he caught her hand and pulled her towards him. 'Let's join in.'

Imma felt her heart start to pound.

As they made their way through the crowded yacht she felt even more exposed than when they'd first walked into the hotel together.

Everyone was so beautiful. Particularly the women.

All of whom were looking at Vicè with naked longing. She knew what they were thinking. It would be like seeing a peahen with her mate. They must all be wondering how such an ordinary bird could attract this glittering peacock.

'It's okay,' she said quietly as someone called out Vicè's name. 'I think everyone here believes we're married. You don't need to stay glued to my side all evening.'

His brows locked together. 'I couldn't care less what they believe, *cara*. I'm staying glued to your side because I want to. I like being with you, okay?'

She stared at him, her doubts suddenly losing shape, growing hazy next to his muscular solidity and the steady focus of his dark eyes.

'Okay then…'

It took them some time to actually get anywhere. People kept coming over to talk to him, and every person needed introducing.

'Do you know *everyone* here?' she asked as finally they made their way out into the deck, what seemed like several hours later.

'I suppose I do.'

Glancing back into the crowded saloon, he made a face. 'I know that must seem crazy, but it's what I do—it's who I am.'

She smiled. 'You have a lot of friends.'

And yet he still seemed to prefer her. The thought made warm bubbles of happiness rise inside her.

He smiled down at her. 'They're your friends too now. Now, how about that dance?'

'You took the words right out of my mouth.'

Swinging round, Vicè grinned at the lanky dark-haired man standing beside him. 'Is that the best you've got, Roberto? Really?'

'I'm a starving artist. I'm used to humbling myself.'

'You're an artist?' Imma frowned. 'Are you the Roberto who painted those frescoes in the hotel?'

'One and the same.' He made a small bow. 'But I would much prefer to paint you, *bella*.'

Groaning, Vicè slipped his arm around Imma's waist. 'Get your own wife and paint her.'

'This is your *wife*?' The other man raised an eyebrow appreciatively. 'Lucky man.'

'Yes, I am,' he agreed.

Imma felt a blush suffuse her cheeks as he stared down into her eyes.

'Very lucky...'

Roberto shook his head. 'I think I need to come up with a reason to get you alone, Signora Trapani. Then I can give you the low-down on this guy.'

'She already knows.' Vicè shook his head. 'Now, go and stretch some canvases, or whatever it is you do when you're not bugging me.'

Imma glanced up at him. 'Are you okay?'

'Of course.' He smiled. 'I just want to dance with my wife.'

She looked so beautiful. A little nervous but she was hiding it well, so that only he would have known. His spine tensed. He liked knowing that he could see beneath her poise, but it made him feel responsible.

Only how could he be responsible for Imma? He could barely manage his own life, let alone someone else's.

Taking her hand, he drew her away from the dance floor.

She frowned. 'I thought you wanted to dance.'

'I do. But I want it to be just the two of us.'

He thought back to when she'd said he had a lot of friends. Were they friends? He stared at the faces, feeling suddenly confused. Tonight none of them seemed even the slightest bit familiar. Nor did he feel like talking to any of them.

Normally he liked being at the centre of the crowd, surrounded by happy, smiling faces. But tonight the music was too loud, the lights too bright.

Turning, he led her through a door marked *Private*, up a spiral staircase and back outside.

'That's better,' he said softly. 'I can hear myself think.'

'You need to *think*? What kind of dancing are you planning?' she teased.

He smiled and pulled her closer. He thought about the party downstairs. And then she leaned forward, her cheek pressing into his shoulder, and he forgot about everything but the feel of her body against his and his hunger for her.

He cleared his throat. 'Are you having fun?'

Looking up at him, she nodded. 'Yes, but I'm happy to leave whenever you are.'

Her lips were parted and her eyes looked dark in the moonlight. Without replying, he took her hand and led her back downstairs, his self-control unravelling with every step and turn.

CHAPTER NINE

RAISING A HAND to shield her eyes from the sun, Imma put down her book and gazed across the terrace. It really was very hot today—far too hot to read anyway.

Totti, Matteo's French bulldog, lay panting beneath the wilting shrubs, and down in the bay even the motorboats were still, smothered into silence by the heat haze shimmering above the blue water.

She was lying on a lounger, half shielded from the sun by the trailing wisteria that overhung the terrace. And for the first time since arriving in Portofino she was alone in the villa.

Vicè was dealing with something at the hotel—she wasn't sure what. After a night of making love she had been too sleepy to do more than mumble when he'd said goodbye.

At first she'd been glad to have a few moments to herself. To think back to last night...to how he'd held her close as if she was precious to him. She knew he had held her because he liked her, and in his arms all those years of wondering who she was had dissolved.

But, much as she might have liked to daydream about those blissful hours when he had chosen her over everyone else, she was still Claudia's big sister and after a few days of just texting she needed to check in with her properly.

Feeling guilty, she had called her, expecting her to be tearful and crushed and needing reassurance.

She had been wrong on all counts.

Claudia had been quiet, but calm, and instead of wanting to talk she had been the one to end their conversation.

Imma shifted against the cushions. Of course she was glad that her sister was coping so well, and yet it was a shock. Claudia had always been so sweet and shy. But she had sounded focused, determined—like a different person, in fact.

'There you are.'

She jumped slightly as a cool hand slid over her shoulder and a shadow blocked the sun. Dropping down onto the lounger beside her, Vicè leaned over and kissed her softly on the mouth.

Her heart bumped against her ribs and she tensed, her breath hitching in her throat, her body taut and aching. Surely she should be used to his touch by now? But she was already melting on the inside, her limbs and her stomach dissolving into a puddle of need.

For a moment her lips clung to his, and she was lost in the warmth and the dizziness of his kiss, and then she shifted back, blinking into the light as he lifted his mouth from hers.

'Was it okay?' she asked quickly. 'At the hotel?'

'It's fine. The guests in Room Sixteen decided to record some new songs. At three a.m. Then they got upset when someone uploaded them to the web.' He grinned. 'Here—I thought you might need a drink. I know I do.'

Squinting into the sun, he handed her a glass. 'One perfect Negroni.'

She raised an eyebrow. 'At ten o'clock?'

'It's pretty perfect at any time.' The ice clinked as he tipped his glass up to his mouth. 'Come on, *cara*, this is supposed to be your year of living dangerously.'

As she took the drink, he glanced up at the flawless sky.

'*Accidenti*, it's hot today! If you want we can take the yacht out later. It'll be cooler at sea. We could head down the coast to the Bay of Poets.'

With his shirt hanging loosely open and his dark hair flopping into his eyes he *looked* like a poet, she thought. She felt her stomach clench. He might not be as bad or as mad as Lord Byron, but he was certainly dangerous to know.

Dangerous to her self-control.

'Does that mean you're going to write me a poem?'

His eyes gleamed. 'I might. What rhymes with Immacolata?'

She smiled. 'Poetry doesn't have to rhyme. Free verse doesn't follow any rules.'

'That sounds more like it.'

His dark eyes rested on her face, the corners of his mouth curving up into a smile that was so unapologetically flirtatious that she burst out laughing.

'You're impossible.'

'So I'm told.' He frowned. 'You're not getting too hot in the sun, are you?'

She felt her pulse accelerate, and a shivery pleasure danced down her spine as he leaned forward and ran his fingers lightly over her stomach, stopping at the triangle of her bright yellow bikini bottom.

'Maybe I should rub in some oil,' he said softly. 'Just to be on the safe side…'

That might work for her skin, she thought, but no amount of oil was going to appease the heat inside her.

She lifted her chin. 'Or I could just go for a swim.'

He grinned. 'Chicken.'

Ignoring his teasing gaze, she stood up and walked down the steps into the pool. He watched her as she did a slow length, and then, downing his drink, he stripped off his shirt and dived in, slicing through the water without a ripple and surfacing beside her.

His hands circled her waist.

'You don't need to hold me.' She held his gaze. 'I can swim.'

'That's not why I'm holding you.'

He pulled her closer and her eyes widened with shock as she felt the thickness of his erection through his shorts.

'If I pass out, I'm relying on you to get me to safety.'

His voice had a huskiness to it that made her heart thump out of time.

'So you see me as some kind of lifebelt?'

His eyes dropped to her mouth, then lower to where the water was lapping at her breasts. 'If that means you're going to wrap yourself around my waist, then yes.'

'I think it's you that needs cooling off, Vicenzu,' she teased. And, grabbing hold of his head, she pushed him under the water, then turned and swam away.

He came up, spluttering, and swam after her, snatching for her ankles and making her scream with laughter and terror until finally he caught her in the shallow end.

Laughing down at her, he scooped her into his arms

and carried her out of the pool, his dark eyes glittering. 'You are going to pay for that, Signora Trapani. With interest.'

Her hands gripped his bicep as he lowered his mouth to hers...

'What the—' He swore softly, his face creasing with irritation. On the other side of the terrace his phone was ringing. 'I won't answer it.'

'It's fine. Honestly.' Her body twitched in protest but she managed to smile. 'It might be important.'

Grimacing, he put her down and strode over to his phone. Picking it up, he glanced briefly at the screen, and her throat tightened as he immediately turned away to answer it.

It was Ciro. It must be. There was a tension to his body that hadn't been there before and he clearly didn't want her to hear his conversation.

Moments earlier she had been laughing in his warm arms. Now, though, she felt as if someone had slapped her in the face. For the last few days she had all but forgotten how he and Ciro had plotted together against her family. Now here was a blunt reminder.

Her body stiffening with misery, she watched him pace back and forth, his head bent over the phone, and then, picking up her book, she walked quickly back into the villa.

Inside it was dark and cool and she felt some of her panic recede.

Nothing had changed.

So why did she feel as if it had?

'Imma?'

She turned. Vicè was standing behind her, a frown still touching his handsome face.

'I'm sorry, but I won't be able to take you down the coast today.' His eyes avoided hers. 'Something's come up—'

'What's he done now?' Her heart was suddenly thumping so hard she could hardly speak. Claudia had sounded fine earlier, but—

'Who?' He stared at her uncomprehendingly.

'Your brother.'

'Ciro?' His eyes widened. 'I don't know. I wasn't talking to him. That was my mother.'

Her pulse slowed. She saw that his face had none of its usual animation, and something in the set of his shoulders made her hold her breath.

'Is she okay?'

Vicè had told her very little about his mother. All she knew was that Audenzia had moved to Florence, to live with her sister and brother-in-law.

He shook his head. 'She's had a fall.'

'Oh, Vicè…' Reaching out, she touched his hand. 'I'm sorry.'

'She's okay—just a bit shaken up. She's not alone. My aunt and uncle are with her. But—'

'She wants you.' She finished his sentence. 'Of course she does. We can leave right now. I'll go and get changed.'

'You want to come with me?' He looked confused.

'Of course. You can't go all that way on your own.' Now it was her turn to look confused. 'And besides, won't it look odd if I don't go with you?'

He didn't reply and she stared at him, suddenly mortified. Earlier, in bed and when they'd been laughing by the pool, she had been lulled into forgetting that this was just a mutually convenient arrangement.

But clearly Vicè hadn't forgotten. For him, this was still about sun and sex and drinking cocktails by the pool. It was obvious—*should have been obvious to her*—that his mother would be off limits. He didn't need or want her there for reasons that were glaringly self-evident.

She felt his fingers tighten around hers.

'I'm sorry,' he said slowly. 'I'd love you to come with me. It just didn't occur to me that you'd want to.'

'No, *I'm* sorry.' She tried to smile. 'I mean, why would you want me there? After everything my father's done?'

'I don't care about what your father did.' A muscle flickered in his jaw and he pulled her closer. 'Look at me, Imma. I don't care—not any more. I told you that's over. Done. Finished. Forgotten. I just didn't want you to have to lie to my mother that's all, to pretend that you love me—'

Her arms tightened around him. 'This isn't about me. It's about your mother. So if you want me to be there, I'll be there.'

Tipping her face up to his, he kissed her softly. 'I'd like that very much.'

They were about an hour away from Florence when steam began swirling up from the bonnet of the car. Swearing softly, Vicè pulled off the road and switched off the engine.

'What's the matter?'

'It's overheated. Wait here. I'm going to flip the bonnet and check the radiator.'

Imma leaned back in her seat. Without the air-conditioning the car began to grow warmer immediately, and she was opening the window when he returned.

'Sorry about this. It'll be fine. We just need to wait about half an hour for it to cool down a little, and then I can add some water. It gets a bit moody when it's hot.' He gave her a wry smile. 'Which you'd probably worked out already.'

'Actually, I don't know anything about cars,' she admitted. 'I can't even drive.'

'What?' He was staring at her in disbelief. 'Why not?'

She felt her cheeks grow warm. 'There was no point. Papà wouldn't have liked me going out on my own, and anyway I have a driver.'

Her heart began to thump. Why had she mentioned her father? The confusion between them back at the villa seemed to be forgotten, but reminding him why his mother was now alone had been stupid and insensitive.

But after the briefest hesitation his eyes met hers. 'I'll teach you to drive, if you want. Maybe not in this one—like I say, she's a bit moody. But I've got other cars.'

'You'd do that?'

'Of course. A year's plenty long enough.'

She kept on smiling, but the implicit reminder that this was a temporary arrangement stung a little more than she knew it should. Not liking the way that made her feel, she searched her mind for something neutral to say.

'So why did you drive this car today if it's so moody?'

His face stilled. 'My mother likes to see me using it. It was my father's car. His pride and joy. We used to work on it together when I was a teenager.'

She felt her stomach knot. He seemed distracted by the memory—wistful, even.

'I bet he loved spending man-time with you and Ciro.'

He hesitated. 'Ciro wasn't there. He couldn't see the point in wasting half a day getting covered in oil. It was just me and Papà.'

The ache in his voice made that knot tighten.

'You must miss him so much.'

This time there was a definite pause before he answered. 'Every day.' His mouth tensed. 'I'm sorry you didn't get to meet him. You would have liked him and he would have liked you.'

'I wish I'd met him,' she said truthfully. 'From everything I've heard he was a true gentleman and a good man.'

Alessandro Trapani's reputation was, in fact, the antithesis of her father's.

Vicè smiled, but the expression in his eyes was bleak. 'He *was* a good man. He had no failings, no flaws.' His mouth twisted. 'Actually, that's not true.'

He glanced away, and now the knot in her stomach was making her feel sick.

'He had one major flaw. Me.'

She stared at him in silence, shocked and distressed by the pinched lines around his eyes as much as the brutality of his statement.

'I don't think that's true,' she said slowly.

'Yeah, you do.' A muscle pulled at his jaw. 'You saw right through me.'

Slowly, she shook her head. 'If that were true then I would never have slept with you.'

'Oh, you would still have slept with me, *cara*. You

would have told yourself that I needed saving, or maybe that I was misunderstood,' he said calmly. 'That's what you do, Imma. You take care of people…you protect them.'

'And so do you. You take care of people. That's why they like you.'

Now he shook his head. 'They like me because of how I look and how I make them feel about themselves.'

'Your father didn't feel that way.'

'No, he didn't. My father knew everything about me. He saw my weaknesses and he loved me anyway. He loved me completely and unconditionally and that was his weakness—like I said, I was his flaw.'

He smiled at her crookedly.

'You asked me why he didn't come to me and Ciro for help. Do you remember? You said that neither of his sons had what was needed to save him.'

'I was angry.'

'But you were right. Almost right.' His shoulders tensed. 'He couldn't come to me. He knew I didn't have any money because I'd just asked him for a loan. Another loan.'

The tension was spilling over into his shoulders now. And his spine was so taut it looked as though it might snap.

'He could have gone to Ciro. But he didn't. He wouldn't—he didn't want to do that *to me*. And that's why he's dead. Because he wanted to protect me—my ego, my pride. Just like he did my entire life.'

Imma felt sick. 'That's not true, Vicè.'

'It *is* true.' His voice cracked. 'You were right about me. My whole life is a charade and my father played along with it until it killed him. And, you know, the worst part is that since his death I've had to just get on with it—and I have. So I could have done it all along. I could have been the son he wanted...the son he needed. Maybe if I had he'd still be alive.'

Tears pricked the back of her eyes. The pain in his voice cut her like a razor.

Reaching out, she took his hand. 'You *were* the son he wanted. The son he loved. And if he protected you then it's because he was your father and that was his job,' she said, her longing to ease his pain giving emphasis to her words. 'And I don't think that's why he didn't ask you for help. With his reputation he could have gone to any number of people. But good men have their pride too.'

His fingers squeezed hers. 'You're a wonderful person, Imma. And I hate how I've hurt you.'

'That's done. Finished. Forgotten.' Lifting her hand, she stroked his cheek. 'You've forgiven my father and I've forgiven you.'

'I don't deserve to be forgiven. I should have made Ciro wait. Let his anger cool. Then probably none of this would have happened. But I felt guilty—guilty that we'd lost our father because of me.' His face creased. 'And then I messed it up anyway.'

Imma shook her head. 'You didn't mess it up. *He* did. Claudia heard him leaving you a message. I checked your phone afterwards, just to be certain. It was Ciro who messed up. Not you.'

Vicè stared at her in confusion.

Ciro had messed up? He almost wanted to laugh.

But then he caught sight of Imma's face. Her green

eyes were wide and worried, and—his heartbeat stalled—she was worried about *him*.

'It doesn't change anything.' His chest felt tight. 'It's still on me, Imma. I was ashamed and angry with *myself*. But it was easier to blame your father, and that's why I went along with everything. And now I've hurt you, and you're having to live my charade too.'

'Okay. But if you're to blame, then so is Ciro,' she said firmly. 'And your father. And my father. They're all responsible for their actions.' She frowned. 'And so am I. I'm not just a victim, and you're not the villain.'

Her eyes met his, and he felt something inside him loosen.

'Everyone is a work in progress, Vicè. Every new day is a chance to start again and do better. And it's being with you that's taught me that. Maybe you need to accept that too, and let go of the past?'

He stared at her, her words replaying inside his head, the rhythm of her voice soothing him. For the first time since his father's death, maybe even before, he felt calm. The heaviness inside him that he hid so well was lifting.

She was right. Before, everything had always seemed so fixed, so definite—his failings, his relationship with his father and Ciro—so that for years he'd just been blindly following the script. But already he knew that he had changed, and was still changing.

Leaning forward, he tilted her face up to his and kissed her softly. 'I've never met anyone like you, Imma. You're a remarkable woman, and I am so very sorry for how I hurt you.'

Her eyes were bright. 'I know. But I meant what I said. I really have forgiven you.' She hesitated, her fingers trembling against his arms. 'And that's why I want you to have the business *now*. I don't want to wait a year. When we get back to the villa I'll sign it over to you.'

He stared at her in stunned silence. It was the reason he had married her. He had turned his life upside down to pursue this very moment. Only now that it was here he realised he no longer cared about it.

'I don't want it.'

As the words left his mouth his body loosened, his shoulders lifted free of some invisible burden. Ciro could rage all he liked. He was done with revenge.

Now it was her turn to stare. 'I don't understand.'

He pulled her closer. 'Getting even was never really my thing, *cara*. And anyway, I'm too good-looking to be the bad guy.'

Watching her mouth curve into a smile, he felt a rush of relief. He'd hurt her, and he couldn't change the past. But if he let her keep the business then he could at least look her in the eye.

Only what did that mean for their 'arrangement'?

His pulse slowed. Theoretically, there was no reason for them to stay married. Or rather for him to stay married. But the thought of not waking up next to her made something tighten in his chest for one very obvious reason.

He hadn't finished with her, and he knew from the pulse beating in her throat that she felt the same way.

His eyes locked with hers. 'But I still want you to have this year. Actually, I want us both to have this year. We can work on ourselves.' He smiled. 'Or, better still, each other.'

And at the end of the year she would leave and, having had his fill, he would go back to the life he loved. That, after all, was what he wanted—wasn't it?

Reaching into the back seat, he grabbed a bottle of water.

'I'm going to top up the radiator—and then I think we should probably go and see my mother.'

Following his uncle Carlo through the beautiful fifteenth-century apartment, Vicè felt his heartbeat speed up. Carlo had reassured him that Audenzia was doing well, but after what had happened with his father he wanted to see her with his own eyes.

'This way.'

Carlo pulled open a door, stepping aside as a uniformed maid scurried past, blushing as she caught sight of Vicè.

'They're in the salon, and I should warn you that emotions are running high,' he said dryly to Imma. 'They both dote on Vicè—'

Vicè grinned. 'Understandably...'

'Inexplicably was the word I was seeking.' Carlo winked at Imma. 'But when you walk in the room, *mia cara*, I fear that things could get quite out of hand.'

'It's what always happens to me,' Vicè said softly, pretending to wince as Imma punched him on the arm.

He glanced sideways into her beautiful face. He still couldn't quite believe he'd had that conversation with her in the car. He had never talked about his relationship with his father to anyone. Never admitted his worst fears. Not even to Ciro or his mother.

Especially not to Ciro or his mother.

But talking to Imma had been so easy. She had listened and she hadn't judged. She had talked gently and calmly, almost as if he'd been in some kind of accident.

He certainly felt as if he'd been in one—except there

were no physical injuries…just the pain of grief and the ache of loss.

But now he felt lighter. She had helped reconcile the past for him, and for the first time in months he could think about his father without a suffocating rush of guilt or rage or misery.

'Vicenzu, my darling boy. And Imma too—this is so wonderful!'

The room was suddenly filled with noise, laughter and tears.

'Come on, Mamma, don't cry. I'm here now. These are for you, Zia Carmela.' Kissing his aunt, he handed her some flowers, and then, crouching down, he kissed his mother on both cheeks. 'And these are for you, Mamma,' he said gently, his heart swelling with love and relief as she took the huge bunch of palest pink roses.

Her ankle was a little swollen, and she looked pale, but she was still his mother—and she was smiling now as Imma stepped forward, also smiling shyly.

'And here is my beautiful *nuora*. Imma, thank you so much for coming to see us. I really am so glad you came.'

'Thank you, Signora Trapani—'

'*Mia cara*, call me Audenzia, please. Now, come and sit next to me. Both of you. And you, Carmela. I want to hear all about your beautiful wedding, and of course see the photos. Carlo, will you take these flowers, *per favore*, and put them in water?'

Lazing back in his seat, Vicè watched his mother scroll down through the pictures on his phone, clutching Imma's hand and occasionally wiping away a tear. He felt relaxed, calm and happy. Life had never felt sweeter.

'I would like a copy of this one, Vicenzu.'

His mother was holding up his phone and, glancing at the photo, he felt his pulse stumble. It was a beautiful picture—a close-up, not a selfie. The registrar must have taken it. They were gazing into each other's eyes and there was a sweetness in Imma's face that made him want to pull her into his arms right now and hold her close.

And apologise. Again.

How could he have married her in that two-bit way? He'd let her wear that same dress she'd worn to her sister's wedding and exchanged vows with her in a ceremony that had lasted only slightly longer than it would have taken to open a bottle of Prosecco.

That photo was a beautiful lie, and he was ashamed of being a part of it, but he was even more ashamed of having made her part of it too.

'And this one, too. You look just like when you were a little boy. I have a photo in one of my albums…'

'Maybe after lunch, Mamma,' he said, smiling mechanically at Carlo's expression of despair.

As Carmela led Imma away, to show her the rest of the apartment, his mother took his arm and gave it a quick squeeze.

'I know you must have wanted to give her a more special day, *babà*. But you were in a rush—I understand.'

But she didn't. Not really. He'd seen his parents' wedding album and, although their day had clearly not been as over the top as Ciro and Claudia's, it had been undeniably romantic.

He felt sick with remorse. For a fraction of a second he was glad for the first time that his father was not alive to bear witness to his incompetence and insensitivity.

'I'm sorry, Mamma—' he began, but his mother shook her head.

'For what? Falling in love and wanting your life with Imma to start as soon as possible?' Her eyes were gentle and loving. 'You will make every day from now on special. And you are so *simpatico* together. I wish your father was here to see the two of you. He would be so very happy, and so proud of the man you have become. A man who can love and be loved in return—isn't that how the song goes?' She patted his cheek. 'He loved that song.'

He smiled down at her, but inside he could feel something tearing. It was crazy, but he kept forgetting that he and Imma were not a real couple. Watching her with his mother and aunt, he'd almost forgotten that theirs was a marriage of convenience not love.

Only now his mother was praising him for something he hadn't done, something he wasn't capable of doing, and he felt guilt and panic unfurl inside him.

He knew what his father had wanted him to be. But he wasn't that man and nor could he ever be him. And besides, in the long-term Imma wanted her freedom. They both did.

'Oh, Carlo, you clever man! How perfect!' Audenzia looked up at her brother-in-law, her eyes sparkling like the glass of Prosecco he had handed her. 'A toast to my darling son and his beautiful bride. To Vicenzu and Imma. *Cent' anni!*'

A hundred years.

It was just a toast, Imma told herself, glancing at the hibiscus flower at the bottom of her glass of Prosecco. But every time she remembered Audenzia's joyful words she felt a sharp nip of guilt. And something else—something she couldn't quite place.

They had just finished lunch on the balcony overlooking the garden. The food had been sublime and the view was incredible, but she kept losing concentration, her mind returning like a homing pigeon to that moment when Vicè had held up his glass and toasted their marriage.

As his eyes had met hers she'd forgotten to breathe, much less raise her glass. But it wasn't those few shared half seconds that were making her heart pound—it was the memory of that half hour in the car, when he had let his mask slip and needed her for something more than sex.

Audenzia reached out and took her hand. 'Now, Imma, I love my boy, but he has a few tiny faults. He can't have too much red wine. It makes him grumpy.'

Vicè rolled his eyes. 'I'm still here, you know!'

'And he puts too much of that product in his hair.'

Imma giggled.

'And I'm *still* here.' Shaking his head, Vicè grimaced.

'Well, you shouldn't be. Go with Carmela and get my albums. We must show Imma *all* the photos before you leave.'

'Must we?' Groaning, he stood up. 'This is just a ruse to get me out of the room, isn't it?'

'Of course.' His mother smiled. 'We want to talk about you in private. Now, go.' She turned to Imma, her eyes sparkling. 'It's important to keep a man on his toes.' She sighed. 'If only I could show you the garden.'

Imma followed her gaze. 'It's beautiful.'

'Oh, it's not my efforts. Carlo is the gardener—the

same as my Alessandro. He could grow anything. That's why he bought the estate on Sicily.'

Imma managed to keep smiling but her chest felt tight, and maybe something of what she was feeling showed in her face, because Audenzia reached over and patted her hand.

'Oh, child, don't be upset. I loved my life there, but Florence is where I grew up, and I'm happy to be back here. It was different for Alessandro. It was in his blood...in his heart. Vicenzu feels the same way.'

Imma stared at her in confusion. *Did he?* He had never so much as hinted that was how he felt about the estate. On the contrary, he seemed to love his life at La Dolce Vita.

'Did he ever want to take it over?'

'When he was a little boy it was all he talked about. And of course Alessandro wanted that too. But he didn't want to put pressure on him.' Her smile faded. 'Vicenzu idolised his father, only I don't think he ever believed he could step into his shoes so he stopped trying. But Alessandro would be delighted to know the business is still in the family. And to know that Vicenzu has met and married you.' She squeezed Imma's hand. 'You've seen who he really is and you love him.'

Imma nodded. 'Yes, I do.'

She had agreed automatically but her heart swelled as she spoke, opening like the petals of the hibiscus flower in her glass, and with a shock she realised that she wasn't lying or pretending.

She loved Vicè.

Stunned, disbelieving, she repeated the words in her head.

It was true.

Her heart beat a little faster.

And maybe…possibly…he might feel the same way about her.

Okay, he had never said he loved her, but perhaps, like her, it hadn't occurred to him. Perhaps all he needed was someone to point it out to him.

The drive back to Portofino was quicker and quieter than the trip down.

Fixing his eyes on the road, Vicè was aware that he wasn't saying much. But Imma hadn't noticed. In fact, she seemed distracted, wrapped up in her own thoughts, and that was fine.

There had been enough drama for one day.

The villa felt quiet, almost subdued after the laughter and chatter of Florence, and it fed into his mood so that he felt oddly flattened as he walked up to the bedroom. Maybe a swim would help. Or a drink.

'Do you want some wine?' He turned towards Imma, smiling. 'You look like I feel, *cara*. What we need is a couple of late nights.'

She smiled, but it didn't reach her eyes, and the heaviness in his chest seemed to swell and press against his ribs.

'I'm teasing. I know you're tired. I am too. It was a long day.'

She shook her head. 'It's not that. I want to go back to Sicily with you.'

He felt a rush of relief. *Of course.* That was why she was on edge. Seeing his mother had made her homesick. But it was easily fixed. He wasn't willing to see Cesare, but he could visit friends while she saw her father.

'That's fine. We can fly back tomorrow. We can stay for a couple of days—'

She hesitated. 'I don't mean for a visit. I want to move back. To live there. With you.'

'That would be a hell of a commute,' he said lightly.

Glancing down, he saw the tension, the hope in her eyes, and felt his stomach clench.

'What's brought this on?'

'I suppose it was seeing your *mamma*. It made me think about things…about what we're doing…'

He felt suddenly short of breath. 'I know it's hard, having to pretend. I hated lying to her too.'

'But that's just it. I wasn't lying,' she said slowly.

His heart was beating out of time. 'I don't understand—'

Except he did. He knew what she was saying even if she hadn't said the words—he could read it in her eyes.

Looking down into her face, he felt a sudden rush of panic. Her eyes were wide with hope, with trust.

With love.

'You said you'd give me a year so I could find out what I wanted. But I don't need a year, Vicè. I already know what I want. I want us to go back to Sicily together.'

He held her gaze. 'I have a business here—a life. I can't just go back to Sicily.'

'I thought we could run your father's business together.'

Once upon a time that had been his dream. For a fraction of a second he saw the warm olive groves in his head…could almost feel the dry ground beneath his feet. And then he pictured his father's face, the reassuring smile that hid the disappointment in his heart.

He couldn't face seeing that same disappointment on Imma's face.

'I don't want to do that, *cara*. That's why I live here.'

She looked confused—no, more than confused… crushed.

'But… I just… I thought you— We— Your mother—'

He shook his head. 'My mother misses the past. She misses my father. But I'm not my father.'

He felt suddenly furious with Imma. Why was she doing this? Saying these things. Everything had been just fine. Why did she have mess it up?

'I love my life as it is,' he said stiffly.

She jerked back, as though he had hit her, and he knew that her pain was as real as if he *had* hit her. He knew because the pain in his chest hurt so badly it was making him feel ill.

'This year is about helping you. I wanted to do you a favour, that's all,' he lied.

For a moment she seemed too stunned to speak, and then slowly she frowned. 'I don't think I need your help, actually. I can manage just fine on my own.'

The hurt in her voice made his body tense. 'I'm sorry, Imma.'

'Don't be.'

She lifted her chin and he saw the sheen of tears in her eyes. 'We said no more lies, remember? I don't think there's any point in my staying now, do you?'

In the silence that followed her question, her hurt was palpable. But what could he say? *Yes, I want you to stay so we can keep on having sex?*

With an effort, he shook his head, and after a moment, she said quietly, 'If you really don't want the business then I'll sign it back over to my father.' When he didn't respond, she gave him a small, sad smile. 'I'll go and pack.'

He watched her walk upstairs. He'd never known a feeling like this—not even when his mother had called to tell him his father had died. His heart was like a living, struggling creature trapped inside his chest.

Only what choice did he have? He couldn't do to her what he had done to his father. He couldn't be responsible for her love. Nor was he worthy of it. Not when he was so flawed, so imperfect, so bound to mess up.

CHAPTER TEN

'GREAT PARTY, VICÈ!'

Vicè turned, flicking on his hundred-kilowatt smile automatically as the pop-star-turned-actress who was standing in front of him tilted her head in provocation.

'Thanks, Renée—and congratulations on the nomination.' He raised the glass of champagne he was holding. 'There's a bottle of Cristal at the bar with your name on it.'

'Care to come and share it with me?' she invited, her mane of auburn hair falling into her eyes and the hem of her shimmering red minidress riding high on her thighs as she pouted up at him. 'We could have our own private party.'

His pulse accelerated. She was beautiful, willing, and she had booked a suite, and yet…

He shook his head slowly, pretending regret. 'I need to make sure this party keeps rolling, Renée.'

He had never been too hung up dotting the *i*'s and crossing the *t*'s, but mixing business and pleasure was one rule that should never be broken, no matter how much pleasure was being promised.

His chest tightened.

What a load of sanctimonious drivel!

He liked Renée—she was sweet—but he wasn't going to sleep with her, whatever the circumstances. There was only one woman he wanted, and he had let her slip through his fingers just over five weeks ago.

His mouth twisted. Actually, he'd driven her to the airport.

Way to go, Vicè. Drive the woman you love to the airport and wave her off.

His heart was suddenly thumping so hard against his ribs he was surprised the shock waves didn't shatter the glass he was holding.

He *loved* her?

For a moment he turned over his words in his mind, waiting for the denial that would surely follow. Instead, though, the echo grew louder, rebounding and filling his head.

He loved her.

But of course he did.

Only he had pushed her away rather than admit it to himself. Or to her. And now she was gone. And he was going to have to live without her in an agonising charade of his own making for the rest of his life.

'Sorry, Renée. I didn't mean to sound so pompous.' Holding up his hand, he tapped the ring on his finger. 'It's just that I'm missing my wife.'

A flush of colour spread over her face. 'I'm sorry... I didn't know you were—'

'It's fine.' He pasted a smile on his face. 'Look, you have a great night.'

'You too, Vicè.'

She blew him a kiss from her bee-stung mouth and he watched her sashay off on her towering heels.

Eyes burning, he turned away from the laughing,

dancing mass of people. Last time he had been on the yacht Imma had been by his side. Now, without her, he felt empty. Without her all of this—his life, his much-prized *dolce far niente*—was literally nothing.

It was ironic, really. She had told him that she wanted to find herself, and he had blithely told her that he would give her a year, never once realising that *he* was the one who didn't know who he was or what he wanted.

But he did now.

And pushing her away hadn't changed a thing. Wherever she was in the world, she had his heart. He belonged to her. He would always belong to her.

Only it was too late.

Even though all the dots had been there in front of him he had been too scared to connect them—too scared of the picture they would make. So he had let her leave. Worse, he had let her end it. He hadn't even had the courage to do that.

He was a coward and a fool. For in trying to play it cool he had simply succeeded in making his own world a lot colder.

The ache in his heart made him feel sick, but he didn't care. He couldn't lie to himself any more and pretend he felt nothing for Imma. His 'sweet life' tasted bitter now. The pain of loving had been replaced with the pain of loss, as bad as when his father had died.

Closing his eyes, he pictured Alessandro's face. He still missed him—probably he always would. And yet it didn't hurt quite as much as before. The tension in his shoulders eased a little.

Now it wasn't the funeral he remembered, but happier times. Meals round the table. Stories before bedtime. And watching his father dance with his mother,

her head resting against his chest and Alessàndro singing softly.

Now he could think about his father without flinching, and that was thanks to Imma. She had helped him grieve and had put words to his unspoken fears so that they had stopped being the terrifying larger-than-life problems he had always refused to face.

Like the words of another of his father's favourite songs, he had let her get under his skin and found he was a better person with her. Or at least good enough for her to confide her own fears.

His heart began to beat a little faster.

Imma had drawn strength from him too. Holding his hand, she had leapt into the unknown. That night on Pantelleria she had even trusted him to take her virginity, and then later entered into a marriage of convenience with him.

She had even trusted him enough to love him.

Staring out across the dark sea, he felt his fingers tighten against his glass.

Maybe it was time he started trusting himself.

Pushing her sunglasses onto the top of her head, Imma stopped beside the market stall. For a moment her hand hovered over a crate overflowing with lemons, and then, changing her mind, she selected a couple of peaches.

Once—a lifetime ago—this would have been her dream. The freedom to wander alone among the colourful stalls, to linger and to chat to people without the continual unsmiling presence of her security team.

But that dream felt childish now, in comparison to the loss of her dream of love with Vicè.

Smiling politely at the tiny, leathery old woman who

ran the stall, she took her change and made her way back past the boutiques and ice-cream parlours.

She had chosen the small town of Cefalù in northern Sicily on a whim, but after nearly five weeks of living here she liked it a lot. It would be a good place to stay while she worked out what to do next.

The villa she was renting was outside the town, a good ten-minute walk away from the noisy hubbub of the market. It was quiet—isolated, even—but right now that was exactly what she wanted. Somewhere quiet, away from the world, where she could lick her wounds.

Thinking back to those horrific last hours with Vicè, she felt a rush of queasiness. She'd been so excited, so caught up in the thrilling realisation of her own love for him, that she'd completely misjudged his feelings. And in the face of his less than enthusiastic response to her suggestion that they take over his father's business together she'd had no option but to face the facts.

He didn't need or want her.

He certainly didn't want her love.

And, to be fair, he hadn't ever offered her a real relationship. As he'd said, he'd only been doing her a favour.

She had wanted to call a taxi, but he had insisted on driving her to the airport. She would never forget that silent, never-ending journey to Genoa.

As they'd left Portofino he had asked her if she wanted to listen to the radio. Then he had asked if she wanted him to turn up the air-conditioning.

At no point had he asked her to stay.

At the airport he had offered to go in with her, but her nerves had been in shreds by then and she had simply shaken her head.

Her throat tightened. He hadn't used his legendary

powers of persuasion to convince her otherwise. Maybe he had been daunted by her silence.

The other, more devastating but more likely explanation was that he had been desperate for her to be gone so that he could get back to the sweet, easy life he'd had before meeting her...

Walking into the villa, she forced herself to unpack her shopping and put it away before checking her phone for messages. At first she had checked it obsessively, but as the hours had turned into days and the days had become weeks she had forced herself not to look.

Before leaving, she had agreed with him that they would say nothing to their families. She couldn't remember who had suggested it, but she was glad. There was no way she could face her father's I-told-you-so reaction—or, worse, his clumsy attempts to try and make amends. Nor did she want to confide in Claudia. She was doing so well right now, and she feared offloading her problems on to her sister would ruin the fragile peace Claudia had found.

Peace, and happiness at the discovery she was having a baby.

Her breath twisted in her throat.

She had wanted to go to her, of course, but Claudia had been firm and, hearing the flicker of determination in her voice, Imma had understood that her sister needed to prove she could cope alone.

So she had carried on speaking to both of them every couple of days, acting as if nothing had happened, making sure that the conversation merely touched on Vicè.

Her stomach clenched. Against her will she was living another charade, and it was only through sheer effort of will that she dragged herself out of bed each morning, got dressed and made herself eat breakfast.

Incredibly, the one person she found herself wanting to talk to was Audenzia. During those few hours in Florence she had found herself admiring her quiet strength and love of life.

Under other circumstances she would have liked to get to know her better.

But now, of course, that was impossible.

Almost as impossible as stopping all these incessant what-if and if-only thoughts.

Glancing out of the window, she felt her heartbeat slow. She couldn't see Portofino from the villa, but that didn't stop her from closing her eyes and imagining. *What would he be doing right now?*

Opening her eyes, she pushed the thought away before it could spiral out of control. Each morning she promised herself that she wouldn't think about Vicè until lunchtime, and today she had almost managed it—that was something to celebrate.

In fact, she *was* going to celebrate. She was going to take her lunch to the beach and have a picnic. Even though the 'beach' was not really a beach at all—more a patch of sand in a rocky alcove.

After she'd finished eating, she watched the Palermo to Naples ferry heading off towards the mainland. It made her feel calmer, thinking about all those people on board, with all their hopes and dreams buzzing inside their heads.

Her heart might have been broken by Vicè but that didn't mean her life was over. She was going to be all right. He might not love her, but she couldn't regret the time they had spent together. He had taught her to be brave, to take risks.

Yes, she loved him still. Maybe she always would. But she was ready to face the world. On her terms.

Standing up, she brushed the sand off her legs and began to walk carefully across the rocks and back up to the house. But as she reached the villa her feet suddenly faltered.

A man was waiting for her.

Her heart began to pound.

Not because he was a stranger.

But because he wasn't.

She stared at him, stunned and furious. Even if she wanted to run—and she did—nothing seemed to be functioning. Instead she stood woodenly while Vicè walked slowly towards her.

How had he found her? And, more importantly, why was he here?

He had no right to come here—not when she was finally beginning to get him out of her head, if not her heart, she thought as he stopped in front of her, his dark hair blowing in the breeze.

He was dressed incongruously, in a dark suit and shirt, only it wasn't his clothing that made her throat tighten. But she had learned from her mistakes, and she wasn't ever going to let herself be distracted by his beauty again.

'Hi,' he said softly.

She lifted her chin. 'How did you find me?'

'With great difficulty.' He smiled, and then, when she didn't smile back, he shrugged. 'My lawyer Vito knows some people who keep their ears to the ground. He uses them to find clients that skip bail.'

'And I thought it was my father who had the shady friends.'

His expression didn't change—but then why should it? If he had ever cared what she thought of him, he certainly didn't any more.

'Why are you here, Vicè? I mean, I take it this isn't a social call?'

'I had a meeting with Vito this morning.' He stared at her steadily. 'I had some paperwork to complete.'

Inside her head his words were bumping into one another in slow motion, like a train and its carriages hitting the buffers. Glancing down, she saw that he was holding an envelope. Her heart shrivelled in her chest.

Paperwork. In other words, he wanted a divorce.

Pain seared every nerve. 'I thought you were giving me a year?'

He glanced away. 'I can't wait that long.'

She wanted to scream and shout and rage—at the unfairness of life and at the unknowable cruelty of loving someone who didn't love you. But she had laid enough of her feelings bare to this man.

'Fine. Just give me the paperwork and I'll sign it.'

'It's already signed.'

He took a step closer and she backed away from him, not caring that he could see her pain, just wanting him gone.

'Your father signed it this morning.'

She stared at him in confusion—and then suddenly she understood. 'You came back for the business. That's why you came to Sicily. For your father's business.'

He stared at her, his gaze steady and unflinching. 'He signed it over to me this morning.'

Why did it hurt so much? She'd known right from

the start that he'd only ever wanted that. Whatever he'd said in the car on the way to Florence and then at the villa, it obviously was still.

Her chest tightened.

But why had her father agreed to hand it over? Had Vicenzu told him the truth about their marriage? Even though he knew what it would mean for her.

'Did you tell him about us?' she asked slowly.

He shook his head.

'Then how—'

His eyes met hers. 'I threatened him. I told him I had enough on him to make sure he'd lose everything he cared about. Just like my father did.'

On one level she knew her father deserved it, but it hurt hearing Vicè talk in that way.

'Blackmail and extortion? That sounds more like my father than you.'

'I said all that afterwards.' He ran an agitated hand through his hair. 'First I met him for breakfast. I told him that I wanted to buy back the business and that I would pay what he thought was a fair price.'

'What…?' Imma felt as if she was in a daze.

'I'm not like your father, *cara*. I don't bully or black-mail people into doing what I want. I paid him what he asked—twice what he paid my father—so that you and I can start with a clean sheet.'

Her heart was in her mouth. 'I don't understand…'

'You asked me why I was here.' His eyes found hers. '*You're* why. I've bought the business back. For us.'

She shook her head. 'There is no us.'

'There is. Only it took you leaving for me to see it.' He took another step closer. 'I love you, Imma. And

I want to be with you. Not for the cameras, or for the business, but because you're in my heart.'

His voice was shaking now, and she could see tears in his eyes.

'You helped me find out what and who I want to be. And I want to be your husband. For real. Forever.'

Reaching out, he took her hands.

'I'm sorry I didn't stop you leaving, but when you said you wanted us to run the business together I panicked. I mess up all the time, *cara*—with family, with work, with you. And I've hurt people, you especially, and I didn't want to hurt you any more. I don't ever want to hurt you.'

He shook his head.

'I should never have let you go. But I thought that making you stay would have just been me being selfish—that it was what the old Vicè would have done. And I wanted to be a better man. So I let you go and I pretended everything was cool.'

His mouth twisted.

'Only it wasn't. I missed you like crazy. So I went and saw Mamma and I told her everything.'

'Everything?' Her eyes widened with shock.

'Everything. I was sick and tired of lying to everyone. To her…to you. To myself.'

Screwing up his face, he shook his head.

'I think it's the first time she's ever lost her temper with me. *Cavolo*, she was mad at me. Like, furious. Every time I thought she'd finished she'd start up again. She told me she was ashamed of me, that my father would be ashamed of me, and then she told me I had to put it right.'

Imma bit her lip and, reaching out, placed her hands

against his chest, feeling his heart beating into her fingertips. 'Did you tell her about what my father did?'

He pulled her closer. 'A bit.'

'Is that why you threatened him? For your *mamma*?'

'No. I wanted him to know what it felt like to be cornered and helpless.' He gave her a small crooked smile. 'And then I made him donate a lot of money to my mother's favourite charity. Weirdly, it was the difference between what he paid my father and what I paid him.'

She smiled. 'That won't have helped his heart.'

'*What* heart?'

He gazed down into her eyes and she felt her own heart flutter inside her chest.

'I thought I wasn't worthy of your love, *cara*. Probably I'm not. But I'm going to do whatever it takes to be worthy.'

'So you don't want a divorce?' she asked softly.

'*No.*' He stared down at her, his arms tensing around her. 'Do you?'

She shook her head and, breathing out unsteadily, he buried his face in her hair.

'In that case, I have something for you.' Reaching into his jacket, he pulled out a small square box. 'You never had an engagement ring, so I thought I'd get you an eternity ring instead.' His eyes were bright. 'That's how long I want to be with you. For eternity.'

Tears slid down her cheeks as he opened the box and slipped a beautiful emerald ring onto her finger. 'Oh, Vicè…'

Laughing softly, he wiped her tears away with his thumbs. 'I had some change left over…it was that or blow it all in a high-stakes poker game—'

'Change from what?' She looked up at him in confusion.

He hesitated, and she felt the muscles in his arms tighten.

'I sold the Dolce.'

She gaped at him. 'You *sold* it? But why?'

'I needed the money to buy the business back. It was that or go to Ciro.' He grimaced. 'So, as I say, I needed the money.'

'But you love the Dolce.'

'I did—I do. And I've kept a stake in it. But I don't need it any more.'

His gaze rested on her face, and his love was there for anyone to see.

'You're the sweetness in my life, *cara*.' His eyes dropped to the ring sparkling on her finger. 'Now and for eternity.'

EPILOGUE

It WAS A hot day in late September—one of the hottest on record, according to Manfredi, the Trapani estate's longest-serving member of staff. But the weather was the last thing on Imma's mind as she walked slowly through the olive trees.

She had spoken to Claudia that morning, and her sister's news had pushed every other thought out of her head.

Almost every other thought.

But right now that would have to wait.

Breathing in the scent of warm earth and grass, she replayed her conversation with Claudia.

Claudia and Ciro were together. They were in love. Both of them this time.

It was a lot to take in—too much for one person on her own.

A tremble of happiness ran over her skin.

But she wasn't on her own any more.

Her eyes fixed on the group of men standing beneath the trees at the other side of the olive grove. Or rather on one particular man.

Vicè was gesticulating energetically, his dark eyes moving over the other men's faces as he spoke, and she felt a sharp, almost unbearable urge to push them all aside and drag him back to the villa and upstairs to their bedroom.

'Imma!'

She looked up at the sound of his voice, her heart leaping as it still did, maybe three, five, sometimes ten times a day, whenever she remembered that Vicè was her husband 'for real' and 'forever'.

Pulse jumping, she watched him excuse himself, and then he was walking towards her, his long legs making short work of the uneven ground and a slow, curling smile pulling at the corners of his mouth.

She felt her stomach flutter. She had thought that he couldn't look any more desirable than he did in a suit, but she'd been wrong. In scuffed work boots, faded chinos, and with the sleeves of his denim shirt rolled up he looked impossibly sexy.

'Signora Trapani…'

He pulled her against him, his mouth seeking hers with an urgency that made her whole body twitch with desire.

Behind them, a cacophony of approving whistles and shouts filled the air.

'Vicè, everyone is watching us,' she whispered.

'So let them watch. I'm just saying good morning to my wife.'

His voice was warm, and she felt an answering warmth across her skin.

Her eyes met his. 'You did that already.'

The corner of his mouth tugged upward. 'I'm thinking that was more of a *ciao* than a *buongiorno*.' His dark gaze drifted slowly over her face. 'How do you feel about going back to the villa and brushing up on our greetings?'

'It wouldn't hurt,' she said softly. 'I mean, just because we're married it doesn't mean we should take each other for granted…'

Watching the flush of colour suffuse her cheeks, Vicè felt his body harden. That she should want him at all still felt like a miracle, but that she loved him…

There were no words that could adequately capture how that made him feel. All he knew was that he was the luckiest man in the world.

The doubts and regrets of the past were forgotten now. Imma loved him, and he knew that her love and the efforts he'd made to deserve it would have earned his father's respect.

Life had never been sweeter.

Uncurling his arm from around her waist, he took her hand and led her back across the field.

'I like this dress.' His eyes ran over the curve of her breast. 'Although I think it will look even better once you've taken it off.'

She smiled, hesitated, then said, 'Claudia called.'

Cavolo. He swore silently.

'Yeah, Ciro called me too.' He'd been so caught up in this morning's meeting he'd actually momentarily forgotten about his brother's call. 'He sounded pretty happy. Is that how Claudia sounded?'

She nodded. 'It's all she's ever wanted, but—'

'But what?' Turning towards her, he caught her chin. 'What is it, *cara*?'

Her green eyes were so open, so unguarded, and he felt a sudden urge to tell her how much he loved her, how necessary she was for his own happiness. But he didn't need to say anything. She already knew, and that made him love her even more.

'You can tell me.'

She bit her lip. 'It *is* real, isn't it? This time? He does love her? I mean, he's not just saying it because your *mamma*—'

He hated seeing her so worried—hated that he had something to do with her doubts.

Pulling her closer, he shook his head. 'Mamma didn't speak to him until after he and Claudia had sorted it out between them. You don't need to worry, *cara*. Honestly, I've never heard my brother sound like that before. He's crazy about her.'

Ciro had been so emotional. For once, he had actually felt like the big brother.

His fingers tightened around hers. 'I promise it's real, *cara*. As real as you and I. All of what happened—it's in the past for Ciro, for me.'

It was a past that didn't feel so much like another country to him as a different planet.

'I feel the same way,' she said.

He stroked her cheek. 'Have they told anyone else?'

'Claudia told Papà.' Her eyes met his. 'But she agreed that the same rules I insisted on will apply.'

Vicè nodded. Imma had gone to see Cesare the day after they had got back together. Glancing down at her beautiful face, he felt a rush of pride in his wife for facing up to the man who had once dominated her whole life.

She'd given her father an ultimatum: change, or she and Claudia would cut him out of their lives forever.

And Cesare had capitulated. In fact, he had blubbed

like a child, apologised, and then made promises which, so far, he was keeping.

'Why are you smiling like that?' she asked slowly.

'I was just thinking what a great aunt you'll be, Zia Imma. Of course I'll be the most fantastic uncle too.'

She laughed. 'That won't be hard as you'll be the only uncle.' Her face softened. 'Vicè, if you're half as good at being an uncle as you are at being a husband and a boss, you'll be better than fantastic.'

'Let's see if you still think that after the harvest,' he said lightly.

'I will.' Her eyes met his. 'I spoke to Manfredi this morning. He said that you have the same feel for the olives as your father.'

He felt his heart contract.

Stepping into his father's shoes had been nerve-racking. He still had doubts about his ability to pull it off. But with Imma by his side...

He felt a fierce, unpremeditated quiver of anticipation. She was his partner, his equal. Together they had already faced their fears. And together they would meet whatever happened in the future.

Watching the mix of sadness and pride in Vicè's eyes, Imma felt her heart swell.

She knew how much this estate meant to him. It was his father's legacy and one day it would be his.

Her breath caught in her throat.

'So, are you going to be Zio Vicenzu or Zio Vicè?'

'Not Vicenzu.' He shuddered. 'Too serious. Vicè is what a cool uncle would be called, and I am definitely going to be a cool uncle.' His eyes gleamed. 'I cannot wait until this baby is born. Hopefully he's going to be just like me. That'll keep Ciro on his toes.'

'It might not be a boy.'

'It is.'

She raised an eyebrow. 'And you know this how, exactly?'

'Man's intuition.' He grinned. 'It's very rare—only the most impressive males of the species have it.'

'Right… And I'm guessing it's infallible?'

He nodded, and keeping her expression innocent, she took his hand and rested it gently on her stomach. 'So what are *we* having, then?'

He stilled, his eyes widening with shock. 'You're pregnant?'

She nodded. 'I did a test after Claudia rang. Actually, I did two. Just to be sure.'

'And it's definite?'

She drew a deep breath and nodded again. 'I was going to wait for the perfect moment to tell you, but then I realised that every moment is perfect with you.'

There was a shake in her voice that matched the tremble in his hands as they tightened around hers.

Looking up, she bit her lip. 'Are you pleased?'

'Pleased?' His eyes filled with tears. 'I'm ecstatic.'

He pulled her against him, burying his face in her hair, pressing her close to his heart, which was hammering as wildly as hers.

'You're having my baby.'

He kissed her gently on the lips and she felt his mouth curve into a grin.

'Of course, with my man's intuition I already knew that—'

She punched him lightly on the arm. 'You are such a bad liar, Vicenzu Trapani.'

'Thanks to you,' he said softly.

His smile sent a shiver of heat down her spine. 'I love you, Vicè.'

Tipping her mouth up to his, he kissed her again. 'I love you too, Imma. That's the truth and it's going to stay true forever.'

She felt her pulse twitch as he gazed down at her, his dark eyes gleaming.

'That dress, though—that's coming off right now.'

And, scooping her up into arms, he carried her into the villa and upstairs to their bedroom.

* * * * *

Marriage Made in Blackmail
Michelle Smart

MILLS & BOON

Michelle Smart's love affair with books started when she was a baby, when she would cuddle them in her cot. A voracious reader of all genres, she found her love of romance established when she stumbled across her first Harlequin book at the age of twelve. She's been reading—and writing—them ever since. Michelle lives in Northamptonshire, England, with her husband and two young smarties.

CHAPTER ONE

Luis Casillas snatched his ringing phone off the table and put it to his ear. *'Sí?'*

'Luis?'

'Sí.'

'It's Chloe.'

That brought him up short. 'Chloe… Chloe Guillem.' The woman who had spent the past two months treating him as if he were a carrier for a deadly plague?

'Oui. I need your help. My car has broken down on a road on the Sierra de Guadarrama…'

'What are you doing there?'

'Driving. *Was* driving.'

'Have you called for recovery?'

'They can't get to me for two hours. My phone is running out of battery. Please, can you come and rescue me? Please? I don't feel safe.'

Luis looked at his watch and swore under his breath. He was due at the gala he and his twin brother Javier were hosting in half an hour.

'Is there no one else you can call?' Chloe worked for his ballet company in Madrid. In the year the gregarious Frenchwoman had lived in his home city she had made plenty of friends.

'You are the closest. Please, Luis, come and get me.' Her voice dropped to a whisper. 'I'm scared.'

He took a long breath as he did some mental maths. This gala was incredibly important.

Ten years ago Luis and his twin had bought the provincial ballet company their prima ballerina mother had spent her childhood training at. Their aim had been to elevate it into a world-renowned, formidable ballet company. First they had renamed it Compania de Ballet de Casillas, in their mother's memory, then set about attracting the very best dancers and choreographers. Three years ago they had drawn up the plans to move the company out of the crumbling theatre it had called home for decades and into a purpose-built state-of-the art theatre with world-class training facilities and its own ballet school. Those plans had almost reached fruition.

Now they wanted patrons for it, members of the elite to sponsor the ballet school and put it even more firmly on the world's ballet map. Europe's elite and dozens of its press were already gathering at the hotel. Luis *had* to be there.

'Where exactly are you?'

'You will come?'

It was the hope in her voice that did for him. Chloe had the sweetest voice he had ever had the pleasure of listening to. It wasn't girlishly sweet, more melodic, a voice that sang.

He couldn't leave her alone on the mountains.

'*Sí*, I will come and get you, but I need to know where you are.'

'I will send you the co-ordinates but then I will have to turn my phone off to save what is left of my battery.'

'Keep it on,' he ordered. 'Have you got anything to hand you can use as a weapon if you need it?'

'I'm not sure…'

'Find something heavy or sharp. Be vigilant. Send me the co-ordinates now. I'm on my way.'

'*Merci*, Luis. *Merci beaucoup.*'

'I'll be with you as soon as I can.'

Hurrying to his underground garage, he selected the quickest of his fleet of cars, inputted Chloe's co-ordinates into its satnav, then drove it up the ramp. The moment he was clear, he put his foot down, tearing down his long driveway, past the stretched Mercedes with his waiting driver in it.

His clever console, which had calculated the quickest route for him, said he was an hour's drive to her position from his home in the north of Madrid, *if* he kept to the speed limit.

Provided traffic wasn't too heavy this Saturday evening, Luis estimated he could make it in forty, possibly even thirty minutes.

He always kept to the speed limit in built-up areas. The temptation to burn rubber was often irresistible but he always controlled the impulse until on the open road. Today, with thoughts of Chloe stranded in the mountains on his mind, he wove in and out of the traffic ignoring the blast of horns hailing furiously in his wake.

Chloe Guillem. A funny, attention-seeking, pretty child who had grown into a witty, fun-loving, beautiful woman. Truly beautiful.

It had taken him a long time to notice it.

An old family friend, he hadn't seen her for four or five years when she had called him out of the blue.

'*Bonjour*, Luis,' she had said in a sing-song tone that had immediately suggested familiarity. 'It is Chloe Guillem, little sister of your oldest friend, calling to ask you to put friendship ahead of business and give me a job.'

He had burst into laughter. After a short conversation where Chloe had explained that she'd completed her apprenticeship in the costume department of an English ballet company, spent the past two years working for a Parisian ballet company and was now seeking a fresh challenge, he'd given her the name and number of his Head of Costume. Recruitment, he'd explained, was nothing to do with him.

'But you own the company,' she had countered.

'I own it with my brother. We are experts in the construction business. We know nothing of ballet or how to make the costumes our dancers wear. That's what we employ people for.'

'I have references that say I'm very good,' she had cajoled.

'That is good because we only hire the best.'

'Will you put in a good word for me?'

'No, but if you mention that your mother was Clara Casillas's personal costume maker, I am sure that will work in your favour. Provided you are as good as your references say you are.'

'I am!'

'Then you will have no trouble convincing Maria to hire you,' he had laughed.

Luis had thought nothing more of the conversation until around six months later when he'd attended a directors meeting at the old theatre to discuss preparations for the company's move. A galloping gazelle had bounded up to him out of nowhere with a beaming smile and thrown her arms around him.

It had been Chloe, bright and joyous and, she had delightedly told him, loving her time in Madrid. Luis had been pleased to see this face from his past but he'd been too busy to take much notice of his old friend's little sister.

When Luis and Javier had pooled their meagre inheritance to form Casillas Ventures almost two decades ago, they had decided from the start that one of them would always be the 'point man' on each project. This would simplify matters for contractors and suppliers. Luis had taken the role of point man for the construction of the new theatre and facilities. In this venture he had been far more hands on than he would normally be but this was a special project. This was for their mother, a way for the world to see the Casillas name without automatically thinking of Clara Casillas's tragic end at the hands of her husband.

The closer it got to completion, the more hours he needed to put in, overseeing the construction and ensuring Compania de Ballet de Casillas was prepared for the wholesale move to its new premises.

From that embrace on though, whenever Luis visited the old crumbling theatre he somehow always managed to see Chloe.

She always acknowledged his presence, with either a quick wave if working on an intricate costume or a few words exchanged if on a break, her cheeks turning the colour of crimson whatever reception she gave, a little quirk he'd found intriguing but never given much thought to...not until he'd walked past a coffee shop a few months later and caught a glimpse of a raven haired beauty talking animatedly to a group of her peers. Spring had arrived in his home city and she'd been wearing a thin dress that exposed bare, milky-white arms, her thick raven hair loose and spilling over her shoulders.

He would have stopped and stared even if he hadn't recognised her.

How had he not seen it before?

Chloe Guillem *radiated*. Sunlight shone out of her pores, sexiness oozed from her skin. Her smile dazzled.

She must have felt his stare for she had looked up and seen him at the window and the full power of her smile had been unleashed on him and this time it had hit him straight in his loins. He had never in all his thirty-five years experienced a bolt of pure, undiluted, unfiltered lust as he had at that moment.

He'd taken her out to dinner that very night. It had been the most fun and invigorating evening he could remember. Chloe was funny, full of self-deprecating wit, a raucous laugh never far from her voluminous lips. And she was sexy.

Dios, was she sexy. He had been unable to tear his eyes away, greedily soaking up everything about her, all the glorious parts he'd been oblivious to. It was incredible to think he'd been blind to it for so long.

And the desire was mutual. Luis knew when a woman wanted him and Chloe's body language had needed little interpretation.

But when they had left the restaurant she had rebuffed his offer of a nightcap by hailing a taxi.

He had never been rejected before. It had intrigued rather than discouraged him.

'If not a nightcap how about a goodnight kiss?' he'd asked before she could escape into the cab, taking her face into his hands and gently rubbing his nose to hers. Her scent had filled his senses, reminding him of English strawberries and cream.

Her eyes had been stark on his, the flirtatious glimmer that had been prevalent the whole evening suddenly gone, her beautiful plump lips drawing together.

'Next time, *bonita*,' he had whispered, inhaling her scent again.

All the confusion on her face had broken into a smile that had shone straight into his chest. She had stepped back and nodded. 'Yes. Next time.'

'You will let me kiss you?'

The smile had widened, baby-blue eyes glittering with promise. 'Yes, I will let you kiss me.'

But there had been no next time and no kiss. Two days later everything had gone to hell with her brother.

Chloe had cancelled their planned date and stopped accepting his calls. When he visited the ballet company she kept her head down and pretended not to see him.

They hadn't exchanged two words in almost as many months.

Why the hell he was tearing down roads at an average speed of a hundred miles an hour to rescue a woman who had dropped him like a hot brick he could not fathom, and especially on this night of all nights.

A curse flew from his lips when, thirty-four minutes after leaving his home, he reached the co-ordinates Chloe had given him.

It was a passing place on the winding road, with a flat grassy area for day-trippers to enjoy the spectacular view over a picnic. There was no one there. And no broken-down car.

He brought the car to a stop and grabbed his phone from the passenger seat. In his haste to get to her he'd forgotten to turn the ringtone up and only now did he see he had three missed calls from his brother.

He called Chloe. It went straight to voicemail.

Getting out of the car to search for her, he called Javier back.

'Where are you?' his brother snapped, picking up on the first ring.

'Don't ask. I'll be there as soon as I can.'

'I'm grounded in Florence.'

'What?' Javier was supposed to be at the gala already. In Madrid. Not Florence.

'My plane's been grounded on a technicality. It

passed all the safety checks this morning. Not a single issue of concern. Something's not right.'

Luis disconnected the call, a real sense of disquiet racing through him. The sun was descending over Madrid in the far distance but the orange glow it emitted did nothing to stave off the chill that had settled in his bones.

His brother was grounded in Florence and suspected sabotage.

Luis had been lured to the middle of nowhere in the Sierra de Guadarrama in his dinner jacket, on a rescue mission where the damsel in distress had disappeared.

He checked the co-ordinates again.

This was definitely the right place.

So where the hell was she? And why was his sense of disquiet growing by the second?

Chloe Guillem took a seat in the first-class lounge at Madrid-Barajas airport and removed her phone from her carry-on bag.

She had six missed calls and seven text messages, all from the same number. She deleted the messages without reading them and fired off a message to her brother.

Mission accomplished. Waiting to board flight. x.

The glass of champagne she'd asked for when entering the lounge was brought to her table and she took a large sip of it at the moment her phone rang.

Cursing to herself, she switched it to silent and threw it down.

Two minutes later it vibrated in a dance over the table.

She had a new voicemail.

Her gut told her in the strongest possible terms not to listen to it.

She pressed play.

Luis Casillas's deep, playful voice echoed into her ear. 'Good evening, Chloe. I hope you are safe wherever you are and have not been kidnapped by a gang of marauding youths. You might wish you had been though because I *will* find you. And when I do…' Here, he chuckled malevolently. 'You will wish you had never crossed me. Sleep well, *bonita.*'

It was the emphasis on his final word rather than the implied threat that lifted the hairs on her arms.

Bonita.

The first time he had called her that she had thought she would never stop smiling.

Now she was overcome with the urge to cry.

He was not worth her tears, the two-faced, treacherous, conniving, evil bastard.

Thank goodness she'd had the sense to resist his offer of a nightcap…

Chloe downed the rest of her champagne and grimaced.

It hadn't been sense that had stopped her accepting his offer or his goodnight kiss. It had been fear.

Her date with Luis had given her a sense of joy she hadn't felt since her early childhood where she had spent innocent, happy days climbing trees and running around with friends, cocooned with love, blissfully unaware life could be anything other than wonderful. Luis was tied up in those memories.

Once upon a time she had been smitten with him.

She'd wanted to be sure his feelings for her were genuine and that he wasn't looking at her only as a potential conquest. As hard as it was, she'd wanted to trust him. She'd wanted his respect.

At the end of their date when his nose had rubbed against hers and every ounce of her being had strained on an invisible leash to escape her brain and *kiss* him, she had almost given in. She'd spent their entire date imagining him naked, something she'd blamed on the erotic dream she'd had of him the night before but which she'd known, deep down, was her own hidden sexuality breaking free for this man who'd stolen into her teenage heart and now demanded to be heard.

What had she been *thinking*?

Luis had no respect.

He had made a mockery of her brother's trust in him and by extension made a mockery of her and her dead mother. He was as bad, no, *worse*, than her pathetic father.

She knew his brother was equally culpable for ripping her brother off but Javier hadn't been the one to embrace her tightly at her mother's funeral and promise that one day the pain would get better. That had been Luis. Witty, sexy, fun-loving Luis, the only man who had ever captured her feminine attention. The only man in her twenty-five years she had ever dreamed of.

Whatever Benjamin had planned for him could not come soon enough.

The board on the wall with the constantly updated list of all departures and arrivals showed her own flight was now boarding.

Hurrying to her feet, Chloe made her way to the departure gate.

Now she knew what Luis Casillas was capable of she had to take his threat to hunt her down seriously.

Only when she looked out of the window of her first-class seat on the flight paid for by her brother and watched Madrid shrink from view did her lungs loosen enough to breathe easily.

Luis thought he'd be able to find her? Well, good luck to him. She would be the needle to his haystack.

The Grand Bahaman suburb of Lucaya was, Chloe could not stop thinking, a paradise. Her brother had set her up in a villa in an exclusive complex where all her needs and whims were taken care of and all she had to worry about was keeping her sun lotion topped up.

She had spent her first six days there doing nothing but lazing by the swimming pool and refreshing her social media feeds, her worries slowly evaporating under the blazing sun. As far as boltholes went, this was the best. It had exclusivity but also, should Luis carry out his threat to hunt her down, the comfort of safety in numbers.

She doubted he was sparing her a moment of his thoughts. The fallout in Madrid and the rest of Europe was growing in intensity. Chloe read all the news and gossip torn between glee and heartbreak.

It should never have come to this. Luis and Javier should have done the right thing and paid her brother the money they owed him, all two hundred and twenty-five million euros of it.

Seven years ago, on the day Chloe and her brother were told their mother's cancer was terminal, Luis had called Benjamin for his help, dressing it up as an investment opportunity.

The Casillas brothers had paid a large deposit on some prime real-estate in Paris that they intended to build a skyscraper on that would eclipse all others. The owner of the land had suddenly demanded they pay the balance immediately or he would sell to another interested party. He'd given them until midnight. The Casillas brothers did not have the money. Benjamin did.

He gave them the cash, which amounted to twenty per cent of the total asking price. It was an eye-watering sum.

Tour Mont Blanc, as the skyscraper became known, took seven years to complete. Two months ago, Benjamin had received his copy of the final accounts. That was when he realised he'd been duped. The contract he'd signed, which he'd believed stated his profit share to be twenty per cent as had been verbally agreed between him and the Casillas brothers, had, unbeknown to him, been altered before he signed. He was entitled to only five per cent of the profit.

His oldest, closest friends had ripped him off. They'd taken advantage of him at his lowest point. They'd abused his trust.

When they'd refused to accept any wrongdoing Benjamin had taken them to court. Not only had he lost but the brothers had rubbed salt in the wound by hitting him with an injunction that forbade him from speaking out about any aspect of it.

Chloe would never have believed Luis could be so cold. Javier, absolutely, the man was colder than an ice sculpture, but Luis had always been warm.

Now the press was alive with speculation. Benjamin whisking Javier's prima ballerina fiancée away from the Casillas brothers' gala and marrying her days later had the rumour mill circling like an amphetamine-fed hamster on a wheel. An intrepid American journalist had discovered the existence of the injunction and now that injunction was backfiring. So far only the injunction itself was known about but a frenzy of speculation had broken out about the cause of it, none of it casting the Casillas brothers in a favourable light.

Let them be the ones to deal with it, Chloe thought defiantly, shoving her beach bag over her shoulder and slipping on her sparkly flip-flops. She was safe here in the Bahamas and her brother was safely cocooned with Freya in his chateau.

Leaving the tranquillity of the complex for only the third time since her arrival a week ago, she spent an enjoyable fifteen minutes strolling in the early-morning sun to Port Lucaya, very much looking forward to a day of island hopping on the complex owner's yacht.

The invitation had been hand delivered by the manager the evening before, the man explaining it was an excursion the owner provided for favoured guests whenever she visited. A guest had been taken ill so the invitation was Chloe's if she wanted it. Thinking she couldn't come to much harm if it was a woman hosting the event—she'd read too many horror stories about young women and rich men on yachts to have been comfortable with it being run by a rich male stranger—she had been delighted to accept. She couldn't spend a fortnight in the Bahamas hiding away.

Chloe liked to keep busy. She liked to be with people. Being alone with only her thoughts for company meant too much time to think. Better to let the past stay where it was by always looking forward and keeping her mind busy and her life full.

She found the port easily, the pristine yachts lined up in the small bay an excellent giveaway. Opposite it was the Port Lucaya Marketplace she'd heard so much about and which she had promised herself a visit to. Looking at the quaint colourful tourist trap bustling with life and exotic scents brought a big smile to her face. She would go there tomorrow.

Turning her attention back to the yachts, Chloe scanned them carefully, looking for the one named *Marietta*. Her excitement rose when she finally located it. At least four decks high, the *Marietta* was the biggest and most luxurious-looking of the lot. Not quite cruise-ship size, it looked big enough to accommodate dozens of guests with room to spare.

But where was everyone? The metal walkway for passengers to board had been lowered but she saw and heard none of the sounds and sights you would expect of a large party going off on an all-inclusive day trip.

As she hesitated over whether to step onto the walkway, a figure wearing what she assumed was captain attire appeared on deck.

'Good morning,' he said, approaching her with a welcoming smile. 'Miss Guillem?'

She nodded.

'I am Captain Andrew Brand. Let me show you in. I'll give you the mandatory safety talk as we go.'

Chloe joined him on the gleaming yacht with a grin that only got wider as he showed off the magnificent vessel, pointing out the bar, swimming pool and hot tub on the next deck up, then taking her inside.

This yacht had *everything*, she thought in awe as she tried her hardest to pay attention to what she was being shown and told.

After showing her the Finnish sauna that had a window looking straight out to sea, he took her to the top deck to what was appropriately named 'the sky lounge' and left her with a young woman with tightly curled hair who made her a cocktail of coconut blended with mango and rum and served it in the coconut shell with a straw. This stretched Chloe's smile so wide her mouth must have reached her ears. She enjoyed it so much she readily accepted a second, then took a seat on one of the plentiful cappuccino-coloured leather seats encircling the lounge.

She gazed out of one of the many windows, imagining the spectacular view of the stars at night from this wonderful vantage point, and hoped she would be lucky enough to experience it for herself. The estimated finish time of the day's excursion had been vague.

Which reminded her that she still seemed to be the only guest.

And where had the barwoman gone?

Unease crawling through her, Chloe opened her beach bag to search for her phone.

Just as her fingers closed on it, a tall figure stepped into the lounge.

Although the figure was only in the periphery of her vision, it was enough for her stomach to roil and ice to plunge into her veins.

Feeling very much like a teenager watching a horror movie and wishing she could cover her eyes to hide from the scary bit, she slowly turned her head.

And there he stood, filling the space around him like a dark, menacing shadow, a grim smile on his face.

Luis.

'Hello, *bonita*. It is a pleasure to see you again.'

CHAPTER TWO

LUIS FELT IMMENSE satisfaction to read the horror in Chloe's baby-blue eyes.

'Nothing to say?' he taunted. 'I have travelled a long way to see you, *bonita*. I would have thought that deserved an enthusiastic welcome.'

Those wonderful pillowy lips he'd fantasised about kissing parted then snapped shut as she swallowed, shock clearly rendering her dumb.

'You're not normally this shy.' He folded his arms across his chest and stroked his jaw. 'Is it delight at seeing me that has struck you mute?'

Her wonderfully graceful throat moved, colour creeping over her cheeks. 'What...? How...?'

'Is that the best you can come up with?' He shook his head with mock incredulity.

She blinked rapidly and blew in and out. 'I've been set up.'

'The sun hasn't damaged your observation skills, I see.'

The baby-blue eyes stared straight into his. 'You bastard.'

'If we are moving straight to the name-calling, I have a select number of insults I can apply to you. Which shall I start with?'

'Forget it.' Hooking her large bag over her shoulder, she got to her feet. 'Let's not waste time. Say what you need to say. I have a holiday to enjoy.'

He gazed at the long legs now fully on display, only the top half of her supple thighs covered by the tight blue denim shorts she wore. *Dios*, for a She-Devil she had the most amazing body. Beauty, heavy breasts covered in a red T-shirt, a slim waist and a pert bottom... he defied any red-blooded heterosexual man out there not to fantasise about bedding her.

'My apologies,' he said sardonically. 'I didn't realise you were on a holiday. I thought you had run away.'

'No, it's definitely a holiday. Sun, sea, pina coladas and hot men.' She smiled as she listed the latter, a jibe he knew perfectly well was intended to cut at him. 'Getting far away from you was an added incentive but not the main consideration.'

'Would your brother have paid for you to holiday in the Bahamas if you hadn't agreed to do his dirty work?' The booking for her flights and villa had been paid for personally by Benjamin.

'*Au contraire,*' she said, switching from English to her native French. Between them they spoke each other's languages and English fluently. 'I didn't agree to do his dirty work. I insisted on it.' The smile she now cast him was pure beatific. 'Your gallantry at rescuing a damsel in distress does you credit. Knowing you were on those mountain roads searching for me is a thought I will cherish for ever.'

The rage that had simmered in his veins since he and Javier had pieced all the parts of the jigsaw together flashed through his skin.

Luis hadn't expected contrition from her but her triumph was something else.

Chloe had sent him on a wild goose chase so he would be late for the gala. Her brother had conspired to ground Javier's flight to Madrid so he too would be late for the gala. With both Casillas brothers out of the way and the world's media present, Benjamin had pounced, stealing Javier's fiancée away and taking her to his secure chateau in Provence. And then he had proceeded to blackmail them: Javier's fiancée in exchange for the money he claimed they owed him. If the money wasn't forthcoming he would marry her himself.

Luis could not remember the last time his brother had been so coldly furious. Javier had dug his heels in and refused to pay. For Javier it was a matter of principle. They had done nothing illegal and a court of law agreed with them. They didn't owe Benjamin a cent.

For Luis, Benjamin's actions were a declaration of war. All the guilt he'd felt and his plans to put things right between them had been discarded in an instant.

The press photographs of Freya leaving the gala hand in hand with Benjamin had captured a certain *something* between the pair of them that had made Luis wince for his brother. Whether Javier's fiancée was an unwitting tool in the plot or a willing supplicant was irrelevant. Those pictures had shown his brother's fiancée gazing into his enemy's eyes with a look of rapture on her face. Javier would rather starve than take her back.

His brother had been right not to take her back. Their enemy had married Freya two days ago, barely five days after stealing her away. The fallout against the Casillas brothers had accelerated.

Chloe had willingly played her part in this. She would find herself playing a role to end it and whether that was willingly, he could not care less.

'Cherish those memories, *bonita*,' he said, hiding his anger with a beatific smile of his own. 'You earned them. You have proven yourself to be a fabulous actress.'

She fluttered her long black eyelashes at him. 'Were you worried about me? How touching.'

Remembering the burst of raw panic that had grabbed him to find her car missing from the place he had expected it to be… Worried, Luis concluded grimly, did not begin to cover it.

It was only because he had known her since she was in her mother's stomach, he told himself. For the first three years of Chloe's life he, Javier and Benjamin, all ten years older, had been her chief babysitters. None of them had been enthusiastic about the job, especially when she'd entered toddlerhood and turned into a pint-sized She-Devil.

More fool him for being so blown away by her adult beauty that he'd failed to see behind the fun-loving façade to the fully grown She-Devil beneath the milky skin.

'I would not be human if I hadn't been concerned,' he said blithely.

'I think it's debatable whether you and your brother are human at all.'

He spread his arms out and winked. 'Oh, I am *very* human, *bonita*, as I am more than happy for you to discover for yourself.'

A tinge of colour slashed her pretty rounded cheeks. She scowled at him and pulled her bag even closer into her side. 'Are we done yet? Have you finished with your fun?'

'Finished? *Bonita*, my fun with you has only just begun.'

Indeed, this was already much more fun than he had envisaged. Chloe's belligerent discomfort and outrage were things of beauty, acting like salve to his rabid anger.

'Yes, well, *my* fun is over. I'm going.'

'Going where?' he asked as she stomped to the door, giving him an extremely wide berth as she moved.

'Back to my villa.'

'How?'

It was the way he said that one word that made Chloe pause and her heart accelerate even faster and the sick feeling in her stomach swirl harder.

It didn't matter that Luis had found her, she kept telling herself. It had been inevitable that their paths would cross again one day. At least it was done with and she could stop worrying about it.

'Have you been so enraptured by my presence

that you failed to notice we're no longer at port?' he mocked.

She turned her head to look out of the window to her left. Then she turned it to the right.

Then she spun round to face the front, curses flying through her head.

The captain had set the *Marietta* to sail and she hadn't even noticed.

'Get this thing turned around right now!' she demanded, eying him squarely.

He rubbed his chin. 'No, I don't think I will.'

'The captain will turn it round.' She took three quick paces to the door and pressed the green button beside it.

'That won't work,' he commented idly. 'The crew have been instructed to leave us alone until further notice.'

'Take me back to port right now or I'm calling the police.'

He strode to the bar and laughed. It had a cruel, mocking tinge to it. 'Why ruin this wonderful reunion with talk of the police?'

She could have easily stamped her feet. 'Because you're holding me here against my will.'

He turned his back on her to study the rows of spirits, liqueurs and mixers lined up on the bar. 'Drink?'

'*What?*'

'I need a drink. Do you want one?'

'I want you to take me back to port. This game has gone on long enough.'

'This is no game, *bonita*.'

'Stop *calling* me that.'

He looked at her and winked. 'I remember when it made you blush.'

'That was before I knew what kind of a man you really are, you unscrupulous jerk. And stop winking at me. If this isn't a game, stop acting like it is.'

'If I am acting like it's a game, you conniving witch, it's to stop myself from grabbing you by the shoulders and shaking you until your teeth fall out.' He flashed his perfectly white and perfectly straight teeth at her. 'Or from taking the kiss you owe me.'

She sucked in a sharp breath.

His threat didn't bother her because she instinctively knew Luis would never lay a finger on her in anger.

But the mention of the kiss she owed him…

Chloe spent her days surrounded by dancers. The male ones had the most amazing physiques and they worked hard to maintain them, the look they strove for lean and strong. To her eyes they were beautiful sculptures but not sexy.

Luis was a hulk of a man, burly and rugged, a man for whom chest waxing would be considered a joke. If he had any vanity she'd never seen it. Even his dark hair, which he kept long on top and flopped either side of his forehead, never looked as if he did more to it than run his fingers through it when he remembered.

Square jawed, his hazel eyes surrounded with laughter lines, his nose broad, cheekbones high, lips full but firm, the outbreak of stubble never far beneath his skin.

In a world of metrosexual men, Luis was a man who drank testosterone for breakfast and made no apologies for it. He would be as comfortable chopping wood with an axe as he would holding a meeting in a boardroom and she found him *very* sexy.

She'd dreamed of kissing him when she was seventeen years old, dreams that had faded to a hazy memory over the years but then re-awoken with a vengeance when she had started work at Compania de Ballet de Casillas. Months after she'd joined the company Luis had turned up. She had been delighted to see him, had spontaneously thrown her arms around him and been completely unprepared for the surge of heat that had bathed her upon finding herself pressed against his hard bulk in that fleeting moment.

That heated feeling had been with her ever since. All she'd needed was one glimpse of him and her heart would pound. She would smile and try to act nonchalant but had been painfully aware of her face resembling a tomato.

That heat was there now too, vibrating inside her. Not even the knowledge of his treachery had dimmed it. She hated herself for that.

He looked up from the bottle of black vodka he was examining and smiled unpleasantly. 'The insults hurt, don't they?'

'You deserve yours and more for what you did to my brother.' And to me, she refrained from adding.

Learning how deeply he'd betrayed her brother had cut her like a knife. The more she and Benjamin had put the pieces together, the deeper the cut had gone, all the way back to her earliest memories.

Had Luis and Javier always had contempt for her family? Or had the damage done by their mother's horrific murder at the hands of their father been the root cause of it?

Their mothers had been closer than sisters. As far back as Chloe could remember Luis and Javier had been a part of their lives. They would come and stay with them for weeks at a time in the school holidays then, when she had reached eight and them eighteen and they had snubbed university to set out on their own path, they would still drop in for visits whenever they were in Paris.

Their visits had always made her mother so happy. When she'd been diagnosed with lung cancer they had been there for all of them. Luis had visited her mother so many times in hospital the staff had assumed he was one of her children.

Had the supposed feelings he'd had for her family all been a lie? If not, then how could he have tricked her brother into signing that contract on the day their mother's condition was diagnosed as terminal?

Luis replaced the bottle of vodka in his hand with a bottle of rum, twisted the cap off and sniffed it. 'Whatever we did to your brother he has repaid with fire. He has gone too far and so have you. Thanks to you and your brother conspiring against me and *my* brother, our names are mud.'

'Good. You deserve it.' She hated the quiver in her voice. Hated that being so close to him evoked all those awful feelings again that should never have sprung to life in the first place.

Her heart shouldn't beat so wildly for this man.

She swallowed before adding, 'You took advantage

of him when our mother was dying. I hope the journalist investigating the injunction unveils your treachery to the world and that everyone learns what lying, cheating scumbags the Casillas brothers are.'

Hazel eyes suddenly snapped onto hers, a nitrogen-cold stare that sent a snake of ice coiling up her spine. 'We did not cheat your brother.'

'Yes, you did. I don't care what that court said. You ripped him off and you know it.'

His nostrils flared before he stretched out a hand to the row of cocktail mixers. 'I am going to tell you something, *bonita*. I had sympathy for Benjamin's position.'

'Of course you did,' she scorned with a shake of her hair.

'The terms of profit were reduced from twenty per cent to five per cent under the advice of our lawyer. Your brother's contribution to the project was a portion of the funding whereas Javier and I would be doing all the work.'

Luis remembered that conversation well. It was one of only a few clear recollections from a day that had flown by at warp speed as he and Javier had battled to salvage the deal they had put so much time and money into.

'You agreed on twenty per cent. That was a verbal agreement.'

He added crushed ice to the concoction he'd put in the cocktail shaker. 'Benjamin was sent a copy of the contract to read five hours before we all signed it. He didn't read it.'

Javier had been the point man on the Tour Mont Blanc project and emailed the contract to Benjamin. Luis had been unaware of his twin's failure to mention the change in the profit terms in that email. When they had gone to his apartment to sign it, the atmosphere had been heavy, the news of Benjamin's mother overshadowing everything.

Luis had only discovered three months later, at Louise Guillem's funeral of all days, that Benjamin still thought he would be receiving twenty per cent of the profit. It had been a passing comment during the wake, Benjamin nursing a bottle of Scotch and staring out of his chateau's window saying he didn't know how long he would have to keep the wolves from the door and ruefully adding that, if only the Tour Mont Blanc project could be speeded up and he had his twenty per cent profit now, all his money troubles would be over.

Luis had had many arguments with his brother through the years but that had been the closest they had ever come to physical blows. Javier had been immovable: Benjamin should have read the contract.

His twin was completely hard-nosed when it came to business. Luis was generally hard-hearted when it came to business too. They weren't running a charity, they were in the business of making money and at the time their bank balance had been perilously close to zero.

But Benjamin had been their oldest friend and Luis had been very much aware that Benjamin's frame of mind on the day of the signing had been anywhere but on the contract.

With Javier digging his heels in, Luis had decided that it would only cause bad feeling and acrimony if he told Benjamin the truth. It had been better for everyone that Luis wait for Tour Mont Blanc, a project that would take years, to be completed and for all the money to be in the bank before speaking to Benjamin man-to-man about it and forging a private agreement on the matter.

'He didn't read it because he was cut up about our mother. He *trusted* you. He had no idea the terms had been changed. He signed that contract in good faith.' Chloe's eyes were fixed on his, ringed with loathing. 'He gave you the last of his cash savings. That investment meant he couldn't afford to buy the chateau outright and he had to get a huge mortgage to pay for it so our mother could end her days there. He almost lost everything in the aftermath. You took his money then watched him struggle to stop himself from drowning.'

'We were not in a position to help him. It gives me no pleasure to admit this but we were in as dire a financial situation as Benjamin was. We'd grown too big too soon and over-extended massively. The difference between us and Benjamin was that Benjamin saw no shame in admitting it. We did, and I am only sharing this with you so you understand that I'm not the treacherous bastard you think I am. At that time we were *all* trying to save ourselves from drowning. I'd always had it in the back of my mind that when the Tour Mont Blanc project was complete I would come to a private agreement with Benjamin and pay him the extra profit he felt he was due…'

'You didn't do that though, did you? The first he knew of it was when he saw the final accounts!'

'I'd been overseeing a project in Brazil. Javier sent the accounts before I had the chance to talk to Benjamin about it. I flew back for Javier's engagement party and your brother came in all guns blazing firing libellous accusations at us. Call it human nature, call it bull-headedness but when someone threatens me my instinct is to fight back. I admit, ugly words were exchanged that day—we were all on the defensive, all of us, your brother included. He would not discuss things reasonably...'

'Why should he have?' She stared at him like a beautiful, proudly defiant elfin princess, arms folded belligerently across her ample chest, as sexy a creature as could be imagined.

Luis still struggled to comprehend how he'd been oblivious to her beauty for all those months or how he could be standing there with the woman who had conspired against him and his twin and find his blood still pumping wildly for her. He didn't know which need he wanted to satisfy the most: the need to avenge himself or the need to throw her onto the nearest soft furnishing and take that delectable body as his own.

Soon he would do both. He would screw her over in more ways than one.

'Humans respond better to reason. Fight or flight, *bonita*. Benjamin made threats, we dug our heels in, then he hit us with the lawsuit and we had no choice but to defend ourselves. But I still had sympathy for his position. In truth it is something that hadn't sat well with me for many years. I'd hoped to speak to him privately and come to an agreement once the litigation was over with and tempers had cooled and we could speak as rational men. Legally, I had nothing to prove. Javier and I had done nothing wrong and that's been vindicated in a court of law.'

'If you really believed that, why take the injunction out on him?'

'Because there has been enough rubbish in the past two decades about my family. Do you have any idea how hard it is being Yuri Abramova and Clara Casillas's sons?' Luis downed his cocktail and grimaced at the bitter taste that perfectly matched his mood.

He tipped the glass he'd filled for Chloe down the bar's sink and reached for a fresh cocktail shaker.

'We are the sons of a famous wife killer,' he continued as he set about making a more palatable cocktail, one that would hopefully wash away the bile lodged in his throat. 'It is one of the most infamous murders in the past century. There have been documentaries made about it, books and endless newspaper articles. A Hollywood studio wanted to make a movie about it. Can you imagine that? They wanted to turn my mother's death at the hands of my father into entertainment.'

Chloe tried her hardest not to allow sympathy to creep through her but it was hard. Luis's past was something that never failed to make her heart twist and tears burn her eyes. She blinked them back now as she imagined the vulnerable thirteen-year-old he would have been.

She had been only three when Luis's mother had

been murdered, far too young to have any memories of it.

But she *had* been there.

Clara had been performing in London on the night of her murder in a production of *Romeo & Juliet*. Yuri, a ballet dancer who had defected from the old USSR in the seventies and whose career had gone into free-fall, had watched the performance convinced his wife was having a real-life affair with Romeo. When the performance had ended, Yuri had locked Clara in her dressing room, preventing dancers and backstage staff from entering when the screams and shouts had first rung out.

By the time they'd smashed the door open, Clara was dead, Yuri's hands still around her throat.

Luis and Javier had been in the hotel across the road from the theatre babysitting Chloe with Benjamin.

Chloe and Benjamin's mother, Louise, who had loved the twins fiercely, had been the one to break the terrible news to them.

He poured the fresh cocktail into two clean glasses. 'Imagine what it has been like for us growing up with that as our marker. We are hugely successful and rich beyond our wildest dreams but still people look at us and their first thought is our parents. You see it in their eyes, curiosity and fear.'

He pushed one of the glasses towards her and put the other to his lips. He took a sip and pulled a musing face. 'Not too bad. Better than the last one but I think I'll stick to construction and property developing.' He took another sip. 'As I was saying. My parents. A legacy we have tried hard to escape from while still honouring our mother.'

'Is that why you took her surname?' The question came before she could hold it back. It was something she'd been intensely curious about for years.

'We took it because neither of us could endure living with our father's name. We have worked hard to disassociate ourselves from that man and to make our mother's name synonymous with the beauty of her dance and not the horror of her death, but now everything has been dredged up again and *you* are partly responsible. Our lives are back under the media's lens and again we find the world wondering how much of our father's murderous blood lives in our veins.' He inhaled deeply. 'We took out the injunction to stop this very thing from happening because we knew Benjamin was an explosive primed to detonate. We are close to signing a deal to build a new shopping complex in Canada. Our partner in this venture has stopped returning our calls.'

'Then he's a smart man who knows he will be ripped off.'

The flash of anger that rippled from Luis's eyes was enough to make her quail.

'We did *not* rip him off and if anyone says otherwise we will sue the clothes off their back.'

'You ripped my brother off,' she said defiantly. 'Feel free to sue me. I would love my day in court.'

'I have a much better way of dealing with *you*, *bonita*, but as for your brother, I will not say this again— we did not rip him off. I was going to get the gala out

of the way and then call him but, instead, Benjamin
stole Freya and tried to blackmail us. All my sympathy left me then. As far as I'm concerned, your brother
can go to hell. The press speculation his actions have
wrought are untenable. My assistant found comments
on a newspaper website querying whether Freya ran
off with Benjamin because she feared she would end
up like my mother.'

Chloe winced. She had many issues with Luis and
Javier but they could no more help their parentage than
she could help hers. 'That's disgusting.'

'I'm glad you think so because you are going to help
put things right. If you hadn't called with your tale of
terror I would have been at the gala before Benjamin
stepped foot inside it. None of this would have happened.'

'He believed you owed him two hundred and twenty-
five million euros,' she spat, her fleeting compassion
overridden by anger. 'Did you expect him to roll over
and accept that? Did you expect *me* to? I was there with
him at the hospital when you made that call begging
for his help and his money.'

She'd been there, at the first turn of the wheel of
the whole mess.

Chloe had been sitting on a bench in the hospital
garden with her big brother, both of them dazed; her
crying, he ashen, both struggling to comprehend the
mother they loved so much was going to die. That was
when Benjamin had received the call from Luis asking
for his financial help.

'If you felt Javier had been cheated would you sit

there meekly and allow it to go unchallenged when there was something practical you could do to help?'

'Probably not.' He shrugged. 'But would I have conspired to kidnap a woman and hold her to ransom…? No, I would not have gone that far if the first throw of the dice had not already been rolled.'

'I did not conspire to kidnap Freya! I helped whisk her away from a potential marriage made in hell and…'

'Is that how you justify it to yourself? I must remember to dress my actions up in a similar fashion when I tell you that you won't be returning to port until you have married me.'

CHAPTER THREE

FOR A MOMENT there was an intense buzzing in Chloe's
ears. She shook her head to clear it, being careful not
to take her eyes from Luis, who was now leaning forward with his elbows on the bar.

'What are you talking about?'

His eyes were intense on hers. 'I've not kidnapped
you, I've borrowed you. Would that be how it's said?
Is that how I can justify it?'

'No, what was that rubbish about marrying me?'

'That? That's the next stage. If you want to go home
you have to marry me first. But let us not call it blackmail. By your logic it will be…an incentive? How does
that sound?'

'It sounds like your cocktail has gone straight to
your head.'

'And you haven't drunk yours yet. Try it. You might
surprise yourself—and me—and like it.'

'Not if it makes me as drunk as *you* clearly are.'

'Regretfully, I am not drunk but I *am* serious.'

The hairs on her arms lifted, coldness creeping up
her spine and into her veins. She hugged her bag closer

to her. 'Okay, this game stops now. I'm sorry for my part in the affair. Is that what you want to hear? Okay then, how about this? I was wrong, I apologise. I'm sorry...*je suis desolée...lo siento...mi dispiace...*'

Amusement flickered in his hazel eyes. 'Can you apologise in Chinese too?'

'If that's what you want I'll teach myself it and say it to you, just *let me go.*'

The spacious windowed walls of the lounge were closing in on her. Suddenly it felt imperative to get off this yacht. She needed dry land and space to run as far and as fast as she could. Luis's defence of himself, his hulking presence, his magnetism...it was all too much.

It had always been too much but it had never scared her before, not like this.

She had such awareness for this man. She remembered all the visits he'd made to the theatre when she'd been working there, how she would sense his presence in the building long before she caught sight of him, almost as if she had an internal antenna tuned to his frequency. That antenna was as alert now as it had ever been and vibrating like the motor of a seismograph recording an earthquake.

She needed to find safety before the ground opened up and swallowed her whole.

He studied her silently, the brief amusement disappearing into seriousness. 'I warned you in my message that I would find you and that you would live to regret crossing me,' he told her slowly. 'You have known me long enough to know I am not a man to make idle threats.'

'Believe me, right now I am regretting it.'

'You're only regretting that I found you, not your actions.'

She opened her mouth to lie and deny it. His denials about not being party to Benjamin signing the contract under false pretences and that he'd wanted to put things right had sounded so sincere that there had been a few moments when she'd wondered if he might be speaking the truth.

His threats to marry her made her glad she hadn't swallowed those lies.

It would never happen. *He* could go to hell first. Hell was where he belonged, him and his cold monster of a brother.

'I can see the truth in your eyes, *bonita*,' Luis said grimly before she could speak. 'You don't believe me and you don't regret your actions. In many respects I commend you for your loyalty to your brother.'

It was a loyalty he understood.

Luis and Javier had always been loyal to each other. Though far removed from the other in looks and personality, they had grown and developed in the same womb and the bond that bound them together was unbreakable, tightened by the tragedy of their lives.

'Benjamin's own sister marrying me will kill the rumours and stop people believing that Javier and I are the devil's spawn. It's the only way to repair the damage.'

'I would rather swim to shore than marry you,' she spat, not caring at that moment that she'd never even mastered a basic doggy paddle.

'It will be the only way you get home if you don't agree to it.' He placed his chin on his knuckles. 'But have no worries, *bonita*. I am happy to wait for as long as is needed for you to come to the correct decision.'

'Then we will sail these seas for ever because I will never, ever, marry you and there is nothing you can do to make me.' She smiled tremulously. 'You can't threaten to fire me—I've already quit.'

It didn't escape his attention that she was inching her way to the door. Any moment she would bolt on those long gazelle-like legs.

Let her run. Chloe would soon discover there was no escape.

He returned the smile. 'You have not worked your notice period. I can sue you for that and I can sue you for breach of contract.'

'What have I breached?'

'You passed on confidential information about one of our dancers to your brother.'

'Freya's not an asset, she's a person.'

'She's a company asset. You acted as a spy against our interests.'

'You would have to prove it. Look at their wedding photo. It's obvious they're in love with each other.' Her beautiful smile widened but there was a growing wildness in her eyes. 'See? My instincts were right. Benjamin took her to punish Javier but he already wanted her for himself and she wanted him. You can sue me for whatever you want but if you won it wouldn't matter; Benjamin would pay any fine.'

'I could make sure you never work in the ballet world again.'

'I'm sure you could and without much effort but I don't care. I survived on an apprentice's salary, I'll cope. I don't care what job I do. I'll wait tables or clean bathrooms.'

'You would throw your career away?'

Her heart-shaped chin lifted. 'Some things are more important. I knew the risk I was taking when I made the call to you.'

'Interesting,' he mused. 'You will be pleased to know I have no wish to destroy you. Your brother? *Sí*. I would gladly destroy him but the feud can end here and now—call it an additional incentive. All you have to do is marry me and all the bad blood will be over.'

'You call that an incentive?' she said disdainfully. 'There is nothing more you can do to hurt him than you have already done.'

'Any hurt caused was not deliberate,' he asserted through gritted teeth.

'You would say that. You wanted me to feel guilty enough that I agreed to your nefarious plan. Well, it hasn't worked. I don't believe you ever intended to give him any of the profit you denied him and I regret nothing. I will never marry you.'

The last of Luis's patience snapped.

He'd only been prepared to make up the profit shortfall because Benjamin was his oldest friend. In truth, despite his bulging contact book, Benjamin was his only real friend.

But Benjamin had not just crossed a line, he'd

hacked at it with a chainsaw and the damage caused by his actions had the potential to destroy both Casillas brothers. Reputations could be broken by the smallest means and businesses ruined. Luis had not been exaggerating when he'd spoken of the financial troubles he and Javier had got into seven years ago. There had been an eighteen-month period when they had struggled to find the cash to put petrol in their cars but then three projects were completed within months of each other and suddenly the money had started rolling in. Almost a decade of complete focus and hard work and suddenly they were richer than they had ever dreamed possible. Their fortune had only grown since.

He would not be poor again. He would not have his or his brother's reputation battered any more. Chloe could put a stop to all of it with two simple words: I do.

'I have explained the facts of the situation,' he said tightly. 'If you choose not to believe them then so be it but this ends now. Too much damage has been caused. Marry me and no one else need be hurt.'

'Apart from me.'

'How will marriage hurt you? You're a single woman—'

'We went on one date two months ago,' she interrupted hotly. 'You've no idea who I've seen since then.'

He mustered a smile. 'You said only an hour ago that you were on a holiday that involved hot men. That implies you are either single or a cheat. Which is it?'

Her cheeks had turned red enough to warm his hands on them. 'I'm a grown woman. How I conduct my personal life is my business.'

He shrugged. 'Lover or not, you're an unmarried woman. Your career is in tatters... What will you be giving up to marry me and rectify the mess you helped create? It wouldn't be a permanent marriage, only one that lasts long enough to shut the wolves up and restore my and my brother's reputations. In return, I would give you everything your heart desires.'

'My heart does not desire *you*.'

'Your body does.' At the outraged widening of her eyes, his smile broadened. 'I do not forget the kiss you owe me or the way your hungry eyes looked at me.'

Somehow her cheeks managed to turn a shade darker but she tossed her hair over her shoulders defiantly. 'That was the wine talking.'

His laugh at her barefaced lie was genuine. Even now, with all the acrimony and anger between them, that undercurrent remained, thick enough to taste. 'Do you want to prove that?'

'I don't have to prove anything. I don't want to marry anyone, not even for a short time, and if I did you would be the last man on the list. I won't do it. Promise what you want, make all the threats you like, I'm not going to marry you. The end.' Her hand grabbed the handle of the door that led outside. 'This isn't the Middle Ages. Women are not chattels to be bought or traded. As fun as this conversation has been, I'm going.'

Turning her back to him, Chloe stepped out onto the deck. After the air conditioning of the sky lounge it was like stepping into a furnace, the sun high above them and beaming its rays onto her skin.

She would find a way off this yacht even if she had to row her way back to shore. She'd just have to wear a life-jacket.

All she could see to the horizon was the Caribbean Sea, shining brilliantly blue under the azure sky.

She shivered to think what creatures lay beneath the still surface.

She spotted the stairs that led to the deck below and hurried down them.

'Where are you going to go?'

Heart pounding, she paused to look up.

Luis's arms were hanging over the balustrade at the top of the stairs, his handsome, sexy face smirking down on her but that hardness still glinting in his eyes.

'I'm going to find the captain and tell him to take us back to shore,' she told him with all the defiance in her veins.

'I bought the *Marietta* from her namesake three days ago. The captain answers to me.'

'But the manager said it belonged to the owner...'

'I bribed him,' he said matter-of-factly, without an ounce of shame. 'Marietta doesn't own the complex in Lucaya.'

She stared up at him as she processed what he'd said. 'You bought a yacht to trap me on?'

'I have often considered the idea of a yacht and now I have one.'

'Just like that?'

'I had a spare two hundred million sitting in a bank account. I was going to use that money to settle with your brother…that money enabled me to make Marietta an offer she couldn't refuse.'

Her stomach cramped to imagine what other factors he had brought to the negotiating table with Marietta. If his reputation was anything to go by it was more likely to have been a negotiating bed.

Wherever he'd done his negotiations for it, knowing he'd bought this yacht with the primary purpose of trapping her almost had her struck dumb.

Seven years ago it would have thrilled her.

From the age of seventeen she'd developed an intricate fantasy in her head where Luis waited for her to become a fully mature woman then declared his undying love for her and whisked her down the aisle.

That memory, not thought of in years, lanced her.

Once upon a time she had dreamed of marrying *him*.

How idyllic she had been. And how starved for affection.

She'd woven the fantasy while living under her father's roof for the first time in her life, mourning the mother she had loved with all her heart and coping with her remaining parent's indifference. His indifference shouldn't have hurt, not after a life spent where he'd been nothing but a name, but he was her *father*. His blood ran in her veins. They shared the same nose and ears.

Once she had moved out of that awful, unloving home the fantasies about Luis had petered away. She'd had a career to embark on and she'd been determined to put the past behind her and get out there and live her life to the fullest.

It had been the biggest shock to her system to re-enter Luis's orbit and discover her old craving for him hadn't withered into nothing, just been pushed into dormancy.

It felt like poison in her veins to imagine the debauched parties he would host on this beautiful yacht.

He moved from the balustrade and put his hand on the rail as he made the slow walk down the steps. That dangerous glint remained in his eyes but there was amusement within the hazel swirl too. 'Have you not yet realised I am a man who plans everything down to the last detail?'

Her throat closed at his approach. She stepped back, off the bottom step and onto the safety of the deck.

His smile grew with every step he took closer to her. 'Your brother is good with details too. I have thought about how he was able to steal Freya and keep her under lock and key. Seclusion with only trusted employees was how he achieved it. He even got her to marry him, the clever man. I thought if such a ploy is good enough for Benjamin then it is good enough for me. All I had to do was work the details. The yacht is mine and the crew are in my employ. They obey orders directly from me and I am paying them enough to ensure their loyalty.'

She took another step back. 'Not everyone's loyalty can be bought. And don't come any closer.'

The faint amusement that had lurked in his eyes faded away as he came to a stop barely two feet from her.

For a long moment neither of them spoke. Chloe,

trapped in the sudden intensity of his stare, felt her heart clench into a fist then burst into an erratic beat that echoed up her throat.

Then a tight smile formed on those sensual lips and he spread his arms out. 'Search wherever you like. Speak to whoever you like. When you are satisfied you have nowhere to escape, come and find me.'

And then he walked back up the steps, leaving her standing there, her nails digging into the palms of her hands.

She would find a way off this yacht. She would. And then she would bring the full force of the law down on him.

Luis disconnected the call from his brother and bowed his head to dig his fingers through his hair, doing his best to rub the forming headache out of his skull.

He had finally got hold of George, their Canadian partner in their venture to build the largest shopping complex in the northern hemisphere. George was one of the richest and most powerful men in North America. After much coaxing, he had agreed to a video conference. However, he had insisted it be held in the morning.

Just as they had suspected, George was seriously considering pulling out of the agreement. Without George as their partner, the permits needed would be revoked.

Unfortunately he'd insisted Javier be in attendance for the call too.

Luis swore as he thought of his brother's foul mood.

His brother was like a stick of old highly temperamental dynamite ready to explode at the slightest provocation.

Even if he succeeded in getting Javier to put on a human front, Luis knew it would not be enough. Their Canadian partner was an old-school tycoon who believed in a man's word being his bond. It was the injunction he and Javier had taken out against Benjamin that would be the biggest hurdle to overcome.

That damn injunction. At the time, with Benjamin then the one behaving like a stick of temperamental dynamite, it had seemed necessary. They had rushed it through, knowing time was of the essence. Now it only served to make them look guilty over a matter in which they had broken no law.

If George pulled out of the project, the consequences were unimaginable. It wasn't the money, it was what it represented. If he pulled out he was essentially telling the world that the Casillas brothers were not men who could be trusted to do business with. It would prove fatal to their already battered reputations.

With Chloe as Luis's wife, all of George's doubts would be allayed and the dominoes would stop falling but until he got his ring on her finger he would have to play for time.

He'd known from the first look at the pictures of Freya and Benjamin leaving the gala hand in hand how the situation would be played out in the media. He and his brother would be painted as the devils. Their parents' history would be dredged up and played to fit the media's narrative of them. The idea of marrying Chloe had floated into his mind almost immediately bringing with it a flicker of excitement through his loins. Punishment and vindication all in one neat move.

Chloe had become an itch he could not purge in more ways than one, a taunt in his dreams, and suddenly he'd been presented with the motives to scratch it all away.

He'd known her well enough to know she wouldn't agree to marriage without a fight. Chloe had been born stubborn...

The door from the deck suddenly flew open and she burst into the lounge, raven hair spraying in all directions.

In one skip of a heart his burgeoning headache and weariness disappeared and his mood lifted.

He straightened in his chair, taking in everything about her afresh.

She glared at him, her chest heaving as she struggled for breath.

Then those wonderful voluptuous lips parted. 'I *hate* you.'

CHAPTER FOUR

TWO WHOLE HOURS Chloe had wasted going from room to room, speaking with crew member after crew member, her panic growing with each brief conversation. Surely her pleas for help would be met with sympathy from *someone*? Instead she had gained the distinct impression they didn't understand what she was complaining about.

Either that or they were used to histrionics. They probably assumed she was some spoilt rich girl who'd had a fight with her boyfriend.

The worst of it was that Chloe had always prided herself on *never* having histrionics. Only once had she succumbed to it and it had ended with her moving out of her father's house and moving in with her brother. She hadn't spoken to her father since that awful argument.

Luis sat casually on a chair with his elbows resting on his thighs, his hazel eyes fixed on her with what looked like calm amusement that raised her blood pressure to critical levels.

How could he be so calm when her entire life was being pulled out from beneath her?

'When I get away I am going to make it my mission in life to destroy you.'

'I'm terrified.' He stretched his back. 'I assume you didn't find an escape route?'

How badly she hated him, his arrogance, his cruelty, his entitlement.

And how badly she despised herself for having a heart that still jolted violently just to look at him.

Why were these awful emotions for this man still inside her, after everything he had done? She could forgive her just-turned-seventeen-years-old self for blithely overlooking his reputation as a ladies' man in the dreams she had created about him but she was an adult now, with adult thoughts and responses.

She could not forgive herself for it still being him, with all his treachery and lies, evoking so *much* inside her.

'How much are you paying the crew to turn a blind eye? It must be a fortune. Not one of them is prepared to help me.'

'I hope they refused politely.'

'They are incredibly well trained and polite.'

'Good.' He smiled with satisfaction. 'Marietta assured me they were the most loyal crew on the seas.'

For some reason the name Marietta only enraged her further.

She didn't want to think about the negotiations that had taken place for Luis to take ownership of this floating prison in such super-quick time. It made her feel as if she had ants crawling all over her skin.

'Now you are back we can have something to eat.'

Chloe breathed heavily, trying her hardest to keep some semblance of control when all she wanted to do was kick and punch him into reason. She had known there was a risk in crossing Luis but she had never dreamed he would go to these lengths.

She had no means of escape until they reached land.

'I'm not hungry.'

'Yes you are. How can you hope to escape if you're faint with hunger?'

'How can you be so blasé?' she demanded angrily. 'You have *kidnapped* me.'

'Borrowed,' he corrected as his phone suddenly rang. He stretched an arm out to pick it up.

His infuriating arrogance, already burrowing under her skin like a pulse, pushed her over the edge, all her fears and panic peaking.

She could contain it no more.

Chloe charged at him, snatched the phone from his hand before he could speak into it and threw it onto the floor as hard as she could. Only two humongous arms wrapping around her waist and yanking her backwards into a solid wall of man stopped her from stamping on it.

'Let me go,' she screamed, struggling against the vice-like hold she'd been put in, but it was like fighting against a solid strait-jacket.

His hold around her tightened and then she was lifted off her feet and placed unceremoniously onto a sofa. She hardly had time to catch a breath before her arms were pinioned above her head, her wrists secured together with one of his hands and Luis was on top of her, using the strength of his legs and his free hand to stop her from bucking and kicking out at him.

She opened her mouth to scream at him again, to demand he let go of her at once but nothing came out. Her tongue had become a stranger in her own mouth, unable to form the needed words.

Far from recoiling at being trapped in his hold, she felt the fight inside her morph into something equally ferocious but of a shockingly different flavour as his scent found its way into her bloodstream. Pulses flickered to life, electricity zinging over and through her.

His dark hazel eyes hovered only inches above her own, staring down at her with an intensity that made her chest expand and her abdomen contract.

'Are you going to behave yourself now, *bonita*?' he asked with a husky timbre she'd never heard before. A fresh pulse of heat ripped through her, filling her blood and her head with the fuzziest, dreamiest of sensations.

She could not tear her eyes away…

'Make me.' Her whispered words came unbidden from a voice that belonged to someone else.

Their gazes stayed locked until she found herself staring at the sensuous mouth she had so yearned to kiss.

And then that mouth fitted against her own and claimed her in a hard, ruthless kiss that sent her head and her senses spinning.

All her defences were stripped away from the first crush of his lips. Her mind emptied of everything except this moment, the heat that engulfed her… It *filled* her, from the tips of her toes all the way up, snaking into every crevice of her being.

With a greed she hadn't known existed within her, she kissed him back, wrapping her arms around his neck and cradling his head with her hands, digging her fingers through his hair to his scalp.

She had dreamed of kissing Luis for close to eight years. On cold nights she had imagined him lying beside her and keeping her warm with that hulking, magnificent body.

She had never imagined it could be like this. Warm? Her body had become a furnace, desire running on liquid petroleum in her very core. The heat of his kisses fuelled it beyond anything fantasy could evoke. His dark, chocolatey taste, the thickness of his tongue playing against her own, the weight of his hands roaming down her sides… those fantasies had been dull compared to this giddy, urgent reality.

Scratching her nails down the nape of his strong neck, her fingers had slipped under the collar of his T-shirt when a door into the sky lounge opened.

In the breath of a moment reality reasserted itself.

Wrenching her mouth away, she turned her face from him and saw a pair of legs exiting the room as whoever had walked in on them left abruptly.

The ignobility of the situation they had been found in was starkly apparent.

She snatched her hands away from his skin and bucked against him. 'Get *off* me.'

The sensuous lips pulled into a smile as Luis levered himself back up.

The moment he was upright, Chloe twisted herself off the sofa and fell in a graceless heap onto the floor.

She stared at him, wishing she could crawl away and hide for ever.

Chloe had been kissed before. She might be a virgin but she wasn't completely innocent. She'd experimented like everyone else but nothing she had done—which admittedly wasn't much—had been anything like this.

This was something else.

This kiss had come directly from heaven.

She had to remember it had been delivered by the devil himself.

'You did that on purpose,' she said in a breathless voice that made her wince. It was no consolation that Luis's breathing was as ragged as her own.

He arched a dark brown eyebrow. 'Kissed you?'

'You knew someone was going to walk in,' she hissed, grasping for excuses, anything to negate what she had just experienced. 'You wanted us to be caught like that to discredit me.'

What madness had taken control of her?

She imagined that within minutes their passionate embrace would be known by the entire crew, including the captain, who had locked himself in the bridge when she'd been seeking help to escape. They would all conclude that they had been right to deny her help. They would never take her entreaties seriously.

'I have many talents but mind control is not one of them.'

He could have fooled her. She would swear he'd just used a form of mind control. Something in his eyes, a magnetism, it had hypnotised her. It must have. Something that would explain the madness that had possessed her.

'I kissed you because you asked it of me.'

'I did *not*.' Scrambling to her feet, she smoothed her T-shirt over her belly, trying desperately to look composed on the outside even if on the inside she had turned into a hormonal, blubbering mess.

'What was *"make me"*, if not a challenge to kiss you?' He spread his arms across the back of the sofa in a nonchalant fashion that made her fingers itch all over again to smack him.

'It was not a challenge.' She was painfully aware her cheeks must be the colour of tomatoes.

Her lips had tingled for him. They still did.

His gaze stayed unwaveringly on hers. '*Bonita*, your eyes begged for my kiss. You kissed me back. You ran your fingers through my hair. Faking virginal outrage does not change any of that.'

'Shut up.'

'You blush like a virgin too.'

'I said, *shut up*.' Storming to the bar, Chloe grabbed the first bottle that came to hand and poured a hefty measure into a glass.

She felt his eyes watching her every move.

'*Dios*, you're not, are you?'

'Not what?' She took a large sip hoping whatever the potent liqueur was would numb her insides.

'A virgin.'

The fiery liquid halfway down Chloe's throat spluttered back out of her.

'You *are*.'

The sudden fascination in his voice made her want to hurl the remnants of her glass at him. Instead she tipped them into her mouth and forced herself to swallow.

Oh, wow, it *burned*.

She coughed loudly and blinked back the tears produced by her burning throat, hating the amusement she found in his gaze.

'Being a virgin is nothing to be ashamed of,' he said when she had herself back under control. 'And I would go easy with that—that's Cuban rum. It's very potent.'

Staring at him insolently, she poured herself another measure. Now the burn had abated she was left with a pleasant after-taste. 'I'm not a virgin. I've slept with tons of men. Many more and I'll be on the same number of conquests as you.'

Luis ignored her gibe. Her lie was written all over her flaming-red face and trembling hands.

His heart twisted.

It had never occurred to him that Chloe was a virgin. And why would it? She was twenty-five, an age when a person would have had a number of lovers in their life. This was the twenty-first century. Women were as entitled to take lovers as men were. He had never met a woman who hadn't embraced the liberation that came with it.

Until now.

He thought of how her cheeks had always turned crimson when he saw her at the theatre, the look in her eyes when he had rubbed his nose against hers...

'It explains a lot,' he mused, shaking his head, in-credulous at the turn of events since she had stormed back into the sky lounge.

Their kiss… It had exploded out of nowhere.

One moment he had been restraining her, the next their mouths were locked together, their hands burrow-ing hard enough to dig through flesh.

There had been no finesse. They had come together in a brief fusion of unleashed desire.

'Because I refused a nightcap?' She tossed the drink down her throat with a grimace. 'That's called having self-respect.'

'If you've had a *ton* of lovers, why refuse to sleep with me? Your self-respect would already have been out of the window if that's what you were hoping to preserve.'

'Maybe I just didn't fancy you enough to come back to your house? Maybe I didn't want to be another con-quest in a long line of many.'

'If it's the former then you lie—your body language is very expressive, *bonita*.' Her blush was delicious.

She was delicious.

Her sweetness lingered on his tongue, the softness of her skin still alive on the pads of his fingers.

'If the latter, why worry about being a conquest when you have such a long list of your own?'

She poured herself some more rum. 'I do not have to explain myself.'

'I'm merely curious as to why such a sensual woman would deny herself the pleasure that makes the world turn around.'

'Pleasure—sex—counts for nothing. There are far more important things. Like loyalty,' she added pointedly.

'We are already agreed on the importance of loyalty but only someone with minimal experience would deny that sex is an important part of life, especially someone who has slept with *tons* of men.' He hooked an ankle over his knee and enjoyed the fresh batch of colour flaming her cheeks.

Her presence alone invigorated him. He'd felt a lifting of his spirits when he'd first stepped into the sky lounge and surprised her with his presence. The hammers that had pounded at his head when she'd disappeared on her quest for escape had been driven out again with one look on her return.

Their kiss had pumped something else inside him, a buzzing in his veins.

He remembered their date; that buzz had been with him throughout it then too, an electric charge in his cells that had driven out the strains of his daily life and the weight that always seemed to be pressing on his shoulders.

'If you have slept with the number of men you claim you have and can still state that sex is unimportant then that would suggest you have either been doing it wrong or have been picking the wrong partners.'

'Is this where you tell me that having sex with you will awaken me to all the things I've been missing out on?' She rolled her eyes with a snort.

Laughter bubbled up his throat. Chloe had the face of an angel, the body of a siren and a melodious voice that sang to a man's loins. It had only taken him so long to become fully aware of it because of all the years he'd seen her as a child.

He doubted there was a heterosexual man who'd met her and not felt a twinge of awareness for her.

Had she really, as he now strongly suspected, turned down every man who'd shown an interest in her?

And if so, why?

'Close your eyes, *bonita*, and let your senses guide you. What do you taste? It is the chemistry between us seeping into the air we breathe.'

If he hadn't suspected before that they had the potential to be incredible together, their brief, furious kiss had proven it.

She scowled as she poured herself more rum with a still-shaking hand. 'The only thing I can taste is the hot air you keep spouting every time you open your mouth.'

His laughter came out as a roar.

No wonder he felt so invigorated to be with her. Chloe had a zest about her that he fed off. She'd always had it.

He remembered seeing a glimpse of the woman she'd become when they'd celebrated her seventeenth birthday at the chateau mere weeks before her mother had died. She'd been a gangly teenager still growing into her face, the beauty so evident today nothing but potential back then.

She was a full decade younger than the rest of them but her indefatigable spirit during those awful months her mother had been dying before their eyes had been inspiring.

Chloe had been the one to keep everyone's spirits lifted. She had kept that smile on her face during the worst of times, never once letting her mother see the pain that had been hidden behind it, always turning the stone over to find the ruby underneath. She would speed from school to the hospital and later Benjamin's newly bought chateau where Louise had ended her days, armed with cosmetics and other feminine products, doing her mother's hair, massaging her feet, painting her nails, all the little tactile things that had shown her love. All of it conducted with a smile and that raucous laugh that had lifted everyone and pulled them all together in a web of joyous love.

Her hidden pain had only come out at the funeral.

The memory of her tears soaking into his shirt that day and the tremulous look in the baby-blue eyes staring at him now cut the laughter from Luis's lips.

Whatever mistakes he had made, he had done his best by Chloe and her family. He had loved her mother and her brother. He had loved all of them. That she could believe him capable of using that awful time for his own financial gain sliced like a dagger through his chest.

Hindsight gave him much to regret but the past was the past. It was the future he had to think of and that future involved Chloe by his side as his wife.

Sentimentality had no part in it.

She held the glass of rum to her lips. 'Does the possibility of me being a virgin not make you pause and think that what you're doing is wrong on so many levels that Dante's *Inferno* would have run out of space for you?'

'You are thinking ahead to us sharing a bed?' he asked, fresh sensation awakening in his loins as he brushed the last of the memories away.

'*Never.* I despise you.' She swallowed the rum in one hit.

'No, *bonita*, you hate that you desire me.'

'Don't tell me what I feel,' she snapped, pouring herself yet another glass. By Luis's estimate she had drunk over a third of the bottle in a very short time.

She downed it and fixed her eyes on him with a glare. 'I will *never* be yours,' she repeated, then gave a hiccup. Then another.

She reached for the bottle again.

'Are you sure that's wise?'

'Stop telling me what to…' another hiccup '…do.' Her hand went to her mouth. When she next looked at him her face had lost much of its colour.

He leaned forward, preparing to get to his feet. 'Feeling woozy?'

'No.' As if to prove her point she took two steps towards him but then stopped herself and grabbed hold of the bar.

'I did suggest you eat something. All that rum on an empty stomach…'

She swallowed then took some long, deep breaths before raising her chin and studiously walking to the nearest seat. Seated, she gripped onto the arms of the sofa she had put herself into and flashed a grimace at him. 'See? I'm fine.'

He raised a brow, torn between guilt at driving her to attacking the rum, admiration at her refusal to submit and amusement at the hangover he was certain was coming for her.

'Ready for some food now? A bread roll or some toast to soak the alcohol?'

Her beautiful, stubborn mouth opened. He could see the refusal ready to be thrown at him. But then the mouth closed and she seemed to shrink a little into the chair.

When she met his eye there was a glimpse of vulnerability in her returning stare that made his heart twist and his chest tighten.

She gave a short jerky nod. 'Just something light, please. I think I'm suffering from seasickness.'

Dios, she was amazing. Clearly inebriated as she had suddenly become, she still had the wit to try and turn it to her advantage.

'You suffer from seasickness?' he asked with faux sympathy.

She gave another nod. 'You should put me on dry land...unless you want me to vomit all over your new toy?'

'That is certainly something for me to consider,' he said gravely.

'I would consider it quickly if I were you or I won't be...hic...responsible for the consequences.'

'If it gets too bad I will get the ship's doctor to give you something. He has a supply of anti-nausea injections and pills for such an eventuality. In the meantime, I'm sure some food will help.'

Whistling, Luis strolled out of the sky lounge with the weight of Chloe's glare burning into his back.

CHAPTER FIVE

'FEELING BETTER?'

'A little.'

'Still seasick?'

'Yes. Very seasick.'

Luis's cynical laughter ringing behind her ear sounded like a hammer to Chloe's brain.

She tightened her grip on the railing and kept her gaze fixed on the clear waters surrounding her. She had been standing at the front of the yacht for almost an hour, inhaling the fresh air to clear her banging head.

She knew she wasn't fooling him with her woes of seasickness.

Faking seasickness had been better than admitting she was slightly—okay, a touch more than slightly—drunk.

The last time she'd consumed that much alcohol she'd been living in London but that had been spread over a number of hours, never in such a short space of time.

She had never drunk as much black coffee as she had since either. Cut her and she was quite sure she would bleed caffeine.

She'd needed the alcohol's numbness to smother the tortured emotions that had been engulfing her. There was nowhere to escape, nowhere to flee the heat his kiss had generated and her excruciating embarrassment at being called out as a virgin.

How had he known that? *Did* he have psychic powers? Or had he been with so many women that he could tell an innocent by one kiss?

Reaching the age of twenty-five a virgin was just something that had happened, not something intentional and not something she had been embarrassed about before.

When she'd moved to London months before turning nineteen to take on her apprenticeship with the ballet company, all the freedom in the world had suddenly been in her lap. It hadn't been that she'd been denied her freedom before then; she'd lived with her father and stepmother for the year following her mother's death and neither of them had shown the slightest concern for her whereabouts, then she'd spent a year living with her brother, who had watched her closely but never stifled her. This had been a different freedom.

Her whole life had opened itself out to her, unanswerable to anyone. She had embraced that freedom with gusto.

She had loved her life in London. Living in a shared house with three other young women had meant lots of partying and a growing number of friends. Long days and long nights, young enough to burn the candle at both ends without any ill effects…yes, she had loved her life back then but not as much as her house-mates had.

Rarely a morning had gone by when Chloe would go downstairs for breakfast and not find a man or two in the kitchen, different faces on a seemingly daily basis. She'd recoiled from such casual hook-ups for herself. She'd dated though, even kissed a few of them, but nothing more. The mechanism inside her friends that allowed them to discard their inhibitions and embrace sex whenever and wherever they could seemed to be faulty in her.

'You're too choosy,' her best friend Tanya had drunkenly told her one night. And she had been right. Chloe loved her male friends but she did not trust them. There were only two men she'd trusted. One was her brother, the other had been Luis.

She hadn't deliberately sought Luis out. When she had seen his ballet company advertising for a costume maker she'd been ready for a fresh challenge.

To discover her old teenage feelings for him had been merely dormant and then to find her resurgent desire reciprocated had been both exhilarating and terrifying.

She had spent the past two months consoling herself that at least she hadn't accepted his offer of a nightcap.

Everything she had believed about Luis for her whole life had been torn asunder.

He had ripped her misplaced trust to shreds.

And now she knew her self-consolation had been pointless too. She still desired him. She'd been pinned beneath him and instead of kicking him where it hurt she had melted for him.

Worse, he knew it too.

'You will be glad to know we will be docking within the hour,' he said nonchalantly placing his hand on the railing beside her.

Chloe's heart leapt, although whether that was at his sudden closeness or his announcement she could not be sure.

She stepped to the side, away from him, not quite daring to get her hopes up. 'You're going to let me go?'

'No, *bonita*. I'm taking you to my island.'

'*Your* island?'

'*Sí*. I bought it with the yacht.'

'You bought an island to trap me on as well as a yacht?' Her leaping heart sank in dismay as that tiny glimpse of freedom disintegrated.

'They came as a package. I had intended to stay at sea a few more days so that Marietta's furniture could be moved out but necessity has brought the schedule forward. I have a video conference in the morning. This yacht, as magnificent as she is, was designed as a pleasure vessel and does not yet have business facilities.'

A swell of something hot and rabid pulsed in her chest. 'You bought the island off Marietta too?'

'I've met her a few times socially—I'd attended one of her parties on this yacht. When I learned where you were hiding and its close proximity to her island, I called her with my offer. The stars aligned for me that day, *bonita*.'

'If the stars aligned for you then God knows what

torturous trick they were playing on me,' she whispered bitterly.

'What can be torturous about staying in paradise?'

'How about that I'll be staying in it against my will?'

His tone became teasing. 'At least you won't have to worry about seasickness.'

She tightened her hold on the railing and breathed in deeply. 'How long will we stay there?'

'You will stay until you agree to marry me. It really is very simple. Marry me and then we return to the real world.'

'The real world where I'll be your wife?'

'That's what marriage means, *bonita*. We marry, make some public appearances together to kill the heinous rumours and speculation being spread about me and my brother and then you go free. It will all be over. You will be free to resume your life and your brother will not have to spend *his* life watching his back for my vengeance. You can put an end to all of it. The power is in your hands.'

She stared down at Luis's hand, tanned and huge, holding the rail so loosely beside her own. *That* was a powerful hand, in more ways than one. It could swallow her own hand up.

If she didn't find a way out of this mess *he* would swallow her whole.

But this was a mess she didn't know how to resolve. She *couldn't* marry him.

Just having him there beside her, that masculine scent her nose hungered for catching in the breeze and filtering through her airways had her senses dancing with awareness.

But she couldn't stop her eyes darting back to those hands. They had pinned her wrists together without any effort at all.

Her abdomen clenched, warmth flooding her to imagine them touching her again...

She would not let that happen. Luis would never lay a finger on her body ever again and she would not allow herself to touch him either, whether she married him or not.

Suddenly it occurred to her that Luis was taking her to an island which meant new people, telephone lines—her phone had no means of communication on this yacht—and transport. Which all meant potential escape routes...

But what if he meant it about ending the feud with her brother? Her being trapped here in his power proved the lengths Luis would go to.

She could laugh at her naivety. As if she could trust a word Luis said, after everything he had done.

Gathering all the raging emotions zipping within her and squashing them into a tight ball, Chloe twisted to look him right in the eye and then immediately wished she hadn't.

She was trapped, in more ways than one.

All she could do was gaze into the dark hazel eyes staring at her with a force that made her stomach melt and her fingers itch to touch him all over again.

Those strong fingers she had only moments ago

stared at with a strange aching feeling reached out to smooth a lock of her hair behind her ear.

'Marry me, *bonita*,' he whispered, then craned his head towards her and brushed those sensuous lips over hers.

Chloe's feet were still stuck to the decking when he pulled his hand away and strode back into the sky lounge. It wasn't until the door closed behind him that the strange fog-like thing that had happened in her head filtered out to be replaced with anger, at Luis and especially at herself.

So much for never allowing him to touch her again. She had barely lasted a minute from making that vow.

In disgust, she wiped her still-tingling mouth with the back of her hand.

Must try harder, she thought grimly as she stared back out to sea with a heart still thumping madly.

Chloe came to a stop on soft golden sand upon which dreams were made. In front of her, gleaming like a Maharaja's palace under the descending sun, set in an island within the island, was a whitewashed mansion with a terracotta roof from which even more fantastical dreams were made.

They had been met off the yacht by a skinny boy of around ten, who skipped alongside her, clearly bursting with excitement. In rapid-fire English he happily told Chloe that he was the caretakers' son and had lived on the island his whole life.

His cheerful presence was a welcome respite from

the turbulence she had been through that day, although did nothing to lessen the coils knotted tightly in her belly.

Luis walked some way behind them, deep in conversation with the yacht's captain. She felt his presence like a spectre.

Determined to blank him out while she could, she tried hard to concentrate on the child's chattering while taking in everything around her.

The closer she got to the palace-like structure, the more she realised her initial thoughts were an illusion. What she'd thought was one palatial villa was a complex of interlinked homes around one huge main house nestled with high palm trees and traversed by the longest swimming pool she had ever seen, snaking the perimeter and weaving between the individual beautiful buildings. Only as she crossed a bridge over the swimming pool did she realise it was a saltwater pool filled with marine life that must feed directly from the sea.

Following the wide path, she saw what was undoubtedly a traditional pool snaking the main house like a moat, more bridges leading to the smaller homes.

Chloe sighed with pleasure then hated herself for it, immediately following her self-castigation with the thought that it was better to be locked away in paradise than in a cell.

She'd thought the complex she was staying on in Grand Bahama was paradise. This was nirvana.

'Who else lives on the island?' she asked the boy when she could get a word in.

His nose wrinkled but before he could answer, Luis got into step beside her.

'No one,' he answered cheerfully, the look in his eyes telling her clearly that her hopes of finding escape off this island were as futile as her hopes of finding help on the yacht. 'I will bring new staff in soon.'

'Jalen!' a loud, harsh voice called out. 'Come here.'

The little boy's skinny frame froze momentarily before he pulled himself together and ran off, back over the bridge they had just crossed to a scowling, weather-beaten man who'd emerged from the side of the main villa.

'Who's that?' Chloe asked, following Jalen with her eyes.

'Rodrigo. His father.'

She looked at Luis and found his gaze was also following the boy. 'The caretaker?'

He nodded, his attention still on the boy. 'He looks after the island with his wife, Sara.'

'Jalen said they've been here for a long time.'

'Sara's lived here for ever. Her parents were the caretakers before she took over.' There was a grimness to his tone.

Chloe looked back at Jalen. He'd reached his father and his head was bowed. He was obviously on the receiving end of a scolding. 'What do you think he did wrong?'

'I have no idea. I met the family three days ago when I took possession of the island. I know nothing about them.' Luis shook his head and pushed his attention away from the young boy and back to the beautiful woman at his side.

Small boys always pushed their luck. It was a parent's job to discipline them. Just because Luis's father's methods of discipline had been extreme did not mean Rodrigo used the same methods.

But when he met Chloe's gaze he saw the same concern ringing out from her as needled in his own skin.

'Where do they live?' she asked.

'In one of the staff cottages at the back of the main house.' He pushed Jalen and Rodrigo more firmly from his head. He would have plenty of time to observe them interact and, he was sure—hoped—he would find the father-son relationship that he had spent so many years wishing for.

His own history was not òthers' reality. That was a truth he had always been aware of.

Luis had long ago accepted that there had been something in his genetic make-up that had triggered his father's violence towards him, something dirty and rotten.

It had to be inherent otherwise Javier would have been on the receiving end of it too. He'd never bought Javier's reasoning that he'd got away with only mild chastisement and a rumpled shake of the hair because their father had looked at Javier's face and seen a mirror of himself.

There was no denying that Javier had inherited their father's looks while Luis had inherited a masculine version of their mother's, and there was no denying that only Luis had been Yuri's whipping boy, right until the day their father's drunken, jealous rage had turned on their mother.

His father had served ten years of his sentence for killing his mother. A year after his release he'd died of pancreatic cancer. Luis sincerely hoped he'd suffered every minute of his death.

Dios, would it always be like this? Would he be condemned to a life where every time he saw a father chastise his child the memories of his own childhood would smack him in the face afresh?

Would the past ever set him free?

Strolling along another bridge that led to the door of a pretty villa, he said to the woman who could kill the demons from the past affecting his future, 'This will be your villa while we're here...'

She raised a startled eyebrow. 'I get my own villa?'

'Did you want to share one with me?' he mocked, glad to be back on familiar ground with her.

'No!'

He pushed the door open and winked at her.

This was better. Flirtation and teasing. Let it flow between them. Let it warm the coldness that had settled in his veins.

'If you change your mind, I will be in the villa next door.'

'Get over yourself.'

'I'd rather have you over me but I can wait.'

'You'll be waiting a long time.'

He gazed at her flushed cheeks and smiled. 'We shall see.'

She scowled but there wasn't the force behind it that had been there throughout the day.

She had made no effort to step into her new home. 'Are you not going to live in the main house?'

'Not until Marietta's possessions have been shipped out. I'll show you around it tomorrow but, for now, I have a conference call to plan for and I need to make sure everything's set up. Tonight, *bonita*, you get to amuse yourself. Sara will be with you shortly and will go through everything. She knows the island better than I do and has arranged the villa for your arrival. If there is anything you're not happy with, take it up with her.'

'You're not scared I might try and escape?'

He laughed. 'There is no escape. And no rescue, if that's what you're thinking. This island is an unnamed dot on the map.'

'What about the ship that's coming for Marietta's stuff?'

He noticed the darkening of her eyes as she spoke Marietta's name. It was the same darkening he'd noticed earlier.

'She's in no hurry for it.'

'I can hijack the yacht.'

'I'm afraid not. Captain Brand's taken it back to the mainland. He will return in a week and then he will marry us.'

'He can't.'

'He's a recognised officiate.'

'What does that mean?'

'That he can marry us.'

'But I haven't agreed to marry you!'

'You will and the sooner you accept it and say yes, the sooner we can marry and the sooner this nightmare will be over for the both of us.'

He could manage a week away from the business but, he had realised earlier, no longer than that. He was still in communication with those he needed to communicate with but this island, for all its beauty, was cut off from civilisation as he knew it. For this to be a true holiday home he would need to purchase a helicopter to be permanently manned there and possibly get a landing strip put in and buy a smaller version of his private jet.

He was confident he would gain Chloe's acceptance to marry him in the seven-day deadline he had imposed.

He could sense her resolve failing her. She knew there was no escape. If she wanted to leave the Caribbean she would have to marry him.

She was the reason he was having to scramble together a conference call the next morning to salvage a deal that had been in the bag and stop the business he and his brother had worked so hard for from crumbling around them.

Before she could respond, a slender, tired-looking woman with frazzled hair crossed the bridge to them.

Luis shook Sara's hand then introduced her to Chloe. 'Please see that Miss Guillem has everything she needs,' he said, then turned back to Chloe.

Was it his imagination or was that panic resonating from those beautiful blue eyes?

He reached out a hand to stroke her soft cheek.

The pupils of her eyes pulsed at his touch.

'I will find you after my conference call tomorrow,' he said. 'Until then, stay out of trouble.'

Chloe watched him walk away with the strangest desire to call him back.

She managed a small smile at Jalen's mother and was relieved to receive a warm, if tired, smile back.

The villa she was shown into was charmingly beautiful if a little old-fashioned and fitted with its own kitchen and all the amenities a woman could want. The swimming pool curled past the bottom of the pretty garden her living room opened out to.

'I hear you've always lived on the island,' Chloe said when Sara was about to leave.

Chloe *hated* being alone at the best of times but with her head so full of the day's events, so full of Luis, the thought of only her own company terrified her.

Sara nodded and put her hand on the door. 'I was born here.'

'What's Marietta like?' she couldn't resist asking.

Why she couldn't stop imagining the mystery woman she could not begin to fathom but the name had lodged itself in her head like a spike digging into it.

Luis had bought Marietta's yacht and island off her and taken possession of them both in mere days. He'd met her socially.

Chloe knew all about Luis and his sociability. His party-loving ways were legendary. She remembered the leaked photos of his thirtieth birthday party, a joint event with his twin at which her brother had, naturally, been a guest. Someone had captured pictures of Luis dancing, beer in hand, surrounded by a hive of semi-naked women, all with their attention fixed firmly on him.

A quote in the paper by an unnamed source had described it as the party of the decade. To the question of which of the beauties Luis had ended up with, the answer had been, 'Knowing Luis, it could have been all or any of them.'

Recalling that picture made her want to vomit.

Had Marietta been at that party? Had she been one of those beauties draped all over him?

Sara's face lit up into a smile that momentarily transformed her tired features into beauty. 'She's an amazing woman.'

Later, alone on her villa's veranda after a light supper eaten alone, Chloe sat under the starry night sky nursing a glass of water.

Other than the crickets chirruping madly to each other, the silence was absolute. There was no sign of life from the villa next door, no lights, no sound.

She could be the only person on this earth.

Luis must still be in the main villa preparing for his video conference.

She should be happy to be rid of him, not reliving their kiss for the fiftieth time.

Dieu, now she was alone with her thoughts it was *all* she could think about, their lips and bodies fused together and the *heat* that engulfed her.

She rubbed her eyes and breathed even more deeply.

Why did any of this have to happen?

If Luis and Javier had been straight with Benjamin all those years ago instead of luring him into a lie then she would...

Would what?

She would have gone on that second date with Luis. She would have accepted his offer of a nightcap. She would have let him kiss her. And then she would have let him make love to her.

And then he would have broken her heart.

In a way, he had broken it already through his treachery to her brother and all the memories that had been shattered as a result.

He had a ruthless streak in him she would never have guessed ran so deep.

But, as her memories continued to torture her, she thought back to his vehement denials of treachery.

Now she had a little distance from him and could think without his magnetic presence disturbing her equilibrium, she couldn't help but wonder if there was some truth in his defence of himself.

As a child Luis had been her favourite visitor to their home. She had loved it when he and Javier had come to stay, had a strong memory of climbing to the top of the fifteen-foot tree at the bottom of their garden but then losing her nerve and being too scared to climb back down.

She had sat at the top of it, crying her head off, terrified of the drop, which to her five-year-old self had looked petrifying.

Luis had been the one to haul himself up and get her down. She had clung to him like a limpet but he had got them both down safely. She had hero-worshipped him for that. His steady presence when her mother had become ill had been such a comfort to all of them. His visits had brightened her mother's mood, invigorated her brother and made her own heart lighten a little.

Had that *all* been a lie? Had twenty-five years' worth of memories all been false or distorted?

And then she thought of the social media comments he had mentioned, the sick ones that had equated Freya leaving Javier out of fear of ending up like Clara Casillas. Fear of ending up murdered at Javier's hands.

Had there been cruel comments aimed at Luis too?

The rustle of movement nearby pulled her back to the present, a door being closed softly.

Footsteps crunched and, although their individual gardens gave them privacy, she knew in her bones that Luis had stepped outside into his villa's garden.

Chloe held her breath. Her heart beat maniacally beneath her ribs, all her senses pinging to life. The knots in her stomach had tightened to become a painful ache inside her.

Could he sense her, feet away, separated only by the hedgerow filled with an abundance of beautifully scented flowers?

A short while later she heard the distant splash of water. Luis had gone for a midnight swim.

Still holding her breath, she took that as her cue to bolt back inside.

Her head felt hot and thick when she slipped under

the cool bed sheets a short while later. A riot of images flashed behind her closed eyes that no amount of trying could dispel.

Luis swimming.

Luis naked.

Luis, Luis, Luis…

CHAPTER SIX

THE IMAGE OF Luis swimming naked was the first thing Chloe saw in her mind's eye when she awoke the next morning after a turbulent night that had not involved much in the way of sleep.

Throwing the bed sheets off, she hurried into the bathroom and took a long shower, washing the images—which weren't even images, just something conjured by her pathetic imagination—away.

With a towel wrapped around her torso and another wrapped around her head, she opened the dressing-room door to see what clothes had been brought in for her. Inside she found a collection of beach and summer wear, all in a variety of sizes.

She supposed she should feel grateful that Luis had made sure there would be something that would fit her. She wasn't the easiest of women to dress. At five foot eight, she was taller than average. If not for her breasts, she would be considered slender. Her breasts had been the envy of her friends when she'd been a developing teenager. She'd always considered them to be a nuisance. Dresses were a nightmare to buy, always a compromise between fitting from the waist down or the waist up. If she wanted them to fit the rest of her without looking as if she were wearing a tent, she was forced to cut the circulation of her breasts off. The times she found a dress she liked and that fitted perfectly she would buy it in all the available colours.

She'd been wearing one of those dresses in the Madrid coffee shop the day she had seen Luis through the window, she suddenly remembered, hit afresh with the liquid sensation she had experienced as their eyes had met and, for the very first time, she had seen interest in his eyes.

The date that had followed had been the best evening of her life. She hadn't wanted it to end.

It had taken all her willpower to get into the cab and return to her apartment without him.

Inhaling deeply, she selected a blue bikini and covered it with a denim skirt that fell to mid-thigh and a black T-shirt, both of which fitted well.

She left her damp hair loose, put the coffee on as Sara had shown her and opened the front door to the glorious bright Caribbean sunshine.

As she had promised, Sara had left a tray of food there for her. Sitting next to the tray and looking straight at her was a two-inch-long gecko.

Chloe crouched down to look properly at its cuteness. 'You are adorable,' she said, smiling at the reptile that appeared unfazed to have a strange woman making cooing noises at it.

'Stay where you are,' she told it, leaving the door open as she backed into the villa.

She'd left her bag on the dining table and quickly upended the contents to find her phone.

Her intention to take a picture of the cute gecko came to nothing when she stepped back out and found it gone.

With a sigh, she carried the tray in, shoving her mess to one side to fit it on the table.

About to put her phone down and pour the coffee out, she suddenly noticed the Wi-Fi icon showing itself.

Luis must have got the Wi-Fi working for her phone had logged in to it, no password needed for access.

She had no signal to make phone calls but she could communicate with the outside world.

The first thing she did, while absently chewing on a freshly baked croissant, too intent on her potential freedom to taste her food, was search the island's co-ordinates.

A message flashed up warning her that her Internet safety settings did not allow her to search this.

She tried again but to no avail. Equally, she found herself blocked from accessing her emails and social media.

She could scream.

Foiled again.

As always, Luis was two steps ahead of her.

Luis...

Remembering his claims about malevolent comments on the Internet, she wrote his and Javier's names into the search box.

Her search engine announced there were over two hundred thousand results.

She clicked on the first news article, a gossip piece about Freya and Benjamin's 'secret' wedding. She scrolled to the comments section.

Twenty minutes later she switched her phone off and threw it onto the heap of stuff from her emptied beach bag, nauseated.

How could people write such things? And on public forums too?

She wished she could scrub her eyeballs out and cleanse them from the poison she had just subjected them to.

Had Luis read those comments?

She fervently hoped not. She hoped Javier hadn't either.

No one deserved hateful comments like that. No one should ever have to read faceless, anonymous opinions that they had evil in their eyes, were inherently bad, were secret psychopaths, were women-beaters, that they'd inherited their father's violence.

What the hell were the moderators of these news sites doing? she wondered angrily. How could they let such toxic bile onto their sites?

This was worse than she had imagined. A thousand times worse.

She closed her eyes as a memory hit her of when she'd been really young. It might have been the same summer she had got stuck in the tree. The Casillas twins and Benjamin had sat around her kitchen table playing a board game she'd been too young to join in with. She couldn't remember the game itself but vividly remembered the booming laughter that had echoed through the walls of her home, remembered stealing into the kitchen in the hope of sharing the array of snacks her mother had laid out for them. One of the boys—she wished she remembered which—had ruffled her hair and slipped her some crisps.

In her mind back then, the three had been giants fully grown in comparison to her puny self, but now she knew they'd been kids in frames their brains were trying to catch up with. Two of the three had been living with a trauma her own young brain had been unable to comprehend.

That those two vulnerable boys should have such spite aimed at them now made her heart ache.

Chloe was comfortable with the world at large questioning the Casillas brothers' business integrity but this...

This was sickening. This was personal.

She had never, would never, could never, have wanted this. Not for anyone but especially not for them.

Luis closed his laptop with an exasperated sigh.

The video conference with their Canadian partner had not gone well.

He had a bad taste in his mouth and was thankful his brother was thousands of miles away so he couldn't give in to the urge to punch him in the face.

'We do not have to explain ourselves to you,' Javier had said from his home office in Madrid. 'The litigation between ourselves and Benjamin Guillem is not a matter of gossip.'

'I am not a man who deals with gossip,' George had

retorted, visibly affronted. 'But I am a man who needs to feel comfortable with who I do business with. The rumours are that you ripped Benjamin Guillem off on the Tour Mont Blanc development. If you cannot refute those rumours then I cannot be expected to put my name and money to this development with you.'

'We do not need your money,' Javier had said coldly.

'But you do need the access I can provide. Without my backing this project is dead in the water.'

That was when Luis had stepped in. 'The litigation between us is sealed for confidentiality reasons. However, I can assure you Benjamin Guillem was paid every cent owed under the terms of the contract we all signed seven years ago.'

'I'm afraid your assurances are not enough. I will need to see that contract and the full accounts for the project if I am to proceed.'

'If our word is not good enough for you then it is *us* who needs to rethink this deal,' Javier had retorted, ice seeping through every syllable. 'We will not do business with someone who takes the salacious word of the tabloid press over ours.'

And then his brother had cut himself off from the conference.

Luis had kept the deal on the table only by apologising profusely and explaining the tremendous strain his brother was under.

A huge part of him had been tempted to tell George to take a hike and pull the plug on the project himself, write off the money they'd already spent and the hours he'd spent as point man on it, but that would mean giving in.

His brother had since turned his phone off, no doubt taking himself off to pound the hell out of a punching bag as he always did when his anger got the better of him. Living with the shadow of their father's violence had affected them in different ways and it was in their own reactions to anger that they diverged the most. Javier closed himself off and showed his true emotions only to inanimate objects. Luis was as comfortable with anger as he was with pleasure. Harness it in the right way—a lesson learned by always doing the opposite of what his father would have done—and the anger could be used as fuel.

Javier might be prepared to throw in the towel but Luis was not. Why should they allow the business they had worked so hard for be destroyed? Was it not bad enough that their reputations were being destroyed, their names dragged through the mud?

He would not let it all go without a fight.

And from Chloe not the slightest bit of contrition.

He hadn't seen her since he'd shown her to the villa that would be her dwelling for the immediate future.

She had been on his mind every minute of her absence, even during that damned video conference.

Fed up of the cloying walls of the room he'd turned into an office for himself, Luis left the main villa and headed over the moat to the beach.

His beach.

This whole island, bought as an insurance policy to keep Chloe tied to his side, belonged to him.

Rolling his sleeves up, he welcomed the sun's rays onto his skin as his attention was caught by two figures on the golden beach…

Was that *music* he could hear?

He pulled his loafers off and stepped onto the soft sand, walking closer to the figures that revealed themselves to be Chloe and Jalen. They were dancing…or something that looked like dancing, the kind of moves the more drunken revellers at his parties would make as the night wore on, body popping, robot moves; the pair of them facing each other having some kind of dance-off, oblivious to his presence.

Not wanting to disturb them, he sat on the sand, enraptured with what was playing out before him and enjoying the beat of the hip-hop music.

The longer he watched, the thicker his blood ran, awareness spreading like syrup through him.

This was the Chloe he knew, joyous, enjoying a spontaneous moment, her beautiful face lit up and glowing, her raven hair spraying in all directions and… *vaya*, that body.

After a good ten minutes of frenzied dancing, Chloe stopped and doubled over to massage the side of her stomach. By the grimace on her face she was the victim of a stitch.

She twisted slightly and that was when their eyes met.

After a long moment of hesitation, she turned away and said something to Jalen, who immediately looked at Luis, grabbed what was recognisably an old-fashioned boom-box and scarpered.

Slowly she trod barefoot to him, one hand holding her flip-flops, the other still massaging her side, breathing heavily, her eyes not leaving his face until she stood before him.

For a passage of time that seemed to last for ever, they stared wordlessly at each other until she took one last inhalation and sank onto the sand, lying flat on her back beside him, clearly exhausted.

'I didn't know you were into hip-hop,' he said wryly, bemusement and awareness laced together in his veins.

She gave a ragged laugh, her gaze fixed on the sky. 'Neither did I. Sara told me you were still on your conference call so I went for a walk and found Jalen.' She took a breath that turned into a groan. 'I'm shattered. I've become so unfit.'

He stared at the flat of her white stomach, exposed where her T-shirt had ridden up her midriff, and resisted the temptation to run a hand over it. 'Not from where I'm sitting.'

She followed his gaze with a flush creeping over her cheeks, then tugged the T-shirt down over her navel. 'Some ground rules. If I'm going to be your wife then no flirting.'

'My wife?' His heart jolted then set off at a thrum. 'You are agreeing to marry me?'

The breath she took before inclining her head lasted an age. *'Oui.'*

He studied the beautiful face that was no longer looking at him. 'What made you change your mind?'

The last time they had spoken Chloe had been vehement in her refusal. He'd known she would agree eventually but had been sure it would take a few more days for her to see reason.

'I read the comments you spoke of.' Her brow furrowed. When she continued, there was real anger in her voice. 'They are *vile*. How people can even think such things…it is beyond anything I have ever seen. To post them on public forums like that…? Vile, vile, vile.'

'Let me be sure I am understanding you correctly,' he said slowly. 'You are comfortable with my business and reputation suffering through your actions but take exception to mindless fools' comments on the Internet?'

Chloe turned her head to stare into the hazel eyes that were studying her with an expression she did not understand.

'Those comments are *vile*,' she repeated fiercely. It was the only word she could think of that fitted. 'You and Javier are not your parents. Your father's crimes are not yours. You have suffered enough from what your father did, you shouldn't have to suffer in this way too.'

Because in essence that was what the cruel, ignorant commentators were saying, that the apple didn't fall far from the tree and that Yuri Abramova's violence had been inherited by his sons and that they must have used their wealth and power to cover it up.

Oh, it made her *rage*. The more she had thought about it over the morning, the greater her anger had grown, reaching a boiling point when she had bumped into Jalen walking around with his beloved boom-box on his shoulder.

The simple, uncomplicated innocence she had seen

on his young face had been the exact tonic she had needed while she waited for Luis to be done with his video conference.

'You'd manipulated things so I would have been forced to marry you eventually but this made my mind up for me,' she said into the silence that had broken out, reminding herself of his actions that *were* reprehensible and deserving of her fury. She might be having doubts on whether he had intentionally ripped her brother off but that did not excuse what he had done to *her*. 'I don't want to be stuck in limbo here for the rest of my life.'

'Being forced to spend your life on these beautiful shores sounds like a real hardship.'

For some reason, the dryness of his tone tickled her funny bone. She covered her face with her hands so he couldn't see the amusement he'd induced.

She didn't want him to make her laugh. It hurt too much.

'Are you crying?'

'No, I'm holding back a scream.' A scream to purge all the torment building itself back up in her stomach.

'What was that? I can't hear you.'

Moving her hands away, she was about to repeat what she'd said when she found he'd shifted to lean over her, his face hovering above hers.

'Do you mind?' she snapped, frightened at the heavy rhythm her heart had accelerated to in the space of a moment.

'You want me to move?'

'Yes.'

A gleam pulsed in his eyes. 'Make me.'

Instead of closing her hand into a fist and aiming it at his nose as he deserved, Chloe placed it flat on his cheek.

An unwitting sigh escaped from her lips as she drank in the ruggedly handsome features she had dreamed about for so long. The texture of his skin was so different from her own, smooth but with the bristles of his stubble breaking through…had he not shaved? She had never seen him anything other than clean-shaven.

His face was close enough for her to catch the faint trace of coffee and the more potent scent of his cologne.

Luis was the cause of all this chaos rampaging through her. She hated him so much but the feelings she'd carried for him for all these years were still there, refusing to die, making her doubt herself and what she'd believed to be the truth.

Her lips tingled, yearning to feel his mouth on hers again, all her senses springing to life and waving surrender flags at her.

Just kiss him…

Closing her eyes tightly, Chloe gathered all her wits about her, wriggled out from under him and sat up.

Her lungs didn't want to work properly and she had to force air into them.

She shifted to the side, needing physical distance, suddenly terrified of what would happen if she were to brush against him or touch him in any form again.

Fighting to clear her head of the fog clouding it, she

blinked rapidly and said, 'Do I have your word that your feud with Benjamin ends with our marriage?'

Things had gone far enough. For the sake of the three boys playing board games in her kitchen all those years ago, it was time to put an end to it.

'*Sí*. Marry me and it ends.'

She exhaled a long breath. '*D'accord*. If I am going to do this then there will be some ground rules. Our marriage will last as short a time as is possible.'

'Agreed.'

'And it will not be consummated.' Aware of her face going crimson again—*Dieu*, the heat she knew that was reflecting on her face was licking her everywhere—she scrambled to her feet.

A few inches of distance was not enough. Not when it came to Luis.

Two months of distance hadn't been enough.

How was she going to get through this? How was she going to cope with living with him, even if it was only for a few months, and keep her craving for him contained?

Somehow she would find a way. She could not give in to it; the dangers were too great.

This was *Luis* she was going to marry. The only man she had ever had feelings for, the man she had fallen for when she had been only seventeen, the only man other than her brother she had thought she could trust. Even if he'd spoken the truth about not deliberately betraying Benjamin, she knew it had only been the headiness of newly discovered desire that had made her want to trust him before.

She could never trust this ruthless, pleasure-seeking hedonist, not with her body and especially not with her fragile heart.

She could feel his eyes burning into her as he clarified, 'No sex?'

'Our marriage will be short and strictly platonic.' She strode away over the warm, fine sand, heading for the footpath that led back to the villas, needing to escape from him.

'Still holding on to your virginity?' he called after her.

She closed her eyes but didn't break stride.

She would not give him the satisfaction of a response.

The hairs on the back of her neck lifted as he easily caught up with her.

'Captain Brand's bringing the yacht back in six days. We will marry then. In the meantime, I'll get the pre-nuptial agreement drawn up.'

'What pre-nuptial agreement? If you think I want your money you're crazy.'

She didn't want *anything* from him.

'I am not interested in protecting my wealth, only my reputation and my future. You will sign a contract that forbids you from discussing our marriage.'

She stopped walking to stare at him in disbelief. 'You're going to put a gagging order on me?'

'I will not have you sharing with the world that you only married me because you were forced to.'

'Haven't you learned your lesson about stifling free speech from my brother?' she snapped, affronted.

'That injunction you put on him worked out so well, didn't it?' she added over her shoulder as she set off again.

The only reason she was agreeing to marry him was to stop the cruel things being stuck all over the Internet about him, not to add fuel to the fire.

Those cruel comments had hurt as much as if they had been personally directed at her. More.

As she was about to step onto the bridge over the seawater moat, a strong hand snatched hold of her elbow and spun her around.

Where moments ago there had been a casual, almost lazily seductive look to his eyes, now there was a hardness. 'The injunction against Benjamin was necessary. He was a loose cannon—'

'Only because he felt you took advantage of him when our mother was dying.' She grabbed hold of the outrage that filled her, negating the growing guilt at what her actions had helped lead to. 'You can shout it as loudly as you like that you were going to give him that money but where's the evidence to back it up? It's been two months since the truth came out and all you have done is fight him in the courts. One phone call could have put an end to it.'

His hold on her elbow loosened but his angry face leant right into hers. 'Your brother hit us with the lawsuit two days after our confrontation when I was still furious at his accusations. You speak of betrayal, well, what about your brother's betrayal to friendship? He turned this into war, not us, and you were happy to join in with it. The only thing Javier and I are guilty of is protecting ourselves and if you would pull those damned blinkers from your eyes you would know it too, but you won't because then you would have to accept responsibility for *your* actions and accept that it suits you to cast me as the monster in the scenario.'

'In what possible way does it *suit* me to cast you as the monster?' she demanded to know as the rest of his accusations dragged through her skin as if they were attached to barbs.

She had never been *happy* to join her brother's side. She had been heartbroken for him…

But what if Benjamin had been wrong? What if his fury at the supposed betrayal had driven his actions to the point where reason was something no longer available to him?

'Because you, *bonita*, are running scared and have been since you ran off like a frightened virgin at the end of our date. Your brother's war with me was the excuse you needed.'

'*Excuse?* Listen to yourself! Your ego is so big you should buy another island to contain it in.'

Her heart thundering and her skin feeling as if the barbs of his words were being pulled through it, Chloe marched away. There was a cramp in her stomach far sharper than the stitch she'd had on the beach.

'Chloe!' His deep voice called after her in a growl but she didn't stop, upping her pace, trying her best to keep herself together through the burn of tears growing at the backs of her eyes and the cramp that had spread into her chest.

Hearing his assured footsteps closing in on her, she

broke into a run, almost skidding over the swimming-pool moat bridge that led directly to her villa's path.

That she was doing exactly what he'd just accused her of—running scared—was something she understood on a dim, hazy level of her psyche but enough to propel her faster, a desperation to escape the eyes that saw too much and the emotions brimming inside her.

She pulled the door open with Luis only a couple of strides behind her and slammed it shut.

CHAPTER SEVEN

IF LUIS HAD been one step quicker the door would have slammed in his face.

He turned the handle, had pushed it open an inch when she threw her weight against the other side.

'Stay away from me,' she screamed through the closed door.

'Let me in or I will break it down,' he said with a calmness he did not feel. Right then he felt anything but calm.

He knew he should walk away and wait for Chloe to regain her composure but reason be damned. He would not allow her to walk away. She had run enough from him.

'I don't want anything to do with you.'

'Tough. Last chance, *bonita*. Open the door.'

His ultimatum was met with a choice of rude words.

He sighed heavily. 'Don't say I didn't warn you.' And with that he used all his strength to barge the door open against the pressure Chloe exerted on the other side of it.

But he was by far the stronger of the two and in seconds he had it open.

She clearly had no intention of letting him in without a fight. As he stepped over the threshold, she hurled herself at him, pounding her fists against his chest, kicking him, her long raven hair whipping around her face as she threw curses at him.

He grabbed at her flailing arms and held her wrists tightly as she continued to struggle against him, clearly uncaring that her height and weight against his own made it a fight she could never win.

He managed to manoeuvre her so her back was to the wall and pulled her hands up and above her head and used the strength in his legs to pin her own and stop them kicking.

'Is this how it's going to be for the next few months?' he demanded, staring hard at the beautiful face glaring at him as if condensed with all the poison in the world. 'Is every cross word going to end with you running away or fighting me?'

Those gorgeous, voluptuous lips wobbled. The eyes firing loathing at him became stark, the fight dissolving out of her like a balloon struck with a pin.

'I don't know how to deal with it,' she whispered tremulously. 'It scares me.'

She no longer struggled against him.

His chest twisted to see the starkness of her fear. 'What scares you, *bonita*?'

She inhaled deeply through her nose. Her throat moved, her eyes pulsed and darkened, her lips parted...

And then those soft lips brushed against his and he was no longer pinning her to the wall but pulling her into his arms. The hands that had been hitting at him wrapped around his neck as their bodies crushed together and their mouths parted.

Her taste hit his senses like a knocked-back shot of strong liqueur. It played on his tongue, the sweet nectar that was Chloe's kisses, a flavour like no other.

Every cell in his body caught fire. The fever caught her too; there in the crush of her lips moving greedily against his own and the digging of her nails into his scalp and the hungry way her body pressed itself against him, an instantaneous combustion trapping them in a magnetic grip.

What was it with this woman that he responded to with such primal force? Chloe lit a fire inside him, fuelling it with kisses a man could use for sustenance. It was like nothing he had ever known before, as if all others before her had pitched him to a mere simmer.

Mouths clashing and devouring, Luis swept a hand up her back and under her cropped T-shirt, headily relishing the warm softness of her skin. Such beautiful, soft, feminine skin…

He found the ties of the bikini that contained the breasts he'd fantasised about for so long and pulled it undone. The bikini rose upwards as he traced his hand around her midriff and up to the newly released swell.

She gasped into his mouth as he cupped a breast far weightier than he'd imagined but soft like her lips and her skin. Her hands burrowed under the neck of his T-shirt and grabbed at the material.

The fire condensed into his loins. It burned, a pain like nothing he had felt before.

He'd never felt *any* of this before.

When he pressed his groin against her, his arousal ground against her abdomen, they moaned into each other's mouths before she wrenched her lips from his and rubbed her mouth against his cheek and tugged even harder at his T-shirt.

Together they scrambled to pull each other's T-shirts off and fling them to the floor, and then her arms were hooked back around his neck and her hot mouth devoured him all over again.

In a frenzy of kisses, Luis tugged the ties of her bikini at the back of her neck and whipped it off fully, discarding it without thought.

A pulsing thrill ripped through him at the first press of her bare breasts against his bare chest.

He wanted to taste those breasts and all her other hidden places and burrow his face in their softness.

Everything about Chloe was soft. Everything. And so utterly, amazingly feminine, the yin to his yang, soft where he was hard, porcelain wrapped in silk.

She was a woman like no other. Feisty, stubborn, smart, funny, all contained in a body that could make a grown man weep.

And she was going to be his wife.

Chloe's breaths were coming in pants. She could hear them, could feel herself make them but they seemed to be coming from somewhere else, from someone who was not herself.

She was not herself.

Her body had become something new, a butterfly emerging from its chrysalis, coaxed into the sunlight by the only man she had ever desired or wanted. She had become a vessel of nerve-endings, and they were all straining to Luis, all her hate and rage, pain and sorrow, turned on their head in the time it took for a coin to flip from heads to tails.

She was beyond caring about yet another self-made vow being broken.

If this was what broken promises felt like then she would break a thousand of them.

For two months she had focused on her passionate hatred of him. But her passion for him was more than hate, it always had been, and to deny this part of her feelings for him was like denying herself air. If she were to walk—run—away right now she would forget how to breathe.

Even her skin felt alive. Tendrils curled around her and through her, sensation burning deep inside.

She gasped again when he squeezed her bottom roughly and ground himself more tightly to her, the weight and size of his excitement pressed so deliciously against her loins sending newer, deeper sensations racing through her.

As he held onto her thighs and lifted her up, she wrapped her legs around him and kissed him even more deeply as he carried her to the bed in three long strides.

She had to keep kissing him. She needed the heat of his mouth on hers and that dark masculine taste firing into her senses to drive out the fears that had held her in its grip for too long.

What had there been to fear about *this*?

This was pleasure. Erotic, greedy and needy, not

something to be frightened of but something to be embraced.

He placed her on the bed, her bottom on the edge, her arms still wrapped around him, Luis between her parted thighs.

He was the one to break the kiss.

She moaned her complaint and tried to resist as he put a hand on her shoulder and gently pressed her back.

Her complaints died when she saw the darkness pulsating in his eyes as he lightly circled her breasts with his fingers, sending brand-new sensation over skin she hadn't known could be so sensitive. When he put his lips there too...

She closed her eyes to this new, intoxicating pleasure as he kissed each breast, flickering her nipples with his tongue.

So intense were the sensations that she was only dimly aware of his hands working on the buttons of her skirt and tugging it down her hips with her bikini bottoms, only fully aware that she had helped shed them by kicking them off when he brought his mouth back to her lips for another of his darkly passionate kisses.

When he put a hand to the womanly heart of her, an electric pulse charged through her, strong enough to lift her back into an involuntary arch. She drank his kisses while fresh, new pleasure assaulted her. His fingers gently but assuredly stroked and manipulated her, making her senses spin and rocket to an undiscovered dimension, and she cried a protest when his hand moved away from his heavenly doings and traced up and over her belly and covered her aching breasts.

Time slipped away and lost all meaning, thoughts dissipating to just one concrete thing: Luis.

This, here, now, was everything she had dreamed, everything she had...

Her eyes flew open.

Luis must have removed the rest of his clothing for suddenly she was conscious of a velvety thickness pressing against the apex of her thigh.

She gazed into the dark hazel eyes gazing so sensually into hers but with a question contained in them.

This is the point of no return, they said. *If you want this to stop then now is the time.*

Chloe would rather take a knife to the heart than stop. She had never wanted anything more than she did at this moment.

She placed her hand on his tightly locked jaw. It softened under her touch before he turned his face to kiss her palm.

Then she moved her arms round his back as he kissed her mouth again and put his hand between their conjoined bodies to take hold of himself and position himself at the most secret, hidden heart of her.

A hard, heavy pressure pushed against her but it was a pressure she welcomed; craved, his kisses no longer enough to satisfy the intense heat overwhelming every part of her.

Slowly he inched inside her with a careful tenderness to his movements that drove out what little fear still lived inside her. His lips brushed over her face and his hands stroked her hair, as he filled her bit by bit until he was fully inside her and their groins were locked together.

The newness of the sensation stunned her. She could feel *him*, inside her, over her, on her, two bodies fused together as one.

And then he kissed her again and began to move… and that was when she discovered the true meaning of pleasure.

Her legs wrapped around his waist, Chloe closed her eyes and let Luis guide her.

Luis.

Even with her eyes shut she could see him so clearly. The scent of his skin, a new muskiness to it, the smoothness of his skin, the bristles of the hairs of his chest brushing against her breasts…

He was her everything. Her pain, her pleasure, her desire, her hate, all blended together so there was only him.

Low in her most hidden part an intensity built, every slow thrust raising it higher and yet somehow deeper, everything inside her concentrating into one mass that finally reached a peak and exploded within her. Ripples pulsated and surged through her body with a strength that had her crying out. Pressing her cheek tightly to Luis's, she rode the waves of pleasure, the only thought echoing through her head that she didn't want this feeling to ever, ever leave her.

There was a wonderfully languid weight in Chloe's limbs she'd never experienced before, a mellow buzzing sensation in her veins. Luis's face was buried in her neck, his breath hot on her skin, fingers laced through hers.

Time seemed to have come to a stop.

She sighed when he raised himself up to stare down at her. She couldn't read the expression in his eyes but what she saw made her stomach melt and her heart clench.

His kiss was light but lingering before he climbed off the bed.

'Are you going?' she asked before she could stop herself.

A shutter came down in his eyes but his stare remained on hers. 'Do you *want* me to go?'

She hesitated before answering. She should want him to go. What they had just shared hadn't been planned—*Dieu*, had it not been planned—but the culmination of something that had fired into being months ago and been left to simmer. To tell him to leave would be an admission of regret and a denial of her own complicity.

She did not regret it. How could she? It had been the most intensely wonderful experience of her life.

And she would not be complicit in any more deceit.

There had been enough deceit between them to fill his yacht.

She swallowed. 'No.'

He inclined his head, a gleam returning in his eyes. 'Good. Because I'm not going anywhere apart from the bathroom to dispose of the condom.'

That made her blink.

When had he put that on?

She watched him stroll to the bathroom, unable to believe she hadn't noticed Luis slipping a condom on.

Wriggling under the bed sheets, she cuddled into the pillow, dazed that passion had engulfed her so acutely that it had swept her away to a place where she had lost all sense.

When Luis came back into the room in all his naked glory her heart skipped up into her mouth.

Her imagination of his naked form had not done him justice. He truly was a titan of a man, broad, muscular, bronzed, unashamed in his masculinity.

A smile curved on his lips as he strolled towards her and lifted the bed sheets to climb on top of her.

Elbows either side of her face, Luis gazed down at the face that had been like a spectre in his mind for so long, drinking in the expression in the baby-blue eyes, the flawless porcelain skin, the voluptuous lips that kissed like the softest pillow.

He dipped his head and kissed her softly. 'Do you regret making love?'

She arched a perfectly shaped brow. Her mouth had quirked with amusement but there was something in her eyes that negated it; a vulnerability. 'Is that what you call it?'

He shuffled down to kiss her neck. *Dios*, barely minutes since they'd made love and he was hard again. 'What do you prefer to call it?'

'Sex?' From the breathless way she suggested the word he sensed her own arousal sparking back to life.

'I thought the French were a romantic people?'

'We are with people we feel more than hate for.'

'You feel more than hate for me.'

'No, I don't.'

He nipped her shoulder. 'Yes, you do. And what we shared was more than sex.'

'No, it wasn't. And stop telling me what I...' he'd encircled one of her nipples with his tongue '...feel.'

'Ah, I forget you have had *tons* of lovers.'

'I might have exaggerated a little.' Now there was a sensual hitch in her voice.

'When are you going to admit you were a virgin?'

'Never.'

He moved his attention to her other breast, enraptured with its texture, its taste, its weight, the sheer feminine beauty of it... 'You didn't answer my question.'

Her hands found his head, her fingers digging through his hair. 'Which question was that? There have been so many.'

He rested his chin on her nipple to look in her eyes. 'Do you regret us making love...having *sex*?'

The returning stare shone at him. 'I should regret it.'

'But you don't?'

'No.' She wound a lock of his hair in her fingers. 'I don't regret it. It doesn't change how I feel about you or anything else. I still think you're the devil.'

Trailing his tongue up her breast and to her neck, he pressed his mouth back to hers. 'Maybe one day you will discover I am not the devil you think I am,' he said before kissing her deeply.

No more words were spoken between them. Not verbally.

* * *

The gecko was back.

Chloe had woken early, much earlier than she usually liked to wake, and had come to an instant alertness.

That had been a man lying with his head on the pillow next to hers, an arm slung across her midriff. She had moved his arm carefully and sat up to stare at Luis's still-sleeping face.

There had been something surprisingly innocent in his sleeping form, his features smoother except for the now thick stubble around his jawline.

Resisting the urge to press a kiss to the stubbly cheek, she had torn her gaze from him and got out of bed, pausing only to put her thin robe on. Then she had made herself a coffee and slipped through the sliding door and onto the veranda, which was where her two-inch friend had found her.

Of course, it could be a different gecko. Luis's island was full of them. She was sure their parents could differentiate but they all looked the same to her, all except for this one.

This one was cute. It had perched itself on top of the seat next to hers and was staring at her with what she liked to think was interest.

'What do you want, little one?' she asked softly. 'Food? Drink? I would share but I don't think coffee is good for a little thing like you. Are there any bugs you can eat for your breakfast?'

As ridiculous as she knew it was to talk to a reptile, there was a comfort to it. Focusing on the cold-blooded creature stopped her thinking too hard about the warm-blooded creature she'd left sleeping.

This was the first time she'd left the villa's walls since Luis had barged her door open the morning before.

He'd had food brought to them at varying points with jugs of cocktails of varying strengths. She couldn't remember any of it, not what they'd eaten or drunk. The only image with any solidity to it was making love… having sex…with Luis.

The desire that had simmered between them for so long had finally been unleashed and she was in no hurry to tie it back up, not when the things he did to her felt so utterly wonderful.

Luis had taught her things her imagination had never conjured, taught her pleasure that was about so much more than the mechanics of sex.

What had surprised her the most was how fun it had all been. There had been passion—lots of passion—but there had been laughter too. Dirty jokes. A shared bath that had ended with far more water on the floor than in the tub.

She was French, she'd reminded herself many times that day. Taking a lover meant nothing. That her lover was her…fiancé—was that what she was supposed to call the blackmailing, kidnapping devil?—was irrelevant.

But she didn't feel like a kidnap victim. In truth, she'd never felt like his victim. His pawn, yes, that was an apt description but victim, no.

She had known when she'd offered to help her brother

that there would be a price to pay in putting herself up against Luis.

A shiver ran up her spine. She shook it off.

Better to have lost her virginity with a man who made her stomach melt with one skim of his finger on her skin than with…

But that was the problem. There never had been anyone else. When she and Luis were done with she still could not envisage herself with anyone else.

She couldn't reconcile her insatiable hunger for him. It was wrong on so many levels that soon she would be joining him in the special level built just for him in Dante's *Inferno.*

The patio door slid open and Luis stepped out onto the veranda, cup of coffee in hand, charcoal boxers slung low over his hips…and nothing else.

Chloe gaped, struck anew at his rugged, masculine beauty.

With the early morning sun beaming down on him he looked like a statue of a Greek god brought to life and filled with bronzed colour, albeit a Greek god with hair sticking up all over the place and eyes puffy from sleep.

For some reason, seeing him like this made her want to cry.

The smile he bestowed her with made her heart double flip on itself.

'You know that talking to yourself is the first sign of madness?' he said casually.

It took a beat for her to get what *he* was talking about.

She grinned, although it was an effort to make her lips and cheeks comply. 'I've been talking to Greta.'

'Greta?'

'Greta the Gecko.' She nodded to the chair Greta was perched on.

Luis took a step towards it and Greta fled.

'You've scared her away,' Chloe chided.

'I have that effect on women,' he teased, taking Greta's vacated seat.

He certainly did, she acknowledged with a painful twist of her heart.

Luis was a man any right-thinking woman would run a mile from.

She had run, as fast as she could.

And then she had drawn him back.

It suddenly struck her that the method she had chosen to get him out of the way for the gala had put her directly in his firing line when there must have been numerous other methods that wouldn't have pointed the finger at her as perpetrator.

But she had *wanted* him to know her part in it. She had imagined his face when he'd worked it all out and taken bitter satisfaction from it while her heart had splintered.

And why had she chosen to make out she was a damsel in distress? Because she had known he was a man who would never let a woman be alone and in potential danger when he could help her.

He'd carried her out of the tree, hadn't he, when he had been only fifteen…?

Luis's fundamental nature was, not exactly good,

but selfless. He'd put his own life on the line to help a small child.

Had Benjamin got it all wrong as Luis insisted?

Before she could follow her train of thought any further, Luis put his cup on the table and opened his other hand to reveal a rectangular foil package.

CHAPTER EIGHT

LUIS WATCHED CHLOE'S REACTION, being careful to keep his own lurching emotions in check.

Her cheeks were stained red. 'Have you been going through my things?' she croaked.

'No, *bonita*. I saw them on the dining table with the rest of the contents of your bag. They caught my eye. You're on the pill?'

He thought of the trio of condoms he'd had in his wallet, which they'd used up in relatively short order, and the other ways of making love they had embraced that hadn't required actual penetration since.

She stared back at him, the same thoughts obviously going through her mind too because darker colour flooded her cheeks.

Although incredibly willing, there had been a shyness about her over all the new things they had done, a shyness not quite disguised with laughter and quips. He'd found it utterly beguiling, just as he found most things about her.

When they had run out of condoms and he hadn't wanted to break the headiness of the spell they had created together to return to his villa for more, she hadn't breathed a word that she was already protected.

He hadn't wanted to break the spell until their limbs were so heavy and sated that the only bodily command they could obey was the one demanding sleep. In the back of his mind had been the certainty that the moment he walked out of this villa, what they were sharing would be over.

The chemistry between them had in no way been a precursor to what they would be like together.

Spending the day in bed making love…it had made him forget why he had her there, her conspiracy against him and the consequences he and his brother were living through. It had been passionate and, strangely, fun, a heady combination he had never experienced before.

'I had a bad outbreak of acne when I was nineteen so my doctor put me on the pill to help,' she blurted out, cutting through the increasingly tense silence that had formed between them. 'I stayed on it because I found it helped with the monthly pain.'

Luis dragged a hand through his hair and muttered a curse under his breath, suddenly feeling like a heel.

It had been a reflex action. He'd seen the packet, recognised it, and scooped it up to examine it. It hadn't been a conscious decision to confront her over it. What was there to confront? It was *sensible* for her not to trust him or any other man to keep her safe.

Luis knew his reputation with women wasn't the greatest. There was some truth in his playboy reputation, he had to admit, but it wasn't the whole truth. He'd never hopped from one bed to the next like some of the Lotharios he knew, but didn't see the point in pretending to pine for a relationship that had run its course…although, to call these interludes relationships was pushing it a little.

Marriage or anything remotely long-term had never been on the cards for him. None of the women had wanted to be in a relationship with him, Luis, the man, just with Luis Casillas, child of the murdered Clara Casillas and her killer husband Yuri Abramova, generous host of great parties and generous giver of gifts.

The point was, he told himself firmly, he always used condoms. Always. He didn't care if his lover was on the pill *and* had an IUD fitted, he used condoms, end of discussion.

It must be sleep deprivation that made it feel like a stab in the guts that Chloe didn't trust him to keep her safe.

Their relationship was nothing to do with trust. The sex, great as it was, gave it an added piquancy but that was all.

Chloe owed him nothing but marriage.

'You don't have to explain yourself, *bonita*. I apologise for embarrassing you.'

'You haven't embarrassed me,' she insisted even though her cheeks, flaming all over again, contradicted her statement.

'Bueno.'

'No, really, you haven't embarrassed me.' A sudden hint of mischief flashed in her eyes. 'After all, I am a woman of great sexual experience.'

Her obvious and deliberate lie was so outrageous that he burst into laughter.

She caught his gaze and burst out laughing too.

It was only a minor moment but the tightness that had formed in his chest loosened and, with it, the tension between them defused.

She did not owe him a thing more than she had already pledged. Chloe had agreed to marry him. That she was now sharing a bed with him was a delicious bonus.

Very delicious.

Luis settled back in his chair and sipped his coffee, admiring how Chloe could look so fresh and ravishing after such little sleep, slouched back in her chair as she was. She had on only a white robe tied loosely around her waist, the V of it gaping enough for him to see the divine swell of her wonderful breasts.

He exhaled a long sigh. A part of him wanted to press her back on the table and make love to her, the other part content to merely sit there and soak in her rare, unblemished beauty.

His suspicions had been confirmed. He really had been her first.

He'd been as gentle as he could be the first time he'd possessed her and if she had suffered any pain from it she had covered it well. They had been amazing together.

It struck him then that if he was her first, it stood to reason that one day some other man would be her second.

'Are you comfortable in marrying me knowing it won't last?' he asked curiously.

She arched a brow. 'Are *you*?'

'Very comfortable. Marriage has never been on my agenda.'

'It's never been on mine, either.' Although the fresh, light stain of colour that crawled up her neck made him suspect that there was something there she was keeping from him. 'Marriage is an outdated institution. People make those vows every day without meaning them. At least there's an honesty in the vows we'll make.'

'Are you speaking of your parents' marriage?'

'Their marriage was never honest.' Her eyes held his. 'Did you know your mother and my mother deliberately planned it so they fell pregnant at the same time?'

'That has been alluded to over the years,' he said. He and Javier were only three months older than Benjamin. Whenever his mother had toured, Benjamin and his mother would go with them, Louise as his mother's costume-maker, Benjamin as their playmate.

'My father was, in essence, a sperm donor. My mother married him because she didn't want to be a single mother but she raised Benjamin *as* a single mother. My father had little involvement or say in his upbringing, which was how he liked it. He got the glory of a son without any of the work.'

'I didn't know your father.' He'd been nothing but a name to them. Benjamin had rarely mentioned him.

'Their marriage was all but dead when Maman got broody again.' She rubbed her nose and gave a sad laugh. 'He was ready to leave her but she got him drunk and seduced him. *Et voilà*, nine months later I was born. He left before I was born.'

Luis ran a hand through his hair at this revelation he had known nothing about. 'Your mother told you this?'

'*Non*, my father told me the day before I left his home. He never wanted me and he hated my mother for tricking him into being a sperm donor for a second time.'

He gazed at the beautiful elfin face staring back at him with the merest hint of defiance to counteract the wobble of her chin.

'You learned all this after your mother died?'

She gave a sharp nod.

'That must have been a hard thing to accept.'

She shrugged but her chin wobbled again. 'It explained why he'd never been in my life. I'd only met him three times before Maman died.'

He gave a low whistle. 'Obviously I was aware there wasn't much in the way of involvement from him but I didn't realise it was that bad.'

'It was good,' she insisted. 'My childhood was incredibly happy. He's the one who chose not to be a part of it.'

'So why did you move in with him? Couldn't you have lived with Benjamin?'

'It wasn't allowed. I had only just turned seventeen, I was still at school and still a minor, so that's how it had to be. One parent dies so you move in with the other even if he is a stranger to you. And at the time Benjamin was struggling to cope financially—it wouldn't have been fair to burden him with me too, not then.'

Benjamin had been struggling financially because he'd taken out a huge mortgage to buy the chateau for his mother to end her days in and then neglected his business to care for her in those last days. The savings he'd had to purchase the chateau outright had been given to Luis and Javier for the Tour Mont Blanc land.

Another unintended consequence of that damned contract that Luis was becoming sure would haunt him in the afterlife.

'But you moved in with him eventually, didn't you?' he asked, his brow furrowed. 'I remember visiting the chateau once and you were there. I remember him telling me his fears about you moving to London.'

'I stuck it out with my dad and stepmother until I completed high school then moved in with Benjamin for a while before I moved to London. When I moved back to France after I'd completed my apprenticeship I split my time between his chateau and his apartment in Paris.'

'You never went back to your father's home?'

'*Non.*'

'Did they treat you badly?'

She made a sound like a laugh. It was the most miserable sound Luis had ever heard from her. 'They didn't treat me like anything. They might as well have had a ghost move in for all the attention they paid me. My mother was dead and they couldn't have cared less. They clothed and fed me and made sure I attended school but that was it. They were always out, seeing friends, going on holidays, but they never included me or invited me anywhere with them. I didn't get a single embrace from either of them in the whole year I lived with them. I could understand it from my stepmother but from my father...'

Chloe blinked back the burn of tears.

She would never cry over her father again.

When she'd left her father's home she'd sworn to forget all about him. She'd survived perfectly well for the first seventeen years of her life without him; she didn't need him.

But it still hurt. It really, really hurt.

Whatever the circumstances of her conception, she had been innocent. Benjamin had been innocent. Their father hadn't just walked out on their mother but his ten-year-old son and unborn child too.

The first time he had met his daughter, Chloe had been three years old. It had been another four years before she'd seen him again.

'They didn't want me there,' she explained, trying her hardest to keep her voice factual and moderate. 'I learned when I turned eighteen that my mother had saved all her child support payments from him. It wasn't a fortune but was enough for me to live with Benjamin without being a financial burden.'

'Your father didn't object?'

She gave another miserable laugh. 'He couldn't wait to be rid of me.'

And that was what hurt the most. Deep down Chloe had wanted him to object. She'd wanted him to raise himself up and insist on being her father. She'd wanted to be important to him. She'd wanted him to love her but he didn't. He never had and never would.

She had never spoken about any of this before. Benjamin knew she'd had a hard time living with their father but she'd never confided the depth of her misery there or the enormous one-sided argument she and her father had had, scared she would come across as a spoilt, needy brat. Her stepmother, in a rare moment of interaction with Chloe, had called her exactly that.

It had been a one-sided argument because it had essentially consisted of Chloe having a complete breakdown. She had screamed at her father, all her misery and pain pouring out of her in an emotional tirade that had been met by her father's cold retelling of the past and her stepmother's cruel words.

The closest she had come to that feeling of betrayal and helplessness and that total loss of emotional control was with the man whose arms she had found such pleasure in.

She hadn't seen her father since the day she'd left.

A buzzing sound rang out.

'That will be our breakfast.' Luis jumped to his feet, grateful for the disturbance.

After defusing the tension between them things had suddenly become extremely weighty.

He admired Chloe's spirit, her beauty, her feistiness…

Her vulnerability was not something he liked to see and there had been more than a flash of it then as she'd narrated a part of her life he'd only known the basics of.

Dios, her father's treatment of his child had been as deplorable as his father's, even if their methods of abuse had differed. Chloe's father had abused her with his indifference. Luis's father had abused him with his hands.

'Stay there. I'll let them in.'

Pulling a pair of shorts on first, he opened the door to find Sara and Jalen. The little boy took one look at him and hid behind his mother.

Sara rolled her tired eyes and said apologetically. 'He was hoping to see Chloe. My son has taken quite a shine to her.'

Remembering the hip-hop dancing the boy had been doing with her, Luis quite understood why.

'I will tell her you were asking for her,' he said to the boy pretending to be invisible behind his mother's legs, before taking the breakfast tray from Sara's hands.

At some point soon he would have to employ more staff for the island. Marietta hadn't been to the island in the three years before she'd sold it to him and had let all the other permanent staff go. Sara had proved herself to be an excellent cook but she had a hundred other jobs to get on with.

He carried the tray out onto the veranda and set it on the table.

Chloe gave him a small smile.

As she helped herself to toast, he said, 'Your boyfriend was asking after you.'

Her brow furrowed in confusion. 'What?'

'The caretakers' boy.'

He did not want to go back to tales of her childhood. Listening had had the effect of a hook being wound around his stomach.

His diversion did the trick.

'Jalen?' Her face lit up. 'Oh, he's a sweet little thing.'

'He hides or runs away whenever he sees me.'

She shrugged with bemusement. 'You're three times the size of him. To his eyes you're a big scary giant.'

'You think?'

'He told me that himself.'

'It's not men in particular that he's fearful of?'

'No—why do you ask?'

'I keep thinking of his reaction when his father called him over the day we got here. He looked terrified.'

Chloe grinned. 'That's because his father had expressly forbidden him from speaking to us.'

'Why would he do that?'

'You're the new boss. They don't know you and they don't know how tolerant you are to children. They're worried for their jobs. They're scared that if you think Jalen is a nuisance you will replace them with childless caretakers.'

'Jalen told you all this?'

'He's a chatterbox without a filter.' Her pretty white teeth flashed at him again. 'I can understand why they're scared of him talking to you.'

'They have nothing to worry about. I appreciate that this is their home…you are sure that that's the only reason Jalen was afraid of his father?'

Her eyes narrowed slightly as she tilted her head. 'He wasn't afraid of his father, he was afraid of the telling-off he knew he would get from him.'

He nodded slowly. It was the way Jalen had hung

his head while speaking to his father that had sent the alarm bells ringing in him. It had taken him back thirty years to how he would stand when summoned to see his father.

'I suppose all children are afraid of their father some of the time.' Luis had been one of the unlucky ones who had been afraid of his father all of the time. The only times he'd ever fully relaxed as a child was when he and Javier had gone on tour with their mother without him.

Chloe was watching him closely. He could see the questions swirling in her head, her curiosity piqued.

The tension that had filled him when he'd discovered her contraceptive pill packet and her matter-of-fact explanation on her relationship with her father crowded back into him.

He got back to his feet and leaned over to place a hard, hungry kiss to her mouth. 'I'm going to my villa. I'll be back in five,' he murmured into the silkiness of her hair before kissing her again.

When he broke away there was a dazed look in her eyes, her questions successfully driven away.

He returned to her in four minutes with his pockets stuffed with condoms and carried her to the bedroom.

CHAPTER NINE

CHLOE FINISHED HER lunch with Jalen on the beach then headed to the main villa where Luis had spent the morning working.

Butterflies rampaged through her belly, the product, she told herself, of nerves that they were going to sign their pre-nuptial agreement, not excitement at seeing him again. That was a ludicrous notion. He'd only left her bed four hours ago.

But it frightened her how much she had missed him in those four hours apart.

No, she told herself firmly, it was the sex she missed. Two days of doing nothing but making love was bound to affect her and, as a lover, although she had no one to compare him to, Luis was amazing. They were amazing together. So long as they kept things physical then everything was fine.

She still struggled to understand why she had divulged her relationship with her father to him. She'd crossed an invisible line there and had only just stopped herself from crossing it again when they had been talking about Jalen.

There had been an undercurrent running behind Luis's questions about the boy, and she'd recalled the fleeting concern she'd seen on his face when Jalen had been scolded by his father.

Scared of being alone with her thoughts, she had sought Jalen out, assuring Sara repeatedly that he was no bother at all. She liked the little boy's company. There was no artifice to him, everything laid out in that innocent way only a child could manage.

Sara opened the door with a welcoming smile and invited her to wait in one of the living rooms while she let Luis know she was there.

The living room in question was an enormous elegant space with a distinctly feminine touch to it. Chloe stared at all the clutter and boxes filling it with awed disbelief. How did any one person accumulate so much *stuff*?

A huge, elaborately framed portrait at the front of a stack of frames resting against the wall caught Chloe's attention. It showed a young, strangely old-fashioned beautiful woman with thick curly black hair, posing elegantly with an enigmatic smile.

'I'm sorry about the mess,' Sara said, slipping back into the room. 'We are packing up Marietta's things to get them shipped to her. It's taking us a lot longer than we thought it would.'

Chloe smiled then pointed at the portrait. 'Is that Marietta?' The armchair the sitter had posed in was in the corner of the room.

'It is.'

Something sharp stabbed into Chloe's heart. So this

was the woman who had sold her yacht and her island to Luis in the space of days.

Her stomach curdled again to imagine the *incentives* Luis must have brought to the table to convince her so quickly.

The ghost of Marietta had haunted her since she had arrived at this beautiful island, a phantom reminder that, to Luis, women were disposable.

'She was only eighteen when this was painted,' Sara explained. 'Her father had it done to celebrate her coming of age.'

'He must adore her,' she said, unable to contain her wistfulness.

Chloe had been living with her father on her eighteenth birthday and he'd still managed to forget it. The huge row that had exploded between them the day before she had moved out of his emotionally cold, horrible house had resulted in Chloe being struck from his address book permanently. She doubted he knew she now lived in Madrid.

Sara laughed. 'I don't know about that. It was the done thing with the gentry in those days.'

'What do you mean?'

'That portrait is over seventy years old.'

Chloe's jaw dropped. 'Seriously?'

'Marietta's going to be ninety on her next birthday.'

She stepped over to look at the portrait in more detail and crouched down. Close up it was even more majestic.

Footsteps sounded behind her.

'It's incredible to think this is seventy years old,'

she murmured. 'It's in remarkable condition, and the detail…'

'It's something special, yes?'

Chloe almost fell backwards onto her bottom. She hadn't heard Luis enter the room, had thought Sara had come to stand behind her.

He held out a hand to her.

Her legs wobbling in protest at her crouching position, she grabbed onto it and let him help her up.

'Thank you,' she murmured, disconcerted to find her heart racing.

His eyes sparkled. 'Pleasure.'

She felt more unsettled than ever. Her insides were a cauldron bubbling with a thousand differing emotions, all of which boiled for him.

But she would not show it. She would never let Luis know how easily and seamlessly he had burrowed under her skin.

Smiling broadly, she pulled out the contract she'd shoved into the back pocket of her shorts. 'Shall we get this signed?'

Sara and her husband Rodrigo were going to act as their witnesses.

'You are happy with the terms?'

'What terms?' she snorted. There had been only one; the one forbidding her from speaking publicly about any part of their relationship. She would be gagged for ever from speaking about Luis in any shape or form.

It was a term she could live with.

She would never do anything to fuel the poison out there about him.

At some point she would need to speak to her brother and warn him. It would have to be done before she and Luis exchanged their vows. How Benjamin would take it she couldn't begin to predict. Her brother's hatred of both Casillas brothers ran so deep she had no way of knowing if he would listen to reason.

Surely he wouldn't have wanted all this poison for them?

But her brother was wounded. Their betrayal had cut him so deeply that his instinct had been to lash out. Chloe understood that because it had been the same for her.

Had Luis been right when he'd accused her of using it as an excuse to run away from him?

'Before we sign, let me give you a tour of the house,' he said, cutting into her thoughts. 'I need a fresh pair of eyes to help me decide how to redecorate this place.'

'Isn't that what interior designers are for?'

'And I will employ one but right now it's your opinion I'm interested in.'

Curiosity piqued, Chloe let herself be guided through the magnificent villa that was more than a match in size for her brother's chateau. But where Benjamin's chateau was decorated and maintained to the highest possible standard, the deeper into the villa she went, the more its neglect shone through.

'Marietta inherited it from her father,' Luis explained as he took her into the library. 'It had been in the family for generations and Marietta was the end of the line.'

'Did she not have children?'

'No. She never married either. She was a socialite who preferred life on the bigger islands and in Manhattan. She used this island as her personal holiday home for her and her closest friends but she never liked living here. She found it too isolating.'

'Is that why she was happy to sell it to you?'

'She hasn't set foot on the island in three years. She lives permanently in Manhattan now. I made her an outrageous offer for the island and the yacht and she accepted on the spot. She'd kept it for so long only out of an old sense of duty. The yacht was just one of her many toys she bored of playing with.'

Chloe looked up at the faded wallpaper fraying away from the ceiling.

To think she had assumed he'd seduced Marietta into selling up...

For some reason to know she had been way off the mark made her feel lighter inside.

A burst of laughter flew from her mouth. 'I still can't believe you would spend that much money just to kidnap me.'

'To make money you have to spend money. In this case, to preserve my fortune and salvage my reputation, I had to spend a good sum. It's money well spent. And I got a yacht and an island out of it,' he added with a grin before pulling her in for one of the heady kisses she was becoming addicted to. 'I'm already thinking ahead to the parties I will host here once I've renovated the place and had a runway put in.'

She hooked her arms around his neck and gazed into his eyes. Luis had shaved since he'd left her bed.

The scent of his fresh cologne danced into her senses in the dreamiest of fashions. 'Won't having a runway ruin what makes the island so special?'

'I'll keep the runway small and discreet. There won't be any jets landing here.'

'Good.'

He grinned. 'You should come to one of my parties. You can do the hip-hop dancing I saw you doing on the beach.'

'By the time you've renovated the house and sorted out a runway, you and I will be long over,' she pointed out.

Instead of the joy she expected to flush through her at the thought of the day her life became her own again, her stomach plummeted.

The gleam in his eyes made the slightest of dims before his grin regained full wattage and he tugged her arms away from his neck.

Keeping a firm hold of her hand, he led her up the winding staircase that creaked on every tread. 'You should still come. Your hip-hop dancing is very entertaining.'

She forced a laugh.

She much preferred it when they were making love and she could concentrate on the physical side of their relationship, because that was all their relationship would ever amount to and there was no point in allowing the old dreams she'd once had for him rear their head again. She wasn't a teenager any more. She'd seen enough of life to know dreams did not come true.

'I've never had much rhythm,' she told him.

'I remember when you were small. You were always wearing a tutu.'

'That's when I was young. I grew up in a house that my brother called a shrine to dance. My mother was crazy about it and had me in dance classes when I was three.'

'Did you not enjoy it?'

She hesitated before admitting, 'My dream was to dance like your mother.'

The shrine to ballet that had been her childhood home should really have been called a shrine to Clara Casillas. Pictures of her in dance had framed all the walls, along with tour posters and pictures of the two women, Clara and Chloe's mother, Louise, together. The latter had been Chloe's favourite pictures. Her absolute favourite had been one taken in Clara's dressing room in New York. Clara had been dressed in a red embellished costume, Chloe's mother on her knees making adjustments to the hem. In the background, sitting squashed together cross-legged under Clara's dressing table were three small boys all with sulky faces. Benjamin, Luis and Javier. That picture had made her smile for so many different reasons.

When their mother had died, Chloe and Benjamin had gone through all her things together. He had been happy for Chloe to have the ballet memorabilia, all except for that one picture. He'd explained that it had been taken minutes after he and the Casillas twins had been scolded for trying to set off the theatre's fire alarm. Their mothers had made them sit in silence for ten minutes, threatening the withdrawal of the promised after-show pizza for non-compliance.

Her eyes met Luis's, the middle child in that long-ago picture. A fleeting sadness passed between them that pierced straight into her heart.

'What stopped you pursuing ballet?' he asked after a sharp inhalation.

'I told you, my lack of rhythm.' Then she sighed. 'To be truthful, I lived in denial for many years. I always hoped that one day the rhythm would find me and I would turn from the ugly duckling of dance to the swan but it wasn't to be.'

'When did you give it up?'

'When I was thirteen and my breasts exploded from molehills to mountains. Have you seen a ballerina with large breasts? They don't exist, do they? I had so little talent that no one bothered suggesting breast reduction surgery for me. I used that as the excuse for giving it up but, really, everyone who had ever seen me dance knew the reason was simply that I wasn't good enough.'

'I'm sorry you had to give up your dream.'

She shrugged. 'There are worse dreams to give up…'

Like the dream of having a father who actually wanted to be a father. Living under his roof for barely a year had been the final proof that dreams really did not come true no matter how hard she wished them.

Her ballet dream had always been more of a wispy cloud than anything concrete.

Her dreams of a miracle cure suddenly appearing

for her mother… Chloe had seen the cancer ravaging her mother with her own eyes and known that to focus on a cure when the present was all she had left with her would ruin the remaining time they had together. But that dream had still been there, buried deep, getting her through the nights until time had finally run out.

She'd never realised how concrete her dream of wanting her father to *be* her father had been until she'd learned that it was never going to come true. That was a dream that couldn't come true not through a lack of talent or a lack of a medical cure but because *he* didn't want it to happen.

Dreams did not come true. Chloe would never be Clara Casillas. Her mother had died. Her father would never love her. And Luis would never…

Luis would never what? Love her either?

She didn't *want* his love. All she wanted from him was her freedom.

'And I always liked watching Maman create costumes,' she continued, blinking back the sting of hot tears that had sneaked up on her without warning. 'It turned out that costume-making was a talent I did have and the good thing about it is I don't have to watch what I eat or exercise for a hundred hours a day.'

She'd realised in the first week of her apprenticeship at the London ballet company that she would not have made it as a professional ballet dancer even if she'd had the talent. To reach the top as a ballet dancer required self-discipline and a *lot* of sacrifice. She'd had the dream but it had never been matched by the needed hunger.

She liked the niche she'd carved as a costume maker, liked that she'd followed her mother's footsteps, liked the camaraderie and the creativity. She had the best job in the world…

Anger and pride had had her denying to Luis that she cared about losing her career and in that heated moment on his yacht she had meant it. But now, with tempers cooled, it chilled her skin to think how perilously close she had come to throwing it all away.

She had to hope that when this was all over with Luis she would find another ballet company to take her on.

'It does take dedication to reach the top,' he agreed, opening another door. As with all the other doors he'd opened, Chloe took only a cursory look at the room behind it, her attention on their conversation.

'Did you ever dance?' she asked. Luis was the son of two professional dancers. The masculinity issue that prevented many boys from trying ballet would not have applied in his household.

'Me? *Dios*, no. My mother tried to encourage us but neither of us had the slightest interest in it. We just wanted to play.'

She hesitated before asking, 'What about your father?'

A hardness crept into his voice. 'What about him?'

'Did he not encourage you and Javier to follow in his footsteps?'

'Not that I remember.' He opened another door and smoothly changed the subject. 'This was Marietta's bedroom. I'm debating whether to turn it into my own bedroom. What do you think?'

She thought that she needed to respect his reluctance to speak about his father but that undercurrent was there again and, against her better judgement, she said, 'What was your father like?'

'You know what he was like. The world knows what he was like.'

'If I ever met him as a toddler I don't remember it. Benjamin never spoke of him. I know what I've read about him but I would think only a very small part of it is based on truth.'

'No, you will find the majority of it is based on truth. I hated him.'

At the widening of her eyes, Luis took a deep breath, fighting for air in his closed-up lungs.

'Was he always violent towards your mother?' she whispered.

'As far as I know—and your mother confirmed this to me—my father was never physically violent to my mother until the night he killed her.' He relayed this matter-of-factly, hiding the manic thrumming of his heart that even the mildest of allusions to that night always broke out in him. 'I took the brunt of his anger.'

'In what way?'

'In the way that involved belts across naked backsides. It was a form of corporal punishment that was accepted in those days.'

'Just you?'

He nodded curtly. 'He never touched Javier. When we got into trouble together the blame would be put on my shoulders.'

'Even if Javier was at fault?'

'In fairness to Javier, he rarely instigated any trouble. I was the ringleader. I was drawn to trouble like a magnet. When your brother toured with us he was a far more willing accomplice than Javier.' He took another long breath and put a hand to the flaking doorframe, ready to put a stop to this conversation immediately. Instead, he found himself saying, 'Our father was a bitter man. You know he defected from the Soviet Union in the early seventies?'

She nodded, wide-eyed.

'He was a star to the western world back then, another Nureyev. When he met my mother in London she was an up-and-coming ingénue fifteen years his junior. Her star was not supposed to eclipse his but eventually it did and he hated her for it. Our mother carried us twins and returned to the stage stronger than ever. As her star rose his faded. He was always a drinker and prone to outbursts of temper but when he started fighting choreographers and fellow cast members, he no longer had the star power for companies to turn a blind eye. Work dried up. His resentment towards my mother grew. There were months when we wouldn't see anything of him—those were the best times—then he would reappear on the scene and act as if he had never been away.'

'Didn't your mother mind?'

He shook his head as bile curdled up his throat. 'Theirs was a strange relationship. The power balance always tilted from one to the other. They both had lovers. They both flaunted it. But then my father found the young lovers he wanted no longer wanted him; and why would they? He was a drunken mess. He couldn't touch my mother so he took his anger out on me.'

'Didn't she stop him?'

'He was my father. To her mind it was his duty to punish me when it was deserved. She was no disciplinarian herself.' He felt the smallest of smiles break over skin that had become like marble to remember his mother trying to hide her amusement at their japes by putting on her 'stern' face. 'She never raised a finger to us. If my father's punishments went too far she would cup my cheeks and tell me to smile through the pain.'

He heard Chloe suck in a breath.

'My mother understood corporal punishment,' he said, compelled to defend the mother he had loved. 'Her own parents would often use it to punish her. To my mother it was normal and, though she couldn't bring herself to physically punish us herself, she cited it as toughening her up and giving her the tools she needed to succeed in such a competitive world. Her ballet training had taught her to smile through the pain and she wanted me to have that resilience too.'

There was a long period of silence before she asked, 'Why do you think he chose to punish only you?'

'He never liked me. There was something in me that pushed his buttons; I don't know what it was. He adored Javier.'

'That must have been hard.'

'Harder for Javier,' he dismissed. 'It hurt him to see *me* be hurt. We are not identical but we *are* twins and we've had each other's back our entire lives. It is a bond that no one can come between. He suffered in his own way too—our mother loved us both but she doted on me. That was hard on him. He always tried to protect me. He was always trying to save me from the worst of my behaviour because he could always see what the consequences would be.'

'Couldn't you see them?'

'I could but I didn't care.' Just as he'd seen that the consequences of keeping silent about the profit share with Benjamin could be dire but had kept his mouth shut through the years rather than rock a friendship that had meant so much to him.

His relationship with his brother was like a rock, solid and impenetrable. His friendship with Benjamin, which had been stronger than Javier's and Benjamin's, had had the fun element to it. They had broken the rules together, Javier tagging along not to join in with the rule-breaking but to try and stop them going too far.

Benjamin had been his closest friend. He grieved the end of their friendship but in life you had to look forward. Always look forward. Never let the past hook you back.

But the past was hooking him back. He could feel its weight clasped around his stomach, the tentacles digging in tighter and tighter with each hour that passed.

'Maybe it was because you look so much like your mother,' she said softly.

'What was?'

'Your father... Javier looks so much like him whereas you resemble your mother. Maybe he preferred Javier because he thought of him as a miniature version of himself.'

Her words were a variant of Javier's attempts to placate him over their father's cruelty.

Luis moved his hand away from the frame to run it through his hair then caught the flakes of paint on his palm and wiped it on his shorts instead.

The main house needed to be bulldozed and started again from the foundations upwards, he thought moodily.

Unfortunately he had made a promise to Marietta that he would keep the actual structure intact.

He looked back at Chloe, took in the compassion ringing from those beautiful eyes and suppressed a shudder.

Her experiences, different from his as they were, were similar enough that she would have an inkling of what he had felt when growing up.

He needed to keep the structure of their relationship intact too. A marriage that lasted long enough to kill the nastiness circulating about him and his brother. They would have fun and enjoy the time they had together but there would be no bonds between them other than the bonds made in the bedroom.

'No,' he denied with more ice than she deserved. 'It was nothing to do with any physical resemblance. My father disliked me because there was nothing in me for him to like.'

At the parting of her lips, he pressed a finger to them. 'Enough about my father. He's dead. The past is over.' And why he was rehashing long-past deeds with Chloe was beyond his comprehension. His past had nothing to do with their marriage. 'The future's what matters now. And now I would like your honest opinion about this room as I am thinking of making it my bedroom.'

Only his.

As she had rightly said, he and Chloe would be long over when this house was fit for purpose.

He would be the one to pull the trigger to topple the structures holding them together.

CHAPTER TEN

'ARE YOU GOING to join me?' Luis cajoled from the side of the pool.

Chloe, who'd been admiring his strong, powerful strokes from the safety of her sun lounger, shook her head.

Another day in paradise...

After spending the entire morning in bed making love, Luis had suddenly declared himself in need of exercise.

She'd raised a disbelieving eyebrow at that, which had made him laugh and plant an enormous kiss on her mouth. Then he'd strode naked from the bed, strolled through the villa and down to the bottom of the garden and dived straight into the swimming pool, still unashamedly naked.

And with that glorious body, why should he be ashamed? she'd thought dreamily as she'd spied on him from the bedroom window before slipping a bikini on and moving outside for a better view. Luis was a man made for a physical life and the more time he spent showing that physical prowess off in the most physical way with her, the better...

Her increasingly erotic thoughts about him were cut short when Luis hauled himself out of the water and scooped her into his arms.

'Into the water with you,' he said with a grin as he carried her effortlessly to the water's edge despite water dripping off him.

'Put me down,' she squealed, panic setting in instantaneously as she threw her arms around his neck and clung on tightly.

He held her over the water. 'Scared of getting your hair wet?' he teased.

'I can't swim!'

He took an immediate step back and stared down at her with a combination of bemusement and concern. 'Are you serious?'

'Yes!' she yelled. 'Now, put me down!'

Carrying her back to the sun lounger, he gently deposited her on it then grabbed the towel she'd brought down for him and rubbed it through his hair.

'You really can't swim?'

She rolled her eyes. 'I really cannot swim.'

'Why not?'

'Because I hate getting my hair wet.'

He wiped his hand over the droplets of water shining on his chest and flicked it at her hair.

'Behave.'

He laughed and helped himself to a glass of the orange juice Chloe had also brought out. He drained it, wrapped the towel around his waist and sat next to her.

'You're not vain enough to care about your hair getting wet,' he observed with a grin.

She grinned back at him. 'Benjamin tried to teach me when I was little but I hated the shock of the cold water and refused to go any deeper than my thighs.'

'So you never learned?'

'I hate the cold. And I was a stubborn thing.'

'Some would say you still are.'

She mock-glowered at him and, to better show her disdain, swung her legs round to rest on his wonderful, muscular thighs.

He shook his head mockingly and rubbed a hand on her calf. 'The water here is the perfect temperature. I could teach you.'

She made a non-committal grunt. Chloe had managed perfectly well without swimming and didn't see that she'd missed out on anything by preferring to be on land.

'It's better to be able to swim,' he pointed out. 'You never know when it will come useful.'

'Says the man who was probably born able to swim like a world champion.' His prowess in the water was a thing of wonder.

Now he was the one to make a grunt-like noise. 'Hardly. I didn't learn until I was eight.'

'That's late, isn't it? Benjamin had given up on teaching me by then.'

'I learned on our only family sunshine holiday. Our father decided he was the man to teach us.'

The tone of his voice sent a chill up her spine.

The easy playfulness between them seemed to hover on a pair of scales between them as Chloe weighed up whether to ask anything about it.

Would this be a rare happy childhood tale of his?

It pained her to think that unlikely.

So she went with the most neutral question she could think of. 'Did you pick it up easily?'

'No. Javier did, but like you I was a stubborn thing and did everything wrong.'

'On purpose?'

He nodded. 'One day my father got so angry with me for not trying, he said that in the morning he would throw me in the deep end and it would be up to me to sink or swim.'

Nausea creeping through her, Chloe shifted forward so her arched thighs were pressed against his and stroked his damp arm.

'You believed him,' she whispered, resting her chin on his shoulder. She did not doubt for a second eight-year-old Luis had believed his father would let him drown.

His jaw clenched. 'Javier believed it too. He dragged me to the beach with him—we'd found a cove near the resort that was really secluded and calm—and made me learn.'

'You were eight?' she clarified, stunned to think of two such small boys being allowed to go off on their own.

'It was safe,' he insisted. 'The cove was next to the resort. My parents were having one of their good spells and had gone off for what they called a siesta. We had free rein.'

Chloe knew better than to comment on this, did nothing but continue stroking his arm, making her way down to the palm of his hand and tracing circles around it.

'Javier took me out into the sea and made me lie on my back while he held an arm under me to keep me afloat. He kept telling me that if I could float I would never drown. Chloe… I cannot tell you how scared he was, much more than I. He was crying and begging me to trust him. And I did trust him. He was my twin. Who else in the world could I trust more than the boy who was always trying to save me from myself?'

Chloe closed her eyes, trying hard not to allow sympathy into her heart for the small boy Javier would have been, the boy terrified his father would let his beloved twin drown.

'You floated,' she said softly.

'*Sí*. I floated for my brother's sake. By the end of the holiday we were racing each other in the water.'

'How did your father react when you floated?'

'He didn't do it. I don't know if it was a burst of his meagre conscience or if he forgot but he never did throw me in.'

'I'm glad.'

'So was I.' He took a deep breath then carefully moved her legs from over his thighs and got to his feet.

When he looked at her she could virtually see the shutters that had come down in his eyes.

It was the same look as when he'd told her about his father's abuse. End of discussion.

After the strangest pause where he gazed at her as if seeing her for the first time, he blinked.

The shutters had gone and now he stared at her with that hungry look she knew so well.

He grinned widely and held his hand out to her. 'Come, *bonita*. If you won't get your hair wet in the pool with me then you can get wet in the shower.'

Her heart hurting for him, she let him help her to her feet then, when she was upright, wound her arms around his neck and kissed him deeply.

His fingers speared her hair as he kissed her back, his arousal undeniable despite the thick cotton towel draped around his waist.

How badly she wished she could kiss away his past and drive out the pain she knew on an instinctive level still haunted him.

But then, when he lifted her into his arms and carried her back into the villa, the moment overtook her and all thoughts were driven from her mind as she revelled in the heady pleasure they had found together.

Chloe sat on the beach digging her toes into the soft sand and stared up at the sky. There was no moon that night and the stars were in abundance, twinkling down on her like tiny dazzling jewels.

She had been unable to fall asleep. Her mind was filled with too much for it to switch off.

Her resolve over Luis was made of the same fine sand as this warm beach. She could laugh at her weakness but it frightened her too much to be funny.

In two days she would marry him.

She had lain in the bed with him breathing deeply

and rhythmically beside her, her lungs getting tighter and tighter until she couldn't draw air any more.

There was a turbulence in her stomach that had grown stronger with each passing hour spent with him.

She spent *all* her time with him, laughing and making love. She would gaze into his hazel eyes and feel all the breath leave her in a soar.

And then she would recall their conversations about his childhood and her chest would cramp so tightly she couldn't breathe the air back in.

His childhood had been more violent and tempestuous than she could have imagined. The old stories about his violent father that she'd assumed had been embellished by an insatiable media had, if anything, been underplayed.

He'd come so far, both he and Javier. What they had lived through in their formative years could have destroyed lesser men. Not them. Not Luis.

And then he had shut her out. It had almost been a physical act; a blink of the eye and then shutters appeared in them. She understood it was his way of telling her, without words, to back off, to keep things between them on the loose footing they had agreed on, his way of telling her not to get too close.

There was a reason Luis had reached the age of thirty-five without a single long-term relationship under his belt and she strongly suspected it had its roots in his relationship with his father.

She shouldn't *need* telling. She didn't want their marriage to be anything other than temporary either and had no clue as to why that turbulence in her stomach felt strong enough to dislodge her heart.

This craving for him, which had grown so much more than physical, had to stop.

'Chloe?'

She turned her head to see Luis emerge from between the palm trees lining this stretch of beach.

'Hi,' she said softly, her pulse surging just to see his silhouette.

He walked to her wearing nothing but a pair of navy shorts and his deck shoes. 'I wondered where you'd got to.'

'I couldn't sleep,' she confessed.

'You should have woken me. Are you okay?'

Her heart twisted to hear the concern in his voice. In his own way, he did care about her.

She nodded. 'I just needed some air.'

He sat down beside her and stretched his long legs out. 'Something on your mind?'

She gave a hollow laugh. 'Right now it feels as if I have the whole world on my mind.'

Silence bloomed between them and then stretched, a tension in it that she soon found herself desperate to break.

'I keep thinking back to our childhoods,' she said, speaking without really thinking of what she was going to say, just aware that all the stuff that had accumulated in her head as Marietta's possessions had accumulated in the main house needed an outlet. 'Do you remember my mother's funeral? You found me crying and you comforted me. You let me cry in your arms and said things that really resonated and gave me the courage to hope that one day the pain would become bearable. You understood what I was going through. I always remembered that. I carried your words with me for so long… When Benjamin told me about the profit terms with Tour Mont Blanc I felt betrayed, not just for him but for myself and our mother too. I'd been with Benjamin at the hospital the day you made that call to him asking for the money. We'd been told barely an hour before that our mother was dying. I remember him telling you the news. I was holding his hand.'

She felt his eyes burn into her but kept her gaze out on the still sea, black and sparkling under the night sky.

Luis's heart had clenched itself into a fist.

He'd awoken alone in the bed to find Chloe missing. Intellectually he'd known she wouldn't have gone far but there had been a punch of nausea to see the indentation of her head on the pillow.

The hook that had wrapped around his stomach was now so tight it threatened to cut off his blood flow.

If not for the starkness in the way she'd spoken, he would drag her back to bed and distract her in the only way he knew how.

'Being told about your mother's diagnosis is why I have little memory of what occurred the rest of that day,' he said, recalling how Benjamin's news had lanced him.

The Guillem siblings hadn't been the only ones hoping for a miracle.

'Javier and I were fighting to save our business.

To then hear your mother's condition was terminal… Chloe, it cut me to pieces.'

'Really?'

The simple hope that rang from her voice sliced through Luis as if it had a blade attached.

'When we went to Benjamin's apartment to sign it that night I barely gave the contract a second thought. I thought Javier had told him we wanted to renegotiate the terms…'

'But he hadn't.'

He breathed heavily. No. His brother hadn't done. For seven years Luis had believed it to be an oversight on his brother's part but now, as he relived that time in full, he had to wonder…

'Our lawyer and his paralegal came with us to witness it. The contracts were laid out on Benjamin's dining table. He wanted to get it signed and done with. Neither Javier nor I had any way of knowing he hadn't read it. We all signed it, Benjamin transferred the money, Javier and the lawyers left, then Benjamin and I got drunk together.'

'Didn't Javier stay with you?'

'Someone had to finalise the deal with the seller and that someone was Javier. Besides, he doesn't drink.'

His brother had never drunk alcohol. The healthy hell-raising that was a rite of passage for most young men had been left to Luis and Benjamin.

'I drowned my sorrows with your brother because, *bonita*, your mother had been a part of my life from when I was in the womb.' He breathed the salt air in deeply as even older memories hit him in a wave. 'Did you know I was named after her?'

'Non!' she gasped, her head turning to face him. 'You were named after my mother? No one ever told me that.'

He smiled to see how wide her eyes had gone with her disbelief. 'I always felt a bond with her because of it. I will never forget the way she broke the news of my mother's death to us and the kindness and love she showed us that night. My grandparents took good care of us when we became their wards but they were old and would never talk about my mother. They found it too painful.'

The loss of their only child had devastated his grandparents, who had been in their forties and resigned to a childless life when they had unexpectedly conceived Luis and Javier's mother. When they had taken their twin grandsons into their home they had been in their seventies, old-fashioned and set in their ways and unprepared for the mayhem bereaved teenage boys would bring to their orderly lives. When they had tried to discipline Luis in the manner they had disciplined their daughter all those decades before, he'd stood his ground and refused to accept it.

He'd vowed on the death of his mother that he would never again be a whipping boy for anyone. He would never let another person raise a hand to him or look at him with the contempt he'd always seen ringing from his father's eyes.

In Louise Guillem's home Luis had found a modicum of peace. The Guillems' suburban house was near to the Parisian apartment he and Javier had called home with their parents until their lives had been destroyed. Being under Louise's roof with his brother and his best friend, speaking the language that had come more naturally to him than his own had been the only light he had found in those years.

'Your mother found it painful to talk about her too but she was always willing. She kept my mother's memory alive for me. She became the surrogate parent my grandparents weren't capable of being. Carrying her coffin was one of the hardest things I have ever done. Saying goodbye to her was like saying goodbye to my mother all over again.'

A tear glistened on her cheek. She wiped it away and gave a deep sigh. 'I'm glad you loved her. She loved you and Javier very much.' She wiped another spilling tear. 'Can I ask you one more question?'

How could he refuse? 'Anything.'

'Did you ever see your father again, after…?'

After he'd killed Luis's mother.

'Never. I never visited him in prison and I never visited him on his deathbed.'

Their father successfully pleaded diminished responsibility and got convicted of manslaughter. He served only ten years of his sentence, nothing for extinguishing such a precious life.

It had felt fitting that he should die of pancreatic cancer less than a year after his release, alone and unloved.

Only as the years had gone by had regrets started to creep in.

'Do you regret not seeing him?'

Her question was astute.

'My mother has been dead for over twenty years and I still miss her. My father has been dead for half that and I have never missed him but now I wish I had accepted the visiting orders he sent me from prison and taken the opportunity to look him in the eye and ask him how he could have done what he did.'

Her voice was small. 'He did want to see you, then?'

He sighed heavily. 'Yes. He asked for me in the hospice too. He died a very lonely man.'

He pressed his head to hers.

There didn't seem any more need for words. In their own wildly differing ways each had suffered at the hands of their fathers. And in their own way each still suffered at them, Chloe with the indifference she lived with each day, he with the legacy of his mother's murder, a story that would not be extinguished.

Another tear rolled down her cheek. She brushed it with her thumb before lying down on the sand. 'I am so sorry, Luis.'

'Sorry for what?'

'For conspiring with Benjamin against you. I should have known it had never been a deliberate act on your part...'

He wished he could say the same for his brother.

'Hush.' Laying himself down next to her, he gently took her chin and turned her face to look at him. 'Your brother had good reason to think we ripped him off. I regret not handling it better when he confronted us about it but what's done is done. All we can do is put things right for the future.'

'But we have caused such damage, and after everything you've already…'

He put his lips to hers and slid a hand down the curve of her neck. 'Damage our marriage will repair.'

She burrowed her fingers into his hair and gazed intently at him.

The lights from the stars glittered from her tear-filled eyes, desire mingling with her pain, all there ringing at him. Another solitary drop spilled down her cheek.

Suddenly unable to bear looking into those depths any longer, he kissed the tear away then plundered that beautiful mouth with his own, taking her pain away the only way he knew how.

Her response was as passionate as it always was, their desire for each other a simmering flame that only needed the slightest coaxing to bring fully to life.

It was so easy to lose himself in her softness and her passion. There was such openness in her lovemaking; no pretence, no artifice, nothing hidden, just a celebration of the joy their lovemaking evoked, there in her every touch and moan.

As he pulled her dress off and kissed the breasts he just could not get enough of, it came to him that he'd changed as a lover. The pleasure he gave Chloe was far more intoxicating than the great pleasure she gave him, never an exercise in ticking boxes until the time was right for him to take his pleasure but an erotic, heady experience all of its own.

When it came to giving pleasure there was nothing he would not do for her.

And it was the same for her too.

Chloe was the most unselfish lover he could have dreamed of.

Trailing his tongue down her soft belly to the pretty heart of her femininity, he used his tongue in the way he knew she loved, enraptured with the melodious mews that escaped her throat and the scraping of her nails on his skull. He savoured her special, inimitable taste, the downiness of her hair, the silky texture of her skin, all unique to Chloe. Blindfold him and he would know her from the imprint of her mouth and the scent of her skin alone.

The nails scraping into his skull pulled at his hair, urging him on, her moans deepening, her breaths shallowing until she was crying out, his name spilling from her tongue and echoing through to his marrow.

Chloe sighed happily and gazed up at the stars while the stars Luis had set off in her twinkled with equal joy.

His touch alone was enough to soothe her. When he made love to her nothing else existed but them and the moment they were sharing.

So many moments. So many memories to take with her when they were over...

A pain sliced through her chest so sharp she gasped.

Luis, his wonderful mouth making its way back up her belly, must have assumed it was a gasp of pleasure for he took her breast into his mouth and encircled her nipple with his tongue in the way they had discovered she liked so much.

Fresh sensation building back up in her, Chloe closed her eyes and welcomed the pleasure, let it drown out the fleeting pain. When he reached her lips she kissed him greedily and looped her arms around him, needing to feel the solid warmth of his skin beneath her fingers.

She could have had the ton of lovers she'd once lied about but nothing would have compared to what she and Luis had. She didn't need to be experienced to know what they had was special and unique and belonged only to them.

She could drink his kisses for ever.

And, when he was finally inside her, fully sheathed, filling her completely, she wound her legs tightly around his waist and let go of everything but this most beautiful of moments.

CHAPTER ELEVEN

Tiny sharp prickles dug into Chloe's cheek, as she roused into consciousness.

Absently running a hand over her face, she found sparkling grains of sand clinging to the pads of her fingers.

She smiled sleepily and rolled over, memories of Luis making love to her under the twinkling stars on the beach awakening other parts of her...

Luis shuffled in his sleep and groped for her hand.

She laced her fingers through his and stared at him. The sun had almost fully risen, its light filtering through the curtains. Luis's features were clear and strong. Thick dark stubble had broken through his skin since he'd shaved the morning before. When he had made love to her that stubble had scratched her breasts in a way that had been half pain and half pleasure.

Everything about them was like that. Half pain. Half pleasure.

So much had been revealed between them in the days they had spent on this island.

She felt wretched about the hand she had played in Benjamin's revenge.

It had been her revenge too, she had to acknowledge painfully.

Luis had never set out to cheat her brother.

He had kidnapped her and blackmailed her but that all felt like a lifetime ago, actions done to and conducted by two different people.

The man she had once believed herself in love with *did* exist.

And if he did exist then didn't that mean…?

That their marriage could be for real…?

'You've got that look on your face that tells me you are thinking,' he whispered, his voice thick with sleep.

She blinked, reopening her eyes to find his gorgeous hazel gaze fixed on her.

You don't want to know what I'm thinking.

Or maybe he did.

Maybe it wasn't just the desire they shared.

Oh, what was she *thinking*?

She would still be entering a marriage based on revenge.

But that had been agreed before they'd made love and before they'd opened up to each other.

Before she'd accepted that she loved him.

And even if his feelings for her were as strong as hers were for him, that didn't mean they had the basis of anything that could last.

Luis was a twin. He and his brother had a bond she could not begin to understand and it pained her to know that even if she and Luis were to have a proper future together, she would always come second to Javier.

This was a dream she didn't dare hope for.

'I'm just thinking it's been a few hours since you made love to me,' she whispered back, putting her hand on his cheek.

Her brain hurt from sleep deprivation and too much conversation. Now she was hallucinating thoughts.

Love?

No, that was taking things too far.

She felt a lot towards this man, but love…?

Proper, uninterrupted sleep was needed. Then, when her brain and body were refreshed, she would be able to think properly.

But first she wanted the closeness she felt when he was deep inside her.

Snuggling into him, she welcomed his arms wrapping around her, a blanket in their own right, and closed her eyes to the heady power of his intoxicating kiss.

Sleep. Everything would look different after she'd had some.

Everything was the same.

Everything.

Chloe was lying on her back in the calm sea, Luis's arm acting as a float.

After making love and then falling into a deep, pure sleep, she had woken with the urge to swim. He hadn't questioned it—she didn't allow herself to think too deeply about it either—just led her to the section of beach where the water was calm and so clear she could see the tiny pebbles on its bed.

The most important part, he'd reiterated seriously, was being able to float. And to be able to float, she needed to relax in the water.

They had taken it slowly.

'Are you ready for me to remove my arm?' he asked.

The patience he'd shown in getting her to this stage filled her heart with the buoyancy she needed to stay afloat.

She trusted him. To not let her drown. To keep her alive.

With her heart.

For the better or the worse she did not know but loving Luis had changed something fundamental in her.

When he looked in her eyes she almost dared hope she saw the same reflected as shone from hers.

And if it wasn't there yet then she had to take the chance that one day it would be.

She had allowed her father to destroy her fragile heart for too long.

She had carried his rejection every day for seven years… No, she'd carried his rejection her entire life.

He was the reason she had kept men at arm's length, she'd come to realise. Her father had rejected her twice, the first time while she had still been in the womb. The second rejection had been the one that had destroyed her and shattered any trust she might have. She'd always told herself it was men she didn't trust but the truth, as she could now see clearly, was that her father's rejection of the almost fully grown-up Chloe had left her feeling inherently unlovable. If her own father couldn't find anything to love about her then why would anyone else?

Tomorrow she would exchange her vows with Luis. If she didn't take the chance and trust the passion and friendship that had grown between them then she would never find it with anyone else and she would grow into a lonely old woman.

There would never be anyone else for her.

She looked into Luis's eyes and smiled.

His eyes sparkled. 'Is that a yes?'

Her smile widened.

She couldn't speak. Not with words.

She loved him.

He let go.

She floated.

When Luis opened his eyes into the duskiness of early morning he thought for sure he was still sleeping. This had to be a dream. A wonderful, heady, sensuous dream.

Dreams of Chloe were nothing new. He'd woken with erotic dreams of them simmering in his blood so many times over the past few months that it was more a surprise when he didn't have them. The intensity of them had only grown since they had become lovers.

They never felt this real though.

He closed his eyes and hooked an arm above his head with a sigh.

Dios, that felt good.

Chloe was underneath the sheets, between his legs, pleasuring him with her tongue.

He groaned as she slid him into her mouth, groaning even louder when she cupped his...

Dios.

This was incredible.

In his dreams he was always left unfulfilled but now he could feel telltale sensations tugging at his loins.

And then she stopped.

This time his groan was one of frustration that was cut off from his tongue when she pulled the sheets off him and crawled over him.

Putting her hands either side of his face, she stared down at him with a soft gleam in her eyes. 'Good morning.'

And then she sank down on his burning erection.

Luis gasped.

There had been a very real danger then that he would have come undone with one thrust.

But, *Dios*, this was like nothing he had ever felt before. This was something new.

They had never made love without a condom before.

He had never made love without a condom before.

He could not have comprehended how different it would feel being completely bare inside her or the sensations that would course through his blood and loins.

Adjusting herself so she was sitting upright with him fully inside her, she rested her hands lightly on his chest.

Luis gazed at her, now quite certain that he wasn't dreaming and that this was real, that this was Chloe waking him in such a pleasurable way, Chloe, the woman he would be marrying that day.

He raised a hand to cover one of her breasts. *Dios*, he loved her breasts. Loved her soft, rounded belly. Loved her supple thighs currently squeezing against him. Loved the raven hair falling in waves over her breasts and down her back.

And then he loved when she began to take her pleasure from him, finding a rhythm, leaning forward to stare deep into his eyes as her breasts gently swayed with the motion.

He couldn't take his eyes from her face. Her eyes had darkened in colour, becoming violet, her cheeks slashed with the colour of passion. Harder and deeper she ground against him, tiny moans flying out of those gorgeous lips that became louder when he grabbed hold of her hips to steady her and drive himself up into her.

Colour heightened on her cheeks and then he felt her orgasm build inside her as vividly as he felt his own, her muscles thickening and tightening around him as, with a loud cry, she fell against him at the exact moment he lost all control of himself.

For long moments the world went white.

'We didn't use a condom,' he said a short while later when they had finally caught their breath.

He didn't know if it was an oversight on her part or if she had meant it.

He didn't know which he hoped the answer would be.

Since they had become lovers they had only ever used condoms, which he'd armed himself with from the numerous boxes he had thrown into his suitcase on a whim before he had kidnapped her. He made sure to always have some handy wherever he went, their passion for each other often finding them making love in the most unlikely places, like on the beach in the middle of the night.

Neither of them had mentioned her being on the pill since he had confronted her with the packet.

She was still on top of him.

He was still inside her.

She nuzzled into his neck. 'I know.'

Then she raised her head and put her chin to his.

The look in her eyes was one he had never seen before. 'I trust you, Luis.'

He forced a smile to lips that had become leaden.

The euphoria of the moment died as a klaxon set off in his guts at this declaration of trust that instinct told him meant much more than had been said.

In truth, he had felt that klaxon warming up since he had taken her swimming the day before.

There had been a moment when he had been encouraging her to try and float when she had looked in his eyes and he'd felt as if she had seen right down to his soul.

The only thing that made him certain she hadn't seen right down into it was that she hadn't run away screaming.

His yacht was on its way to the island, the captain and crew preparing for the ceremony that would make him and Chloe husband and wife. The press release had been prepared, the champagne was on ice, everything that could be controlled taken care of.

And yet he felt his control over the situation slipping through his fingers and he didn't know how to claw it back.

Luis pounded along the beach, stretching his legs as he jogged, running as he hadn't run in too many years to count.

He hadn't wanted to swim. He'd needed to do something physical that didn't remind him of the woman he'd left burrowed under the covers, her lips curved in a beautiful smile as she slept.

The sun rising over the Caribbean like an enormous jewel was a glorious sight but not one he could appreciate. The knots in his stomach were too tight for him to appreciate anything at that moment.

In a few hours he would be a married man to the most beautiful woman in the world.

Their marriage was supposed to be an exercise in damage limitation.

It was not supposed to feel like this.

He was not supposed to let her get close to him.

A short, entertaining marriage that fixed all the problems she had helped create. That was all it was supposed to be.

He was not supposed to feel her presence like a pulse.

How the hell she did it he did not know but Chloe had a talent for drawing things out of himself that he'd hardly acknowledged to himself. She was better than any priest for making a man want to bear his rotten soul. Not even Benjamin knew he'd been his father's whipping boy.

He had never had to physically drag himself away from a woman before.

After running for an hour he headed back and went straight in the shower without checking in on her.

The knots in his stomach hadn't gone.

Almost ten miles of pounding his legs and he felt as out of sorts as when he'd set off.

Only when he had dried and dressed did he check his phone and find a missed call from his brother.

As if he didn't feel crap enough as it was.

Javier had ignored his calls since that disastrous video conference with the Canadian. He'd messaged him a few times about the business but voice-to-voice conversations had been blacklisted.

His brother really could be a cold bastard when he wanted. Add injured pride—and Javier's pride had been enormously injured by Benjamin stealing his fiancée away from him and in such a deliberate and public manner—and his brother was a tinderbox primed to explode.

Luis wanted to help him but had learned through their thirty-five years together that there was no point in putting pressure on his twin to see reason. When he was in a mood like this it was best to keep his distance and wait either for Javier to open up or for the darkness to pass.

With a heavy sigh, he stepped out onto the balcony and called Javier back.

'Why are you with Chloe Guillem?' Javier asked, not even bothering with a cursory greeting.

'I am saving our backsides,' Luis informed him

calmly. He had hoped to have this conversation after the deed was done. He'd known from the outset that his brother would not approve this plan of action. How he had discovered that he was with Chloe was a mystery to be solved another time.

'By getting involved with that poisonous bitch?'

'Do not speak of her in that way,' Luis cut in, his hackles rising at the insult to Chloe.

She was the least poisonous woman he knew.

'She is a Guillem. Everything they touch is poison.'

Luis counted to ten before responding.

He had to remember that it was Javier's fiancée Benjamin had stolen away with Chloe's assistance. For Javier, it ran much more deeply.

'I'm marrying her today. Having Chloe as my wife will prove to the world that the rumours of what happened between us and Benjamin are unfounded. George will be placated. It will save the Canadian project and kill the rumours flying around about us.'

'I don't care about any of that.'

'We have already invested fifty million euros in it. That's money we will never get back. Investors on other projects are asking questions too. I'm not telling you anything you don't already know.'

'The other investors won't do anything, you'll see. It will blow over and, even if it doesn't, I would rather take the financial hit than have a Guillem marry into our family.'

'Don't be so petty. I'm saving our business by doing this.' He almost added that marrying Chloe was an excellent form of revenge on Benjamin but stopped himself at the last moment.

It felt like a lifetime ago that revenge had been the driving force behind all this.

When had that motive disappeared?

He shrugged the thought away and concentrated on the conversation at hand.

'Our backsides don't need saving any more than our business does. Our fortune is safe. We might take a short-term hit but we can claw the long-term back, and we can preserve our reputations by other means.'

'*What* other means?' Luis demanded to know.

'We would have thought of something already if you hadn't gone running off on this hare-brained scheme.'

'You were not in the mood to talk,' Luis reminded him with equal venom. 'Need I remind you that your whole attitude was to sit and seethe with only yourself for company?'

'I was thinking.'

'And I was doing. Marrying Chloe is the best solution for everyone.'

'Have you lost your mind?' his brother demanded with incredulity. 'We have overcome worse than this by working together and putting on a united front. That's all we need to do. Ride it out. We don't need her and I cannot believe you would think otherwise. That woman conspired with her brother to destroy us and now you want to marry her into our family? No, you *have* lost your mind, and over a *woman*…' His disgust was clear to hear. 'Has her pretty face blinded you to her poison?'

'Do not be ridiculous,' Luis snarled, the end of his

tether reached. 'Chloe regrets the part she played and wants to put things right.'

'You *defend* her?' Javier's laughter was hollow. 'Marry her if you must but do not pretend it's for our sake. We do not need her to get through this and for you to think otherwise only proves your head has been turned.'

Then the line went dead.

Anger fisting in his guts, Luis threw his phone on the floor.

How dared his own twin question his judgement in such a way? And as for saying he'd lost his mind over Chloe...

Luis accepted that he'd let her get closer than he'd ever intended but he had not lost his head. He could walk away from her right now and not feel an ounce of regret.

In an instant the anger was replaced by a wave of relief so strong he could almost see the ripples in the air as it left his shoulders, all the tension and knots that had grown in him these past few days leaving with it.

Javier was wrong about his feelings for Chloe but in one respect he *was* right.

It always had been the two of them, the Casillas brothers against the world. Everything the cruel world had thrown at them had been faced and defeated together. Why should this situation be any different?

And why had it taken so long for him to recognise it?

Whatever the reason, his relief was absolute.

He didn't have to marry Chloe.

CHAPTER TWELVE

CHLOE STEPPED OUT of the bathroom with only a towel around her. Luis was sitting on the edge of the bed.

One look at his face told her something was wrong.

'What's the matter?' She walked to her dressing table to put her watch on.

'Nothing's wrong. Quite the opposite.'

'What are you talking about?'

'Our wedding is off.'

She laughed. 'Funny. You should be a comedian.'

'Our wedding is off. I've let the captain know. I've had a helicopter flown in which will transport us to Lisa Island and…'

'Are you being *serious*?' she interrupted.

'Yes.'

She searched his face. 'But why? Is it something I've done?'

'No, *bonita*. You have done nothing wrong. *Au contraire*, as you would say. I have spoken to Javier. We are in agreement that it is unnecessary for me to marry you. We have decided to proceed as we have always done; together, putting on a united front to the world.

Be happy. You can be out of my life sooner than you had hoped.'

Chloe felt the blood drain from her face. It happened so quickly she had to grab hold of the dressing table tightly as the room began to spin.

It took a few goes before she could open her throat enough to speak and when she did, her words were croaky. 'Our marriage is no longer necessary?'

'I apologise for wasting your time.'

'Are you for real? Is this a joke?' This absolutely did not make sense. The look on his face did not make sense, a mixture of lightness and grimness, a strange combination that terrified her.

'I am for real and this is not a joke.' He got to his feet. 'The helicopter will leave here in an hour and I've arranged for a jet to take you from Lisa Island back to Grand Bahama. Let me know when you wish to fly back to Europe and I will get that arranged for you too.'

He headed out of the bedroom door, hands in pockets, as nonchalant as if he'd just told her breakfast was about to be served.

This could not be happening.

This *was* happening.

Violent storms churned in her belly, hot and cold darts bouncing in her dazed head.

Forcing her newly leaden legs to move and holding tightly to her towel, Chloe hurried out of the room behind him. 'Wait just one minute.'

He couldn't end it like this. No. This was all wrong. Not now, not after everything.

He was halfway down the corridor.

'Wait just one minute,' she repeated, raising her voice so he could not pretend to ignore her.

He stopped.

'Why are you doing this?'

'I just explained it to you.'

'No, you didn't. And please show me the courtesy of looking at me when you are speaking to me.'

He didn't move. 'I thought you would be happy.'

'Will you turn around and *look* at me?' she begged. 'Please, Luis, just look at me. *Talk* to me.'

If she had something to hand to throw at him to compel him to turn and face her she would take it gladly.

She needed to look in his eyes, really look, make sense of this grenade he had just thrown at her feet.

All she had was her towel.

He slowly turned.

When she finally got to look in his eyes she quailed.

There was nothing to read in them.

The shutters had come down and locked themselves shut.

'You only agreed to marriage because I blackmailed you,' he reminded her steadily, his frame like a statue. 'Neither of us wanted it.'

'I don't care about the marriage. I care that you're walking away from *us* without a word of discussion about it.'

'*Bonita*, there is no us. There never was.'

'Then what was the last week all about? That felt like an *us* to me.'

She had seen tenderness in his eyes. She had felt his tenderness in his kisses.

Surely, surely that hadn't all been a lie? Surely she hadn't dreamt it all up?

Her brain clouded in a steamy fog as she realised what she had done.

She had allowed herself to dream.

A fiery burn stabbed the back of her retinas and she blinked rapidly, driving the tears back, begging them not to fall, not to humiliate her.

'I am not responsible for your feelings,' he told her in that same steady voice. 'We were both very clear that our marriage would be a temporary arrangement to quell the stories and preserve my business. Javier and I...'

'Was it *him*?' Ice plunged into her spine at the mention of that hateful man, the ripples driving out the fog in her brain and bringing her to a form of clarity.

She believed Luis had had nothing to do with her brother signing the contract under false pretences but she would bet her brother's chateau that Javier had known.

'Talking to Javier made me see that this route was unnecessary. I acted rashly in demanding marriage from you. I should have thought things through in more detail but I was angry. Your brother had declared war on us.' He shrugged, a nonchalant, dismissive gesture that had her clenching her hands into fists. 'As regretful as it is with hindsight, anger leads to impulsive actions.'

She stared at him, trying her hardest to get air into her lungs. 'So I've given you all of this for nothing?'

'All of what?'

The tears she had come so close to shedding were sucked away as fury finally cut its way through the anguish.

She dropped her towel and held her arms out. 'This! Me!'

Let him see her naked. Let him see what he had taken, what she had given him, the very thing she had never given to anyone. Let him see her heart beating so frenziedly beneath her skin and the chest struggling to get air into it.

Let him see *her*.

Finally there was a flicker of something in his eyes.

'Oh, you liked this part, didn't you?' She laughed mirthlessly. 'You couldn't get enough of it. I bet you were laughing through your teeth every time you made love to me. But there was no love in it, was there? It was all just *sex* to you—'

'Chloe,' he tried to cut in, but she was on a roll, anger and humiliation and a splintering heart too much to bear with any form of stoicism.

'Was it all a joke the pair of you dreamt up? Did I give you my virginity as part of a screwed-up *game*?'

His face contorted. 'You are making too much of this. We were never going to be for ever.'

'Of course we weren't going to be for ever. You don't do for ever, do you? Too busy hiding your feelings, scared someone will see too deeply and think the same as your father did. That's what scares you, isn't it?'

'How dare you?' The statue suddenly came to life with a roar.

'No, how dare *you*? How dare you make love to me like I mean something, how dare you comfort me, how dare you confide in me, how dare you make me dream when dreams were something I had given up?' Aware of angry tears splashing down her cheeks, she swiped them away.

'I have never lied to you,' he snarled, storming over to stand before her, as tall and as broad as she had ever seen him. 'You are the one who has made too much of what we've shared here. How would you have liked me to make love to you? With indifference?'

'I wish I'd never let you touch me in the first place!'

'But you did, didn't you?' He took hold of her chin roughly but painlessly and stared at her with eyes that spat fury. 'Do not blame me for *your* desires. We were never going to last. We've had fun together—I admit, I never expected to enjoy our time here as much as I have but now it is over. All I'm doing is bringing the end date forward and allowing us to pick up our lives.'

Chloe's open hand was inches from connecting with his hateful face before she became aware that she was on the verge of slapping him.

Even with all the hurt and fury unravelling like a nightmare kaleidoscope inside her she could not bring herself to physically harm him, not now, not with the tales of his father's violence so fresh in her mind.

What kind of a person would that make her?

She had lashed out at Luis before and he'd overpowered her easily but that meant nothing.

If she struck her hand to him that would make her as bad as the dead man she hated.

She *wanted* to hurt him. But not like that.

She would rather rip her own heart out than strike him in anger again.

Taking a deep breath, she dropped her hand and, with all the dignity she could muster in her naked state, looked him straight in the eye.

'You call what we have shared *fun*? Fun is for the parties you like to throw and for the women whose beds you hop in and out of without a care. I bared my soul to you. I confided things in you that I have never shared with anyone because I trusted you. I deserve better than to be discarded like an unwanted puppy that's outgrown its cuteness.'

But the dignity was fleeting for as soon as she had said her piece she could feel the bones in her legs begin to crumble.

Terrified he would see the depths of her pain, Chloe turned on her heel and fled back to the bedroom.

The door shut with a bang loud enough to damage the hinges.

Luis closed his eyes and blew out a long puff of air.

After taking a few moments to gather his composure and rub his forehead to lessen the forming headache, he bent down to pick up Chloe's discarded towel. Discarded as she claimed he was discarding her.

He'd known she would be shocked that he was ending things so abruptly but never had he expected her to react like that.

He hadn't expected to see the pain in those blue eyes.

Dios, his head was really hurting.

Slinging her towel over his shoulder, he headed

down the stairs to the kitchen and poured himself a glass of water and scavenged for painkillers. He found a packet stuck in the back of one drawer and popped the tablets out.

This was not his fault, he thought angrily. He was guilty of many things—kidnap, blackmail; the pain in his chest deepened just to think of it—but he had never led her on. Not by word or deed had he done anything to indicate he wanted a future with her.

She should be grateful. Better he ended it now, before she looked hard enough at him and she saw the rottenness that lay in his core. She'd alluded to it, to his father, but how she couldn't see it already was beyond him. He had kidnapped her. He had blackmailed her.

And she acted as if he'd wounded her by setting her free early.

He tossed the pills down his throat and drank the water. Maybe they would help the pain that had erupted in his chest as well as his head.

He should never have let it get this far. He should have worked harder to keep things on a purely physical level as he had always done before. Maybe then the sting of her words wouldn't feel so acute.

Hearing footsteps on the stairs, he braced himself for another onslaught.

Chloe appeared in the doorway.

She'd thrown on the shorts and red T-shirt she'd been wearing the day he had kidnapped her and had her beach bag stuffed tightly under her arm.

She walked to him, her gait stiff, stopping far enough

away that there was no danger in either of them touching, accidentally or not.

'I apologise for bringing your father into it,' she said tightly. 'That was uncalled for.'

He inhaled deeply then inclined his head. His throat had closed.

But what could he say? There was nothing left *to* say. Everything that could be said had already been said.

'I would be grateful if you would allow me to travel on my own in the helicopter,' she said into the silence, no longer looking at him.

By the time his throat had opened enough for him to speak, Chloe had walked out of the front door.

He let her go.

Chloe opened the letter with a shaking hand.

The large padded envelope had the official Compania de Ballet de Casillas logo embossed on it. It had been forwarded from her shared apartment in Madrid to the house she was currently staying at in London, where she had taken sanctuary with her old friend, Tanya. She hadn't called it sanctuary, of course, had said only that she was taking a break and begged use of Tanya's spare room.

Inside the envelope was a letter of reference written by Maria, the Head of Costume.

It was a glowing reference too.

She held it to her chest and blinked back tears.

Luis had authorised this for her. He must have done.

Maria, as wonderful as she was, would not dare write a reference for her without permission.

Chloe hadn't asked for a reference. She'd assumed that there was no chance of her getting one, not after she had quit without working her notice and then for her hand in stealing their principal dancer away from the co-owner. She'd assumed her name would be mud in the whole company.

A separate, smaller envelope had fallen out of the package and landed by her feet. She picked it up, opened it and pulled out a goodbye card signed by the entire costume department and many of the other back-stage crew. Even a few of the dancers had scribbled their names in it. There was also a personal handwrit-ten note from Maria wishing her all the best for the future and telling her to seek her out the next time she was in Madrid.

The postscript at the end was what got her heart truly racing.

My daughter was going to have this ticket but she can no longer attend. It's yours. Please come.

Tucked in the envelope was a ticket for the opening night of Compania de Ballet de Casillas's new theatre.

Chloe resisted the instinct to rip it in two.

Instead, she placed it on her dressing table and pinched the bridge of her nose to keep the tears at bay.

She'd cried too much in the past month.

The worst of it was that she couldn't tell anyone, not even Tanya.

How could she admit that she'd been stupid enough to fall in love with the man who'd kidnapped her and blackmailed her? They would think she was suffering a version of Stockholm syndrome.

She wished she could explain her pain away on that. That would be easier to cope with.

Easier to cope with than to accept that she, the woman who had learned the hard way that dreams did not come true, had allowed herself to dream of a future with a man incapable of returning her love.

The flash of cameras that went off as Luis stepped out of the limousine with his brother would have blinded a less practised man.

Unfazed, the Casillas brothers cut their way through the reporters all eager for a sound bite, past the chanting crowd all hoping to spot a famous face, and up the stairs and through the theatre's doors.

The new theatre that homed Compania de Ballet de Casillas was, Luis thought with satisfaction, a perfect blend of new and old. They had employed the best architect to work on it, Daniele Pellegrini, and he had produced the same magic that had won him so many awards through the years.

The fifteen-hundred-strong audience crowded inside were enjoying a drink in one of the five bars or finding their seats, excited chatter filling the magnificent bowled space. He and Javier had made the conscious decision to give only a third of the tickets to VIPs. The remaining two thirds had been sold through a form of lottery, reasonably priced so any member of the public should be able to afford it, something they both felt strongly about, that the arts should not be the domain of the rich. Every member of the audience, whether rich or poor, had made an effort with their appearance and it warmed his cold heart to see the glittering dresses, smart suits and tuxedos.

The press were out in force, not from a desire to see the theatre's grand opening or to review the performance of *The Red Shoes*—although the bona fide critics had been allocated seats—but because two of the parties of the love triangle would be under the same roof for the first time since Benjamin had stolen Freya two months ago.

It would be the first time Javier had come face to face with the woman who had dumped him so publicly.

The tension emanating from his brother's huge shoulders let Luis know the strain Javier was under. He hadn't loved Freya but his pride had suffered an enormous blow.

It would not be easy for Javier to see the woman he'd intended to marry dancing on his stage, the star of the performance. Despite the animosity that curdled between them, Luis felt for him.

Things had been strained between the brothers since Luis had returned from the Caribbean. They continued to work together, conducted their regular meetings, nothing changed in that respect, but a coldness had developed between them, unlike anything they had been through before.

However, Javier had been correct that they would get through the bad press that had been unleashed on them. They'd written the Canadian project off—damn, that had felt great telling that sanctimonious oaf George where to go—and it had generated the expected flurry of headlines. But with all the parties in the Javier, Benjamin and Freya love triangle remaining tight-lipped, the press had run out of new angles for the story. The ever-moving news cycle had moved on to new fodder... until that evening.

Although this was an opinion he chose not to share with his brother, Luis was grateful that Freya had some loyalty left in her. She had, naturally, handed her notice in with Compania de Ballet de Casillas but had agreed to honour her commitment to this opening performance. They kept their star performer for one last night and, without actually saying a word, Freya was telling the world that they couldn't be the complete monsters the cruel Internet commentators gleefully insisted they must be.

Whenever Luis thought of those comments now, he thought of Chloe. She had been far more outraged by them than he had been. It was as if she had taken them personally.

Sometimes, alone in his bed, Luis would gaze at the ceiling and wonder where the madness had come from that had made him think marrying her would be the solution to all their problems.

His brother had been right: he *had* lost his mind.

And then he would stop thinking.

Or try to stop thinking.

He couldn't rid himself of her. Everywhere he went his mind played tricks on him. He'd walked past the coffee shop where he had first been so dazzled by her and had seen her in there, laughing, her raven hair flowing like waves around her. And then he'd blinked and she'd gone.

Drinks in hand, faking cordiality, he and Javier settled themselves in their private box, which they had chosen to share that evening with senior members of the Spanish royal family. Sitting on his other side was a ravishing princess. Four months ago he would have decided on the spot to get her into bed. Now he couldn't even muster basic interest.

There had been no one since he had left the Caribbean. Not even a twitch in his loins. There had been no one other than Chloe since their one date all those months ago…

The curtains fell back and the performance began.

Within minutes Luis experienced his usual boredom when watching the ballet. He much preferred watching an action-packed movie to this, and he found his gaze drifting over the audience.

Minutes before the interval, he saw, hidden at the back of the box on the other side of the theatre, the unmistakable dark features of Benjamin Guillem.

Putting his binoculars to his eyes, he trained them on him to confirm it.

Yes, it was Benjamin.

Luis had not expected him to be there. Indeed, if he were a gambling man he would have put his money on Benjamin staying away.

Admiration flickered in him. Benjamin had voluntarily entered the lion's den. That took balls…

And then he saw the expression on his old friend's face and moved the binoculars to the stage where Freya was dancing a solo. Then he trained them back on Benjamin and he understood, his heart suddenly thumping rapidly, why he had come.

He was there to support the woman he loved.

Luis's thoughts flashed to Chloe.

His thoughts *always* flashed to Chloe.

'What is she doing here?' Javier hissed in his ear. He too was looking through his binoculars.

'Who?' He would not mention Benjamin's presence.

'Chloe.'

Whipping his binoculars to where his brother's were trained, high up in the gods, Luis sucked in a breath as he worked on the lens's focus.

He made sure to blink before looking again, certain that his eyes were playing their familiar trick on him.

Dios, it was her, ravishing in a black lace dress, her raven hair framing her face in a sleek, coiffured style he had never seen before but which enhanced her elfin beauty.

'What is she doing here?' Javier repeated.

'I don't know.'

He had no idea where she had got a ticket from or why she had come.

Or why his heart hammered so hard his ribs vibrated with the force.

CHAPTER THIRTEEN

CHLOE WATCHED THE performance without paying any attention to what was happening on the stage. She managed to keep her frame still but emotionally she was all over the place.

She had a good view of the Casillas brothers' private box and had spotted Luis the moment he'd entered it. That one look had been enough for her heart to set off at a thrum and for her palms to become clammy.

That one look had been enough to prove she had made an enormous mistake in coming here.

On one side of him sat his hateful brother. On the other side a beautiful woman dressed in crushed velvet whispering intimately into his ear.

Chloe had put her binoculars back in her clutch bag and refused to look in his direction again.

What was she trying to prove to herself? she thought miserably as the performance went on. That she was over him?

The ticket had been sitting on her dressing table for a week when, after another terrible night's sleep, she had decided to go.

She needed to see him one last time, in circumstances over which *she* was in control.

She'd had it all planned out. She would find him during the interval or the after-show party—she knew enough people to be confident of someone helping her sneak in—and then she would graciously thank him for the reference and sweep out with all the grace she had been practising all week.

It destroyed her to know his last memory of her was as an hysterical wreck.

She hadn't even cared that coming here would mean she would see Javier or that there was the chance she would bump into her brother. She hadn't seen Benjamin since she'd returned to Europe.

Her wounds were too fresh for her to see anyone who cared enough to notice the insomnia-inflicted bruising beneath her eyes. Tanya cared but she was busy with her work and still the party animal of old. In Tanya's home, Chloe found the peace she craved but also the time she'd always shied away from that allowed her to think.

Oh, what had she come here for?

More humiliation?

Luis didn't love her. He wouldn't care that she had made a deliberate effort with her appearance or for any graceful sweep away from him. She would have been relegated to his past. She doubted he'd given her more than a fleeting thought, other than arranging her reference.

She had to do what he had always said and look to the future. She could do nothing about the past but she could pick her life up and move forward. She could complete the application form for the ballet company in New York and make a fresh start.

Another fresh start.

But this would be the last.

She wouldn't go chasing a dream; she would create her own.

Suddenly filled with determination, she straightened her spine and waited for the performance to end.

How Luis remained in his seat through the rest of the performance he would never know. He kept his binoculars trained on Chloe, willing her to look his way.

But she didn't. Her eyes stayed fixed on the drama unfolding on the stage, oblivious to his presence and oblivious to the drama unfolding in the pit of his stomach.

Dios, she looked so beautiful. The way she was holding herself too... When they'd been together she had been a great one for slouching and putting her feet up wherever she went. Tonight she looked as regal as the princess sitting beside him, who had given up her attempts to draw him into conversation.

It must have taken real guts for Chloe to come here tonight.

Which begged the question of why she had come. Was it merely that she'd procured an invitation and, being a ballet lover, had decided to use it? That was the only logical explanation he could think of. He hadn't seen or spoken to her in over a month.

Whatever her reasons, the Guillems had more guts

than an ice-hockey team. Both of them had entered the lion's den.

But Benjamin had entered it to support the woman he loved.

After the way things had ended between him and Chloe he could say with one hundred per cent confidence that she was not there to support him.

But she was there.

And he couldn't take his eyes off her.

And he couldn't fight the knots in his stomach that were pulling tighter and tighter in him.

'I'm going to have a word with Security and make sure they know not to let her into the after-party,' Javier murmured as they rose to their feet at the end of the performance.

As Luis was craning his neck to keep watch over Chloe, it took a few moments to understand what his brother was saying.

He turned his attention to him. 'You will leave her alone,' he said sharply.

Javier's face darkened into something ugly. 'You still defend her? After what she did?'

'She was defending her brother, doing what either you or I would do if we felt someone had hurt us.'

Their royal guests had got to their feet.

Remembering his manners, Luis managed to exchange a few words with them as they exited the box.

Right at the last moment he turned his head for one last sight of Chloe but found her row empty.

Swallowing back the bile that had risen up his

throat, he forced a smile to his lips and joined the throng in the corridor.

The after-show party was being held in one of the theatre's underground conference rooms and, trying hard to keep his attention on his honoured guests and not allow his eyes to keep darting about in the hope of catching a glimpse of a raven-haired beauty, Luis headed to it.

When the group took a left where the corridor forked, he saw, in the distance, the tall figure of Benjamin.

Not hesitating for a moment, Luis put his hand on his brother's back and steered him in the other direction, calling over his shoulder to their guests that they would join them shortly.

'What's the matter?' Javier asked, staring at him with suspicion as they walked.

'I wanted to talk to you alone.'

He hadn't realised until he said the words that he *did* want to speak to his brother.

Avoiding a confrontation with Benjamin was the impetus he needed to confront his brother with a conversation they should have had a long time ago.

'You knew we were ripping Benjamin off all those years ago, didn't you?'

It was the first time Luis had vocalised this notion.

His brother's face darkened. 'We didn't rip him off. He was the fool who signed the contract without reading it.'

'And you should have warned him the terms had changed as you'd said you would do. You didn't forget, did you?'

His brother merely glowered in response.

'I knew it.' Luis took a deep breath, trying hard to contain the nausea swirling inside him that was fighting with a swell of rage. 'All these years and I've told myself that it had been an oversight on your part when I should have accepted the truth that you never forget. In thirty-five years you have never forgotten anything or failed to do something you promised.'

'I never promised to email him.'

'Not an actual promise,' Luis conceded. 'But look me in the eye and tell me it wasn't a deliberate act on your part.'

But all he saw in his twin's eyes was a black hardness.

'For what reason would it have been deliberate?' Javier asked with a sneer.

'That is for your conscience to decide. All I know for sure is that Benjamin was our friend. I have defended you and I have fought your corner...'

'*Our* corner,' Javier corrected icily. 'I assume this burst of conscience from you is connected to that damned woman.'

His temper finally getting the better of him, Luis grabbed his brother by the collar of his shirt. 'If you ever speak about Chloe in that way again then you and I are finished. Do you hear me? Finished.'

'If you're still defending her to me then I would say we're already finished, *brother*.' He spat the last word directly into Luis's face.

Eyeball to eyeball, they glowered at each other, the venom seeping between them thick enough to taste.

Then Luis released his hold, stepped back and un-clenched the fist he hadn't been aware of making.

His eyes still fixed on the man he had shared a womb with, had shared a bedroom with, had fought with, had protected, had been protected by, had grieved with, the other side of the coin that was the Casillas twins, Luis took backwards strides until he could look no more and turned his back on his brother for the last time.

With long strides, Luis walked the theatre's corridors, hardening his heart to what he had just walked away from, his focus now on one thing only: finding Chloe.

He had the rest of his life to sort out his relation-ship with Javier. And if they couldn't sort it out? He would handle it.

An incessant nagging in his guts told him he had only one opportunity to make things right with the woman it had taken him far too long to realise he was in love with. He did not think he could handle it if his attempts didn't work.

As he picked up his pace, scanning the crowds ahead for a tall, raven-haired woman, he collided with a much smaller blonde woman with a face he vaguely recog-nised.

'Sorry,' he muttered.

'My fault,' she whispered, looking over his shoul-der. 'I wasn't looking where I was going.'

Forgetting all about her, he continued to scour the corridors and bars, put his head into the conference room where the after-show party was being held three times, until he had a burst of inspiration and hurried to the costume department.

By the time he reached it, he was out of breath.

He pushed the door open and there she was, chatting with Maria over a bottle of wine.

Both women looked at him, startled at his appearance.

Only Chloe turned a deep red colour to match her lipstick to see him there.

'Maria, can I have a minute alone with Chloe, please?' he asked as politely as he could.

She must have read something on his face for she shot to her feet and hurried out of the door. 'I'll be at the party,' she murmured as she closed the door behind her.

'Can I have some of that?' he asked, nodding at the bottle of white wine.

Chloe handed him her glass without a word.

He drained it and handed it back to her. 'I was thirsty,' he said in an attempt at humour that failed when her lips didn't move.

And then they did move. 'I'm here legitimately. I was given a ticket.'

'I'm not here to question your legitimacy.' He took Maria's vacated seat and rolled his shoulders.

Chloe pushed her chair back, away from him. 'Then why are you here? I assume you've been looking for me.'

'I saw you from my seat.'

'I saw you too. You looked very cosy. Have you abandoned your date?'

'I don't have a date,' he said, confused.

She raised her brow and pursed her lips.

Then he understood who she meant and gave a hollow laugh. 'The women who sat with us are members of the royal family. We invited them to share our box out of courtesy. There is nothing in it.'

'I wouldn't care if there was.'

But he recognised the look he'd seen fleetingly on her face from the times he had mentioned Marietta, before she had realised Marietta was nearly ninety years old. It was the first time he recognised that look as jealousy.

That jealousy allowed him to breathe a little more easily.

'How have you been?' he asked.

'I've been having a great time in London, thank you.'

'London?'

'Yes. I've been there since I left the Caribbean and I'm flying back there in the morning. Now, did you seek me out to make small talk or was there a purpose to it?'

'Have mercy on me, *bonita*. I know I don't deserve it but allow me the small talk. What I have to say is hard for me. I need to build up to it.'

She looked at her watch.

Was he imagining it or did it look loose on her wrist? Had she lost weight?

'My cab is collecting me in thirty minutes. I will need ten minutes to get to the front, which gives you twenty minutes to say what you need to say.'

'I can give you a lift to wherever you want to go.' Hopefully home with him.

Unmoved, she looked again at her watch and said pointedly, 'Twenty minutes.'

He nodded and took a deep breath. 'Okay. Did you get the reference?'

'Yes. Thank you for arranging that. I assume you authorised it?'

'I did. And now I would like you to rip it up and return to Madrid.'

'You want me to come back and work for you?'

'No, I want you to come back and be my wife.'

There was a moment of silence before a grin broke out on her face. It didn't meet her eyes and there was no humour in it. 'You really are a comedian.'

He cursed under his breath. 'I am not being funny, *bonita*. I want you to marry me.'

'And I am not being funny either, but if you call me *bonita* one more time I will pour the contents of the bottle over your head.' The fake smile dropping, she got to her feet. 'Excuse me but I don't have time for any more of your games.'

He managed to take hold of her hand before she could snatch it away.

'Please, sit down. I'm not playing games. I know I am doing this all wrong but I have never told someone I love them before.'

Her eyes widened, a pulse ringing through them before she blinked all expression out of them.

Snatching her hand from his, she said, 'I thought Javier was the cruel one.'

'He is cruel,' Luis agreed sombrely. 'Our childhoods

screwed with our heads. He has to live with seeing our father's reflection every time he looks in the mirror.'

'And how did it screw with yours?'

'I have to live with seeing the reflection my father hated.'

She studied him in silence then carefully sat back down. 'I have to live with seeing the reflection my father didn't want every day,' she said slowly.

He couldn't tell if she was relaying this as a fact or to empathise. Her usually melodious tones were flatter than he had ever heard them.

'I know you do. How you have turned into such a vivacious and loving woman is inspiring. You could be bitter with the world but you're not. People like you.'

'People like you too,' she pointed out.

'They like my money. They like the parties I host and the presents I give. I've had to buy my friendships.'

Something flickered in her eyes. 'That's not true. You've always been a fun person to be around.'

'I like to have fun,' he conceded. 'But I am talking of real friendship. You and Benjamin are the only people other than my brother that I have been able to let my guard down with.'

'Because you have known us all your life?'

'With Benjamin, yes. We grew up together. He knew me before the nightmare, but you were just a child then and remained a child in my eyes until you came to Madrid and I suddenly saw the beautiful, vibrant woman you had become. I looked at you with brand-new eyes and I fell in love, and I never even knew it. I ended our date filled with emotions I can't explain because I have never felt them before, and then everything blew up with your brother and you, rightly, didn't want to know me any more. Through all the litigation we were going through, you were always there in my mind. I couldn't stop thinking about you. When you called me to say you had broken down in the mountains... *Dios*, I have never driven so fast in my life. To learn it had been a trick to get me away from the gala...ah, *bonita*, I was furious—please don't pour the wine over me—but my revenge was never focused where it should have been, on your brother, but on *you*.'

He paused for breath and gave a shake of his head. 'Javier says I lost my mind insisting that you married me and now I can see that he was right. Of course, back then I didn't see it—in truth, it's only becoming clear to me now as I say it to you.'

'Truth?' she said with only the slightest hint of cynicism. 'You're saying you kidnapped me and blackmailed me because you love me? Do you have any idea how screwed up that sounds?'

He ran a hand through his hair. 'Don't you know by now that I *am* a screw-up?'

'Then explain this. If you did all that because you love me, why did you end it so cruelly?'

'I was scared,' he replied simply. 'What I felt for you was like nothing I had ever felt for anyone. It scared the hell out of me. And I was scared that you were falling in love with me, scared that if you fell much harder you would see me too clearly.'

'I did see you clearly,' she said slowly. 'I always did. Even when I hated you I understood you. I understood you more when I learned about your relationship with your father. In many ways we are kindred spirits, two children longing for love from a parent who refused to give it. I fell in love with you when I was seventeen years old. I dreamed of marrying you…and then I grew up and learned the truth of my conception and had to come to terms with my father…' She took her own deep breath. 'But you know all this. I confided it in you. I had never told a soul. No one knew. It was too raw and too personal but I entrusted it with you.'

'You were in love with me all that time?' he asked in dazed disbelief.

'All that time.' Her smile was sad. 'You were there for all of us when we most needed you. You made my mother smile on the days she was so ill and so low from her treatment that she could hardly lift her head. You brought joy to all our lives and then on the day we buried her, when I so desperately needed someone to hold onto, you were there to hold me up and give me the strength to keep going. Of course I fell in love with you. Over the years I thought my love for you had… not died but been put aside with all my other childish things. And then I saw you again in Madrid and all my old feelings for you erupted.

'When Benjamin told me about the contract it broke my heart. I couldn't understand how you could be there for us during the worst time of our lives and at the same time conspire against us. Of course, I know differently now and as soon as I accepted that I had been wrong, my love for you… Luis, it never died. It's always been with me.'

He sighed. He couldn't hide it from her, not now that he knew the truth. 'Javier did know.'

'What do you mean?'

'When he didn't warn your brother about the change in the profit terms... It was a deliberate act. He didn't forget.'

'I know that.'

Unsure if he understood her correctly, he clarified, 'You know? How?'

She shrugged. 'Benjamin was adamant he mentioned the terms of profit on the night it was signed and that nothing was said to the contrary. That's why he felt so betrayed and why I felt so betrayed. If it wasn't said to you it must have been Javier.'

'I'm sorry.'

'You are not your brother. And he's paid for his deception. I'm sorry you were dragged into it.'

'Don't be. I kept my mouth shut for seven years and ignored the nagging voice that told me Javier's actions had been deliberate.'

'I can't say I wouldn't have done the same if I had been in your shoes. What you two have lived through together...' Her sigh was heavy as she got to her feet and looked at her watch. 'He's your brother. Your loyalty is to him. I understand that. I always have.'

As she headed to the door, he suddenly realised what she was doing and stood, kicking his chair back so forcefully it fell onto its side.

'Where are you going?'

'To my cab. I'm already running late for it.'

'You're *leaving*?'

She closed her eyes and nodded.

'But…' He groped for words, unable to comprehend this turn of events, not after the heartfelt exchange they'd just had that had alternately ripped his soul from him and cleansed it.

'I told you I would be getting a cab, Luis,' she said softly. 'I'm sorry. I can't marry you.'

She could not be serious. Please, God, do not let her be serious. 'You just told me that you love me.'

'I *do* love you but it's not enough. Don't you understand?'

'No,' he answered flatly, walking over to her, trying his hardest to quell the rising panic in his chest. Putting his hand on the nape of her neck, he brought his forehead to hers. 'I love you, you love me, what else is there to understand? You are my heart. Do you understand *that*? I have spent the past six weeks feeling as if something inside me has died and it was only when I saw you in the audience tonight that I realised what was wrong with me. *You* were what's wrong. I love you, more than anything or anyone.'

'I'm sorry,' she repeated, blinking frantically. She slipped out of his hold and wrapped her finger around the door handle. 'Please don't come any closer. I'm sorry. You hurt me too much. I've been in agony without you and have only just patched myself back together. I can't go through that again. I love you but I don't trust that you won't break my heart again. Forgive me.'

Ready to argue some more, to fight, to make every promise that would make her see sense, Luis caught the look in her eyes and closed his mouth.

What little fight was left in him vanished.

The pain he saw reflecting back at him was too acute to argue with.

He could gift-wrap his heart for her and she wouldn't believe it.

Their eyes stayed locked together, a thousand emotions passing between them before she gave a small nod of her head, raised her shoulders and walked out of the room.

Slumping against the door, Luis listened to the click-clack of her shoes fade away to nothing.

And then he fell to the floor and buried his face in his hands, every wretched part of him feeling as if it were being pulled through every circle of Dante's hell.

Chloe walked as fast as she dared on heels she was unpractised in walking in.

She tried to text the cab driver to let her know she was on her way but her fingers were all over the place.

All she had to do was get to the front entrance, get in her cab and get to her hotel. Three simple things easily achieved, or they would be if her feet and fingers would work properly.

In the morning she would fly back to London and complete the application form for the New York ballet company.

That was all she allowed herself to focus on. She would not think of the man she had just left behind.

An usher, who was shrugging a coat on, saw her approach and stepped in front of her. 'Is everything all right, miss?'

'Everything's fine. Why do you ask?'

The usher looked embarrassed. 'You're crying.'

'I am?' Putting a hand to her face, Chloe was horrified to find it wet with tears.

'Can I get you something? A coffee? Something stronger?'

'No, no, I need to get to my cab.' As she spoke her phone buzzed. It was the cab driver telling her she had five minutes to get to her or she would have to leave for her next job.

Panic now setting in, Chloe put a hand on the usher for support and leaned down to pull her heels off.

Shoes in one hand, phone clutched in the other, she set off at a run.

Had she thought the theatre's corridors wide when she'd arrived earlier? Now they seemed to have shrunk, the sides pressing closer and closer to her.

She picked up speed as she spotted the staircase, and kept close to the side as she ran down steps that seemed to go on and on, winding and winding, the exit so near and yet so far.

As soon as she reached the bottom she sprinted, running as fast as she had ever run in her life, the people she streamed past nothing but blurs.

Everything was a blur.

But still she ran until the warm night air hit her face and she was outside.

The cab driver, the same woman who had dropped her off hours before, tooted.

Doubling over as the first signs of a stitch set in, Chloe hobbled to the car, gasping for air.

Hand on the passenger door, she went to open it but then found her fingers still refusing to work.

The driver wound the window down and said something to her. It was nothing but noise to Chloe's ears, that distant sound of interference like a car radio going through a tunnel.

She spun around and stared up at the magnificent theatre, the name 'Compania de Ballet de Casillas' proudly embossed in gold leaf around the silhouette of a dancer in motion above the entrance door.

The Casillas Ballet Company. Named after the beloved mother of two boys whose life had been so cruelly taken at the hands of their father, her own husband.

A ballet company bought to keep her memory alive, a state-of-the-art theatre, dance school and facilities created from nothing to showcase the best that ballet had to offer, all to honour the memory of the woman they had loved.

Luis had loved his mother. Twenty-two years after her death and still he loved her. Javier had loved her too. For the first time in months she allowed a wave of tenderness into her heart for a man who had also lost so much, a man who'd clamped down on his feelings so tightly and effectively that he could deliberately cheat his oldest friend.

Luis hadn't clamped down on his feelings. Luis had opened his heart and embraced them—for her.

He had laid his heart on the line for the first time since his mother had died and Chloe, out of rabid fear, had turned it down.

She had dreamed of the day he declared his love for her then learned that dreams never came true.

But what if they did?

Luis *loved* her.

That was a truth.

He had seen all the good and bad in her just as she had seen the best and worst in him and still he loved her.

If she ran away now...

She would never have this chance again.

This was her time, *their* time, if only she had the courage to accept that sometimes dreams *did* come true, even for people like her and Luis whose own fathers could not bring themselves to love them.

Working automatically, she dug her hand into her clutch bag and pulled out the cash she had ready for the cab and thrust it into the driver's hand, unable to speak, able to apologise only with her eyes.

On legs that felt drugged, she walked back up the stairs and into the theatre foyer. The tears pouring down her face were so thick she struggled to see. She sensed the concerned faces surrounding her but blocked them all out.

Oh, Luis, where are you?

He couldn't still be in the costume room. Could he?

'Chloe?'

She spun round to the sound of the voice she knew so well and loved so much, and there he was, only feet away.

She didn't need her vision to see the haggard state of him.

How had she not seen it before?

'What's wrong?' Concern laced his every syllable. 'Have you been hurt?'

She shook her head, trying desperately to stop the tears that were falling like a waterfall, trying desperately to speak through a throat that had choked.

Her limbs took control of matters for her, legs propelling her to him, arms throwing themselves around him and holding him tightly, so tightly, burying herself to him.

Only his innate strength stopped them buckling under the weight of her ambush and after a moment where he fought to keep them steady and upright, his strong arms wrapped around her as tightly as she clung to him and his face buried into her hair, his warm breath seeping through to her skin.

'Oh, Luis,' she sobbed, 'I'm sorry. I'm sorry. I love you so much it hurts. I'm sorry for hurting you and for…'

But two large hands gently cupped her face to tilt her head back. The dark hazel eyes she loved so much were gazing down at her with a tenderness dreams were made of.

'My love,' he breathed. 'Please, say no more. It is *I* who am sorry.'

She shook her head, fresh tears spilling free. 'I love you.'

'And I love you, with all my heart. I swear, I will never hurt you again. You are my life, Chloe, please believe that.'

'I do. Because it is the same for me. I don't want to live without you.'

'You won't,' he promised reverently. 'You and I will never be parted again.'

'Promise?'

'Promise.'

'For ever?'

'For ever.'

And then his lips found her and they kissed with such love and such passion that neither doubted the other's love again.

EPILOGUE

THE SUN SETTING over the Caribbean like an enormous jewel was a glorious sight and one Luis gazed at with full appreciation.

'How are the nerves holding up?'

He turned his head and smiled at Benjamin. 'No nerves.'

The Frenchman raised a brow that was a perfect imitation of his sister. 'No nerves?'

'None. This is a day I have been looking forward to for so long I think I might burst if she makes me wait any longer.' Chloe had insisted they not rush into exchanging their vows, reasoning that as they were only going to do it the once, she wanted it to be perfect for them.

Benjamin laughed. 'My sister can be very stubborn.'

'It's a family trait.'

'*Oui.*' A flash of white teeth. 'A trait I imagine will be inherited by my niece or nephew.'

'She told you?'

'She told Freya. Who told me…'

Luis burst into laughter.

Chloe had taken the pregnancy test only the week before and had made him swear not to tell anyone until the first trimester had passed.

He should have guessed she wouldn't be able to contain herself from telling Freya.

After the first heady days when they had finally declared their love for each other, days spent in bed, surfacing only for food, all forms of contraception forgotten about, Luis had come out of the daze determined to make things right with Benjamin.

Chloe had elicited her sister-in-law's help in the matter, Freya falling under her spell enough to forgive Chloe's part in Benjamin's kidnapping of her. With his wife and sister both on his case over the matter, Benjamin had eventually given in and accepted a meeting with him, just the two men, in a neutral venue.

Naturally, that had meant Chloe and Freya had come along to the chosen hotel too, doing a terrible job of hiding behind menus at a table on the other side of the room.

Luis knew it was their presence there that had given Benjamin the impetus to hear him out. He'd refused Luis's cheque that equalled the total profit lost, plus interest, telling him to donate it to charity. But he had accepted a beer from him. And he had listened.

Three beers each later and Benjamin had apologised for his own terrible deeds.

Five beers each later and they were cracking jokes together.

And now, two months on, Benjamin was to be Luis's

best man as he married the woman who had stolen his heart then given it back to him whole with her own nestled in with it.

The only fly in the ointment was Javier's absence.

His twin had cut himself off so effectively a French guillotine could not have severed it better.

Chloe kept telling him to give Javier time but Luis knew his brother better than anyone.

For Javier it was simple. By choosing Chloe, Luis had switched his loyalty. His brother could not accept or understand that it hadn't been a choice for Luis; his love for Chloe was all encompassing, his need to be with her as necessary as breathing.

But then he forgot all about his estranged twin for the woman he loved appeared on deck, radiant in a floor-length lace white wedding dress that showed off her mountainous breasts—*Dios*, early pregnancy really suited her—and holding a posy of flowers over her non-existent bump. Her smile illuminated everyone. Even Captain Brand, officiating at the wedding, smiled broadly along with the rest of the crew.

Chloe made no attempt to walk serenely to him, bounding over like the galloping gazelle who had thrown her arms around him all those months ago.

The beaming smile didn't leave her face for a moment as they exchanged their vows. When the time came for them to share their first kiss as husband and wife she threw her arms around him and kissed him for so long they missed the first set of fireworks.

With his beautiful wife snuggled securely in his

arms, Luis watched the spectacular display and reflected that he was the luckiest man to have sailed these waters.

Luis and Chloe Casillas are delighted to announce the birth of their first child, Clara Louise Casillas, born at 5.22 a.m., weighing 7lb 3oz. Both mother and daughter are doing well.

* * * * *

Keep reading for an excerpt of
THE GREEK SECRET SHE CARRIES
by Pippa Roscoe — find this story
in the *The Diamond Inheritance* anthology.

PROLOGUE

Last night...

THERON THIAKOS STALKED the damp London street, cursing the rain. It just never stopped. How could people live like this? he angrily asked himself, longing for the piercing heat and pure bright sun of Greece, the glittering blue sea that sparkled enough to make a person squint. The cloud-covered night gave the Mayfair street an air of mystery as he came to stand before the impossibly exclusive private members club, Victoriana.

Before him, two men stood either side of a door with such thick black gloss the paint looked like running water. The Tuscan columns supporting the portico spoke of riches and a sense of history that struck a nerve. Theron bit back a curse. This was exactly the kind of superior, expensive establishment that would appeal to Lykos's ego. Theron made to step forward when, shockingly, one of the men raised his hand to stop him.

'I'm here to see Lykos Livas,' Theron stated, not

bothering to conceal the distaste in his tone. He had neither the time nor the patience for this. The anger in him was overpowering and he wanted someone to blame. *Needed* someone to blame. And he knew just the person.

The other doorman nodded, holding the door open and gesturing Theron towards a woman wearing some sort of strange green tweed trousers that cut off at the knee and a waistcoat. Lykos had always had a flair for the dramatic, but this was so… English. *Old* English.

The immediate press of warmth that greeted him after the cold London night was a blessed relief. His mouth watered at the thought of the whisky he'd fantasised about for the entire drive down from the Soames estate in Norfolk where he'd left Summer standing on the stone steps, unable to face the look in her eyes as he drove away.

He'd lost everything. Absolutely everything.

Theron followed the hostess weaving her way through a surprisingly large establishment, completely decked out—as one would imagine—in furniture and furnishings from the Victorian period. And, despite the negative bent of his thoughts, he couldn't help but be impressed by the bar that stretched the entire length of the main room. Two houses, at least, must have been knocked together to create such a space.

He caught sight of his quarry, sitting at a booth of deep green leather with a woman no less exquisite than to be expected in Lykos Livas's company. Theron's gaze barely touched the brunette, his mind instead seeing rich golden hair, hazel eyes and lips that were ruby-red when full of desire and pale when devastated.

His fingers pulsed within his fist as Lykos finally turned to acknowledge him.

'This is all your fault,' Theron charged, his tone firm and bitter.

Lykos stared at him for a moment, his gaze so level Theron wondered if he'd even heard the accusation. Then he blinked that silvery gaze. 'I'd say it's good to see you but—'

'We are well beyond niceties, Lykos, so I'll say again, this is all your fault.'

'That depends on what "this" is,' Lykos said over the rim of his glass before taking a mouthful of his drink.

Inhaling a curse, Theron turned to the brunette. 'Leave us.' He hated being so cruel but he was at his wits' end.

'That is hardly necessary,' Lykos protested half-heartedly.

'It's not as if you won't find someone else to play with,' Theron said truthfully, turning his back on the girl as he looked for the hostess. 'Whisky?' She nodded and disappeared into the bar's darkness.

'True,' Lykos replied with a shoulder shrug, watching his companion leave in a huff before narrowing his eyes at Theron. 'I see you once in ten years and now you won't leave me alone?'

It was a relief to speak in his native tongue again. It had been—what?—a week since he'd left Athens and found himself in that hellhole in Norfolk. Some found the Greek language harsh, but to Theron it flowed like *tsipouro* from Volos and tasted like honey in *loukoumades*.

'This is not the time for jokes, Lykos.'

'You never did have a good sense of humour,' he groused.

Theron's drink arrived and he slipped into the now empty seat. He palmed the glass, staring at it as if he hadn't spent the last three hours wanting it.

'You'd best bring the bottle, *glykiá mou*,' Lykos said, leaning well into the server's personal space. Not that she seemed to mind. At all.

'What are you doing in London anyway?' Theron asked before challenging himself to only take a sip of the liquid he wanted to drown in.

'I like it here.'

'I don't believe you. I don't believe that any Greek worth their salt would enjoy all the…*grey*,' Theron said with such distaste it was as if the colour had taken up residence on his tongue.

'Grey? I'm not quite sure I've seen London during the daytime hours. Is it that bad?' Lykos asked, appearing to sincerely ponder it.

'Yes. But Norfolk is worse.'

Lykos's silver eyes narrowed and Theron's dark gaze held the challenge. 'Is that so?' Lykos asked.

'It is. They've even named a paint after it.'

'What, Norfolk?'

'Yes. It's grey.'

Lykos sniggered into his glass, before sobering and then sighing. 'What did you do?'

Theron clenched his jaw at the accusation. For just a moment it had been like it had always been between them. The banter flowing freely from the bone-deep knowledge of each other. But that was before Lykos had walked away from their friendship.

'If you're looking for absolution,' Lykos warned, 'you've come to the wrong damn place,' he went on before eyeing up the bottle of Glenglassaugh the waitress had placed on the table as if he wasn't sure he wanted to waste such good alcohol on Theron.

Theron shook his head, frustrated with the man who'd once been like a brother to him. 'I don't need absolution. I need to know why you called me a week ago.' Theron knew with absolute certainty that he was involved in all this somehow, but he needed to hear it from Lykos.

'To taunt you, of course,' Lykos said with a smile that had more than likely charmed women right out of their underwear. 'When your holiday fling turns up at my door—'

'Watch your mouth,' Theron growled.

'Ooh, touchy.' Watching Theron from the corner of his eye, Lykos continued. 'When the lovely Ms Soames arrived at my door trying to offload a fifteen-million-pound estate in the country for a third of the market value, I just wanted to brag. I've always wanted a castle.'

'It's not a castle.'

'Oh?'

'And it's rundown. There are holes in the walls and it's freezing. All the time. And the damp...' Theron threw his hands in the air as if in despair.

'Oh, well, that wasn't in the sales pitch. Is that why you're here? To talk me out of buying the estate?'

Theron thought about it for a moment too long. 'Buy the estate,' he said tiredly. 'And it's worth the market value, Lykos. Don't take advantage of a vulnerable woman.'

Lykos slammed his glass down on the table, ignoring the stares it drew from the other guests, his eyes shards of ice but the burn in them white-hot. 'There's a line, Theron, and you are skating dangerously close to it.'

Theron wanted to bite back, wanted the anger Lykos threatened. His pulse pounded and he welcomed it, his breath audible now as his lungs worked hard. They stared at each other, while Theron waged an internal war and Lykos waited to see what he would do.

Gritting his teeth, Theron decided it was better to leave than to cause a scene and got to his feet.

'Oh, sit down before you break down,' Lykos bit out.

Theron stared at the doorway long enough to realise that he didn't have anywhere else to go.

'Break down?' he asked.

'I can practically feel the tears from here. Drink that,' Lykos said, passing him a large measure of whisky, 'before you start weeping all over the place. *Then* have the kindness to leave before you scare off the rest of tonight's entertainment.'

'You're a real piece of work, you know that?'

'Theron, as hard as this is to believe, I really don't care what got your knickers in a twist.'

'You would have once.'

'And you chose Kyros,' Lykos growled.

'No,' Theron shot back. '*You* left.'

'And you could have come.'

'And how would that have repaid the man who gave us *everything*?' Theron demanded.

'That was always your problem. What could ever be equal compensation for what he did for us? What could you give him that would repay such a thing?'

Theron turned away from the demand in his oldest friend's gaze and stared into the whisky, trying to ignore the feeling that he might have finally found something worthy of such a debt.

His heart.

And his child.

'Fine,' huffed Lykos. 'You may explain, if it will take that look off your face.'

Summer paced before the fire in the Little Library. Back and forth, back and forth as her eyes went from wet to dry, red to pale. But her heart ached as if she'd never stopped crying.

This room had become her sanctuary in the last two months, every inch of it as familiar to her as if she'd lived here all her life. But instead of seeing books that would make the British Library jealous, she saw eyes, dark like coals, making her shiver from the heat. Eyes that had laid her bare, exposed her soul. Her heart pulsed and her core throbbed as if taunting her, reminding her of the night before, as he'd thrust into her so deep and so deliciously she *still* ached from the pleasure. She turned and paced back past the fireplace where flames danced joyously as if there was nothing wrong, as if her world hadn't just shattered into a million pieces.

She brushed her hair back from her face. Six months ago she had been a naïve third-year geophysics student whose only worry was how to pay her sisters back for working all hours to pay for her to go to university. And now?

She was pregnant.

And yet she couldn't afford to think about it. She couldn't think about Theron Thiakos or even her father, Kyros. Now she *had* to think about her mother and sisters. About finishing the treasure hunt she, Star and Skye had been sent on by the grandfather they'd never met. The task? To find the Soames diamonds, hidden over one hundred and fifty years ago by their great-great-great-grandmother from her abusive husband. Clues had been found, coded messages translated, and her sisters had travelled the world to track down the elements needed to find the jewels.

It had been easy to hide her baby bump three weeks ago, when Skye had flown first to Costa Rica and then to France to locate the map of secret passageways that led throughout the Norfolk estate. And Star had been so full of romance when she had left for Duratra in the Middle East, searching for the one-of-a-kind key made by joining two separate necklaces that her sister had missed all signs of Summer's pregnancy too.

Meeting the terms of the will, she had been forced to stay behind. She had scoured their great-great-great-grandmother's journals, searching for clues about exactly *where* Catherine had hidden her family's jewels, but hadn't been able to find any. But if they did find the jewels, the sisters would have met the terms of their inheritance and be able to sell the estate in order to pay for their mother's lifesaving medical treatment. That was *all* that mattered right now. The jewels. Her mother's health. She couldn't think of anything else.

Especially not a man with eyes as dark as obsidian and a heart protected by granite. A granite, she thought with a sob, she'd hoped to have chipped. She placed her hand over the crest of her bump, reassuring both herself and their baby that they'd be okay.

'It will all work out in the end,' she whispered. 'It's what Auntie Star is always saying. And Great-Great-Great-Grandmother Catherine? Trust, love and faith,' Summer assured her child, wiping away the last of her tears.

The sound of the ancient doorbell ricocheted throughout the sprawling estate that looked—at least on the outside—like Downton Abbey. On the inside? It could have inspired Dickens. For five generations the men of the Soames line had let the estate go to ruin, fruitlessly looking for the Soames diamonds. And the last, their grandfather, in his madness had been driven to knocking great holes in the walls. The irony was how close he had actually come to finding them.

Summer took a deep breath, swept another reassuring hand over her belly and whispered, 'It's time to meet your aunties.'

Summer opened the front door and was instantly

pulled into a tangle of arms that squashed and hugged and she didn't need to see her sisters' faces to know she was *home*. It didn't matter where they were in the world, as long as they were together. Summer breathed them in. She had missed them so much.

'Oh my God, it's so good to see you,' Star rushed out in one breath. 'And oh my God, we have so much to tell you, and oh my... *God, what is that?*'

Summer found herself thrust back as Star stared wide-eyed at her stomach. Over her shoulder, Skye's delighted smile followed Star's gaze down to Summer's waist and her eyes sparked with shock.

'Surprise!' Summer called weakly just before she burst into tears again.

As if the spell had been broken, Summer was instantly pulled back into her sisters' loving embrace and given soothing declarations of support and reassurance. Unfortunately, this only made her cry harder, until Skye took charge and guided them off the steps and into the estate.

They held her all the way to the Little Library, Skye on one side, Star on the other, words of love filling the cold damp estate and easing Summer's hurt just a little. Once they had seen her settled in the large wingback chair, Skye put another log on the fire and ordered Star to make a cup of herbal tea from the kettle they'd set up in the library almost two months ago.

Skye crouched down and levelled her gaze at Summer. 'Are you okay?'

Summer nodded, blushing furiously now that the crying had once again stopped.

'Is the baby okay?' Star asked from behind her sister.

Summer nodded again, her hand soothing over the crest of her bump, and when she looked back up she saw the most beautiful smiles on her sisters' faces—joy lighting their eyes, pure and bright. Summer sniffed and Star passed her a tissue, keeping one back for herself and wiping at her eyes. Summer smiled as she could see Skye trying to suppress an eye-roll at their romantic middle sister.

'Can I ask—?'

'I don't want to talk about it. Now you're here—'

'Summer,' Star chided.

'I don't,' she replied, shaking her head resolutely. 'Besides, we have to find the jewels.'

'But I thought you found the jewels?'

'I haven't actually seen them. I was waiting for you both.'

As if quickly weighing up the importance of things, Skye seemed to come to a decision. 'The diamonds aren't going to disappear overnight,' she insisted gently. 'They can wait. *You* are more important right now. And we're not going anywhere until you tell us what's going on,' she said firmly.

The kettle reached boiling point and clicked off, all the sisters' gazes called to it, and a sudden silence blanketed the room until Star laughed. 'Okay, let's have some tea, take stock and, you know, breathe.'

Skye and Summer shared a look.

'Okay, who are you and what have you done with Star?' Skye demanded.

Star smiled. 'We have a *lot* to catch up on.'

And for just a moment they enjoyed the silence, enjoyed being back together again, reunited after the longest time away from each other. Then, as Star made the tea, Skye told them about her fiancé Benoit and the cottage in the Dordogne they had been staying in for the last few weeks. Star asked a few questions before telling her own tale about the oasis the Prince of Duratra had whisked her away to before his ostentatious proposal and how much she wished she had some *qatayef* to share with them as they had their tea. It was as if they sensed that Summer needed time just to let the heavy emotions settle. Warmth finally seeped into her skin and wrapped around her heart and finally both Star and Skye looked at her expectantly.

'I don't know where to begin.' Summer shrugged helplessly.

'At the beginning, of course,' Star replied, as if she were talking to her primary school class.

Summer took a deep breath, the words rushing out on a single exhale. 'I found my dad.'

'Wait…what?' Skye asked, clearly not expecting that to be where Summer's story began.

'In Greece. I found my father.'

'But I thought Mum didn't know his name?' said Star, frowning. 'Which was why she could never find…' She trailed off, as if suddenly understanding.

'Oh, no,' Skye said. 'Really? She knew the whole time?'

Summer nodded, the ache of all those missed years, of all the questions unanswered for so long, that missing part of her… She understood *now* why her mother had done what she'd done but, with a child growing within her, she knew that she couldn't have made the same choice.

'Why didn't you tell us?' Skye asked gently.

'I didn't want you to think badly of her. *I* didn't want to think badly of her.' Summer shook her head, trying to find the words to explain why she'd hoarded that information, hoarded that hurt from her half-sisters. Skye's father had started another family after he and Mariam broke up, Star's father had died tragically when she was just months old. But Kyros? He was *her* father and a part of her feared they wouldn't understand the need she'd felt to meet him. The need in her to connect with a man she'd never met. And perhaps beneath that, deep down, the thing she hadn't been able to admit… that if he rejected her then she wouldn't have to tell them. No one would have to know.

'I… I wanted to meet him first,' Summer said.

'And did you?'

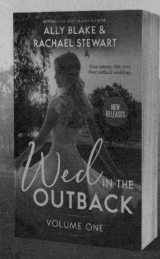 

Subscribe and fall in love with a Mills & Boon series today!

You'll be among the first to read stories delivered to your door monthly and enjoy great savings.

WE SIMPLY LOVE ROMANCE